D0850573

TIDES

Scott Mackay

TIDES

an imprint of **Prometheus Books**
Amherst, NY

Published 2005 by Pyr™, an imprint of Prometheus Books

Inquiries should be addressed to
Pyr
Editorial Department
Prometheus Books
59 John Glenn Drive
Amherst, New York 14228–2197
VOICE: 716–691–0133, ext. 207
FAX: 716–564–2711
WWW.PYRSF.COM

09 08 07 06 05   5 4 3 2 1

Library of Congress Cataloging-in-Publication Data

Mackay, Scott, 1957–
    Tides / Scott Mackay.
        p. cm.
    ISBN 1–59102–334–3 (hardcover : alk. paper)
    1. Life on other planets—Fiction. I. Title.

PR9199.3.M3239T53 2005
813'.54—dc22

2005020493

Printed in the United States on acid-free paper

To my agent, Joshua Bilmes

Part One

VOYAGE

CHAPTER ONE

Hab gazed at the hundreds of red bladders floating on the sea. His men lowered boats over the side. The tides of Foot and Lag mounted from the south, the sky squalled with rain, and the northeast coast of Paras was ragged with intermittent fog banks. Hab glanced over the stern at the tides, then at his first mate, Guenard, who counted the red bladders with his finger. The ship rocked with the tide's first unruly push. As ship's captain, Hab knew his place was on board. But he yearned to join the hunt.

"Guenard," he said, "I'm going with the men. You take command."

Guenard turned to him, his bleary eyes widening. "But Captain," he said, "look at those tides." Rain dripped from the first mate's beard. "I'd feel a lot safer if you stayed on board."

"These tides aren't anything you can't handle," Hab said. "As long as the whales don't drag us beyond the southern tip of the Island of Liars, we should be fine."

Overhead, the mainmast creaked in the wind.

"But why do such a thing?" asked Guenard. "Why ride out in the pouring rain with all those hunters? I can smell them from here."

Guenard stared, waiting for an answer.

"Because I was once a hunter myself, and I sometimes miss it."

"And for this you desert your post as commander?" said Guenard. Guenard just stared. "The moons ride high, and the tides lurch like granite walls toward us. How should I set the jib sail? And what of the kedge?" As the first mate voiced his concerns, the *Minden* rocked again, climbing twenty feet in a matter of seconds. "Should I heave to? Or should I tack directly into the wind? It's a damnably rough watch when tide and wind are adverse to each other, Captain."

"Tack into the wind and furl the jib sail," said Hab. "Set the kedge anchor off the starboard bow. We've faced tides much worse than these, Guenard. What's made you so liverish?"

The first mate cast an anxious glance toward the east. "I should hate to be cast upon the Island of Liars, sir, that's all."

Hab glanced into the misty east, thinking about the Liars.

"You don't have to worry about the Liars, Guenard," he said. "They're human beings, just like you and me."

ᕙᕙᕙ

Hab got into a boat with a hunter he knew well: Jeter, a man his own age. Jeter was tall and lank, with an unruly bang of blond hair hanging over his small blue eyes, a long narrow face, a bony chin, a few pimples, and long yellow teeth crowding the front of his mouth. He loaded the harpoons into the boat.

"I'm coming with you," said Hab.

Jeter looked at him doubtfully. "Is Guenard sure about the pickup?" he asked. "I'd hate to get lost in all this fog."

Hab gave him a gruff nod. "He's an able seaman."

"But not as able as you," said Jeter.

With the help of three other hunters and a puller, they soon lowered the longboat into the water and got the small sail hoisted.

They tacked into the wind, letting the tides push them from behind. Hab helped the puller with the paddling. Over the stern of the small boat, the *Minden* grew smaller and smaller. Storm lanterns, haloed by the mist and rain, grew faint as they drew away. Up ahead he saw the bladders, thick and red, two per whale, each the size of a boat, the animals taking on air, herding on the surface.

"Over there!" he shouted, pointing.

A mother and two calves bobbed on the surface. Jeter came from the bow.

"I'll haul," said the hunter. "You can have this one."

Hab gave the hunter a nod and on sturdy sea legs walked to the front of the small boat. He got his harpoon ready. Jeter and the puller drew closer. The small sail snapped briskly in the freshening wind. The tide swelled behind them, slapping into the stern, sending spume over their backs. Hundreds of red bladders heaved upward on the twenty-foot tide, as graceful as dancers. Hab knelt in the braces and tied his legs into place. Closer . . . closer . . . the cow and its two calves suspected nothing. The cow was big. Her blubber alone would pay rent on at least one of his boats.

"A few spokes to port!" he called.

They veered closer. Once in range, Hab stood up, aimed, and fired the cannon, launching the harpoon toward the cow's left bladder. The slender projectile sang through the air, uncoiling line behind it, and sank deeply into the cow's bladder. She lurched forward at the sting of the barbed point, arched her back, lifted her head out of the salty foam, and opened her jaws. Razor-sharp teeth ringed the gaping chasm of her mouth. Hab saw two blowholes in the roof of her mouth leading to either bladder. She howled, her eyes flashed with rage, and she slapped her tail against the water. She plowed through the tide toward the boat.

Hab lifted another projectile, rammed it down the cannon, aimed, and just as the cow was going to close its jaws over the bow of the boat, fired.

Funny how they sensed a mortal wound. She stopped her attack. Her bladders hissed air. Blood sputtered into the air like a red fountain. The men cheered. But Hab felt anything but cheerful. Where was his spirit? Ten years ago he would have cheered along with the rest of them. Now he felt empty. This was a good kill. This was going to make him a lot of money. He was going to sustain the flagging family fortunes for yet another year. With this kill, he would provide for Gougou the occasional box of bonbons she enjoyed so much. He would pay off some of Romal's gambling debts. He would buy a pretty dress for Thia. He might even have enough to erect to his father a small memorial in the seamen's cemetery at Alquay. But would the money ever fill this new emptiness he felt inside, or quell his growing restlessness? He wanted something, but he wasn't sure what it was.

He watched the whale with joyless eyes. He tried to concentrate on the hunt, to shake these more melancholy thoughts from his mind. Mortally wounded. Funny how they knew. They were smarter than a lot of men realized. Following instinct, the cow turned away and headed toward land, like they all did whenever they were mortally wounded, off to beach itself, to run itself aground in a final bit of shallows before it died. Hab let out line.

"She's heading toward Paras," he said to Jeter. "We might as well settle down for the ride."

"Should we wound the calves?" asked Jeter.

Wound, but never kill. The bladder whale would secrete a poison into its meat if killed outright. A slow ride to shore, while the whale slowly suffocated, made sure the meat remained edible. Hab looked at the calves, raising their own hideous heads out of the water, looking around in bewilderment, wondering where their mother was.

"No," he said. "Let the bulls have them."

Fifty yards to port, the cow lunged out of the water, a dark gargantuan shape in the surrounding gray, her bladders now half full, like ragged red flags, still gushing blood. The harpoons held fast. She fell with the force of her forty tons into the water, sending spray everywhere, slapped her tail three times, then went under once again. Hab let out more line. The boat lurched and headed west, towed by the whale, the age-old pas de deux between the whalers and the whales of this stormy coast. The rain came down harder.

"Light the torch," ordered Hab. "Guenard's going to be relieved when he sees us moving away from the Island of Liars."

One of the sailors lit the torch. The flame cast a fitful white reflection over the surface. The boat lurched again and gained speed as the whale dragged the men through the water.

"How far do you think she's going to take us?" asked Jeter.

"About a hundred miles," said Hab. "She's a strong young cow."

The small craft headed west at eighteen knots, with the tides occasionally sloshing over her port side, at times nearly capsizing her. The sailors bailed her out once in a while. Hab was cold, wet, and tired. He stared out into the rain, making sure the lines stayed untangled, winching the small capstan whenever the cow gave some slack, forcing himself to stay awake. He raised his collar higher and felt some cold rainwater trickle down his back.

When dawn broke, the cow was winched to within twenty-five yards of the bow. The water was dark, with little islands of foam here and there. The fog was gone. The sky was still overcast. The rain had stopped. The cow's bladders lay draped over her back like a couple of collapsed tents. She had to stay surfaced now or she would drown. Seabirds flocked around her, pecking away at the delicate crimson membrane. Hab took out his telescope and scanned the Channel of Liars. Far to the west he saw the coast of Paras, the hilly province of Dagu, not much in the way of beach, bleak and rocky.

"We'll be there in an hour," he said.

"The Golden Land," exhaled one of the sailors.

"We'll all have a taste of blubber," said Hab.

They reached the treacherous coves and inlets of Dagu in less than an hour. With the tides receding, Hab saw both high- and low-water marks along the coast, a difference of fifty feet, the high-water mark strewn with seaweed, the low-water mark a line of foam over the mud flats. Dagulanders waded in the shallows gathering the succulent morsels of shellfish the tides had left behind. The bladder whale veered north, looking for a suitable sandbar on which to beach itself. The cow dragged the boat along the coast for several hours. Rain fell again, but it was a warm rain, pushed northward by the Auvilly Currents.

Up on the hill, Hab saw an encampment. Strange. Who would camp out on that treeless hill this late in the season? He lifted his telescope and had a look. The people up there were dressed in the traditional blue of Jondonq. His own people. Two thousand miles from home. With three ships harbored against the rocks. What were they doing here?

"Are they whalers?" asked Jeter.

"I don't see any whaling vessels." Hab unstrapped his legs and got up from his harpoon chair. "I need a swim after a night in that chair. I think I'll have a look."

"I'll mark the spot on the map," said Jeter.

"Have Guenard pick me up on the way back."

Hab dove over the side and swam for shore. It was, he knew, an uncharacteristic action. To leave the ship and go out on one of the boats was strange enough. But to jump over the side of the boat and swim for shore—that was even stranger. He stroked strongly and surely, his legs scissor-kicking precisely through the waves. The waves lifted him up and down. Here was another side of himself he every so often discovered, a restlessness derived from his poor dead father, Duq. He lifted his head out of the water and stared at the shore of Dagu to see how far he had to go. He was like his father because his father wanted to know. His father wanted to discover. His father could never sit still or stay in one place too long, but had to be roaming or sailing in his ever-insatiable quest to know. Hab kicked harder, stroked harder. Every so often his father came back to him like a ghost. Sheer determined effort at whatever he happened to be doing at the moment seemed to be the only way to appease his father's ghost.

So he swam for shore. Swam as surely as the whales swam. Curious about the encampment on the hill. As a good Parassian, wanting only the truth. As his father's son, wanting only to know.

CHAPTER TWO

The half-mile swim to the encampment, even after a night in the harpoon chair, was easy for Hab. He pulled himself up onto the rocks, found his footing, and climbed the bluff, startling several nuiyau birds on the way up. As he neared the top, he worked his way around an outcropping of rock. With casual stealth, he peered over the top of the outcropping and gazed at the encampment.

Mist rolled down from the barren hills, shrouding everything in a fine gray cloak, and the rain was starting up again. What were they using these barrels and basins all over the place for? Certainly not to catch drinking water—a small stream ran through the middle of the encampment, providing ample water. He walked to the nearest basin and discovered to his great astonishment that it was made of metal. Were these rich men then? He looked around at the other basins and barrels, and saw that they, too, were made of metal. These strangers from Jondonq must be tremendously wealthy. Yet what was the point of making barrels and basins of metal? Using cheaper materials made far greater sense. He ran his hand over the nearest. Bronze. Surely they should have saved such a fabulously expensive material for the making of jewelry. What mystifying endeavor were these Jondonqers pursuing on this windy scrap of coastline?

"Ho, there!" a voice called. He turned around. A young woman, wearing the traditional blue of his province, stood at the edge of the encampment staring at him. She had orange hair. Not one in a thousand Jondonqers had orange hair. She approached him, seeming to glide over the wet coarse grass. "Who are you and what do you want?"

He was surprised to hear such blatant mistrust coming from the mouth of a fellow Jondonqer. He stood up. He scrutinized the woman. She had a small upturned nose, freckles over her face, full pleasant lips, and a well-defined jaw. She looked nineteen or twenty. Her eyes were big, as green as the sea, and pierced through the gloom as if lit from within. Her body, what he could make of it, was lank, thin, and girlish.

"I should ask you the same," he said, gesturing at the twenty tents around the hillside. "What unseasonal gathering is this?"

"Are you from the Island of Liars?" she asked, not at all daunted. She took a few steps forward and put her hands on her hips, as if she were getting ready to scold him. "Well? Are you?"

"I'm Hab Miquay, from Jauny," he said, telling the simple truth, as was the way. "And you are?"

"You look like a Liar to me," she said.

"But I have no brand."

"How do you happen to be standing on this hillside?" She glanced at his wet clothing. "I take it you crawled from the sea."

If nothing else, the woman had endearing gall. "I'm the captain of a whaling ship," he said. "The *Minden*. We've been hunting all night. I saw your encampment from the channel and came to pay my respects."

"Liars are fond of metal, aren't they?" was all she had to say.

Hab frowned. A bell rang somewhere in the camp. "Come now, miss. Enlighten me. You're Jondonqers, one and all. What brings you to this cold wet coast? And what of these basins? What of these barrels? I ask you a direct question. Please give me a direct answer. A barrel is better made of wood, is it not?"

"Aye, perhaps."

"Then why make one of metal? Why waste such precious materials?"

"Because a metal barrel doesn't contaminate water the way a wooden one does."

"A wooden barrel ages water," he said.

"If you call the taste of wood sap age," she said. Her eyes narrowed. "You look cold, Liar."

He frowned again. Obviously insolence was the cornerstone of her personality. "If you offer hospitality, I graciously accept," he said stiffly. "If not, I can crawl back into the sea."

She gave him a crisp nod. "Come to the camp, then."

She whirled around, her cape spinning out from her, and marched into the camp. Hab followed. Other Jondonqers glanced at him. Obfuscation. Did the young woman know anything about the 28 Rules of the Formulary? She was rude, abrupt, and secretive, hadn't even offered her name yet.

He looked around. He saw an elaborate distilling apparatus made of glass tubing, quart bottles, and a fifty-gallon glass kettle in a large tent. A man coaxed flames with a bellows. As the flames grew, the water boiled in the bottom of the kettle. Steam rose through a conical aperture, condensing into droplets here and there, and curled into the tubing. No corn, barley, or sugar, nothing to indicate the making of spirits or strong liquor. Just rainwater. What strange industry was this? Making rainwater from rainwater? The whole enterprise seemed bizarre.

"What is the nature of your work here?" he asked the girl.

"Scientific," she said.

Ah. Science. That was something he understood. "I'm the author of a small scientific treatise myself," he offered.

"Are you?" she said.

He felt his lips stiffen. "Yes. On the Auvilly Currents."

She stopped, looked at him. "Then you're Hab Miquay, of the House of Cloudesley, I presume," she said.

He was surprised that she should know this. "And you are?" he asked again, hoping to get her name.

"Jara," she said. Her lips curved into a smile. "Jara Pepteri." As if the name meant something. And maybe it did. His eyes narrowed. Pepteri. Why did the name sound familiar?

⁊ɕɕɕ

They came to a large tent at the end of the encampment. Jara pulled the flap open. The tent had been converted into an alchemist's laboratory, with tables, benches, and glassware. A man, around thirty-five, sat at a table holding a beaker of rainwater up to a lamp. Rainwater again. What was so fascinating about the rainwater here? The man's black cloak marked him as a doctor. The man looked at Hab from under dark eyebrows.

"Hab Miquay, of the House of Cloudesley," said Jara. "The man who wrote *On the Rotational Movements of the Auvilly Currents*." The man simply stared, as if he couldn't understand why he'd been interrupted. Jara turned to Hab. "This is my brother, Esten Pepteri." Hab now knew why the name Pepteri sounded so familiar. Esten Pepteri. Alchemist, doctor, historian, naturalist, botanist, and biologist. Esten Pepteri, the world's most respected scientist. "He crawled out of the sea," Jara explained to her brother. "He saw our endeavors here on the hillside and couldn't resist his own curiosity. I took him for a Liar."

Esten Pepteri continued to stare at Hab. Then he tapped his lips with his fingers. "Hab Miquay," he said, trying the name out. He nodded to himself. "Yes . . . yes . . . I believe we've met before."

"We have?" said Hab.

"At Summerhouse," said Esten. "At a reception Parprouch held to celebrate the recent nuptials of his youngest daughter."

Hab searched his memory, and yes, he remembered the reception, the women of the high court wearing sumptuous breast-exposing gowns, glittering in the finest cut amber, the tables laid out with an overabundance of fruit and roast joadre, the fountains fixed to bubble not water but wine—a typical court affair. But he couldn't readily recall Esten.

"I'm afraid I don't remember," he said.

"You showed me a new sextant you were working on," said Esten. "An ingenious design."

Hab's eyes widened farther. "That was you?"

"The first design, I believe, that takes into account the curvature of the world." From somewhere outside, Hab heard the bell ringing again. Esten looked at his sister and pointed at the tent flap. "I hear cook ringing the bell, Jara," he said. "Perhaps you can bring us some food." Jara made a face, as if she weren't fond of taking orders. "And please try to be civil to our guest," urged her brother. "I know you can't be civil to me, but make an effort with our guest."

She thrust a hip petulantly to one side. "His manner of arrival wasn't particularly civil," she said. "If he arrives like a Liar, I shall treat him like a Liar." She left the tent.

Esten stared after her as she went, a grin coming to his face. "You'll have to forgive Jara, Hab Miquay," he said. "You see a young woman who has yet to outgrow her precociousness. But she will. She will."

"Her eyes bristle with intelligence," said Hab, trying to remain polite about the girl.

Esten pondered the remark. "Intelligence of an intemperate sort, I fear." And pondered his sister some more, as if she were a source of constant fascination to him. Then he gestured at a stool. "Sit, Hab Miquay, of Cloudesley," he said. "You must be tired after your swim. What brings you to this part of Dagu? Do you captain a penal ship?"

Hab sat down.

"No, sir, I command a whaling fleet."

"Ah, yes, the whales. We heard them singing out in the rain last night. Were you up all night, then?"

"I was."

"And was the hardship worthwhile?"

"It was."

"I'm glad to hear it."

"I saw your camp from a mile out, sir. Not even the nomads camp so far north at this time of year. You must grant me my curiosity. I mean no impertinence by it. What is the nature of your business here?"

But Esten didn't immediately answer. His eyes narrowed; he pointed at Hab, absently shaking his finger at the captain, looking as if he were again trying to recall something about him. "I believe . . . yes, I think I've heard a thing or two about you . . . and I . . . Now, what was it? . . . A story or something . . . of a voyage you undertook when you were young. . . . Was it you? Or was it your father?"

"Sir, my father is dead," said Hab. "And if you allude to the foolhardy sea journey I undertook to the equator when I was a boy—"

"Then my memory serves me well," said Esten, slapping the table with his hand. "You're the only man who's ever seen the tides of Foot and Lag in deep water, aren't you?"

Hab remembered his journey out to the moon-tides. Back in the days when he had thought anything was possible. He remembered his own boundless enthusiasm for the voyage as he had set out, and how as he passed beyond the Great Reef his enthusiasm had turned to trepidation and finally into fear. Yet he had sailed south, against all advice to the contrary. He'd had to see how his father had died. His father had died in the massive tides beyond the Reef, where, when the two moons eclipsed, the swells were as high as mountains. Hab felt a pang. What had happened to his idealism? Why was he at times infected with a sneaking cynicism? Why did he no longer care about the tides?

"Correction, sir," he said, his face settling. "The only man and only fool who's ever seen them."

"You belittle your achievement, mariner."

"As reckless and ill-planned an achievement as you'll ever see, sir. My father died in the tides. I should have taken my lesson from his reckless fascination with them. His fascination killed him."

"Are they as big as all that?"

"The smallest swells out there are ten times the size of the biggest swells at the Cliffs of Alquay. In a word, sir, they're monstrous." Hab gestured around the tent. "But if you please, forestall me no longer. My curiosity bites at me like a swarm of gnats. Give me your leisure. Scientific, so your sister says, but in what sense scientific? Certainly not scientific in the sense of brewing rainwater from rainwater, such as I saw in the next tent but one. So feed my curiosity, sir, just as your sister seeks to feed my stomach. I yearn to know."

Esten stared at Hab, a grin coming to his face. He lifted the beaker of rainwater. He held it to the light of the oil lamp. "Very well, Hab," he said. He swirled the water a bit. "To know is to ask. And I ask you this: What do you see in this beaker?"

Hab gazed at the beaker. "Rainwater," he said.

Esten nodded. "Yes, rainwater, but what else? Look more closely. What do you see on the bottom?"

Hab leaned forward. He detected sediment now, a dark granular material. "I see dirt, sir," he said.

"A quick observation." Esten gave him a cursory nod. "But not a precise one. It's ash, sir." The scientist's face settled. "Volcanic ash, Hab." Hab felt his brow furrowing in mystification. Volcanic ash? "Here you have the whole purpose of our enterprise in these few ounces of water. This volcanic ash." Hab didn't comprehend. He knew with fair certainty that Escalier hadn't erupted recently. How could there be volcanic ash in the rainwater? "Don't look so puzzled, Hab. One can learn a lot from volcanic ash."

"But has Escalier recently grown active?" he asked.

"No," said the scientist. "The last time it erupted was during Kellen's reign, and Kellen died eighty-two years ago."

Hab's eyes narrowed. "Then how can there be volcanic ash in that rainwater?" he asked.

Esten paused, and gazed at Hab with sober, serious eyes. "Because, Hab, somewhere out there . . . beyond the tides, beyond the waves . . . far, far away . . . where no sailor has ever sailed . . . there's another volcano." Esten let that sink in. Hab heard the mournful sound of the surf whispering from down the hill. "Another place, Hab," said Esten, his voice quieter now. "Another land."

Hab stared at the scientist, for the first time feeling the chill of his wet clothes. The rain came down in a sudden squall against the canvas roof of the tent. Another place. Another land. His gaze shifted to the two ounces of rainwater, to the murky sediment on the bottom. How could this be? Never had there been any evidence of any other place besides Paras. As children, they were taught this. In school, they were taught this. And as adults, they accepted it as an inalterable truth. In a world where honesty was the way, the honest truth was that they were alone in the world. Now this scientist was telling him otherwise? All his life he had wanted to believe in another place. All his life he had felt trapped by Paras. His restless spirit could, at times, hardly abide by the notion of being alone in the world. Now there was this other land?

"But how can this be so?" he asked, giving voice to his thoughts.

Esten looked at Hab, measuring his reaction, evaluating the effect of the news on the mariner. Finally he sighed. "It can be so, Hab, simply by being so."

Hab pressed his lips together. "But I've sailed everywhere, Esten. I've sailed in every direction. From Jondonq, Berberton, Zairab, and Dagu. I've never seen so much as a speck of land out there."

The scientist answered by quoting an old childhood verse. *"Paras is the Golden Land, the only land we know. Beyond her shores are only seas, and lonely winds that blow."* He shook his head. "How often we blind ourselves with the truisms of our grandmothers. Hab, it's out there, I know it is. This ash proves it. And if it means we must make a fundamental shift in the way we think about our world, then that's what we must do."

He stared at Hab as if he were again evaluating the seaman's reaction. Hab felt a burgeoning excitement inside him. Another place? Another land?

"I know, Hab," said Esten. "I found it hard to believe at first too."

He lifted the beaker again. "But I have to believe in this. The basins and barrels you see around the camp are helping me quantify the volcanic material," he said. "I plan to take the material back to Summerhouse. Parprouch has expressed an interest. I've done some preliminary analysis. I've discovered a high basalt content in the ash. There's also a high iron content. Wherever this ash is coming from, there's a lot of metal there. Far more metal than the meager ore pockets we have on Paras."

"No wonder Parprouch expresses an interest."

"You disparage your monarch." Esten sat back and took a deep breath. "I was in Carcil last fall. Do you know the Bluffs of Rageau?"

"I do."

"All those bluffs are stratified. You can see the layers clearly."

"I've seen them."

"Each layer represents a certain length of time, in geological terms, a thousand years, perhaps."

"So I've heard."

"At periodic intervals, these layers contain exactly the same kind of ash I've got in this beaker. That means our volcano, wherever it is, has erupted before." Esten put the beaker down. "Our volcano has a long history, Hab. It's been around for a long time. It's been out there for millions of years, and it's big. If Escalier can spawn a formation as large as the Island of Liars, this new volcano can easily spawn a land as massive as Paras."

"If it's so huge, why haven't we seen it before?"

"Because the tides turn us back before we get the chance."

The two men fell silent. Hab watched Esten. The scientist was deep in thought. Finally he roused himself and looked at Hab.

"You were probably nearly there, Hab," said Esten, "when you traveled to the equator as a lad."

"I saw nothing out there, Esten. No land, no birds, not even any driftwood."

"Maybe if you'd gone a little farther," said Esten.

"As you say, the tides turned me back."

The two men contemplated the inalterable fact of the tides in silence for a few seconds.

"We haven't got the ships to ride such swells, do we?" asked Esten.

"No, we don't," said Hab. "The boat I took was more a barrel, fit for a circus, not a long voyage. I nearly starved."

"But are the tides really that big?" asked Esten, his eyes filling with perplexity.

"In deep water, yes, they are. Picture Weathervane Tower at Summerhouse, how it stands on Pontefeau Cliff, how it vaults into the air as if to touch the sky. Now try to imagine a tide that high. Mountains of water, Esten—that's what I saw out there. Massive, boiling, surging mountains of water. There hasn't been a ship built yet that can keep its keel head to toe in such water. You'd need to line the bilge with lead to keep her upright, and where would we find such exorbitant amounts of lead? Even if we did, we'd still have a rough ride. Half our vessels would be lost. No, you can't defeat those tides. My father was lost in those tides. Anyone fool enough to make another attempt would suffer the same fate."

᠎᠎᠎ ᠎᠎᠎ ᠎᠎᠎

Such strange behavior in one who had been for the last ten years so completely predictable. How could Hab explain it to Guenard, who was now looking at him with perplexed eyes from the helm of the ship as they sailed south to the warmer waters off the coast of Jondonq? He stood beside his first mate, put the palm of his hand on the crown of his head, a childhood habit he had never outgrown, an automatic gesture of worry, puzzlement, and exasperation.

"Tell the hunters they'll get the wages I promised," said Hab.

"But how can you afford to pay such wages," asked his first mate, "when you abandon the hunt halfway through?"

"By paying them with our profit."

"That leaves so little profit, we won't have enough to buy tackle for next year's hunt. Why make yourself a guest of that scientist and his shrewish sister for a whole ten days when such a visit has proved ruinous to your more practical ventures?"

Hab now rubbed the crown of his head with his big palm. He was a big man, towered over the slight Guenard, and had shoulders wide and broad, with a square but at times stern face fringed with a traditional seaman's beard. How could he explain to Guenard the changes he felt inside himself? He glanced toward the bow of the boat, where Jara Pepteri stood watching the waves. The shrewish sister, he thought. Despite her at times surly disposition, Hab was starting to like the young woman. And as for Esten, he could listen to the man talk for hours. How could he explain to Guenard that for the last ten years he had buried his dreams and notions of a wider and greater existence for the sake of hunting whales and supporting his family in Jauny? How could he tell Guenard that there might not even be a hunt next year, that a new dream had taken hold, this dream of a new place, a strange and unknown continent out beyond the waves?

"I'll sacrifice my wages to buy more tackle," he said.

He let his palm drop from his crown, as if exhausted by his reply. The certain plodding round of the seasons in his life were no longer so certain. Guenard said nothing. By the way the small man stared straight ahead Hab knew his first mate wasn't pleased. So he left Guenard at the helm. He walked to the bow of the ship and joined Jara Pepteri. They were taking the Pepteris as far as Cranelle, where brother and sister would then travel inland to the Lake of Life and Winterhouse to study the Great Code.

"He's not happy, is he?" said Jara.

Hab grinned, but it was a wistful grin. "He rarely is. He has a brooding nature, Jara, and so he broods."

"And what of your nature, Hab Miquay? Do you brood, or do you have a sunnier outlook?"

Hab was surprised by the question. But, as honesty was the way, the lifeblood of Paras, he tried to tell the truth, even though he wasn't sure what the truth was.

"I try to be good, Jara," he said. "I try to be fair. I try to be honest. And I try to be happy."

"And do you find happiness an easily available commodity?"

The bluntness of her inquiry disquieted him. "No. I don't. I lack the means to find a common sort of comfort in myself. I'm never satisfied with who I am. And I'm never satisfied with where I am. I'm always going someplace else, and when I get to someplace else, I'm not satisfied there either." He laughed, made a joke of it. "It's a torturous existence, to be sure."

She laughed too. He was always surprised by the sound of it: sweet, musical, with a natural cadence that enhanced the light trill of her voice.

"And so you wish to go to that other place out there," she said, gesturing southward over the waves.

What she said was true. From a small bit of ash in the bottom of a glass beaker had sprung this grand new scheme. For such a scheme he would gladly abandon fifty whale hunts. Here was a new truth. The truth that Paras was no longer alone in the world. And in a world where honesty was the way, that meant a lot to Hab.

"I mean to try," he said.

In a world where honesty was the way, but where so many people simply used the 28 Rules of the Formulary as a convenient way to hide their lies, Hab felt this new truth was important.

"And once you get there are you going to be satisfied?" she asked.

She was being playful, but he couldn't be playful back, and when he looked over the bow of the ship with an intense longing, her eyes grew serious, and her manner solemn. He felt exposed in front of her, vulnerable, couldn't hide the strength with which he felt about this new land. He knew what it was. He had felt it many times before. It was hope. Desperate, clutching, but determined hope.

"Yes," he said. "I will at last be satisfied."

CHAPTER THREE

Hab sat in the kitchen of the family compound in Jauny contemplating his mother, Gougou. She sat in a wheelchair, her mountain of a body draped in a blue gown. Chouc, his younger brother, stood beside her, feeding her choice chunks of roast joadre. Several thousand decou sat in five different piles on the table, the money he'd earned from his whaling expedition. Gougou gestured indifferently at the money.

"I was expecting a lot more," she said. "You brought back twice this much last year."

Hab leaned forward, folded his hands on the table. Another place. Another land. That's all he could think of now. "I abandoned the hunt halfway through," he said.

Her small blue eyes widened. The folds of fat underneath them sagged. She pushed Chouc's hand away. Chouc looked at the greasy piece of meat, then ate it himself.

"Is this Hab who tells me this?" asked Gougou.

How could he explain this to his mother so that she would understand? She was like everybody else. All her life she had believed that Paras was the only place. He wished there were some way he could make up the shortfall in his income. But even some of this money on the table was going to have to pay crew wages. He'd thought he would feel guilty. But he didn't. His obsession with this unknown continent had taken root too firmly to feel any guilt. All he wanted to do was make Gougou understand.

"Like I say, Esten thinks there's another continent out there," he said.

Yes, another continent, one that brought a keen doubt to his mother's eyes. Gougou stared at him, horrified by the heresy he was speaking. "I think you should go to Pendagal and talk to the priests," she said at last. "What has happened to my stalwart boy? The one thing I think we all admire about you, Hab, is your dependable lack of imagination."

He felt his anger flare, withdrew his hand. "I have more imagination than you might think, Mother," he said. What had happened to his mother? Why, when she spoke, could he hear nothing but the voice of convention? He knew he shouldn't be angry with her. Her life hadn't been the best. So young to be a widow. And with an eldest son like Romal, who frittered away the family wealth, naturally she was concerned about money. "Gougou . . ." he said, using the intimate address. "Gougou . . . Esten and I have decided . . . we're beginning to wonder whether it might be possible to go to this place, wherever it is . . . that is, if we could design ships strong enough, and resistant enough, whether we might actually be able to navigate the waters beyond the Reef."

His mother's eyes widened, and her lower lip trembled. "What about the tides?" she asked, incredulous.

"We hope to design ships strong enough to—"

"No, Hab." A look of fear came to Gougou's face. "Your father died in those tides."

Here was the sad and common bond between them. Yet at the same time, it was part of the reason he wanted to go so badly. His father had lost his life out beyond the Reef, and he had to go there.

"I know he did," he said. "But we think if we can build a ship, or maybe several ships, that could take us through the tides, we could actually go to this place."

He couldn't go on, not against the intense worry he saw in his mother's face. "This Esten's a fool for putting such an idea into your head," she said. "He should spend a year in penitence at Pendagal." She leaned forward, shifting her considerable bulk with effort. "We love you, Hab. If we can still take any pride in the name of Miquay or in the House of Cloudesley, it's because of your steadfast and caring character. Chouc loves you, don't you, Chouc?"

Hab looked at his young brother, nearly twenty years his junior, a simpleton at his birth, a simpleton still. "Don't go, Hab," said Chouc. "Who would take me swimming?"

Gougou frowned. "Certainly not Romal," she said. "You would never get him out of the gaming house long enough to get him down to the beach."

Hab felt at war with himself. His imagination, for so long suppressed, was now like a wild conflagration. Having kept himself on such a short leash all his life, with all his energies concentrated on supporting his family, he now wanted to roam more than ever. The accumulation and wise husbandry of money seemed beside the point in the face of this other continent out there. He had suffered long and hard for his family. Now it was time that they should suffer for him, and not only for him but for the rest of Paras, because he felt he had to do this for Paras as much as for himself.

Hab mustered his resolve. "There are certain hardwoods in Dagu . . . and there's a shipbuilder in Fadil who . . . a man by the name of Aigre . . . and in fact, Parprouch already has a number of ships in his fleet which might reasonably be converted. If we give them lead-lined keels, and waterproof their decks with extra Affed oil—"

"Hab, please. Stop. You would die in those tides, just like your father did. I won't hear any more about it. If you love your mother, you will forget this nonsense at once."

But he couldn't forget. He didn't want to forget. For the first time in years he actually felt alive, and his chronic emptiness didn't feel so bad now.

ᘓᘓᘓ

Hab walked down to the Estuary. Everywhere around him rose the tan-colored buildings of Jauny, with their rounded archways and doorways, fluted chimneys, and sea-green shutters. Chevul-drawn wagons crowded the streets, old men played cards at the stone tables lining Place Ourrice, and shopkeepers had their windows open and their stalls brimming. A girl of maybe seventeen danced half naked at the mile-stone next to the quay while sailors threw amber coins. Hab made his way out onto Quay Jouliser. He gazed at all the schooners, junks, punts, scows, windjammers, runabouts, and yawls crowding the placid green waters of the Estuary. The air billowed with sails of every description.

As he stared out at the water, where the sand-colored buildings on the opposite bank two miles away were reflected on the emerald sur-face, he tried to stop the narcotic of his own imagination, tried to think of the practicalities. He took a deep breath. No doubt about it, he was short of money. Esten's suggestion of approaching their monarch, Parprouch, about the voyage seemed the only route to go. So short of money, he couldn't help thinking about the iron content in the ash from that volcano so far away. If such iron could be extracted from this unknown continent and brought to Paras, where metal of any kind fetched a handsome price, his money troubles would be over. A ton of iron, and he would be the richest man in Paras. He didn't care about the wealth for his own sake. But such metal would certainly restore the family fortunes.

He walked to the edge of the quay and looked into the water. Fish schooled massively beneath the surface, their scales flashing pink, gold, and green in the sunlight. He picked up a shell and tossed it into the water.

"Hab?"

He turned around. Chouc stared at him with his simple brown eyes.

"You followed me," said Hab.

Chouc looked at the ground.

"You found a shell," said Chouc. "And threw it in the water."

Hab took a few steps toward his brother and tousled the lad's hair. "A shell likes water better than it likes dry land."

"Gougou was crying when you left," said Chouc. The boy looked at the quay, fighting back his own tears, his lower lip quivering. "I've had dreams."

Hab's eyes narrowed. Chouc might be a simpleton, but it behooved one to pay attention to his dreams—more often than not they turned out to be clairvoyant.

"What kind of dreams?" asked Hab.

Chouc's face went blank. "There's a lot of rock," he said. "Nothing grows there. The earth is black." Chouc's eyelids drooped. "I see a lot of blood. I don't know where it all comes from. I see it everywhere. On the beach, up in the hills, in the caves. I see a land where there aren't any people. I see a land where there isn't any mercy." His eyes returned to normal. He looked up at Hab in his usual simple way. "Don't go, Hab. Stay with us here. We need you here."

Hab walked into the compound courtyard, a sunny place with lemon trees in bloom and a fountain splashing in the middle. He found Thia, his twenty-five-year-old sister-in-law. She worked in the kitchen garden, tending to some shallots. This was usually Cook's work, but Hab knew Thia liked to play at gardening, wore the latest gardening fashions from Bondalais Avenue, was dressed in a long skirt of the palest salmon, a blouse with puffed sleeves, and leather gardening gloves from the finest tanner in Fieze Place. She wore a sunbonnet on her head. Inspecting these clothes, Hab saw not a speck of dirt on them anywhere. She was the wife of Lord Cloudesley, after all. She didn't get dirty, even when she was gardening.

As he approached, she stopped her work and stood up. She had a fair face, but today her fairness was marred by an anxious frown. She took a few steps toward him and rested her hand on his arm.

"I've heard the news," she said.

He noted a faded bruise on her left cheek, and not for the first time suspected his brother Romal might mistreat her from time to time. If only Hab could prove it. Or if only Thia would step forward and admit to it, instead of always protecting Romal.

"Then you've heard that I'm sailing soon, Sister," he said.

"Hab, you can't leave us. Who would look after us?"

He gestured at the garden. "You can grow vegetables. You can help supplement Cook's larder."

He meant this as a kindly jest, and she took it as such, a self-deprecating smile coming to her face.

"But this place you're going to," she said. "Won't it be dangerous?"

"We don't know. We're going there to find out."

"I would hate it if you got hurt, Brother."

There it was again, that earnestness in her voice that made him uncomfortable. She looked at him with her wide blue eyes, and he couldn't help thinking that she might in some way have *feelings* for him. He saw it all the time: in the way she touched him, how she looked at him, and how she made sure Cook baked the apple pastries he liked to eat from time to time. She didn't seem to realize that he felt none of it himself. He was simply fond of her in a brotherly fashion. He felt he had a duty to protect her. He knew she was delicate and unschooled, a child really. As Lady Cloudesley, he was honor bound to protect her, and to give her advice when he thought it was prudent.

"You have to stand by Romal while I'm gone," he said. "You know how bad he is with money. Make sure you keep an eye on the family books, and don't let him do anything foolish."

"Romal *is* foolish," she said, the frown coming back to her face. "He'll do foolish things, no matter how I might intervene."

"Aye, but you are his wife, and you must do what you can to support him, and to counsel him in his financial affairs."

Her eyes moistened. "So you're really going?"

With brotherly tenderness he took her right hand in both of his and stroked it the way he might stroke a child's hand, trying to reassure her.

"I'll be back, Thia. And when I'm back, I'll try to make things better around here."

🐚🐚🐚

He found Romal at a gaming house on Ourrice Boulevard. The gaming house was dim and smoky, filled with young nobles, the dissipated sons of dissipated houses, men intent on squandering, like Romal, the last of their inherited wealth in questionable contests of chance. Romal sat at a back table with some friends. He was dressed in high leather boots, white breeches, and a lavender jacket with gold trim. Hab felt out of place in his simple seaman's blues. Romal looked up from his game of cards, his color high from drink.

"Here's our famous whaler," he said, turning to his companions.

"Romal, I've come to say farewell." As usual, he was curt with his older brother. "I sail in a month. The support of the family compound now rests on your shoulders."

He tried to feel a shred of warmth for his brother, but the casual disdain he saw in Romal's eyes made it impossible.

"Go ahead, Hab," said Romal. "Try to find this fire-spewing mountain of yours. I shouldn't be surprised if you should fall off the edge of the world. We'll manage fine without you."

Hab stared at Romal, at the foppish curls of hair massed on his head, at his arrogant thin lips and his twinkling blue eyes. A man who lived for pleasure, who never thought of tomorrow, who held as his birthright the doctrine that the bountiful Paras would always provide.

"Manage how, Romal?" he asked. "You have no work. And the family stipend is nearly gone."

Romal shrugged with a kind of joyous incredulity. "I shall sell Cloudesley, of course."

Hab's eyes widened. "Sell Cloudesley?" Hab thought of the family estate in the foothills of the Lesser Oradels.

"Don't gape at me, Brother," said Romal. "You look like a fish. I'm not about to go harpooning whales, am I? Cloudesley should fetch a good price. Several hundred thousand, I expect. That should keep us going until you get back." Romal grinned. "If you get back."

CHAPTER FOUR

Hab hired a boat and sailed north from Jauny up the River Necontreu toward Winterhouse and the Lake of Life, a journey of five hundred miles, tacking against the wind most of the way, making no more than seven knots an hour. Guenard was with him. So was Jeter. Both were signing on.

"So Esten knows you've made up your mind?" Guenard asked Hab.

The man stank. As usual. He hadn't had a bath in months. Flies circled around his dirty matted hair.

"I have no reason to stay," said Hab.

"Nor any real reason to go," said the tall lank Jeter, who stood at the rudder, steering the longboat abeam of the wind.

"I have so many reasons for going that I can hardly count them all," said Hab. He grinned. "But I think the biggest reason I go is because I'm the only fool who will."

"I've gone through our profits," said Guenard dourly.

"So have I," said Hab.

"Then you know how bleak our situation is."

"We have nothing."

Guenard looked out at the river with dispirited eyes. "You should abandon this voyage, Hab. Go to Parprouch, yes, ask him for a small loan, not to sail to your certain death in the tides but to rebuild your whaling concern. I've never known you to make such questionable decisions before."

"And I've never known you to raise such objections."

"The only objection I have is one of money."

"This new place has iron," said Hab. "We've found it in the ash. Wouldn't you like to buy our own fleet, Guenard? Aren't you getting tired of renting Heugen's old boats year after year?"

Guenard considered, his lips coming together. "Aye, his rent is a hard thing, and getting harder every year."

"So when I say I must go to this place, I haven't entirely abandoned my practical concerns."

Guenard thought some more and finally nodded. "Aye, then we're fools together." A grudging smile came to his face. "A pound of iron, eh, Hab, and we'd be on our feet again."

"Fools together for a pound of iron," agreed Hab.

"And Esten's been at Winterhouse this last month?" asked Jeter.

"He has," said Hab. "He's deciphering the Great Code, or at least trying to. He goes there every year."

"And the priests let him stay at Winterhouse?" asked Guenard.

"He knows every last one of them," said Hab.

"I'm rather fond of word puzzles myself," said Guenard.

"The Great Code is more than a word puzzle," said Hab.

On the left bank of the Necontreu, Hab saw the Lesser Oradels rise in mellow rounded peaks. He saw the giant amber towers of Summerhouse glistening in the sunlight.

"Has Esten made any headway on the Code?" asked Jeter.

Hab continued to stare at the towers of Summerhouse. "Esten is a scientist, Jeter," he said. "When he has something he can prove, he'll let us know."

♪♪♪

They reached Winterhouse four days later. While Summerhouse was an amber palace, Winterhouse was a stone castle, much older, a fort with battlements from the days when Paras actually had wars. Hab saw it from a long way off, a mile or two down the South Road and across the

Grand Sward. He saw the Lake of Life glittering blue through the trees behind. As they reached the Grand Sward, an emerald expanse of lawn immediately before Winterhouse, Hab saw the Great Code: 2,362 enigmatic and undeciphered glyphs carved into a steep bluff of gray granite rising immediately to the left of the Grand Sward. At the base of the Great Code, giant metal struts rose out of the earth. The metal was blotchy, weathered, stained light gray in places.

Hab saw both Esten and Jara up on scaffolding studying the glyphs. While Guenard and Jeter went to ask the priests for lodgings in Winterhouse, Hab walked across the Grand Sward to the scaffolding. The Lake of Life, nearly twenty miles across, murmured peacefully as small waves tumbled against its stony shore.

"Ho, there!" called Hab.

Esten and Jara looked down from their work. Esten wore a baggy gray cap. Jara was in a loose blue shift. Both were red-faced from working in the heat. A great smile came to Esten's face. Even Jara seemed happy to see him. Both left their work and started coming down.

"Stay there," called Hab. "I'm coming up."

Hab gripped the wooden crossbars and climbed. He gazed at the carvings, tried to see a pattern in them, struggled to sort out the wedge-shaped strokes, deep gashes, pinwheels, and sunbursts. As he neared the top he looked up and saw Jara peering down at him.

"Do you need a hand?" she called.

"I can manage," he said.

She reached down and gave him a hand anyway.

"Thank you, Jara," he said. "I hope the season finds you well."

"You've shaved your beard," she said.

"Aye."

She made a face. "I'm not sure I like a man with a bare chin."

"You're here about the sea voyage," said Esten, stepping forward. The scientist rested his hand on the mariner's shoulder as he climbed onto the platform. "You've thought about it. I can see that you have."

"I've thought of nothing else," said Hab. "How does one safely navigate a fleet of boats through killer tides to the other side of the world? An endeavor like that takes a lot of thought, Esten. We'll need at least fifteen ships. Do you think we can get that many from Parprouch?"

Jara spoke up. "Parprouch is a parsimonious fool. You'll be lucky to get a rowboat."

In a milder tone Esten said, "We can only try, my friend. If we convince Parprouch that the voyage might be of some remunerative value, our chances rise immeasurably."

"What about the lead?" asked Hab.

"He'll give you iron and call it lead," said Jara.

Esten smiled nervously at his sister. "Jara, please, temper your remarks when speaking of the monarch. To accuse him of even such a hypothetical falsehood is but a few steps from treason."

"We'll need that lead to line the keels," cautioned Hab.

"I see we've much to plan," said the scientist. "Ships, lead, crews, provisions, sails, rigging, charts, sextants—a plethora of details that must and will be examined each in their turn, and with the closest scrutiny. But you must be tired from your journey, Hab. Let us consider these details when you've had a good rest, and the sweat and dirt of the road aren't mantled upon your brow. You need food. You need drink. You need to reacquaint yourself with the inspiring prospects and views of the Lake of Life, with the glorious pathways along her shores, and with the venerable forests and dales that have so long been a part of her heritage. Our strategies and campaigns can wait a day. There's no need to plan our voyage all on the spot, especially up here on this hot and sun-blasted perch. Stay a week with us at Winterhouse." He glanced at the Great Code, now looking as if he wanted to get back to work on it. "Help us ponder this wondrous work of the ancients." He shrugged. "As to the other, all we need do for now is send a messenger to Lord Teur. He'll arrange for us an audience with the monarch." He waved his palm at the Great Code. "Tell me, Hab, when was your last visit to this holy place?"

Hab glanced at the strange carvings. "Seven years ago." He turned to Jara. "Jara, is the king really so acquisitive?"

She arched her brow dryly. "You don't negotiate with the king. You barter. Why he spends his time at Summerhouse I can't say. He'd be much happier hawking secondhand goods on a street corner."

"Jara, please," said Esten, giving Hab a patient nod, as if his sister were someone who had to be humored. "Winterhouse is a place where we should try to be charitable to everyone, especially to our monarch."

"The monarch doesn't need charity," quipped Jara. "He takes whatever he wants."

"Please!" said Esten, now sounding genuinely angry. "Let us turn our attention to the Great Code. Our time with the king will come, and I'm sure when it does he'll listen dispassionately to our appeal and make his decision fairly. Let us not forget, it was Parprouch who funded our expedition to Dagu last month. And he funds our work on those fossilized bones on the Island of Maju. The Court has been exceedingly kind to the House of Pepteri over the past decade. His support has allowed us to come to the Great Code every summer to study these miraculous carvings."

"I half suspect he believes these carvings are nothing more than a formula for turning straw into gold," said Jara.

Hab was now staring at the Great Code. What did it mean? Who had carved it into this granite wall? The mystery was a deep one.

"Have you ever understood any of it?" he asked Esten.

Esten looked at the wall wistfully. He examined the nearest carving. "No," he said. "I've been coming here every year since my first pilgrimage twenty-five years ago. I've cataloged and grouped the symbols, but I don't think I'll live long enough to find out exactly what they mean." His eyes narrowed under his dark bushy brows. "This wall makes promises, Hab, but it never keeps them."

ᔰᔰᔰ

After Hab had a rest and a wash, he and Jara went for a walk. A forest of conifers surrounded Winterhouse and lined the Lake of Life. They walked in silence along the well-kept pathways through the forest for a while. He couldn't help feeling as if Jara had something on her mind. Her stride had an irascible character, and she often walked ahead and then waited for him to catch up. He kept his pace relaxed. She simmered. He grinned. And she simmered some more.

Finally she said, "You're not going to leave me behind."

These words came out with the force of a cork from a champagne bottle.

"Leave you behind?" he said. "As far as I can see, you're always ten steps ahead of me."

"You tease me, Hab," she said, her brow settling. "I'm not in the mood for teasing right now. My brother says I should stay behind, and though I've always tried my best to obey him, I will not warrant exclusion from such an important undertaking. I study the fossils on the Island of Maju with him. I study the Great Code with him. I don't see why I can't study this new continent with him. You can't begin to conceive of just how much I yearn to go."

He stopped, looked more closely at Jara. Did she yearn like he did? he wondered. To go. To find out. Did they have something more in common with each other than just their kind and civil regard?

"Your brother forbids you?" said Hab.

"He does."

"What are his objections?"

"That there are too many dangers, particularly the tides."

"Do you fear the tides?"

A hard glint came to her eyes. "I fear nothing. You must convince my brother that I should go."

Hab began to walk again, thinking about it. "How shall I convince your brother, though?" he asked.

"You convince him by telling him it shall be so." Her features softened. "Hab . . ." He glanced at her. He had a simple short name, a common name, but somehow when it came from her lips, he felt something jump inside. "Hab . . . when our parents died, Esten became my guardian, and he was my guardian for a long time. True, I'm one year away from legal age. But Esten isn't really my guardian anymore. It's really the other way around. Esten is a brilliant man, but he's not a particularly practical one. I'm the one who looks after all our money. I'm the one who keeps order in our house at home. And when we're abroad, I'm the one who looks after all our travel arrangements. Esten doesn't know how to care for himself. If I didn't go with him, he wouldn't feed himself properly. His clothes would reek from lack of washing. His hair would become a nest for bugs. He would lose track of time. And on a ship he might walk off the deck and not realize it until he's up to his neck in water. Over and above that, I want to go to this place with such a burning desire in my heart that I can hardly sleep at night."

Still a year away from legal age, he thought. But now he saw that every bit of Jara Pepteri was a woman. He put his hand on her shoulder and gave it a friendly shake. "Consider yourself part of my crew, then," he said.

ᔕᔕᔕ

Ten days later Hab and Esten stood before Parprouch in the Main Hall at Summerhouse. Parprouch, of the House of Zadeaux, was an exceedingly tall man. He sat on his amber throne with his back erect, his skinny shoulders as square as a picture frame, and his pale blue eyes looking bored. He wore an amber crown. His jaw-length hair was white. So was his beard. He leaned forward, put his elbow on the armrest of his throne, and rested his bearded chin in his palm like an opera-goer getting ready for an overly long second act. Hab stood behind Esten. Esten knelt before the monarch.

"Very well, Esten," said Parprouch. "You've explained this new continent in enough detail. Too much detail, I should think. Please, get off your knee. Let me hear what the mariner has to say." The monarch looked at Hab. "Mariner, step forward."

Hab stepped forward and bowed his head. "Sire," he said. Esten stood up and backed away, as fearful as Hab was calm.

"What is it that you want from me, mariner?" asked Parprouch.

"Sire, a handful of seaworthy vessels. We voyage to this new place. We offer you the opportunity to grant us your patronage."

The sovereign's eyes narrowed. "You offer *me* the opportunity?" he said. "As a man looking for a handout, your insolence is perhaps misplaced, mariner. Please remember that I'm the one who dispenses opportunities. And I see no opportunity here, except the opportunity to empty the royal coffers to no distinct advantage. What possible return could the government expect from such a voyage besides a half dozen shipwrecks and a hundred dead sailors?"

"Fifteen ships, Sire, refitted, is all we should need."

"Fifteen ships?" said the monarch, his eyes widening.

"Aye, Sire," said Hab. "And they would have to be refitted."

"Refitted?" said Parprouch. "Refitted how?"

"Their keels would have to be lined with lead to keep them upright in the heavy swells beyond the Reef."

"Lined with lead?" said the monarch. "Preposterous!" Parprouch laughed. "Esten, is your mariner of sound mind? Does he think I look like a man who is prepared to sink a dozen tons of lead into the ocean and risk the lives of a hundred seamen so he can voyage halfway round the world to climb a violently erupting volcano?"

Esten stepped forward. "Sire . . . I . . . Hab Miquay is a most worthy man . . . and I . . . ." The scientist lapsed into silence, cowed by the monarch's stern look.

Hab took another step forward and reluctantly bent to his knee. "Sire, I know many men and women who would eagerly volunteer for such a voyage. Forgive me, Sire, but when I look around Jondonq, and I see the pleasant way we live, how comfortable we all are, how we indulge ourselves constantly because we are constantly surrounded by plenty, I can't help thinking that such a voyage might inspire a new, and perhaps a better, way of looking at our lives here on Paras, and make us more grateful for what we possess. We too often take Paras for granted because we have always believed in her supreme place in the world. Now she has become but one of two places in our world. She's not supreme anymore. And we should learn to cherish her more than we do."

"A new perspective hardly fills the government's treasury," said Parprouch.

"I, for one, shall gladly play the part of admiral," said Hab.

Parprouch contemplated Hab. "Mariner, you are bold. I can see that your arms are strong and your hands are blistered, and that your legs are like two mainmasts and that your dark eyes have in them intelligence and integrity. What you lack is sense." Parprouch glanced at Esten. "What you lack is a practical eye for the cost of things."

A footman appeared at the door, dressed in pink satin, and gave Parprouch a courtly bow.

"Forgive me, Sire," he said, "but your guests have arrived."

"See to them," Parprouch said to the footman. The footman retreated. Parprouch rose from his throne. "Gentlemen, I thank you for this most interesting diversion. Unfortunately, diversions are of little pecuniary value to me. Were you to convince me of a substantive and probable return on this ambitious but by no means certain speculation, I might invest, if not the money, then at least a more protracted consideration of your venture. But I'm mistrustful of the things you've told me so far. A continent, yes, but so far away, and so caged by the tides, why waste breath on it? Yes, fun to think about, a prod to my stodgy imagination, but ultimately without material purpose." He descended the steps of his dais. "Good day to you, gentlemen. I really must dress."

Parprouch gave them a final nod and strode down the long glittering hall. Hab and Esten glanced at each other. Then Hab stared after Parprouch. Parprouch opened the arched doorway. The sun glistened off the mother-of-pearl inlay. Hab saw guests out in the drive, nobility of one sort or another, men and women who lived on inherited wealth, who'd found favor with the Court. He grew suddenly angry. He had to go to this new continent, and nothing was going to stop him. This new continent pulled at him. He left Esten's side and hurried after the king. His stride quickened. He heard Esten hurrying behind him. He stopped, turned.

"Stay, friend," he said. "I think a mariner's word alone with the king might suffice in this delicate circumstance."

Esten nodded uncertainly and stayed where he was. "As you wish."

Hab's footsteps resounded on the inlaid marble. Down this hallway walked his only chance, the tall and grasping Parprouch. All the women waiting out on the drive had their breasts exposed. The men wore codpieces, some of them jeweled, some of them tasseled. In a few final strides, Hab, in his obsession, sacrificed his lifelong instinct for small truths on the altar of this much larger truth. The change left him breathless and dizzy, but more determined than ever. Parprouch turned, startled to see the brawny mariner charging so steadfastly toward him.

"Sire, please, I believe I forgot to mention one thing," he said. "If you could give me your ear for one more moment."

A resigned and impatient grin came to Parprouch's face, as if he'd long grown to expect last-minute appeals from his petitioners. He looked down at Hab from his great height, lifting his chin into the air.

"I give you leave, mariner," said Parprouch. "Be quick. The item you missed?"

"Metal, Sire," he said. He watched the monarch's jaw twitch. "Mountains of it. Everywhere you step you can't but find a nugget of lead or a brick of iron." The monarch inhaled suddenly, as if he'd been jabbed with a pin. "Copper can be found as easily as limestone." The monarch's eyes showed not even a hint of boredom now. "Silver shines from open bluffs. Gold is discovered everywhere in the rivers. Nickel glazes the mountainsides."

So there it was. A misrepresentation. Rule 7 of the Formulary, broken as easily as a boy breaks a stick. Hab felt as if he had stepped into a shadow. He should have clarified. He should have said "might," "could," or "maybe." He felt ill. Truth was the way. Honesty was the light. Falsehood was harshly punished with banishment to the Island of Liars. Yet the risk now seemed a paltry thing compared to that undiscovered continent half a world away. The king continued to stare at him.

"Metal?" said the king, his eyes now looking as simple as Chouc's.

Hab nodded sagely. How strange it felt. To never lie in his life, to live rigorously by the 28 Rules of the Formulary, and then, for his first misstep, to lie so grandly, and to the monarch no less! He felt diminished by his lie.

"The ferrous content of our volcanic ash confirms it." How glibly the lies slipped from his tongue. If Rule 7 could be broken, why not go all the way and sacrifice Rule 9 as well, the one about exaggeration? Anything to convince the king. "Enough metal to fill all of Summerhouse, all of Winterhouse, and all of Gorolet Palace." These careless felonies were enough to send him to the Island of Liars for life, but he pressed on, using these lies as the necessary currency of discovery. "Enough metal to fill the Lake of Life, Sire."

The king lifted his fingers and absently tapped his lips, already counting up the mountains of metal. How easily the great grow stupefied, thought Hab.

"Can such bold extrapolation be true?" asked Parprouch, his voice raspy in its quiet rapaciousness.

"It can't be but otherwise, Sire," said Hab. "In every pound of ash, we find significant quantities of iron. If this new place spits up iron the way an infant spits up mother's milk, can we but doubt that the whole place shines with metal?"

The king looked suddenly doubtful. The king, apparently, was above Rule 18 of the Formulary, the one about distrust. "Why didn't the scientist tell me of this? Esten!" he called. "Esten Pepteri, step forward, please."

Esten approached and bowed. "Sire?"

"The mariner tells me this new continent is a place of metal."

Esten glanced at Hab, his face turning red. "We have found iron in our ash, Sire, it is true."

"In what concentration?" asked Parprouch.

"In a concentration sufficient enough to be detected," said the scientist.

The king cocked his brow. "Sufficient enough to be in any way remunerative?"

"From the ash itself, Sire, no. From this new continent, perhaps."

"The mariner says there's enough metal there to fill the Lake of Life."

Esten blanched but otherwise controlled himself. Collusion. Rule 14 of the Formulary. "That might be so, Sire."

Parprouch's eyes were wide now. He'd forgotten about his guests. His eyes glittered with these untold mountains of metal. "Speculation I admire," he said. "Exaggeration's a crime. The mariner says everywhere you step you find a nugget of lead or a brick of iron, that copper can be found as easily as limestone, and that silver shines from open bluffs." Parprouch arched his brow. "Does such speculation, in your estimation, Pepteri, stray within the forbidden bounds of exaggeration?"

Esten looked at Hab, reddening even further. "Our evidence supports his speculation," he said, in a small weak voice. He turned back to the monarch. "The iron content of the ash is high. Other metals will likely be abundant. Exaggeration is the stuff of dreams. In this case, the mariner speculates admirably."

"Then the return might reasonably be expected to be high?"

"Yes, Sire."

"We want ten percent," said Hab.

Here was an argument the sovereign could understand, and one that didn't break any Rules of the Formulary. After all, one of Hab's own reasons for going was money. How happy he would be if he never had to hunt another whale in his life. How sorry he sometimes felt for the poor lumbering creatures, harpooning their bladders, forcing them toward shore to slowly suffocate in the shallows.

"Ten percent!" said Parprouch. To even get the king talking percentages was, he knew, a great step forward. "Would you rob me of one in ten chevuls? Would you filch from me one in ten concubines? Would you take from my larder one in ten loaves?"

"Sire, I would," said Hab. "You say I have no sense. But I'm not stupid. Ten percent of everything we find out there. The rest we claim in the name of the House of Zadeaux."

"Seven percent," said Parprouch.

Hab remembered Jara's words. You don't negotiate with the king. You barter.

"Nine," he said.

"Eight," said the king. "Providing you grant me the following conditions."

"And what conditions might those be, Sire?" asked Hab.

"That should you fail, the House of Cloudesley will indemnify the House of Zadeaux for every ship lost. This means that should you fail, the House of Cloudesley will be destitute. So please talk to your brother, Hab Miquay. You must vouchsafe Lord Cloudesley's consent. If you are in agreement with this preliminarily, and he agrees in principle to consent, then I'll have Lord Teur draw up the papers."

CHAPTER FIVE

Not fifteen ships, but seven. They lay at anchor high in the water of the Estuary, side by side, their multitude of masts rising into the pale yellow sky of morning like a forest, their bowsprits thrusting southward as if in eager anticipation of the voyage that lay ahead. Hundreds of smaller boats crowded around these seven noble vessels. The good burghers of Jauny were out in their finest blues to witness the historic event.

Hab stood on the royal platform a few paces from Parprouch. He felt ridiculous. His capacious three-cornered hat all covered with pink plumes felt too heavy on his head. His navy-blue admiral's coat with its tails hanging down to his ankles and the sword made of real metal dragging on the ground made him feel encumbered and hot. Worst of all, his ceremonial codpiece, curved and long, sticking straight up in the air, left him red-faced with embarrassment. He would have preferred his regular seaman's blues. Not only that, he was so clean, washed, and perfumed by his court-appointed valet that he felt he could easily roll around in the guts of a beached bladder whale just so he could smell like himself again. The bare-breasted Ladies of the Court stared at him with undisguised interest. At the party last night, he'd been propositioned by seventeen of them.

Parprouch finished his speech. The crowd roared in approval. They tossed their hats in the air. A quick-swooping nuiyau bird made off with one of the hats. Parprouch turned to the trumpeter and gave him a signal. The trumpeter turned to the others in his horn-blowing guild, and together, they filled the air with a majestic flourish of sound.

The pomp seemed hollow to Hab, so much gloss, like rouge on the face of a decrepit old courtesan. Seven barges emerged from Parprouch's private dock near Gorolet Palace. Hab felt his palms growing suddenly cold.

"What's this, Sire?" he asked the monarch.

Parprouch eyes glittered. "You'll be taking these barges along with you."

"What for?"

"For my metal," said Parprouch. "What else?"

"But Sire, to tow these barges along might endanger the stability of our launches when we encounter the deep-water tides," he said.

"I'll trust your able seamanship to solve such problems, mariner."

"But, Sire—"

"I decree it, and so it shall be," said Parprouch, his voice hardening. "Now, please, let's enjoy the spectacle."

But Hab couldn't enjoy the spectacle. A sick thing indeed, the 28 Rules of the Formulary, if even the monarch would stoop to such misrepresentation.

***

The seven ships of exploration sailed from Jauny down the Estuary. The water changed color—from muddy green to sparkling aquamarine—as they crossed the Sea of Maju. The tides came, but because they sailed behind the bulwark of the Island of Maju, the tides were broken into easily navigable twenty-foot swells, nothing but a series of gentle lifts, the sea rising a few hundred feet in a period of six hours.

By late afternoon, the Island of Maju hove into view to the south. Though still several hours away, Maju was like a beacon to Hab, the last port of call before open seas, a tropical place where the air was filled with the scent of spice, and where the dark-skinned women wore hardly anything at all. It was here that his father had last stopped before sailing to his death in the tides. Hab had also made a stopover here during his own reckless voyage to the tides. Here was the traditional last sight of land, the Island of Maju, a place he loved because it was also the first sight of land whenever he returned from a southward voyage. He prayed to Ouvant that he might see it again someday.

"We'll anchor in Perro for the night," said Hab to Esten, "then circle round in the morning. The tides will be retreating, and we should be well clear of Paras by tomorrow evening."

Esten looked as if he were hardly listening. He held a telescope to his eye. "You can see it," he said. "The ash." He took the telescope away from his eye and handed it to Hab. "Have a look."

Hab looked through the telescope at the sky. The air a thousand feet up seemed to break apart into tiny white specks, a barely discernible band of volcanic confetti floating from horizon to horizon in a white river of high-flying ejecta. Hab took the telescope away.

"Then we're on course," he said. "As much of a course as there can be."

"I can't help thinking we should have traveled north," said Esten. "This high-flying ash seems thicker in the skies of Dagu and Zairab than it does down here."

"The sea freezes six months a year up there," said Hab.

"I think our northern coast is closer to the source of this ash than our southern coast."

"Yet to sail north we tack right into the wind," said Hab.

"True," said Esten, "but by sailing south we tack into the wind on the way back."

"Unless we decide to circumnavigate and come through the polar sea on the way back," said Hab.

They reached Perro, the capital of Maju, at sunset. As the anchor chain clanked out the hawser hole, Jara came to the taffrail and stood beside Hab.

"A gaudy display, is it not?" she asked, pointing to the sunset.

The sun sank like a great orange ball into the sea, blazing through the volcanic cloud in a dozen shades of red, pink, mauve, turquoise, and amber.

"It is indeed," he said. He looked at her curiously. "Are you . . . always with Esten, then?" he asked. "Has he reconciled himself to your presence on this voyage?"

She looked down at her hands. "He has. And, yes, I'm always with him. Ever since our parents died when we were young. He's my brother, I'm his sister, but we're also good friends."

Hab thought of Romal. Brothers yes, friends no. No consent from Lord Cloudesley, just his own forged version of his brother's signature. Romal had no idea Hab had wagered the family fortune on this voyage, another rule of the Formulary broken.

"Your hair is the same color as the sun," he said.

She glanced at him. A softness came to her eyes. "Aye, and I have spots all over my face, too," she said, smiling. "I've escaped from a circus, you see. You'll have to watch me, Hab Miquay. I can be a mischievous woman when I haven't got a ringmaster to watch me."

He grinned. "I'll watch you, Jara," he said. "I'll watch you every day."

✦✦✦

Three nights later, a thousand miles south of Maju, they reached the outer limit of the Great Reef of Alquay. Hab was up on deck with Esten. They were on late-watch. Foot hovered in the sky, a misshapen moon with a ruddy cast, so close they could see its craters clearly. Lag, of course, lagged. It was a lot farther away, spherical, the color of quicksilver.

"Three nights to go," said Hab, "and the moons embrace. Then you'll see tides, my friend. Then you'll know what I mean when I say they're as high as Weathervane Tower."

Esten seemed preoccupied tonight. "Do you ever go to Pendagal?" he asked. "Do you ever talk to the priests there, Hab?"

Hab looked away. "I haven't gone in a long time," he said.

"I've gone five times in the last year," said Esten. "That might surprise you. But I think about Ouvant these days. Strange, isn't it? Usually scientists are so divorced from their religion. Ouvant. There's a word for you. A word that means six different things, depending on the way it's used. Of course it means God. But it also means everything we hold most dear in the Golden Land: honesty, fidelity, integrity, loyalty, friendship. Then you can use it the way our ancestors used it. Ouvant to them meant work and toil, and they were proud of their work. Then you can use it in the political sense, a word to describe those who are liberal and forward-thinking. It also means open-mindedness. But I like its last meaning best. Ouvant. The great eternal unknown. The great mystery of everything."

Three or four pekra jumped out of the water, arched through the air, and dove back in, a sure sign that the evening tides were on their way.

"I must confess, Esten, you don't strike me as a particularly religious man."

Hab contemplated the unknown southern horizon. Far in the distance, he heard a rippling sound. He unhooked his telescope and hoisted it to his eye. He saw a massive slope of water approaching from three miles off, like the sea tilting toward him. A flock of nuiyau birds swooped again and again toward the surface of this tipping wall of seawater as the current of the tide forced the fish up through the surf.

"Here's the first of them," he said, handing the telescope to Esten.

While Esten held the telescope, Hab blew his captain's whistle. Guenard stumbled onto the deck, his eyes bleary with sleep.

"Captain?" said Guenard.

"Tides athwart on the portside," he said. "Trim the sails to run them stem to stern on a port tack. Sound the bomb gun to let the other ships know. We've got a night ahead of us, Guenard."

"Aye, aye, Captain," said Guenard.

The first mate hurried to the poop deck and rang the duty bell.

"I can see the second one now," said Esten. He took the telescope from his eye and gave it back to Hab.

"You can generally expect ten or twelve out here in open seas," said Hab. "If we finely tune our labors, we should be able to weather them without mishap."

He lifted the telescope to his eye and had a look. Rising to twice the height of the first tide was the second tide, heaving itself out of the aft well of the first tide, a uniform ridge of seawater sixty feet high, steeper than the first tide, lifting at a thirty-degree angle, its spine curling in a froth of white foam. Hands emerged from the forecastle and galley. The men and women of the dogwatch hoisted the throat halyards and raised the gaff sails. From the poop deck came a hissing sound, then a great boom as Guenard set off the bomb gun. The sound of the tides reached them more loudly now.

Hab scanned the southern horizon from west to east. He saw not a single break in the tide, not a single passageway. This was what he remembered. Beyond the Great Reef of Alquay, there were never any whale tides, as they were called, not many breaks in the water, no trapdoors for a sailor to slip through.

"I wish the wind would freshen," he said. Even as he spoke, the ship began to rise on the first tide. Esten looked at him blankly. Hab gave him a glance and grinned. "We find out now if all that lead is worth it."

Over the rippling of the tide he now heard a new sound, the keel and deck creaking under his feet.

"They're a good deal bigger than they are north of Maju, aren't they?" said Esten.

Across the water, Hab heard the other duty bells ringing on the other ships.

"Their dimensions are indeed bewildering," he agreed.

A sleepy-eyed Jara emerged from the forecastle and looked around. Guenard ran to Hab, now fully awake.

"Requesting a course, Captain," he said.

"Seven spokes hard aport," he said.

"Aye, aye, Captain."

"Clear the decks when the sails are trimmed," he commanded. "I want everybody strapped in below."

"Aye, aye, Captain."

"We'll need the lifelines," he said. "And have the ship's carpenters ready aft."

"Aye, sir."

He turned to Esten and Jara. "You two, below."

Jara was staring at the tides. "They stun the mind, don't they?" she said. "There's the third one. Look at the size of it."

Hab lifted his telescope. Two miles behind the second one, he now saw the third tide, massive, twice the size of the second one, rising to kiss the night sky, sending a fine mist into the air, the mist cloaking Foot and Lag so that now both moons shone murkily, each the color of a squashed gourd. Hab slid the telescope into his belt and turned to Esten and Jara.

"Go," he said, pointing toward the forecastle. "Forestall no longer."

The two made their way along the deck. Hab looked out over the slope of the first tide where his seven tiny ships struggled arduously up the incline, their sails barely puffed, Parprouch's ridiculous booty barges tight out behind them like so many drag anchors. How puny the ships seemed, bobbing in this massive slope of water. He looked up at Foot and Lag. Measured by a sextant, they were still at least a dozen notches apart, nowhere close to the bilunar eclipse. He wasn't a spiritual man, preferred to count on the sense of his eyes, but he now found himself thinking of the Great Ouvant, praying this night that a God he didn't believe in would be merciful to sailors on the open sea.

The ship heaved bow-first into the tide. Hab climbed the slope of the deck to the forecastle. He looked over the bowsprit, glanced behind his shoulder, watched his crew make fast the guys and stays, and, satisfied that all was in order, went to the helm, where Guenard had his hands on the wheel.

"I'll take the helm!" he cried to Guenard. "Let's get those lifelines around our waists!"

"Aye, aye, Captain!"

Guenard hurried to the tackle locker and unhooked two lines. He came back and the men quickly harnessed themselves in, hooking the lines around the nearest scuppers.

"Stand by, Guenard," said Hab. "I may need your help. We can only hope that the rudder holds in this surge!"

Guenard braced himself against the forecastle head while Hab gripped the wheel.

He drove the ship right into the tide, five minutes of an uphill pull, until he reached the crest. The ship balanced precariously on the top of the tide, then slid down the other side, into the two-mile well. The ship heeled back and forth, lurching to port, then to starboard, and the air became suddenly humid, thick with the smell of the sea. Down, down, down they went, sledding like from the slopes of the Oradels, the bow splashing up a heavy spray, the sound of water rushing all around them, Hab's hands so tight on the helm they ached.

The second tide surged toward them, sucking saltwater from the depths, building itself into a massive wave, angling sharper and sharper. The ship slammed bow-first into the second tide, plunging deep into the water with a shudder and a loud crack. The second tide spilled over the ship as if the Lake of Life itself had been emptied from the sky all at once.

Hab gripped the helm, but to no avail. Tons of water surged against him, and he was ripped free from the helm. The water pushed him backward. He slammed into the tackle locker. The foremast snapped from the deck like a toothpick and was washed away in the surging white foam. The water rose quickly over the deck, and he floated free of the tackle locker, his lifeline the only thing holding him to the ship. He tumbled in the current. He didn't know if he was right side up or upside down. He stroked madly, hoping to break free from the current's vicious grip, knowing that he had a minute or two at most to find the surface before he ran out of air. His harness line went taut, and he realized that the ship was submerged below him. The water tossed him around like a piece of driftwood, and he still couldn't find the surface. Why had there been so much heeling on the downward? he wondered, thinking a seaman's thoughts automatically even in this moment of chaos. Should he face the tides abeam instead of stem to stern? The line dug into his skin. He struggled to loosen it, but the knot was too tight. He was running out of air. He finally drew his dagger and cut the line . . . and shot straight to the surface like a cork.

He sputtered through the backside of the second tide. He took several deep breaths, wiped the water from his eyes, looked around.

The third tide, even more massive than the second, rolled toward him, an ominous wall of water. He looked around for the ship but couldn't see it anywhere. He feared she might have gone down. The third tide reared up toward the moons, as tall as any tide he'd ever seen, advancing with a gargantuan and killing grace. He knew if he didn't find something to hang onto soon, he would be sucked to the bottom in the tide's undertow. Huge tides! Monstrous tides! And still three nights away from the bilunar eclipse!

He looked around for survivors. Far to the left, he saw the water suddenly bubble against the backside of the second tide. Then the ship's bowsprit broke the surface and she hobbled out of the water and heeled from side to side again, trying to gain her balance. Her masts were gone. Her keel was cracked. She was hardly seaworthy, but at least she was afloat. He swam toward her. He would stand a better chance against the third tide even if he could simply cling to her side.

He saw sailors scramble from her hatches and man the lifeboats. Good. In a covered lifeboat they might survive. He redoubled his effort—he was their captain and they needed him—but before he could get more than a half dozen strokes, a spar, broken from the ship's deck, launched itself out of the churning water just beneath him, banging him on the side of his head, knocking stars into his eyes with a ferocious blow. He grunted. His vision blurred, darkened, and all strength left his arms and legs. He looked at the ship, watched the crack amidships widen as plank and rib tore apart like paper, saw her take on tons of water as a sudden riptide spilled into her hold, heard the thin cries of those trapped below desperately trying to get out. And that same riptide—that riptide of doom that was now sinking his ship—drew him precariously close to the stricken vessel, sucking him in as it pummeled its way through the interior of the boat. His vision darkened further. He saw blood in the water. His own blood. He was losing consciousness. Esten pointed at him from over the side of the ship. Jara and Guenard stared down at him. Esten pulled off his cape and jumped in after him.

And that was the last thing Hab remembered. Unconsciousness overwhelmed him.

ᔚᔚᔚ

Hab dreamed he was on a ship, that he was looking out over the rail at small waves lapping a rocky shore as the moons shone on a calm sea. He saw something swimming through the water toward him, coming from the direction of the beach. His eyes narrowed as he tried to see what it was. He waited as the thing disappeared under the shadow of the ship's stern. He heard it climb the ladder. He watched it crawl over the taffrail. What was it? He'd never seen anything like it before. He watched the thing approach, not man, not beast. A creature as black as night, with legs rippling with huge muscles and eyes that burned like coals. The creature came right up to him. The creature raised a sword above its head. The creature was going to kill him. . . .

Then the dream faded and a happier one took its place. A dream of his father, Duq Miquay, poring over his sea charts, figuring out his equations, forever trying to understand the tides, obsessed with the tides, just as Hab was obsessed with the unknown continent. He beckoned to Hab. Duq stood on the foredeck of the family ketch, while Hab remained on the dock. In his dream, Hab watched his father point to a sea chart, an accurate and highly detailed rendering of the Sea of Maju, heard his father's gentle voice tell the young Hab why the tides varied so widely, how in the many inlets along the east coast, where one would expect them to be large, they actually came up small; how, in the open ocean south of Maju, where one would expect the deep water to actually make them tiny, they came in gigantic waves, one after the other, for twelve hours straight; how in the Estuary the fluctuation was fifty feet while in the Bay of Vabreulle it was a thousand; and finally how he thought the twin moons and an imbalance in Paras's geological makeup—as if perhaps Paras was weighed with a copious amount of heavier elements in a lopsided way—caused the unruly tides.

And now the ketch was pulling away from the dock, and his father was drifting down the Estuary on the ebb tide with a look of obsession in his eyes. And all Hab had left were Duq's ambiguous sea charts with tidelines drawn one over the other in a series of swooping arches, like the marks of a fingerprint. All he had left were the 632 mathematical equations his father had devised in a futile attempt to explain a system of tidal movements that could best be described as chaotic. All he had left, as his father disappeared from sight down the Estuary, never to return again, were five pages of handwritten speculation about the gravitational pull of Foot, Lag, and the Sun; the possible contours of the ocean bottom; the natural breakwaters of the polar ice cap and the Great Reef of Alquay; and a geological imbalance beneath the suboceanic mantle. . . .

He felt a strong arm shake him. He opened his eyes. His dream disappeared.

"I've got a dry box of dressings from the ship's lazarette," said a voice.

He recognized the voice. "Esten?"

"You're bleeding badly, Hab."

Hab lifted his head and looked around. He was inside a covered lifeboat. He saw Jara looking at him, her eyes like jade in the lamplight. He saw Guenard and Jeter.

"Where's the ship?" he asked. He winced in sudden pain.

"She's gone, Hab," said Esten.

"You saved my life?" he said.

Esten didn't answer. He was busy with the dressing. The boat rocked and heaved in the surf. Hab's head flopped. His eyes closed. "The tides . . ." he murmured. He forced his eyes open. "You can't fight them. You've got to let them have their way."

"Easy now, Captain," said Guenard. "Rest now."

"Let's see if we can get that blood stopped before the next tide comes," said Esten.

Esten pressed the dressing firmly to Hab's head wound. Jeter brought the lamp closer. Hab put his hand on Jeter's wrist and in desperation said, "You've got to ride the tides abeam." He nodded weakly. His throat felt raw from too much saltwater. He could hardly speak. "You've got to ride the wells aslant."

"There'll be no steering of boats just now, Captain," said Jeter.

Hab strained to lift his head again. "How many ships lost, Guenard?"

"There'll be no knowing, Captain, until we're through this. The boatswain reports the fourth and fifth tides aren't as big." Guenard turned from him and looked nervously at the hatch. "We'll hope that morning brings calmer waters, sir." The boat began to climb. "Then we'll get a better reckoning of who's been lost."

ᶜᶜᶜ

By morning, the tides ebbed, and the sea was calm. Three ships remained. The Auvilly Currents eased them homeward. Jara leaned over Hab with a cup of water. She gazed at him with patient, worried eyes, her red hair blowing across her freckled face, her green eyes squinting in the sun. He tried to lift his hand to her face, but he was too weak from blood loss. His hand fell to his side.

"Here," she said.

She put the cup to his lips and he drank. The water soothed his salt-swollen throat. She took the cup away.

"We failed," he said.

She looked away. "In our first attempt, yes, we did, Hab."

Hab let the thought settle. "How many dead?"

"Forty-seven," she said. "Another forty-two missing. We're trying to make the Reef before nightfall, before the tides come again. All the king's barges, by the way, are gone."

"No loss there," he said, managing a grin.

Esten approached from the lee-rail. "You're awake."

"I owe you my life," he said.

Esten looked out at the sea. He seemed uncomfortable with the idea. "We still have three ships," he said.

Yes, three ships, Hab thought, but he now realized they were hardly the kind of ships that would survive the massive tides of Foot and Lag, even if their keels were lined with lead. *Our first attempt*. He thought of Jara's words. What of a second attempt? Was it possible? Especially now that the House of Cloudesley faced ruinous indemnity payments to the king? A second attempt seemed fraught with even more obstacles than this first one. He looked up at the sky. He saw ash glistening in the sunlight—the volcanic confetti of that far-off mysterious continent.

"Aye, three ships," he said, giving them a weak smile.

But neither of them knew how he had broken Rule 8 of the Formulary to manage their misplanned and so utterly failed first attempt. Neither of them knew how he had committed yet another felony by forging his brother's signature on the instrument of consent. Neither of them knew how he had risked everything, including his own banishment to the Island of Liars, for this one precious opportunity to stand on the shores of that distant land.

CHAPTER SIX

Hab stared at Chouc. The boy's eye was black, his lip was broken, and a healing gash marked his forehead. Romal had beaten the boy, all because the boy had accidentally put black shoe polish on his riding boots instead of brown. Gougou looked on with trepidation.

"And when did this happen?" asked Hab.

"This morning," said Chouc, in a meek, tremulous voice. "I told him I wouldn't do it again. I told him I would be more careful next time . . . only he has so many jars of things, and I always get them mixed up, and I was trying only to do what he asked." The boy's eyes filled with tears.

Hab stroked his arm. "It's all right, Chouc," he said. "It's not your fault. Romal's a grown man, the head of our household, and he should better command himself in his anger." He turned to Gougou. "Where is he? At his club?"

Gougou gazed at him in trepidation. "Hab, you're still not well. You should rest in bed. You shouldn't confront Romal. He's been doing his best."

"Don't defend him, Gougou," said Hab sharply. "He's a profligate. He's a fool. And now he's beaten his brother. I must express to him my extreme displeasure in the strongest way. Is he in the south wing?"

"I don't think so," said Gougou, now frantic with anxiety. "This is so upsetting, Hab. You're back not three days and already you're fighting with Romal."

"Did you see him go out?" asked Hab.

Tears came to her eyes. "I don't know." She gestured vaguely toward the south wing. "Maybe Thia knows. Shouldn't you calm your anger first?"

"My anger won't be calmed, Gougou, not under this despicable circumstance," he said. He inspected Chouc's beaten face again. "I can't abide such abysmal behavior. Nor will I tolerate it. The Rules of the Formulary won't be broken in *this* household."

ᘒᘒᘒ

Hab crossed the courtyard and climbed the back steps to Romal and Thia's chambers. His anger seethed like a thing alive. Yet he also felt heartsick. He felt like a hypocrite. *The Rules of the Formulary won't be broken in this household.* He hardened his resolve and forgot about his own recent transgressions. In this circumstance, the rules couldn't be broken. Chouc was an innocent. Chouc was defenseless. Chouc would never raise his hand against anybody. Hab loved him. No one was going to get away with hurting him. Especially not Romal.

He didn't bother to knock. He barged right in.

"Ho, there!" he called.

He looked around the dim stone interior. Through the open window he saw a bird singing in a lemon tree outside.

"Hello?" a voice called from the end of the hall.

Thia's voice. As sweet as a flute. She appeared at the end of the corridor wearing a gown—it looked as if she was getting ready to attend a musical soiree. She was backlighted by a small window at the end of the corridor. Her blond hair was pinned up with a number of combs. Bronze earrings dangled from her ears.

"Where's Romal?" he asked.

"What do you want Romal for?" she asked.

"Your husband has beaten Chouc," he said. "I must find him at once. Where is he?"

But she looked distracted and worried about something.

"There was a man here asking for you this morning," she said. "Something about a summons." Her eyes narrowed, and she gazed at him with a great deal of concern. "Are you in trouble, Hab?"

Hab avoided the question. "You should have this divan done again," he said, pointing to a shabby piece of furniture to his left. Avoidance. Rule 16 of the Formulary.

"He wore the crest of the Court," she said.

He felt suddenly cold inside. So, word was out. Parprouch knew he was back. "I really must find Romal, Sister."

"Perhaps he was from the navy," she said, stepping forward and resting her hand on his arm. "You're still an admiral, aren't you? Maybe it was just something to do with navy business." But then her brow arched with perplexity. "Still, why did he have a summons, Hab? I would hate it if you were in trouble of some kind."

He should have told her straight out that he was a felon, that he'd risked the entire family fortune on the voyage, and that they were all ruined. But he couldn't.

"Forgive me, Sister," was all he could say.

She stared at him. He knew she could tell he was prevaricating. Prevarication. Rule 26 of the Formulary.

"You really *are* in trouble, aren't you?" Her look of distress deepened.

He forced himself to think about Chouc. Poor beaten Chouc. "Where's your husband?" he asked again.

"At the law courts," she said. "Arranging the sale of Cloudesley." She arched her brow. "This man from the palace, dear brother," she said, looking even more worried, "will he come back for you?"

His brow stiffened. He wasn't going to discuss it. "I must bid you good day, Sister," he said. "I must find your husband."

◢◢◢

The Law Courts of the Fanille, occupying three sides of Place Giofre at the end of Avenue Eleger, were not far from Gorolet Palace, Parprouch's place of residence in Jondonq's capital. Unlike most buildings in Jauny, which were made of sand-colored stone, the Fanille was made from black stone quarried in the Oradels and shipped by river barge down the Necontreu 250 miles to Jauny. Eighteen black pillars rose out of the tawny cobblestone of the square, each supporting a giant pediment richly carved with heroic depictions of Jondonq's past. Behind these pediments, the building, a massive and sepulchral edifice, rose to a gigantic black dome resting on top of the central wing.

Hab climbed the steps. He knew his way around the Fanille well. Much of the family business had been conducted in the Fanille for years and years. He was afraid that at any moment a civil guard might accost him. He was a felon, after all. He entered the building. He knew he didn't have much time.

The corridors were crowded with law clerks and solicitors, all in their legal blues, wearing traditional four-cornered hats, bustling from chamber to chamber, holding legal briefs under their arms. He felt like a brute in this place of scholarly men. He knew he should direct every waking moment toward a second voyage, but he first had to make sure that Romal wasn't going to hurt Chouc again. He wouldn't be able to leave without knowing Chouc was safe.

He worked his way to the back of the Fanille, where the corridors branched off toward the offices of the private-practice lawyers, his anger simmering, his apprehension as taut as a wind-lyre string.

At last he came to the studded motwood door of the offices of Marrouin and Vencal, the Miquay family lawyers for generations. He didn't knock. He pushed his way right in.

His brother was sitting there in front of Orvint Vencal. Romal looked up, his eyes dull, dopey—too much brandy had deadened their light over the years—and grinned at Hab as if Hab were the biggest joke in the world. Orvint Vencal—a man in his early sixties, with

round wire spectacles, a coat of indigo silk, and tight beige breeches
that made his skinny legs look like broom poles—rose quickly and
bowed to Hab, knowing that, while Romal might be the titular head
of the household, Hab was its de facto head.

"Mr. Miquay . . ." said Vencal.

No doubt Vencal saw the anger in his eyes. "You will stop this
transaction immediately," said Hab.

Vencal's lower lip bobbed against his upper. "There's no transaction here, Mr. Miquay," said the lawyer. "We are simply drafting an
intent to sell for your family property in the Lesser Oradels."

"Until Lord Cloudesley consults properly with me," said Hab,
"there'll be no intent to sell. My father's testament demands a consultation."

"That might be so, Brother," said Romal. "But my signature pro-
vides the final authority."

The two brothers stared at each other. Why did it have to be this
way? wondered Hab. Why should their animosity toward each other
rankle so deeply, so that even when they were in the same room
together the air was heavy with threat? Why, even in the anger of this
moment, did he coldly scheme to swindle his brother so completely
out of the proceeds from the sale of Cloudesley? Were it anybody else,
he would have hesitated. But he had lost so much already, he knew he
had to risk the rest. And that meant Cloudesley. They hated each other.
They couldn't hide it from each other. And Hab detested himself for
hating Romal. As for Cloudesley, he believed it a necessary expedient.

Vencal shifted nervously. "Perhaps the anonymity and bustle of the
outside corridor might suit the purposes of a family consultation better
than my office," he said. "I'll gladly wait upon you when you're finished. My sincere hope is that an amicable arrangement might be
devised."

The lawyer gave them an obsequious bow. The brothers went out
into the hall.

Hab immediately clutched Romal by the front of his shirt and pushed him against the stone wall. The first Rule of the Formulary, broken, the one about violence, dismissed as a trifle. But his love for Chouc was such that he couldn't control himself.

"If you ever touch Chouc again," he said, "I'll kill you."

Romal's face remained set in a careless grin. The stink of brandy was enough to choke Hab. "The boy must learn how to listen. He must obey my wishes."

Before he could stop himself, Hab drew back and punched his brother in the mouth. "May the fire of Oeil devour you," he said.

Romal's eyes widened and he pulled back, surprised but not particularly frightened. Blood beaded up through the split in his lip. He drew out his frilly monogrammed handkerchief and dabbed his injury. "Are we finished with our consultation, dear brother?" he said. "I should so like to get the sale of Cloudesley under way."

"I don't care what you do with Cloudesley," said Hab. But even in this utterance he broke at least a half dozen rules of the Formulary. The higher truth of the unknown continent demanded it. "But lay one finger on Chouc, and you will die."

ᴕᴕᴕ

Hab couldn't sleep that night. In his room overlooking Bosiler Boulevard, he twisted first one way then the other. A muggy heat climbed out of the Estuary, the first heat of the summer, and the air was close and thick. He tossed his thin sheet from his shoulders, got up, and walked across the cool stone floor to the window. A few fish-wagons rumbled by, merchants getting to the market early, the sound of chevul hoofs echoing over the cobblestones.

What price truth? he wondered. He drummed his fingers on the windowsill. He loved his family. But the proceeds from the sale of Cloudesley were going to be his so he could mount a second voyage.

He knew what would happen to the proceeds of Cloudesley if Romal was allowed to keep them. They would be squandered.

He heard a light knock on his door. He left the window and answered it. Chouc stood there in his nightshirt.

"Can I sleep here tonight?" he asked. Chouc looked scared.

"What's wrong?" asked Hab.

"Romal's drinking with his friends in the south wing, and I'm scared he's going to beat me again," he said.

Hab felt his anger return. No one should have to sleep in fear in their own house. He put his hand on the slender teen's shoulder and led him into the room. "I've got plenty of space in my bed. Crawl in."

Chouc nestled under the thin sheet. He quickly fell asleep. Hab sat on the bed next to him. He still couldn't sleep. He lit a candle, placed it on the table next to his bed, and sat there staring at the stone floor. His mind wouldn't stop. He got up and went back to the window. When he closed his eyes, he saw the continent floating in front of him, a massive peak rising to an impossibly large caldera, with smoke and fire billowing into the sky. He had to see it. Whatever the consequences. Even if he had to lie to every last single Parassian, he would go to that unknown continent.

Down on the street, a black wagon drawn by four black chevuls pulled up. On the sides of the wagon, painted in gold and green, were two sea horses back to back supporting a crown and crossed tridents, the symbol of the Court. Hab's shoulders sagged. Two guards emerged from the back of the wagon, brawny young men in black uniforms, with black truncheons strapped to their belts. He watched them cross the cobblestones. They knocked on the downstairs door. He heard the guards clump up the stairs.

They didn't knock; they burst right in. They presented him with his summons and his indemnity papers. He read over his royal summons, then looked at the tallest guard. "Must I go immediately?" he asked.

"Our orders are to detain you on sight, sir."

Chouc woke up. "Hab?" The defenseless Chouc had come to his room to escape fear; now here was fear itself, in the guise of these two civil guards. "Hab, where are you going?"

"I have some business to settle, Chouc." Hab walked to edge of the bed and stroked the boy's head. "These messengers have been kind enough to remind me about it. Sleep, my brother. Dream well. I'll be back by third bell."

CHAPTER SEVEN

Hab sat in the back of the wagon, a prisoner. No windows, not even a grate for ventilation in the roof. The only light came from an oil lamp. The air smelled of human sweat. The guard with the beard stared at him. The man's eyes were blank. He showed no interest in anything.

"Where are we going?" asked Hab.

"You'll see when we get there," said the guard.

Hab wished the tall one were in the back with him instead. But the tall one was driving. Hab tried to figure out their destination by counting the number of left and right turns, by listening to the street sounds, even by smelling what he could from outside the thin wooden walls of the wagon. And he finally realized they were heading for the Law Courts of the Fanille.

Once they arrived in Place Giofre, Hab followed the tall guard up to the third story of the Fanille. At this time of night there were no more than a handful of clerks and custodians working. Skylights overhead let in a faint trace of dawn. Now that his indemnity papers had been served, he would have to sign the organ of divestiture. He had thought Parprouch might conduct the divestiture personally—stripping him of his wealth and putting it into the royal coffers. But the king had agents for that. No need to perform the unsavory task himself.

The guard led him through an atrium full of trees and plants to a small back office. A lawyer in a traditional four-cornered hat waited for him. The man looked familiar to Hab. Stitched in this small man's legal blues was the crest of the Royal Court: the sea horses, the crown, the tridents.

"Allow me to introduce myself," said the man. "I'm Lord Teur." So this was Lord Teur, he thought, the monarch's number-one aide. The elflike man slid the papers across the dark motwood desk. "Your contractual obligations," he said. He lifted his chin, glanced down through his spectacles, and scanned the document. "Failure to procure for Summerhouse a claim of ninety-two percent of the material metal resources—"

"Who says I've failed?" asked Hab.

Time to scheme again. Lord Teur looked up from the document and peered over the rims of his spectacles at Hab, as if he couldn't understand how Hab could possibly believe four ships, forty-seven dead, and three tons of lead couldn't mean failure.

"I'm afraid I don't follow," said the older man.

Hab gazed at Lord Teur, wondering how shrewd the old aristocrat was. He looked about seventy, had a bald pate with strands of gray hair he wore long over his collar. His nose was thin and delicate, and his nostrils red, as if he suffered from a chronic cold. Hab wondered just how much power Lord Teur might have.

"I have three ships left," said Hab.

Lord Teur continued to stare at Hab. Finally he took off his spectacles, leaned forward, and rested both elbows on his desk.

"Mr. Miquay, I . . . I don't think you realize . . . you're here this morning under the gravest of circumstances. I know you have three ships left, but do you honestly think the monarch will support another attempt after the disastrous failure of the first one? We've seen now that these ships—and I believe the remaining three are similar in design to the shipwrecked ones—can in no way sail successfully through the tides of Foot and Lag without positive threat of destruction. We've witnessed the lamentable loss of forty-seven crewmen. Three tons of lead have gone to the bottom. I can't see how Zadeaux will affix the royal seal to another foolhardy attempt."

Hab got up, walked to the window, opened it, ran his fingers along the sill, came back, and showed his fingertips to Lord Teur. "Do you know what this is?" he asked.

A fine white particulate covered his fingers. "Yes, I know," said Lord Teur. "It's ash. From that place."

"Precisely," said Hab. "Ash. From that place."

"You won't have the king's support," cautioned Lord Teur.

"In any case, I go again, Lord Teur. I admit a setback, out there beyond the Great Reef of Alquay, where four of my ships were wrecked, but I don't admit failure. I have three ships left. I go again. Read our agreement carefully," said Hab, tapping the document with his thick strong finger. "I see no word or line or clause that defines what shall constitute failure on my part. I shall be only all too happy to contest my contract with the king in a civil hearing." He smiled coolly. "You'll find my lawyers well prepared. I shall go to this place," he said, rubbing the ash between his thumb and fingers, "even if I have to support the venture myself. I shall go to this place even if it means a legal battle with the king." Hab took a deep breath and squared his massive shoulders. "Contest our contract if you like, but without a definition of failure to peg your claims on, even the most royalist magistrate will be hard-pressed to rule in your favor."

Lord Teur contemplated the mariner serenely. "And what, Mr. Miquay, would you consider a fair definition of failure?"

Hab shrugged. "Death," he said. "What else?"

⹌⹌⹌

When Hab got back to the family compound on Bosiler Boulevard, he found Chouc sitting on the edge of his bed with wide apprehensive eyes. Early-morning sunlight, as it cut shadows through the bedchamber, brought into sharp relief the oddness of Chouc's features: the close-set unfocused eyes, the small upturned nose with the prominently visible nostrils, the small budlike ears.

"I had another dream," said Chouc.

Hab peered at Chouc. Another dream. "You did?" he said.

Chouc nodded, an uncoordinated bobbing of his head. "I dreamed you sailed off into a sea of ice." The teenaged simpleton licked his lips. "And that you left me behind. And that I never saw you again." Tears came to Chouc's tiny eyes. "You won't leave me, will you, Hab? You'll take me with you, won't you, wherever you decide to go?"

Hab put his arm around Chouc's shoulder. "Don't worry, Chouc," he said. "I'll take you with me." He pulled Chouc near. "Wherever I decide to go."

٭٭٭

Two nights later, as Hab sat at his worktable in the compound library, he heard creaking outside in the corridor, Gougou's wheelchair, and a moment later saw his mother peeking through the door.

"May I come in?" she asked.

He nodded. His mother gripped the rims of her old motwood chair, wheeled herself in, and peered at the drawings Hab was working on. "What's this?" she asked. "A ship?"

He stared at his mother. "Yes, Gougou," he said. "A ship."

"I've never seen a ship like that before," she said, pointing at the design. "What are these cogs for?"

"A system of levers, Gougou," he said. "They allow the masts to be raised and lowered."

She didn't understand. "Movable masts? Why would you want movable masts? Every seaman knows the only thing you raise and lower on a ship are sails. Why would you want to raise and lower masts?" Here it was again: the subterfuge, the omission, the silence, no explanation forthcoming. She pointed to a different part of the design. "And what are these crank handles for?" she asked.

"They open ballast tanks," he said.

"Ballast tanks?" she said. "What do you need ballast tanks for?"

"You turn the crank handles, the ballast tanks fill with water, and the ship sinks," he said.

Gougou now looked at him as if he were mad. "Why would you want to sink your own ship?" she asked. He said nothing. A crease of worry came to her forehead. "You're not planning to . . ." She looked away.

"Mother, I'm diverting myself, that's all."

"Oh," she said. She peered at the strange drawings once more. "Well, I . . . I didn't mean to disturb you, Hab, but I just thought I'd better tell you that the sale of Cloudesley has gone through."

Hab felt his shoulders rise. This was what he had been waiting for. "Thank you, Gougou," he said. He leaned over and gave her a kiss. Her eyes brightened. He knew that nothing pleased her more than getting a kiss from her stalwart boy. "Thank you for informing me."

When Gougou had gone, Hab walked to his cabinet, opened the top drawer, and withdrew a three-page document. He rolled up the document, slid it into an oilskin sheath, put on his hat, his cape, and ventured out into the rainy summer night.

❧❧❧

He found Romal in a different gaming house that night, this one on the edge of the Triser District, where the courtesans on this wet evening huddled under umbrellas and on doorsteps waiting for custom. Romal was stuporous with brandy, struggling to play a game of Brisquette with a number of equally drunk young lords, his usual cronies. Two of the young lords had passed out from drink. A courtesan from Triser was trying to drag one of these to a bedroom upstairs. Romal, his curly pompadour sagging in the humidity, his indigo evening coat casually discarded on the floor, was lying full length on one of the upholstered benches, desperately trying to concentrate on his hand of cards, looking as if he, too, might pass out any moment, his head bobbing and weaving, vapors of alcohol rising from him like methane from a swamp.

"Romal?" said Hab.

Romal looked up while the other young lords grumblingly got out of Hab's way. Hab sat down. Easy enough to forge Romal's signature on the king's instrument of consent, but clerks and lawyers were bound to double-check his file signature for this particular document. Late at night was the best time for this. Romal was usually senseless with drink by this time of night.

"Hab?" said Romal.

"I have some papers for you to sign," said Hab.

"Papers?" said Romal, his head still bobbing and weaving. "What kind of papers?"

"From our vintner at Cloudesley," he said. "The winery has to be sold under a separate bill of sale. Mr. Vencal apologizes for the inconvenience, but the papers didn't arrive until this afternoon and he needs them completed and back in his office first thing in the morning. I don't mean to break up your fun."

Romal struggled into a sitting position. He looked positively ill with drink. A small sore had formed on his lower lip, a fungating little pustule, and his skin was as white as parchment.

"Where do I sign?" he asked.

Was his brother really so helpless? Did he not detect even a whiff of trickery? Hab felt despicable. He held in his mind like a bright candle the higher truth of that unknown continent somewhere out there over the waves. He also hoped that this might force Romal to change his ways. He was convinced this bitter necessity would achieve a higher purpose in more ways than one.

"Down here," he said.

Hab saw no suspicion in his brother's eyes. And why should he? In Jauny, you could leave a bag of metal in the center of Place Giofre overnight and come back to find it untouched the next day. Romal tried to focus on the document. He turned to Hab with a boozy smile and cuffed his brother gamesomely on the shoulder.

"You've missed your calling, Brother," he said. He snatched a nuiyau-bird quill from the center of the table, sunk it into a pot of ink, and scribbled his signature on the bottom of the document. "You should have been a solicitor."

ᔆᔆᔆ

In the Fanille the next morning, Orvint Vencal looked over the document of assignation. The old lawyer smiled, satisfied with its content, and put his own signature to it. He looked up over the rims of his spectacles at Hab.

"I'm so glad you were able to convince Lord Cloudesley to do this," he said. "He's never known how to shoulder responsibility. It's not the cleanest document—you should have had my clerks draft it—but it's legally binding, and I'll be more than happy to have our accountant transfer the funds to your bank in the Escrolage."

"Send it to my bank in Dandan," said Hab. "I travel there this week. I'll be there for the rest of the summer preparing for the autumn hunt."

CHAPTER EIGHT

The three remaining royal launches rested at anchor in the mist-shrouded harbor of Dandan. Having picked out a skeleton crew for each one, Hab now stood on the forecastle head of the lead ship. He felt breathless, surprised at himself, eager to begin but fearful to proceed. He wondered how long it would take before his embezzlement of the family fortune was discovered. A wagon appeared from out of the mist on Dandan's only dirt road, wound its way through the dozen or so houses, and came to a stop next to the water. He knew he didn't have more than a month. By that time he hoped to be on his way. Yet there was still much be done. The driver climbed down and looked around.

"I'm seeking Hab Miquay," he called.

"Over here," called Hab.

The man took a few steps toward the forecastle. "We have two chests here on special delivery. Where do you want them?"

"Just stow them by those dunnage mats over there," called Hab.

Hab watched the men unstrap the chests from the back of the wagon, carry them up the gangplank, and set them down beside the dunnage mats. He had a sudden pang of doubt as he watched them work. He realized he was as much a gambler as Romal was. He watched the men go over to Guenard with their papers. Guenard signed for the chests.

"What do you have in those chests, Hab?" asked Chouc.

He turned to his young brother. "Everything the family owns, Chouc."

He glanced at Lord Teur, who, acting in the capacity of the king's agent, now left his spot by the whaling office and walked toward the gangplank. How long before Lord Teur found out what he had done?

"Permission to come aboard, Captain," called Lord Teur.

"As you will, my lord."

The elfin man climbed the gangplank carefully; the mist had made everything slippery. When the lord reached the forecastle head, he took Hab's elbow and led him away from Chouc. He then gestured around the harbor, nodding at the other two ships lying at anchor beyond, dim shapes in the rolling fog banks.

"You couldn't get any more crew than this?" he asked.

"I'm going to pick up more crew in Perro," said Hab.

"Do the mothers and fathers of these young men and women know where you're taking them?"

Hab's brow settled. "Everything's been made clear."

"And there's nothing I can do to persuade you to desist?" said the small man.

"No," said Hab. "Nothing."

Lord Teur stared at Hab in perplexity. "Then I wish you good luck, Hab Miquay." The old man extended his hand.

Hab looked at Lord Teur's hand.

"May your wish serve us in good stead, my lord," he said.

ᎧᎧᎧ

An hour later, the three ships slipped quietly out of the harbor. Hab wore no fancy admiral's uniform, just his regular seamen's blues. Like ghosts upon the water, the ships moved out, under half sail, easing through the fog banks like barely materialized spirits. Hab felt a stillness settle over him, as if, in that moment, when the dim buildings of Dandan disappeared into the mist, he finally grasped the importance of what he was doing, both in his own life and the life of Paras. He was roaming—roaming like he had never roamed before—

yet in his inner stillness, his spirit, even as it roamed, finally felt at peace with itself.

When they left the Estuary, and were running against a freshening swell in the Sea of Maju, Hab said to Guenard, "Guenard, set a course for the Cape of Alquay."

Guenard's eyebrows rose. "The Cape of Alquay?" he said. "I thought we were going to Perro."

"No," said Hab. "We sail north, to Fadil. Esten and Jara Pepteri will meet us there."

❧❧❧

They sailed along the southeast shore of the Sea of Maju for the next two days and rounded the Cape of Alquay on the third morning out. From here they traveled northward, in open ocean, along the east coast of Paras. Because they were still well within the Great Reef of Alquay, the tides, though at times turbulent, were at least navigable, and the king's ships charted a steady and easy course through the worst of them without mishap.

On the morning of the fifth day, the Auvilly Currents embraced the small flotilla and pushed it northward at ten knots, despite a wind abeam. They arrived in the colder waters off Dagu Province after a full week at sea.

Another week brought them to Fadil, the capital of Dagu.

Hab found Esten and Jara waiting for him there.

"You look harried," said Jara, when they shared a few moments alone together later that evening.

Did it show? The certain knowledge that he was now a fugitive? They walked along the fisherman's beach just north of Fadil. The fishermen sat on overturned boats mending nets as the wind freshened and the tide began to rise.

"A peaceful night's rest, and I'll be myself again," he said. "It's good to see you, Jara."

She looked away, grinning in spite of herself. "My brother's eager to be under way," she said. "And so am I. Is Chouc well? I haven't seen him."

"He's billeted with Aigre, the boatbuilder," said Hab. "And yes, he's well. He's never been to Dagu, and I think the bracing air does him good."

"It's good to see you again too, Hab," she said.

He gave her a friendly smile. "Don't be too glad," he said. "We'll be a long time at sea together. By the time it's finally over, I doubt we'll be civil."

♪♪♪

Aigre, the sixty-two-year-old Dagulander shipbuilder, renowned for the sturdy whaling ships he built, studied the plans for Hab's new submersible boats. He rubbed his grizzled beard, rocked on his heels, and gazed at Hab.

"There's a gum distilled from the sap of the Affed bush," he said. "You simmer vats of the stuff on a low fire, you fill in the chinks of your boat with a whisker brush, and when it dries you have a watertight seal. You have to do it every hundred days or so, or the seal breaks. You'll have to take some with you. It's longer-lasting than the labor oil we usually use for most of our whaling vessels. Tougher too. And less friable. As for the rest of it, these ballast tanks and so forth, it can be done, but it's going to take time. Vekeui's not the easiest wood to work with. And we rarely make boats out of it because it's not particularly buoyant. But of course in this case, we want the boats to sink, so vekeui is the building material of choice. Still, it will take time."

Hab realized that the embezzlement of Cloudesley made time his most precious commodity.

"I have funds enough to employ the whole town," he said. "I've brought extra tools. Enough tools for a hundred workers. I want the job done in a week."

❧❧❧

Aigre employed seventy-five workers in the first day, and another fifty the next. Hab offered such generous wages that some workmen traveled over two hundred miles to hire on. Woodsmen were dispatched to the Pan-Pans to tap the Affed bushes for their sap. The three royal launches were used to haul vekeui wood from the Bay of Vabreulle, corralling log booms and dragging them back through the Channel of Liars to Fadil. Aigre's shipyard was frenetic with activity. Chains, winches, and windlasses lifted the heavy vekeui timbers into place. By the end of the third day, the keels of the new ships, looking like the ribs of three beached bladder whales, were completely laid and ready for planking. The ballast tanks, built separately and hoisted into place with an iron windlass, dovetailed perfectly into the sides of each boat. Smoke billowed constantly from the shipyard—Affed sap simmering in large stoneware kettles.

Hab contracted sixteen cabinetmakers to chisel out the intricate system of levers used to raise and lower the masts. How strange the boats looked, like none ever built, each half the length of the by-now badly scuffed royal launches in Fadil Harbor, but heavy, twice their weight, lined with twice as much lead, dark, wide, ponderous, like port bottles lying on their sides, cradled in their boat launches with extra supports. Boats, not ships, because they weren't big enough to be called ships. Submersible boats. A strange and unlikely invention, but one Hab hoped would work against the tides.

"I commend your ingenuity, my friend," Aigre said to Hab, when the first boat, christened the *Fetla*, was launched for a test run. "An intriguing paradox, a sinkable boat, one that survives the tides simply by submersing itself. One of those rare simple ideas that come to humankind every hundred years or so. I've spent fifty years shipbuilding. I have a reputation as a shipwright whose boats will float in even the roughest seas." He shook his head. "Now I've built one that sinks," he said. "And I've done it on purpose!"

Hab gazed at his new invention with some skepticism. "It seems an imperfect design to me, Aigre," he said. "I built a small model when I was still down south, tested it in the Estuary, and I must confess, it does what it's supposed to do. I didn't think it would sink properly, but after I measured the proportion of wood to lead carefully, it sank fine. Still, once submerged, there's no means of navigation or propulsion. We'll be like bugs in a bottle, tossed whichever way the tides dictate. And we've only so much air to breathe while we're underwater."

"Aye, but at least you'll be safe."

♪♫♫♫

To shore up his money reserves, Hab, as planned, sold the king's royal launches to one of the ten pursers from the Island of Liars, a man by the name of Joulis, not a Liar but an appointee of the penal authorities in Fadil. Joulis brought Liars to Fadil to sail the boats back to the Island. The Liars were all thin and dirty, all with the mark of the Liars—six interlocking circles symbolizing the six meanings of Ouvant—branded onto their foreheads. Hab watched. Joulis stood beside him counting out money.

"Are they good sailors?" asked Hab.

"The best," said Joulis. "They're Islanders. They love the sea." He was a man of forty-five, with long gray hair straggling out from under a soiled bandanna, a few broken teeth, and a face as sharp as a hatchet. "They make their living from the sea, Captain. At least as much as the penal clippers will allow. But it's a hard life for them. You don't see the abundance and plenty on the Island the way you do here on Paras. There's not much that grows there. The soil's too volcanic. And the water's sour for some reason, and that's why the fish stay away. The Liars squabble over food. And who can blame them? There's not enough to eat."

Not enough to eat. The idea was strange to Hab. Fruit trees lined the streets of Jauny, fish teemed in the Estuary, the forests of the Lesser Oradels supplied a profusion of game, Berberton produced more grain than Paras could eat, and the country markets overflowed with goods of every size, shape, and description.

"Summerhouse should send them food," said Hab.

"Summerhouse is too flintish to send anything," commented the purser.

Once the ships were sold, Hab, Guenard, and Esten hired more crew.

"Sign up as many of the locals as you can," said Hab. "If you have to recruit further afield, do it. A crew of fifteen should suffice for each boat. Forty-five in all."

Guenard hired seven Dagulanders from Fadil. Esten hired two from Fadil and two from Retelon, a large town on the Bay of Vabreulle. Added to the current contingent, that left nineteen spots to fill.

"Court guards from Summerhouse were looking for you in Retelon," said Esten. "I'm afraid we can't wait much longer."

Hab took this news quietly. He thought about it, tapped his chin a few times, and said, "We hoist anchor tomorrow."

"But what about the other nineteen crew?" asked Esten.

"We pick up crew across the Channel," he said. Esten raised his eyebrows at the suggestion. "I'm sure we'll have no lack of Liars to choose from. Especially if we offer them three meals a day."

In the morning, they cast off. And none too soon. The sails were just filling, the boats sliding away from the dock at Fadil, when Hab spotted several riders approaching, capes flying, torches held high.

"Stop that man!" one of them cried to the stevedores along the dock, rearing his animal to a stop. "In the name of the House of Zadeaux, I order you to stop that man!" The stevedores did nothing. Hab saw that it was the same bearded guard who'd ridden in the back of the wagon to the Fanille with him the night Lord Teur served

Parprouch's indemnity papers. "That man's a Liar!" cried the bearded guard. And still the stevedores did nothing. They were all related to Aigre in one way or another, and had grown to like Hab.

The strange bulky boats eased away, graceful in an ungainly way, sailing into the gold strip of dawn over the Channel, on their way at last, an unlikely fleet of exploration. Hab watched the riders, frenetic as fleas on a dog's back—watched and watched, thinking how he now indeed officially was a fugitive, a man without a home, a man who would wear the brand of the Liars when he came back. He watched the guards until they were no more than specks, insignificant and ineffective, the true measure, in this great historical moment, of Summerhouse's ephemeral and ultimately futile power. He watched the guards until he understood that he was a far different man than he had ever thought he was; that he was more like his father than he had ever guessed; that he was willing to not only sacrifice the family fortune for the voyage, but also to sacrifice his own life and the lives of his crew members.

His spirit, calm for so many days, again grew uneasy as the coast of Dagu finally disappeared from sight.

CHAPTER NINE

In the dark hours before dawn, as the three ships plowed over the waves toward the Island of Liars, Hab sat with Guenard at the table in the cramped galley of the *Fetla*. Esten, Jara, and Jeter sat there also. Guenard leaned forward and stared at Hab, his brow set, his thin beard hanging limply in the damp, his gray eyes angry.

"You should have told us sooner!" he said to Hab. "You've deliberately misled us." Guenard's lips opened and closed a few times, as if he couldn't articulate the depth of his surprise or sense of betrayal. "The king's guard was right." He recoiled. "You're a Liar!" With the curse out of his mouth, the following words came all in a rush. "For fifteen years I've been your first mate. I signed on when you were barely a man. We've sailed hundreds of thousands of leagues together. I thought I knew you! I thought I could trust you! But I can't trust you at all!" He pointed an accusing finger at Hab. "Look at you! Hunted throughout the realm like a common criminal. Selling Cloudesley out from under your brother's nose so you can pursue this madness! An embezzler! A thief!" Guenard looked around the company with astonished eyes. "And now he plans to take us to the Island of Liars! A place where they eat their own young! He plans to enlist nineteen of the murderous cretins! And these cutthroats are going to be our shipmates! Can you believe this? Have you ever seen such a heinous disregard for the Rules of the Formulary?"

"Guenard," said Esten calmly, "we can't make the voyage without another nineteen shipmates."

The lantern, hanging from the rafter overhead, swayed gently with the movement of the boat, making the shadows grow and shrink against the dark wood interior.

"All my life, I looked up to Hab Miquay as a man of staunch morals," continued Guenard, "as a man who held the word of honesty as strong as any man in Paras. Honesty is our blood. Truth is the meat and bread by which we live. And now we're accomplices to his scheming."

Hab leaned forward. He glanced around the table, first at Esten, who contemplated Guenard the same way he might contemplate a particularly fascinating stone rune of the Great Code. Then at Jeter. Then at Jara. Jara stared at Hab wryly, greatly amused by this. Hab lifted his big hand to the crown of his head, rubbed his hair in exasperation for a few seconds, then eased his hand back to the table.

"Guenard," he said, "I stand by honesty as much as I ever did. In fact, it's honesty that forces these petty and small deceits."

"Embezzling your family of everything it owns a petty deceit?" said the first mate.

"This continent must be known," said Hab. "Parassians must be made to learn that Ouvant hasn't selected Paras as his special place anymore. And I'm sick at heart for Paras. What a land! We drown in its bounty. We atrophy in its plenty. We eat, drink, and fornicate in its easy embrace. Let's find a new land. Let's find a new truth. No matter what the cost."

"Yes, but you lied, Hab," said Guenard. "You lied. Not only to us but to your family. You lied to the king."

"The king is a thief," said Hab.

"Forgive me, old friend, but I earnestly suggest you turn yourself in," he said. "We can't keep you in this boat. Now that we know you're a Liar, the law forbids us to associate with you."

Hab squared his shoulders. "Truth is more elusive than you think, Guenard. Truth to you might be as easy as one plus one. But to me, over these last months, it's become a much more complicated notion." Hab took a deep breath, remaining calm but sure. "If my path is strewn with a thousand petty falsehoods, I shouldn't care because I know these petty falsehoods are the soldiers of a truer and higher honesty, an honesty I intend to show to everybody whether they like it or not. If I have to lie again and again in order to hold up a mirror to the rot, then I'll do it. The conventions of the Formulary won't stand in my way." His face settled, and he regarded Guenard evenly. "Not even the king will stand in my way. I go. We go." He grinned at Guenard. "If you don't want to come with us, my friend, we'll leave you on the Island of Liars. I'm sure they need someone to preach the Formulary to them. I'm sure they need someone to teach them about lying."

෴෴෴

At dawn, Hab climbed topside. He found Jeter standing on the poop deck staring at the rising sun, squinting, his face serious, the limp strands of his shoulder-length hair snapping like small straw-colored whips from under his whaling cap in the brisk wind. Hab put his hand on Jeter's shoulder.

"You didn't say a word last night," he said. "About Guenard."

Jeter, a man with red-blond stubble on his chin, turned to him. Hab was well over six feet tall, but Jeter was six inches taller.

"You know Guenard," said Jeter. "He believes in the Formulary. He's traditional. His father was a clammer from Perro." Hab let his hand slide from Jeter's shoulder. "Rest your conscience, Hab," said Jeter soothingly. "You did the right thing."

"And the tides don't scare you?"

Jeter thought. "No," he finally said. "What I fear is our incompetence against them."

"I was going to give you command of the *Xeulliette*," said Hab, gesturing at one of the other two boats a hundred yards behind them. "I thought I'd let you know now, before we get to Owsheau, so you can start thinking about the kind of crew you want."

Jeter stared at the cumbersome-looking boat and nodded. Simple. Done. Accepted. That's the way it was with Jeter. Jeter was in charge of the *Xeulliette* now.

"Do you talk to Jara much?" asked Jeter.

A wave slapped against the side of the boat and sent a fine spray over the two men.

"Some," said Hab. "Why?"

"She was telling me about the fossils she and her brother found on the Island of Maju." Jeter raised his eyebrows. "Has she mentioned them to you?"

"Yes," said Hab. "The bones of long-extinct animals."

Jeter nodded, then looked out at the water. "It makes you wonder, doesn't it?"

"I find her an odd mix at times," said Hab. "Endearing but galling."

"Who? Jara?"

Hab nodded.

Jeter grinned. "That's just the way she is," said the tall sailor. "Comes with her smarts, I suppose." Then Jeter contemplated the sea again. "But think of it . . . all those bones . . . hard as rock now, she says. Creatures we've never seen before. Semiaquatic, she thinks. Lived half on land, half in the water. I sure would like to see those bones. Jara said she and her brother have a place down there, said I could use it whenever I wanted, that I could go see the bones whenever I liked." He turned to Hab, his grin now a big smile. "Wasn't that nice of her? I don't call that galling. I call that nice."

ʃʃʃ

An hour later, Hab spoke to Jara in the bow of the boat. The mist had cleared. So had the clouds. The sun was up, painting a fiery band of orange over the water.

"Jeter's going to take command of the *Xeulliette* when we get to Owsheau," said Hab. "How would you like to be a member of his crew?"

She frowned. "I would much rather stay here and be a part of yours," she said harshly. "You don't have to worry, Hab. I'll stay out of your way. But please don't banish me to the *Xeulliette*. I would be absolutely miserable."

"Jeter's grown fond of you," said Hab.

"I know he has."

"He has many qualities I commend."

"Then commend them to someone else," she said, and stormed away.

ↄↄↄ

"Don't you see how unfair it is?" said Guenard. "For fifteen years I've sailed with you." Hab and Guenard were alone together in the captain's cabin. "That command should have been mine. And now you've given it to Jeter."

"I did."

"Who's the better seaman?"

"You are."

"And am I your first mate?"

"You are."

"And have you not trusted me with command before?"

"I have."

"Then why for the love of Ouvant did you not give me command of the *Xeulliette*?"

Hab shrugged apologetically. "Because you're inflexible, Guenard. You don't know how to bend. And you might have to bend on a voyage like this."

ᔕᔕᔕ

An hour later, the look out spotted the Island of Liars. It rose out of the gray water, a mountainous and bleak silhouette against the rising sun. Far to the south, Mount Escalier thrust its volcanic peak skyward, the concave dip of its caldera visible in the misty morning light, patches of cloud clinging to its uppermost slopes.

"Turn her two spokes hard aport, Guenard," said Hab.

Guenard, still sullen about being passed over, silently turned the helm two spokes. As the *Fetla*, *Xeulliette*, and *Airamatnas* drew closer to the hard-scrabble island, Hab held his telescope to his eye and had a good look at the penal colony. Of course he'd seen it before, from a distance, but never this close. This close, he was surprised by how bleak and barren it was, no more than a rock cast into the sea. Owsheau was a collection of two dozen stone shacks with thatched roofs, a dock, and the purser's office. Hab had a young sailor from Fadil take a sounding. The sailor cast a kedge anchor over the side and watched the line sink into the waves.

"Fourteen fathoms, sir!" he called.

"Haul about, Guenard," ordered Hab. "And have the boatswain blow the whistle for the other ships. We'll row ashore from here."

"Should we not arm ourselves, Captain?" asked Guenard.

Hab gazed at Owsheau, where he saw a few underfed Liars dressed in rags approaching the dock. "I wouldn't want to scare them, Guenard," he said.

With the ships hauled about, and the longboats lowered, Hab, as always, took an oar and did his share of the work getting them the rest of the way. Yet he found it hard to row with any steadiness, kept turning around to look at Owsheau. Finally he gave over rowing entirely and stood up. Men, women, and children stood along the dock, their faces pale and unwashed, their eyes sunken, their hair bedraggled and lusterless. The longboats heaved in the breaking surf. He saw the whitish branding marks on their foreheads. A few domestic chevuls, of a short and stocky variety Hab had never seen before, nibbled on the sparse grass by the purser's shed. A little boy waved to them, but it was a cheerless wave. The boy had wide hopeless eyes, with ill-looking dark patches under them.

Joulis emerged from the purser's shed. Beyond a promontory to the north, Hab saw the masts of the Owsheau trading and fishing fleet. Tallest among the masts were those of the three royal launches. The purser shouted something to some of the young Liars standing on the dock, and the young Liars waded into the water toward the longboats.

"Ho, there!" cried one of them to Hab.

"Ho, there!" Hab responded.

The young Liars grabbed the sides of the boat and helped them toward shore. "And what brings you to our island?" asked the Liar of Hab.

"Business with the purser."

The young men pulled the boats to the beach, and Hab jumped out. Joulis walked down the beach, limping a bit, as if his leg hurt him, and eyed Hab quizzically. "Captain?" he said, nodding. "This is indeed an unexpected pleasure."

Hab glanced about at the curious onlookers. "The wind bites on this open beach," he said.

"Then perhaps we can go to my shed," said Joulis.

Hab went with Joulis to the purser's shed. Guenard, Jeter, and Eseark, captain of the *Airamatnas*, a stalwart old whaling skipper and Aigre's first cousin, went with them.

When Hab told Joulis he was looking for crew, how he hadn't been able to fill the nineteen spots in Paras, the purser's eyes lit up.

"A voyage like this might not interest anyone in Paras," he said, "but here on the island it'll be like a message of hope. To tell them there might be another place halfway around the world, a place where their children might grow up strong, and with enough to eat . . . Well, Captain, they'll fall to their knees and beg you for the privilege." He put his elbows on the table, leaned forward, and looked at Hab. "You won't have to worry about volunteers, Hab Miquay, not here on the Island. By this afternoon, you'll have a hundred of them outside my shed, ready to sign on."

🌊🌊🌊

By first bell that afternoon, 157 applicants, mostly young men, mulled outside the purser's office. Hab, Jeter, and Eseark began the selection process. Many of the young Liars were quickly disqualified because of poor health. Half seemed consumptive, the other half scurvious. Only a few had color in their faces. One way or another, the nineteen crew were chosen. New shipmates aboard the *Fetla* included three brothers —Olle, Tiq, and Doran. Of those, Tiq, the middle brother, seemed most competent. He had, on many occasions, shipped out as a first mate with Joulis to the trading post in Fadil, and so had a broader experience with the technical aspects of sailing a large ship than some of the others. Not only that, he was quick to master the new routines, both with the masts and the ballast tanks, needed to run Hab's special submersible boats.

At five bells in the morning the next day, Hab bellowed, "Hoist anchor!"

With a rattling of chains through hawser holes and a setting of sails, the three boats strained away from Owsheau into the Auvilly Currents, as inauspicious a leave-taking as could be, these tiny strange vessels in the immensity of the gray ocean, climbing into the highest latitudes of the world, tacking north-by-northwest against a stiff and increasingly cold wind. They could have been whaling vessels, out to make a kill. Or they could have been logging vessels venturing forth from the Bay of Vabreulle. They could have been nondescript trawlers trying their luck in these cold waters off the northern coast of the Golden Land. What made these boats different was their bizarre construction and historical purpose. What made them different were their mixed crews of Jondonqers, Dagulanders, and Liars. And what made them more unique than anything was their method of navigation. For high in the sky, now easily visible with the naked eye, like a pall of darkness a hundred miles wide, floating down from the north, was a dark swath of volcanic ash, a beacon in these icy waters they now couldn't miss, a forbidding signpost that was directing them into the great, the eternal, and perhaps the dangerous unknown.

CHAPTER TEN

The walls perspired. With the ballast tanks fully open, and the *Fetla* five fathoms below, the moisture condensed everywhere, beading on the Affed-treated vekeui. The entire crew was strapped into their tide-riding harnesses and stirrups. The forecastle grew silent and cold. Hab, strapped into his own harness, glanced around at the faces of his crew members. A candle, hanging in a special pivoting mount from the ceiling, its braces weighted on the bottom so that no matter which way the boat heaved the candle would always remain upright, flickered in the slowly diminishing oxygen supply. The movements of the tides were remote underwater, distant, a shadow of what they were when the *Fetla* floated on the surface.

"That was much better that time," said Hab. "The masts were down in three minutes. I wonder if it might be a good idea to start filling the ballast tanks while the crew are still taking down the masts. We might save time that way."

"You might end up with crew trapped above," said Guenard. "The hatches have to be shut before the water comes through the scuppers." Guenard's face was white with apprehension. "I can hardly breathe in here. When are we going to surface?"

"Guenard," said Hab, "command yourself. This isn't so bad. With those heavy seas pounding on the deck for the last two days, I like this quiet. It's peaceful."

"I feel like I'm in my grave," said Guenard. "I'm shivery with cold."

Hab once again glanced around at the other crew members. "How are the rest of you?"

"If this saves us from the tides, Captain," said Tiq, the middle of the three Liar brothers, "then it's nothing we can't bear."

"I agree," said Hadanas, a woman Dagulander, the ship's cook. "Give me the restful embrace of the deep over the murderous tides of Foot and Lag. We've done a good drill this time, and we should be proud of ourselves. We'll be that much safer when the real tides come."

The candle flickered again, guttered, nearly went out, but brightened once more as a rivulet of wax splattered to the floor.

"Crew, prepare to surface!" called Hab.

The crew unbuckled and stepped out of their floor-mounted stirrups.

"All hands, man your stations!" he called. "Ballast tanks open!"

Olle and Doran scrambled to the ballast pump and pumped air into the tanks furiously, using their whole bodies to press the bellows up and down. They used air funneled down a pipe leading to the surface, one of the ship's few metal components. Tiq climbed the companionway to the main hatch. The boat lurched upward, her timbers creaked, the water in the bilge swished about, and the belowdecks sloped upward. Hab walked to the aft hold, where a small square of glass had been fitted into the deck. He saw bubbles, water, a few fish— northern pekra with black scales and white underbellies. The water cleared and, wiping the steam from the glass to get a better view, he saw a clear sky with the first stars of evening shining. Out of the restful silence of the deep grew the dull roar of the ocean above.

"Tiq!" he called. "Open the forward hatch! Let's get some air in here!"

Tiq opened the forward hatch, and a refreshing breeze insinuated its way into the hold. Hab strode to the companionway and climbed topside. Esten followed.

The sea was rough and gray, with six-foot whitecaps. Visibility was a mile, with patches of mist clinging here and there. Fish and seaweed littered the deck. Hands came out the other hatches and began pitching the fish overboard. Some of the fish were thirty-pounders.

Other hands began the laborious job of swabbing while the riggers went to work raising the masts and setting the sails.

"Why does the sea have to beat so infernally hard up here?" asked Hab.

Esten raised his hand and pointed. "What's that?"

A large white shape emerged out of a fog bank. An iceberg, wrapped in its own halo of mist, cleaved its way patiently through the foam-flecked waves.

"We must be a lot farther north than I thought," said Hab.

"I brought up your charts," said Esten, handing Hab a waterproof tube. "Jara's gone to your cabin to get your sextant. You haven't looked since last night."

Jara, wrapped in a blue oilskin coat, emerged from the forward hatch with his sextant. The three walked to the bow of the boat. Hab fixed the sextant to its pedestal and aligned it with the proper stars. The scientist and his sister unrolled the sea charts. Hab checked the sextant several times, glanced at the map just as often, then looked at Esten and Jara with wonder in his eyes.

"Well?" said Esten.

Hab turned toward the bow and stared out over the endless vista of waves.

"We're in uncharted waters now," he said.

✺✺✺

Three days later, it snowed, blizzardlike conditions that, back home, were seen in only the highest peaks of the Oradels. The *Fetla*, *Xeulli-ette*, and *Airamatnas* sailed due north in close convoy. The seas remained rough, but because Foot and Lag were at their farthest opposition, the tides, though at times persistent, could easily be negotiated without having to go to the trouble of sinking the boats.

"I had no idea it would turn so cold," said Hab.

He and Esten stood on the foredeck. Hab had relieved Guenard and was steering the boat himself.

"A voyage like this makes one understand just how ignorant we really are about the world," said Esten. "I don't care what you had to do to achieve this, Hab. Paras owes you a debt."

"We might have to kill a whale or two," said Hab.

"Look at those icebergs," said Esten. "There have to be a hundred at least."

"There's a current over there," said Hab. "They're traveling with the current."

Five sailors shoveled the deck, pitching the snow over the railing into the water.

"Just think, Hab. No one's ever been here before," said Esten. "We're the first ones."

"We should have brought warmer clothing," said Hab.

Esten's bushy brows settled. "You're too practical for your own good, Hab Miquay."

"By anticipating any and all eventualities," said Hab, "I secure the safety of my crew." Hab stared out over the waves and turned a spoke to starboard, widening the distance between the *Fetla* and the icebergs. "That's my responsibility, and I accept it."

৬৬৬

The next day, the snow ended and a fair-weather front pushed in from the north. This brought spectacularly clear skies, calm seas, and bitterly cold temperatures. Icicles hung from all the yardarms. The decks were so slippery that Hab had his hands rig a system of guide-ropes to hang on to. Most bedeviling of all, the icebergs they'd seen floating in a steady stream southward for the past several days had now jammed up, and stood shoulder to shoulder not ten miles away, forming an impassable barrier. How in the name of Ouvant were they going to get by it? wondered Hab. He held his telescope to his eye and surveyed the craggy ice shelf. His breath billowed in great clouds of steam. He couldn't detect any gaps through the icebergs. He swung the telescope to the west, then to east; the icebergs stretched as far as the eye could see.

"We'll sail to within a mile," said Hab to Guenard.

"Will that be close enough?" asked Guenard. "You might miss a passage that far out."

"We can't chance it any closer," said Hab. "There'll be too much ice. And the tides are going to be strong tonight." Hab handed his telescope to Guenard. "Look at that one there. The water's hollowed out an archway."

Guenard looked at a perfect arch of blue ice through the telescope. He handed the telescope back to Hab. "This cold is going to kill us if we don't get out of here soon," he said.

Hab glanced at his first mate. As usual, Guenard was catastrophizing this small obstacle into something much bigger than it really was. "We'll find a way soon," Hab said mildly. "There's got to be a channel through that ice somewhere."

Over the next hour the three ships, under sail in a weak frigid wind, glided over the still blue waters to within a mile of the ice barrier. Jagged peaks etched a white line against the sky. The ice down near the surface, where the tide nibbled, was blue. Hab again inspected the barrier with his telescope. He now saw, just beneath the water, shelves of submerged ice, a daunting fringe of unpredictable shallows.

"What about that channel there?" asked Guenard, pointing.

Hab swung his telescope a few degrees to the left. "You can't see through to the other side," he said. "We might get stuck in there and never get out."

"Can't and might," said Guenard. "These aren't words of command, Captain. You vacillate. We must move in closer to get a better look."

"And risk grounding on the shallows?" said Hab. "Unless we see a true and clear channel through that ice, we'll risk no such venture."

They sailed for another six hours, covering forty miles. The tides came, but the waters remained eerily calm, with the swells blocked by all the ice, and the surges heaving no more than six feet at a time.

"Can you hear them?" asked Esten. "The moon-tides?"

Hab and Esten cocked their ears over the bow. Yes. Faintly. Carried on the weak wind Hab heard the distant crash of the tides against the far side of the ice barrier. An hour later he saw an icy mist in the sky shrouding the two moons, which now rode across the heavens nearly hand in hand. And with this icy mist came a damper and harsher cold.

Esten rubbed his hands together. "I can hardly feel my fingers."

The next morning, one of the women on the *Airamatnas* was found dead of exposure.

"She was on the dogwatch in the early hours of the morning," explained Eseark, captain of the *Airamatnas*. "Her relief fell asleep in the forecastle. She froze to death up in the nest. This cold sneaks up on you, it does. You have to watch out for it."

Hab turned to Jeter. "Captain, anything to report?"

"Three cases of frostbite, Captain," said Jeter.

They continued along the barrier looking for a channel all day. By midafternoon Hab was checking his compass and sextant every five minutes. Chouc stood with him, shivering, his hands deep in the pockets of his seaman's blues, gazing at Hab with dumb concerned eyes.

"I had another dream," he said at last.

Hab lifted his chin and peered at Chouc. "About what?" he asked.

Chouc looked glumly out at the sea. "About all this ice," he said. "About all this water. I dreamed one of these boats sailed too close to the ice."

Chouc's dreams. Somewhere buried in that simple boy's mind were the deeper truths of the unseen and the unknown. "And what happened?" asked Hab.

Chouc looked away, as if embarrassed about his dream. "Everybody froze." His small close-set eyes had grown watery in the freshening breeze.

"Everybody?" asked Hab.

Chouc nodded. "Yes, everybody."

You could sometimes stop Chouc's dreams from coming true. Chouc was here, not left behind, as he had so feared. A dream stopped. Hab would just have to stop this one from coming true. No one was going to freeze. Dream stopped. A forlorn look came to Chouc's eyes.

"What is it?" Hab asked.

"I see them all up on the ice," said Chouc, waving vaguely at the barrier, "boat and all. And they're all frozen."

Esten came up from behind. "Why are you checking your compass so often?" he asked.

Hab picked an ice chunk out of his hair and pitched it overboard. "Because I think this ice has entrapped us. I think it's surrounded us. We've been going around in circles."

Two hours later, as the sun set, Hab's worst fear came true. Tacking east, he spotted the great archway of ice he and Guenard had seen at the beginning of their channel search. Hab stared at the arch, not sure what to do. To add to their jeopardy, their isolated little patch of sea was starting to freeze. A large expanse of ice had spread out from the archway and was inching slowly toward them.

"The sea is freezing," he said to Esten, with perplexity.

Several crew had now come to the rail to look. The ice advanced in a transparent and interconnected plate of frail trapezoids, sketching a thin and delicate framework before piling up more sturdily.

Guenard said, "What now, Captain?"

Sailors aboard the *Airamatnas* lowered a longboat over the side. Hab looked at the longboat with his telescope and saw the bearded and hoary figure of Captain Eseark. He watched the sailors row across the frigid water, their oars dipping into the glassy surface with small white splashes. He glanced up at the sky. Snow clouds were moving in and the wind was picking up. Were they really stranded? He didn't want to believe it. He collapsed his telescope and stuck it in his belt.

"Here comes Eseark," he said.

Hab helped the old captain up over the railing of the *Fetla* when the old seaman's longboat finally came alongside.

"We have to come to a decision about this, Captain," said Eseark. "We've sailed in a circle." He pointed at the archway of ice. "We're back where we started from. The sea is freezing. We're going to be marooned soon." Jeter was now rowing across the water from the *Xeul-liette*. "We have to find a channel through that barrier, and that means getting closer. Blast and damn the shallows. We'll just have to risk it."

Jeter's boat came alongside, and some sailors helped him over the railing. Hab kept thinking about Chouc's dream, how if any of the boats got close to the ice, its crew would freeze to death.

"My brother had a dream," he said, in a distant, tentative way. And he told them about Chouc's dream. They all just looked at him.

"And this is how you're leading us?" asked Guenard, his face a mask of incredulity. "By the dreams of a simpleton who barely has the mental capability of a five-year-old?"

Hab searched for words to adequately explain the strong instinct he had about Chouc's dreams, but none of these men and women knew Chouc the way he did, and he wasn't going to get past their doubt, no matter what he said.

"Set sail for the center of this pool, Guenard," he ordered.

Guenard, his face nearly blue with cold, sneered. "You order us to our deaths. You'll strand us for sure."

Mutiny. Or at least close to it. "I ask you again, Guenard, set sail for the center of the pool. We'll wait for a break in the ice there."

"I respectfully disobey that order, Captain," he said.

The two men stared at each other. Twenty-five years together. They were more than just first mate and captain. They were friends. But now Hab felt as if he were looking at a stranger.

"Then you're relieved of your post, Guenard," said Hab. "Tiq, you're my new first mate."

"Aye, aye, Captain," said the Liar.

Guenard's eyes blazed. He hadn't been expecting this. "You make a Liar your first mate?" he said.

"My orders aren't open to debate, Guenard."

"You counseled flexibility just the other day."

"Flexibility, yes, but not mutiny."

Guenard was both flustered and surprised. He waved his hands at the *Fetla*, then at the *Xeulliette* and the *Airamatnas*. "But don't you see what an ill-conceived thing this is, Captain? You mount the voyage on a foundation of deceit. You man our ships with Liars." He pointed to the center of the pool. "Then you order us to our doom, to cast anchor in a place that will be three feet thick with ice in a matter of hours when we should be using whatever bit of sea remains open to find a likely passageway out."

"My orders stand as they are, Guenard."

But it was as if Guenard hadn't heard. "You dismiss the man who has been your loyal and steady friend for twenty-five years and install in his place a ruffian who wears the ignoble mark of the Liars upon his forehead." Guenard shook his head, his mouth open, his eyes wide, as if his disillusionment with Hab were now complete. "A woman has died, frozen to death on the dogwatch last night. Three others agonize with frostbite. And now you tell us you make your decisions based on the dreams of your simpleton brother."

Hab's lips stiffened and his brow settled. "Guenard, why do you do this? You know Chouc's dreams. You've seen them come true. Why do you misrepresent to these others that you have no idea what Chouc's dreams mean? You've known him all your life."

"You're a fit one to accuse your first mate of misrepresentation, Captain."

"You're not my first mate anymore."

"I have no intention of giving up my post, Captain." Guenard, puffing up, squared his shoulders with righteous indignation. "You are a fugitive, Hab Miquay. You are wanted by Parprouch's sheriffs in Summerhouse. And as such you no longer have authority to command any vessel on the high seas." Hab saw where this was going clearly enough. This was more than just a spontaneous altercation. Guenard signaled two crew from the *Airamatnas*. "Please arrest the captain and put him in manacles. I'm taking command of this vessel."

The two crew from the *Airamatnas* approached.

"Eseark," said Hab, "command your crew to desist."

But the old captain looked away. He wouldn't acknowledge Hab. He stared at the quickly freezing sea with watery gray eyes, ashamed of himself, but doing nothing to stop the mutiny.

"See, here, now," said Jeter. "You two desist. You do as the captain says."

But the two kept coming. They were about to grab Hab by the arms when Tiq, Olle, and Doran, with cool deliberateness, stepped forward, arranged themselves in front of Hab, and savagely pushed the two crewmen away. Hab was as startled as everybody else. He glanced at Tiq, a medium-built youth of about twenty-five with shoulder-length brown hair, dark eyes, and a layer of thick whiskers all over his chin. He saw a fierceness in Tiq's eyes that wasn't commonly found in the men of Jondonq. Then he glanced at Olle. Olle, the eldest, was smaller, darker, and the circles of Ouvant showed up pink on his forehead. Olle looked over his shoulder at Hab. Was that loyalty he saw in the eldest brother's eyes? Fierce, unquestioning, defiant loyalty? If it was, it was of a much more tenacious variety than the kind usually found in Paras. He finally looked at Doran, the youngest of the three, fairer than his older brothers, with a hint of red in his otherwise brown hair, and cheeks that looked like small hollows. These were hardened men, he realized. They were going to defend him, no matter what.

A few more of Eseark's crew came forward. No words were exchanged, and everyone looked on in stunned silence. Not many could warrant the nature of this confrontation out here on the arctic sea. The three brothers drew weapons, crude stone ones fashioned out of flint, knives chiseled and filed to a keen sharpness. Violence. The First Rule of the Formulary. Hab stared at the stone knives, appalled yet fascinated. Was the carrying of concealed weapons commonplace on the Island of Liars?

"Lay one hand on the captain, mates, and I'll slit your throats," said Olle, as evenly as if he were commenting on the weather.

The mates of Eseark's crew stopped. They were Dagulanders, dark, with slight epicanthic folds to their eyelids, mild-tempered men who'd been asked to perform an unpleasant task, desperately cold, driven to this extreme by the dire circumstances. But now they looked at the knives. No one fought on Paras anymore. Murder was unheard-of. As with weapons, war had been outlawed on Paras for five hundred years. But Hab realized that on the Island of Liars, they clearly fought. Tiq particularly looked ready to defend his captain. Hab felt a sudden surge of gratitude to the young Liar.

Guenard gestured desperately at the Liars, trying to save what he could of the situation. "You see the kind of monsters the captain's brought on board?" He spat on the deck. "We might as well stow our hammocks. We won't be safe at night sleeping in them."

Esten stepped forward, a beneficent grin on his face. "There's no need for bloodshed," he said, resting a friendly hand on Tiq's arm. "Put your weapons away." He turned to Hab. "Captain, is there not some way we can reach a compromise in this business?" He glanced at Guenard. "Could we not perhaps send a longboat out to one of these openings Guenard is so eager to explore?" he said, pointing.

"Not with that snow moving in," said Hab.

"Then let us take one of the ships," said Eseark, speaking up for the first time. "This is madness, Hab. I agree with Guenard. This dream your brother has had . . . how can you base such a momentous and possibly catastrophic decision on something so—"

"You will freeze to death if you go near that ice," he said. "I tell you that in all earnestness, and if you don't wish to believe me, Eseark, then I fear for your life. In spite of that, I grant you your leave. You can take the *Airamatnas*. But in granting you your leave I also withdraw my responsibility. If you can find fifteen fools, then go, take your ship. Guenard knows my brother's dreams, but he's chosen to ignore them for reasons I can't readily understand." Eseark stared at him resolutely. He could see that the old man had made up his mind. He also knew the old man was going to die. "Go if you must, Eseark. I send you in good faith, but also urge utmost caution. I see you are a man of good sense, and a well-seasoned sailor." Hab stepped forward, so that he was in front of Tiq, Olle, and Doran. "Everyone else, listen to me. I tell you what I tell Guenard. We on Paras pride ourselves on the truth. But the truth isn't as simple as it seems. Truth and belief, when mixed, become an ambivalent and sly combination. I ask you to trust this dream of my brother's. Guenard asks you to believe the various dead-end openings we've spotted in this wall of ice. You must decide for yourself. But remember this: What you feel and what you see are two entirely different things, and sometimes it's better to trust what you feel rather than what you see."

𝕾𝕾𝕾

That night, the night of the bilunar eclipse, as Lag slowly overtook Foot somewhere beyond the snow-laden clouds, the *Fetla* and the *Xeulliette* lay at anchor in the middle of the seawater pool surrounded by a thin film of ice. Drifting snow scurried over this ice in small ephemeral tendrils, blown by the wind in an ever-shifting and elusive pattern.

"It's cold," said Chouc.

Hab put his arm around his young brother's shoulder, trying to warm him up. They were standing the dogwatch together. Hab peered out over the dark sea. "Do you hear that noise?" he asked.

Carried faintly through the thickly falling snow came a low grinding sound. Several booms followed this grinding sound. Hab looked for lightning, thinking that the booms might be thunder, but the sky remained dark; it was far too cold for lightning, and the booms had a bizarre crunching sound that wasn't characteristic of thunder. He lifted the storm lamp from the hook and held it over the side. From the film of ice below came a crinkling sound.

"Look at that," he said.

Chouc looked over the railing. A fine network of cracks traced its way through the ice. Esten emerged from the forward hatch, sleepy-eyed, and joined them. He looked out at all the cracks. Several more booms came from the north, and the air suddenly got a lot warmer and damper, smelled a lot brinier. Hab walked to the storm cannon and fired a flare. The flare, no more than a whaling harpoon with its barbs soaked in grease, shot high into the air. It quickly sputtered out in the driving snow, but not before Hab got a glimpse of a massive tide moving their way.

"Sound the alarm!" he shouted to Chouc. "We're going down."

Chouc rang the tide bell, and in moments, crew members on both the *Fetla* and the *Xeulliette* scurried to get the masts down and the ballast tanks filled. The ballast tanks began to bubble, hiss, and as the boats inched down through the thin coating of ice, deckhands scrambled to make fast all fittings and sails. Three sailors hooked a large spill-cloth over the bow of the *Fetla*. In minutes, the decks were cleared, and all crew members had scurried below.

The first tide hit two minutes later, wrenching the *Fetla* backward, rolling it to a forty-five-degree angle. The tough vekeui wood creaked but otherwise stayed intact. The crew, strapped in their harnesses, their feet straining in their floor stirrups, rode the surge well. Ten fathoms underwater like this, it did indeed seem the boats would survive the tides, even despite the large chunks of ice knocking against them.

Over the next hour, the tides, at their highest because of the eclipse, rocked the vessel mercilessly. Yet the *Fetla* showed not even the slightest inclination to capsize, so well weighted with lead was her bilge and keel. Even so, the crew's journey through the bilunar ecliptical tides wasn't entirely free of danger. Again, it was the ice. At regular intervals, Hab heard two- and three-ton chunks of ice pounding against the keel and upon the deck. But the boat weathered the onslaught admirably. Aigre the shipbuilder deserved his reputation.

At about four bells in the morning, with the candle sputtering in the nearly airless galley, the sea again grew still, and they were at last able to surface.

Hab opened the hatch and went topside. High summer in the north and the sun was already up, sending a pale golden glow over the water, lighting up a sea that was clogged with millions of pieces of broken ice. Ice chunks littered the deck, some of them waist-high, and he had to struggle over them, sliding this way then that to get to the forecastle head. Once there, he had a clear view of what lay ahead.

The ice barrier was gone. The sea was full of slabs of ice, some twice the size of the *Fetla*, others no bigger than his fist, gray pieces of broken-up icebergs, with tints of turquoise here and there, knocking about, sounding like snooker balls banging each other. The wind blew dead astern and pushed the *Fetla* through these slabs of ice. Far in the distance, about two miles off the port bow, Hab saw the *Xeulliette*. He looked for the *Airamatnas* but couldn't see her anywhere.

Tiq struggled over the ice-strewn deck behind him.

"Awaiting your orders, sir," he said.

He looked at Tiq, again feeling grateful. "Hoist the masts and set a course dead ahead. Have Olle signal the *Xeulliette*. Tell Chouc to climb to the nest and keep a lookout for the *Airamatnas*."

"Aye, aye, Captain," said Tiq, and made to go. Hab stopped him, put his hand on the man's arm.

"And Tiq?"

"Captain?"

Hab gave Tiq's arm a shake. "Thank you," he said.

A surprised grin came to Tiq's face, as if he wasn't used to being thanked for things. "You're welcome, sir."

"How came you to the Island of Liars, Tiq?" asked Hab.

Tiq looked away, the grin slipping from his face. "I was born there, sir. And we who live there don't call it the Island of Liars." He glanced out at all the ice. "We call it Manense."

"Manense," said Hab, trying the name out. "I don't think I know that word."

Tiq shrugged. "It comes from the ancient Dagu, sir. It means 'house of stone.'"

Hab rubbed his chin, thinking of the rocky place of Tiq's birth. "An apt name, to be sure."

In an hour, they were properly under way. Hadanas made a fish chowder out of the pekra that had been collected off the deck, and everyone ate their fill. Jeter came aboard and gave his report: the *Xeulliette* had weathered the full force of the ecliptical tides as well as the *Fetla*.

They sailed northward all morning. By eleven bells, Hab's compass did an odd thing. The needle, over the course of fifteen miles, changed direction, began facing south instead of north.

"We've sailed over the top of the world, Hab," said Esten. "The pole is behind us now. We're sailing south." He pointed at the sky. "And it looks like we're dead on course." A dim gray banner of volcanic ash, looking yet more defined than before, arced over the sky from the south.

By midafternoon, huge icebergs marauded through the sea, and Hab concluded the bulk of the ice barrier had wound up here on the retreating tide last night.

He was just about to have Tiq turn five spokes to the starboard bow so they could avoid these dangerous giants when he saw a thin column of smoke rising from one of them. Hab, Tiq, and Esten stared at the smoke. None of them could figure out how that smoke had gotten there.

Chouc despondently muttered, "It's the *Airamatnas*."

The other three stared at the simpleton. Hab felt his heart thump with apprehension. "Are you sure?" he asked.

"I'm sure," said Chouc.

"Are there any survivors?" he asked.

"No," said Chouc. "No survivors."

Hab took a deep breath and sighed. "Tiq, set a course three spokes to port. We'll have to get in close."

"Aye, aye, Captain."

ᏮᏮᏮ

In the longboat, as Hab, Esten, and six other crew rowed to within a hundred yards, Hab saw a vast subsurface tongue of ice many times the size of the iceberg jutting out below them, not five fathoms deep, unnerving in its closeness, bright blue, glittering with schools of small silver pekra. From behind a jagged hill of snow, the column of smoke continued to drift into the air. As they rounded this hill, they saw the *Airamatnas*, heaved up onto the lip of the iceberg as if it were no more than a toy boat pitched there by a child. The keel was cracked open as surely as an egg and lay on the snow in two distinct halves. The boat was covered with a fresh layer of powder snow from last night's snowstorm. The sails hung in rags, and many of the masts and yards were broken.

"They didn't dive soon enough," said Hab. "The tides got to them before they had the chance."

Several frozen corpses lay scattered about the boat, like rag dolls, looking as if they had just been dropped there. The rowers picked up the pace, and in another five minutes Hab and Esten climbed onto the iceberg.

"There's Eseark," said Esten.

The old captain sat on a crate with his back to the broken hull, frozen stiff in a sitting position. Hab stared at him while Esten climbed into the *Airamatnas*. Everywhere it was the same. Crewmen and crewwomen were frozen stiff. A half dozen lay around the galley stove just inside. A grim and forbidding scene, one that was as distressing as it was saddening, a bad and portentous way to start their voyage.

"Hab!" called Esten. The scientist had climbed up on deck. "I've found Guenard!"

Hab climbed the lopsided and broken companionway through the galley up to the deck. Esten stood on what was left of the poop deck. Guenard hung by the neck from the second yardarm of the mizzenmast, an obvious suicide, his face gray, his beard hoary with frost, his eyes partially open, his tongue bloated and sticking out of his mouth, the trousers of his seaman's blues reeking with the filth of death's incontinence. Hab felt struck through the heart. All the years of his long friendship with Guenard came crowding in around him, bringing with them a myriad of emotions and remembrances. He felt his throat closing up painfully with the pity of it all. The wind spun Guenard's body in a slow counterclockwise motion. Guenard had killed himself because he had been afraid of freezing to death. Hab knew that. With Guenard, it was always fear, something he had never been able to master.

"Chouc was right," said Esten.

Hab shook his head, fighting back his grief tears. "He always is," he said. "And the sad thing is, Guenard knew he was right."

CHAPTER ELEVEN

Hab sat in his cabin listening to the wind snap at the sails. Sixteen straight hours above-deck navigating through the ice, and now his exhaustion was like a weight that was too great to bear. And not only exhaustion, but grief. Grief for everyone aboard the *Airamatnas*, but grief particularly for Guenard. Here on the table before him was the only thing he had left of Guenard, a battered old Formulary with the pages dog-eared and water-stained, and the embossed cloth cover coming apart at the edges. Guenard, a stalwart believer, had, in the end, broken Rule 3 of the Formulary, the one about suicide.

Someone knocked on his cabin door. "Come in," he called.

The door opened and Jara peered inside. Framed in the doorway, with the sun shining in her hair, she seemed to glow with her own light. He now saw tints of gold in her red hair.

"I can't help caring about you," she said candidly.

So. The truth was out. They stared at each other. It seemed he had a whole crew of misrepresenters and omitters. Here was the real reason she had wanted to stay aboard the *Fetla* with Hab. He didn't know if he had the strength for it right now. In the light of his lamp, her eyes shone a pale green in her freckled face.

"Jara," he said, "that's kind."

"No," she said. "No . . . it's not." She looked at the deck. "It's selfish."

He felt overwrought. He felt like crying. He tried to fight his tears, but his eyes clouded with them anyway. He rubbed them away with the back of his big hand, not bothering to hide them from Jara. Twenty-five years was a long time to know Guenard. He leaned for-

ward, put his elbows on his knees, and stared down at Guenard's Formulary, a cheap one, bought from a sidewalk merchant in Perro
decades ago, spattered with dried saltwater. Here was a man. And now
he was gone. He heard Jara walk toward him. She walked around to
the back of his chair. She put her hands on his shoulders and rubbed.
He reached up and put his hand over Jara's. He was surprised by how
delicate her hand felt.

"He followed his conscience," said Hab. "I don't want anybody
thinking he didn't. He did what he thought was right. That's all any
of us can do."

"No one thinks ill of him."

"I forced him into this situation. I shouldn't have done that."

"You can't blame yourself, Hab."

"He believed in this," said Hab, tapping the decrepit Formulary. "I
don't know whether I do anymore."

"It's a guide to be interpreted, Hab."

"I could have been wrong about Chouc's dream."

"But you weren't."

Jara slid her hands down his shoulders and rested them on his
chest. He pressed his head against her abdomen and looked at her
hands. They were as fair as cream and mottled with freckles. He saw
dim blue veins beneath her skin. She had a fresh young smell, like a
girl, only the comfort in her palms was the comfort of a woman.

"When I was a schoolgirl," she said, "I used to study the puzzles of
Iley. Do you know her work at all?"

"The illusionist?"

"She's much more than an illusionist," said Jara. "You look at one
of her pictures and you think you see the face of an old man staring out
at you. But after looking at it for ten minutes you realize it's not an old
man at all but really a young woman standing in front of a large
mirror. Iley taught me to look at things in different ways. I don't see
fifteen dead crew members aboard the *Airamatnas*." She stroked Hab's

head tenderly. "I see thirty living crew members aboard the *Fetla* and the *Xeulliette* who are thanking you for their lives."

ᔒᔒᔒ

Thirty days later, with the food and freshwater running low, the nerves of everyone stretched thin, and no sign of land anywhere, just the dim pall of ash in the sky, those same crew members who'd thanked Hab for their lives were now grumbling about how long the voyage was taking.

"The traditional calculations are off," Hab said to Esten.

Esten nodded. "You can't arrive at an accurate measurement of distance until you've logged at least ninety degrees. All those old mariners from Pieshe never sailed farther than the south coast of Maju. How could they realistically estimate the true length of a degree arc? I've always suspected a bit of bluster on their part."

"So have I," said Hab. "Especially after I made my journey to the equator."

"It's not easy to discard the learning of your predecessors," said Esten. "That's one of the reasons we're out here. To establish some hard facts. To dismantle all that bluster."

"We always thought the world was fifteen thousand miles around. Now we discover it's thirty." Hab grinned. "I would say that's bluster by half. And that makes a degree arc eighty miles, not forty."

Esten looked out over the bow at the warm blue water. "Which means we still have a long way to go."

Hab glanced around at the deckhands. "The crew are surly."

"Maybe we should break out the brandy."

"Some want to turn back," said Hab.

The sun glistened on the water, and the air was steamy with tropical humidity. They were near the equator.

"And what does Jeter say?" asked Esten.

"Jeter says keep going," said Hab.

"What do you say?"

Hab's brow settled. "The same," he said. He shifted restlessly from one foot to the other. "I've got to see it, Esten. I've got to know it." He waved his palm at the sky. "We follow this ash to its source."

✶✶✶

As the moons converged again, the tides got higher and higher. In open seas the tides built to tremendous heights, unbroken by any reef or continental shelf. Not only that, there were more of them, sometimes as many as twenty-five a night.

Hab stood on the forecastle head with his telescope to his eye. Tiq stood beside him.

"So you actually conduct raids on other villages?" asked Hab. Hab was growing more and more fascinated with the Liar way of life on Manense.

"Starvation prompts aggression," said the first mate. Hab took his telescope from his eye and glanced at the young Liar. Tiq was looking out over the bow at the slowly advancing first tide. "Will we be diving, sir?"

"But a raid," said Hab. "Isn't that war?"

Tiq considered, and in perfect seriousness said, "I'd call it supper, sir, not war."

"Did you know war was outlawed on Paras five hundred years ago?"

The first tide rolled ominously closer. "That doesn't surprise me, sir," he said. "None of you look like fighters."

Hab grew suddenly pensive. "I punched my brother in the face," he said. "That's fighting."

"That's a family quarrel, sir," said Tiq. "On Manense, fighting and killing go hand in hand. Striking a brother in the face . . . well . . . anybody can lose their temper."

"You've killed?" asked Hab.

"When I've had to." Tiq stared apprehensively at the water. "Shouldn't we dive, sir? That tide's getting close."

Hab glanced at the tide. "I think we'll ride these ones on the surface. You see the slope of it, don't you? That's nothing but a gentle lift. These ones aren't steep like the ones we'll see five days hence, when our moons are in their eclipse." The boat lurched upward on the first tide. "You see? As stable as a rock, thanks to Aigre." Hab contemplated his first mate with unabashed curiosity. "I can't help wondering why you didn't try to escape from Manense?"

"The king's cutters, sir," he said. "And where would we go? We can't go to Paras—not with these marks on our foreheads."

෫෫෫

In the morning, while Hab was still in bed, Chouc knocked frantically on his cabin door.

"Brother, Brother!" cried Chouc. "Come quick! You've got to see this!"

Hab swung his feet out of his hammock and pulled on his seaman's trousers, certain that the lookout had at last spotted land. But when he came on deck he saw not land but a thousand red bladders shimmering on the horizon, gigantic ones, far bigger than the red bladders of the bladder whales off the coast of Dagu. A great smile came to Hab's face. He tousled his young brother's hair.

"Good going, Chouc."

Esten looked up at the sky. "There's no sign of the ash this morning."

"We'll harpoon a whale," said Hab. "They swim toward shore when they're harpooned. We don't need ash. We've got whales." He turned to Tiq. "Tiq, set a course on the port-beam. And trim the sails to a full gybing."

"Aye, aye, Captain."

"Doran, Olle, break out the whaling tackle."

"Aye, Captain," chimed the brothers.

Hab turned to the signalman, a young man, no more than twenty, from Retelon. "Signalman, let the *Xeulliette* know. Jara, climb to the crow's nest and chart the movement of the pod."

🙌🙌🙌

They were huge. The smallest was ten times the size of its Parassian cousins. Their air bladders rose out of the water, house-sized sacks of red, pulsating and hissing, reticulated with a meshwork of dark purple veins. Hab glanced over the port bow where the *Xeulliette* sailed twenty-five yards away. He saw Jeter hunched over the harpoon cannon. The stench of whale spume filled the air. Hab and Jeter looked at each other.

"Which one do we go for?" called Jeter, raising his hand to his mouth.

Hab scanned the pod, squinting in the spray and sunshine. A huge tail lifted out of the water nearby and slapped the surface, sending geysers of foam twenty-five feet into the air. The whales were getting nervous. And when they were nervous, they charged. Hab was worried about their teeth. Even the teeth on the small Parassian whales were like fence pikes. The teeth on these whales must be the size of small trees. He wondered if their jaws were strong enough to crunch through vekeui wood.

"We'll cull that one over there!" he called, pointing to the smallest whale in the pod.

Jeter nodded, then turned to give orders to his first mate. Hab gave his own orders to Tiq. The boats swerved south. The *Xeulliette* nosed its way through a small channel between the whales. The whales to the right edged away, toward the *Fetla*. The *Fetla* then drove a wedge between this splintered column and the target whale. The *Xeulliette* trimmed its sails to a broad reach and forced the small whale farther and farther away from the column.

"Two spokes hard astern, Tiq!" called Hab.

"Aye, Captain!"

With this maneuver, the *Fetla* found itself directly behind the whale, with the creature's tail not more than a few yards in front of the jib boom. Hab aimed the harpoon cannon and fired. The projectile hissed out of the cannon like a thing alive. The barb thudded into the whale's right bladder, piercing it neatly. The animal lurched around, lifted its head clear out of the water, revealing a face as terrifying as it was ugly—flat, green, with eyes the size of blubber barrels, and a half dozen tentaclelike whiskers extending from its nose. Its teeth, each twelve feet long, were sharp, ragged, and covered with green slime. The whale lunged for the jib boom and snapped it off. It swam around to starboard, carrying the spar in its mouth, an animal easily five times the size of the *Fetla*, its tail splashing the water with a sound like thunder. It shook the spar from its mouth, and bit, with all the terrible force of its mighty jaws, the starboard ballast tank. Hab ran from the harpoon cannon and stood at the railing. The whale's teeth sank a few inches into the hard vekeui but didn't penetrate all the way.

He ran to the forecastle head and signaled to the *Xeulliette*. Jeter waved a strip of red cloth in the air. He was going to strike the other bladder. The tall captain brought the *Xeulliette* into position by backing the sails onto the masts; the wind blew the *Xeulliette* slowly stern-first, toward the stricken *Fetla*. Once in position, Jeter swung the *Xeulliette*'s harpoon cannon round and fired at the whale's left air bladder. A dead strike, right in the center. The whale grew still, as if it had to think about the implications of its injuries, and slowly, like a rusting game trap opening after weeks out in the rain, its jaws parted, and the whale let go of the *Fetla*.

Blood gushed from its bladders, ran over its brown back in cascades of red, and curled into the surrounding seawater. It hissed horribly as it tried to fill its bladders again, snorting a half dozen times through its bilateral blowholes before it gave up. The crews on both boats watched silently. Finally the whale heaved away from the boat, the same way harpooned whales in Paras heaved—lifting its massive tail, casting up a fine spray that the sunlight shot through with rainbows—and headed southeast. The harpoon lines from both ships uncoiled quickly as the whale gained speed.

"Six spokes to the port side!" cried Hab. "Keep us clear of the *Xeulliette*. We don't want to tangle our lines. All hands, a full-out luff, and keep the load light!"

The lines went taut, and both ships lurched forward as the whale took up the slack. Sailors scrambled up and down the ratlines, trimming sails. The sails mercifully billowed. The flap and roar of their bellies filling with wind was like music to Hab. The harpoon lines sagged as the boats began to keep pace with the whale. They could fill their larders again with that whale. The waters hereabouts were curiously fishless. They could replenish their oil supply. The ships quickly picked up speed and in minutes cruised at fifteen knots. Most of all, they could get a good long tow toward land.

⨪⨪⨪

Early in the evening, before the tides struck, they anchored the boats ten yards from each other. Sailors placed a plank from rail to rail, and crew from the *Xeulliette* came aboard the *Fetla* for a roast. They made a fire in a circular stoneware hearth, and soon had a fifty-pound piece of whale liver roasting on a spit. Hab opened three kegs of brandy from the ship's lazarette, probably the last Cloudesley vintage he would ever taste.

Chouc was staring up at the twilight sky with wonder. "We actually have birds again," he said.

Hab looked at the birds, like no birds he'd ever seen before, with wings not of feathers but of membrane, like skin stretched over a delicate framework of fingers, heads like anvils, and talons big enough to clutch a man whole. Big birds, some with wingspans as wide as the top-gallant sail, swooping again and again at what was left of the whale carcass floating a hundred yards astern, landing on the carrion, ripping out chunks of meat, then leaping back into the air. Tiq and Olle watched the birds nervously, the Liar brothers armed with the crossbows from the ship's stores, the crossbows meant for hunting game when they arrived at the place they were going.

"I'm not sure that they're birds, Chouc," he said. "They look more like flying animals."

Sailors were singing an old folksong by the hearth about Atin, the mythological and mischievous sprite who, in times gone by, bedeviled the farmers of Berberton.

"You come in the night when all are asleep,
You steal our fair daughters and make us all weep,
You unlatch our gate and our animals flee,
You must have your fun, you can't let us be.

"You splatter our land with the mud of your bowel,
It kills all our crops and it also smells foul,
We'll throw down our hoes and we'll kick off our clogs,
We'll join with a ship and sail off to the fogs.

"Oh . . . oh . . . oh . . .
Oh, when will you leave us alone, la!
When will you leave us alone, ha!
When will you leave us alone!"

While this singing went on, Jeter sat down beside Jara and put his arm around her. Hab watched uneasily. Jara, who had been enjoying the song with the others, stiffened with displeasure. The smile left her face and her shoulders rose. She grabbed Jeter's hand and flung it off her shoulder. The girl had a fine talent for wrath, Hab had to give her that. She got up and marched to the taffrail. Jeter looked at Hab in innocent alarm. Hab shrugged, shook his head, hoping with these gestures to convey to Jeter the irascible nature of Jara's personality; her personality was a force of nature nobody, not even a well-intentioned suitor, could do anything about.

Jeter scratched his ear, shrugged, then got up and was about to head for the taffrail when Hab shook his head again, this time vigorously. Approaching her now wouldn't do any good. Jeter's eyes went wide with enquiry. Hab nodded and pointed at the bench. Jeter sat down reluctantly and stared into the fire, his face a picture of disappointment.

Hab glanced at Jara. With her slim figure silhouetted against the pink sky of sunset, and the golden waves stretching out endlessly behind her, she was, in her coltish way, enchanting. He thought maybe he should talk to her, but knew it was best to leave her alone. He would stay put. He would stare into the fire like Jeter. And he would try to solve the mystery of Jara Pepteri. She was like one of the puzzle drawings of the great illusionist Iley, whom she admired so much. He thought if he contemplated her long enough, and hard enough, he might finally see a solution, or at least find a new way of looking at her, and understand exactly what it was he was starting to feel toward Esten's brash, hotheaded, and brilliant young sister.

Part Two

DISCOVERY

CHAPTER TWELVE

The moon-tides came again that night. The distant but large Lag piggybacked on top of the smaller, closer Foot, doubling the usual gravitational pull. So big was the first tide that Hab spotted it a half hour before it struck, a rolling wall of water a hundred feet high, stable, slow, and deadly, stretching to north and south vanishing points, its crest glittering with the quicksilver of the bilunar light. Tiq rang the tide bell. Hab heard the responding bell from the *Xeulliette.* In ten minutes both ships, with all masts stowed, sank beneath the waves.

"The night will be a long one," said Hab, once his crew were safely strapped in. "Prepare yourselves well."

The first tide struck a few minutes later. Even ten fathoms under, the *Fetla* was wrenched violently by the tide's vicious current. The boat lurched upward. Hab felt his stomach twist with the sudden rise. He felt as if he had just been shot from a cannon. The boat rolled despite its lead-lined keel, and everyone whirled upside down in their harnesses. The hull creaked, and a loud bang came from the aft hold, sounding to Hab like one of the extra spars breaking loose from its brace. The crew strained in their floor stirrups, holding themselves in place while the boat somersaulted. Then the *Fetla* righted itself as quick as the snap of a whip. Hab felt his neck twist. He heard grunts and groans as the crew grimly bore the punishment. There would be sprains and sore muscles tomorrow, he thought. And this was just the first tide.

The night proved as bad as any they had yet faced. Hab counted thirty-seven tides. Twelve of these capsized the boat. The boat was as good as a barrel when capsized, and remained seaworthy through the heavy pounding. Three hours into the onslaught, their air grew so thin that the candle went out. By the time the tides finally settled, crew were clutching for breath. Even though the sea was fairly rough, with the swells still forty feet high, Hab gave the order to surface.

"It can only get better," he said, as the crew unbuckled and prepared to take their stations. "The moons draw apart tonight. The tides will weaken in the coming days."

Olle and Doran pumped air into ballast tanks, forcing the water out so that at least a few feet of the deck could rise out of the sea. The air was so stale that the crew were dizzy from it. Hab walked to the viewing glass in the ceiling of the hold and watched the water clear from the deck.

"Open the forward hatch, Jamas!" he called to the boatswain, his voice ragged from the strain of the night.

Jamas weakly pushed open the forward hatch. A spray of water burst in, followed by a slow gush of muggy, tropical air. After a night in the damp cool galley, Hab immediately began to sweat. He had never felt air so hot. He momentarily wondered if they had survived the tides only to find themselves in the fires of Oeil.

He climbed topside. He expected to see fish all over the deck, but there were only two or three small ones caught in the scuppers: not pekra, but strange fish, long, sleek, yellow with red stripes, such as he had never seen before. The sun was just up but hidden behind a low gray bank of storm clouds. Though he saw blue sky overhead, he smelled rain not far off, and his body tingled with the suffocating sense of a quickly dropping barometric pressure. Tiq climbed out of the hatch behind him, followed by Esten and Olle.

"No fish again," said Tiq.

Hab pointed. "Except for those few in the scuppers."

Esten looked at one of the striped fish in the scuppers. "Maybe we're outside the pekra's usual migration routes." Esten's eyes narrowed with curiosity. "Let's have a look at these." The three men walked over to the nearest scupper and knelt as the boat heaved and rolled in the after-tide. "It's stuck," said Esten. He gripped the fish and pulled it out of the drain hole, but quickly dropped it.

"Ow!" he cried.

"What happened?" asked Hab.

A knit came to Esten's bushy brow. "It stung me."

"Let's see," said Hab.

Esten showed him his hand. "The spikes on its dorsal fin must have poison in them."

"Maybe you should have Hadanas look at it."

"She's a fishwife, Hab, not a doctor."

"She has a way with herbs, Esten. She might give you something for it, a salve or lotion."

Esten shrugged, then scanned the horizon. "I don't see the *Xeulliette* anywhere."

Hab looked over the waves. "They probably haven't surfaced yet."

Tiq shook his head. "They must be suffocating by this time. I could hardly breathe in there."

The three men scanned the ocean silently for several minutes. Hab finally said, "Don't worry, they'll be up soon. I'll sound the signal cannon in a half hour."

🌊🌊🌊

The sea settled to five- and ten-foot swells. The sun climbed above the bank of storm clouds on the eastern horizon and shone brightly over the water.

"Look at the water," said Hab.

Esten looked. "What about it?"

"It's green. Not blue anymore."

"So?"

Hab lifted his chin. "It means one of two things: a lower temperature or a shallower bottom. I think in this case, because it's so hot here, it must mean a shallower bottom. Which means land."

Esten looked at the horizon skeptically. "We'll see."

Hab pointed. "We'll keep a southeasterly course. In a week or two, we'll be there."

Esten looked up at the sky. "I wonder where the volcanic ash is?"

Tiq fired the signal cannon fifteen minutes later. Hab climbed to the nest, telescope in hand, and scanned the seas for the *Xeulliette*. From high atop the mainmast the ocean stretched to the horizon like a carpet of aquamarine. Despite the blue sky overhead, rain traveled all the way from the storm clouds and fell on the *Fetla*, a sun-shower. A half dozen rainbows formed to the west. Hab, hugging the mainmast with his left arm, held the telescope to his eye with his right. He swung the telescope around slowly in a complete circle. The *Xeulliette* was nowhere in sight. A dark nugget of apprehension settled in Hab's stomach. Jeter was a good seaman and an immensely able captain. But even Jeter might get lost in tides so violent.

"Tiq!" he called. "Sound the signal again."

Tiq fired the cannon. Hab listened for a responding report. Nothing. Just the wind, the waves, and the rain against the deck. He ran his hand through his thick brown hair, held the crown of his head for a moment in consternation, elbow up, then let his arm fall to his side.

"Any sign of them?" Tiq called.

"No," replied Hab.

He stayed up in the crow's nest for the next hour searching the ocean with his telescope. The sails billowed with a strong southwesterly, keeping the *Fetla* steady at ten knots. Jara climbed to the nest with a flask of wine and a piece of hardtack.

"Here," she said. "I brought you something."

He gratefully took the food and drink. "Thank you."

By first bell in the afternoon, with still no sign of the *Xeulliette*, the wind had died, the sea grew bizarrely still, and the sails billowed fecklessly.

"Can I go swimming?" asked Chouc.

Sensitive only in his dreams, Chouc now had no idea of just how anxious Hab was growing over the missing boat. Yet nothing gave Hab greater pleasure than to watch Chouc swim. A teenager needed fun. And because Hab wanted Tiq to take a sounding to see how deep the water was, he had Olle cast anchor. Everyone needed a break after the long night. Crew could relax for a while. Chouc could go for his swim. To watch Chouc swim and enjoy himself might relieve some of Hab's anxiety.

The hands arranged a plank for Chouc, and the teenager dove off the end with a grace that was strange to see in such a crooked little body. Into the warm green water he splashed. Hab and Esten watched him from the taffrail. Despite the unknown whereabouts of the *Xeulliette*, Hab felt his mood lifting.

"How's the water?" he called.

"Warm," called Chouc. "And salty."

The boy swam from one end of the boat to the other, back and forth, with a speed and style all hands admired. Hab felt like going in there with him. At least it would get his mind off the *Xeulliette*. But he knew he had to stay on deck in case the lookout spotted the *Xeulliette*. Tiq approached him from the bow of the boat.

"I've done the sounding, sir," he said.

"And?"

"Twelve fathoms."

"Twelve fathoms?" said Hab. "We'll have an easy night of it, then. The tides will break in such shallow water."

Esten gestured at the sky. "Look, more birds."

The strange bird-animals they'd seen before flew in formation in the distance. Hab looked at Esten's hand as the scientist pointed. "Your hand's swelling from that sting."

"I had Hadanas put something on it."

"Good."

"Begging your pardon, Captain, sir," said Tiq. "But I saw something in the water while I was doing the sounding—a big fish of some kind, twice the size of a man. I thought your brother might come aboard for a bit, until we're sure what it is."

Hab glanced over the taffrail at his brother. As much as he hated to spoil Chouc's fun, caution prevailed. "Chouc," he called. "I think it's time to get out of the water."

"Do I have to?" said Chouc.

But then Hab froze. He saw a blurry green shape under the water, not ten yards from Chouc, like no sea creature he had ever seen before, not a whale or fish, but like some of the amphibious creatures found in the Calundi Wetlands east of the River Gerleni in Berberton, with arms and legs, and a tail, but, as Tiq said, twice the size of a man. Chouc swam indolently to the rigging at the back of the boat, a peevish look on his face, and climbed the rope ladder up to the taffrail. Hab continued to stare at the underwater creature, a brief impression of green scales and a mottled back, then a face looking up at them just a few feet below the surface, primitive and fishlike. But unlike a fish, the thing had eyes on the front of its face instead of at the sides. Red eyes, a snoutish nose, and a glimpse of a mouth with flat small teeth, a harmless-looking creature, a meaty-looking creature. Game, Hab thought. No sign of poison spikes either. What a stroke. A way to replenish their larder in these fishless and now whaleless seas. A flick of its long green tail snapped out of the water. Then the thing was gone, vanished beneath the tepid waves. Supper. A good sign. A bit of luck after this particularly worrisome day.

ᔕᔕᔕ.

"Smoke off the port bow!" cried Jamas an hour later.

Hab climbed to the forecastle head and looked through his telescope. Far to the northeast he saw a smudge of black smoke puffing up from behind the rim of the ocean. Jara stood beside him.

"Are we there?" she asked. "Is that the volcano?"

Hab took the telescope away and looked up at the sky. The pall of ash, having appeared again, drifted from the east, not the northeast. So that smoke definitely wasn't from the volcano. "If only we had a bit more wind," he said. He walked to the steps and called Tiq. "Tiq, trim the sails and bring her five spokes to the port bow. We're going to have a look."

♪♪♪

In the weak wind, the *Fetla* took most of the day to travel to the source of the smoke. Not a volcano, no, not all. Not a volcano but a boat. And not just any boat . . .

The *Xeulliette*.

Though she was still small through the lens of his telescope, Hab saw that her sails were gone, her masts broken, and her decks deserted. Black smoke curled from her amidships. She sat low in the water. She drifted, her anchors hoisted to her hawser holes.

"Do you see any survivors?" asked Esten.

Fire, thought Hab. His shoulders sagged, and the air drifted involuntarily from his lungs as the implications of the disaster took hold.

The *Fetla* crawled at an agonizingly slow pace toward the stricken *Xeulliette* over the next hour. Crew stood apprehensively by the rail watching it get closer and closer. Hab hoped he would see someone walking her decks, but her decks remained deserted. All in all, the stout and odd-looking craft, burning in the waves like that, with no crew aboard, was a bone-chilling sight. He couldn't begin to think what had happened. Only that, as the *Airamatnas* had been devoured by ice, so now the *Xeulliette* had been devoured by fire. The *Fetla* drew to within thirty feet of the *Xeulliette*. The *Xeulliette's* taffrail was broken, her bowsprit cracked, and her capstan pulled from its axle and turned on its side. Except for the constant billowing of black smoke from her hold, she was silent and still, and showed no trace of life.

Hab put his hands to his mouth. "Ho, there!" he called. The waves sounded mournful as they slapped the *Xeulliette*'s side. "Is anyone aboard?" He got no answer. He looked for corpses on her deck but saw none. He turned to Tiq. "Lower a longboat, Tiq. Olle, you help him. We're going across."

"Aye, aye, Captain," said the brothers.

Five minutes later, Hab stood in the bow of the longboat as the brothers rowed toward the *Xeulliette*. The smoke, if anything, was growing thicker, but he didn't see any fire, and he couldn't understand why there was nobody on deck. If he couldn't see any fire, and the boat was still afloat, he was sure there must be at least a few survivors. Did they somehow get trapped below? The *Xeulliette*'s longboats were still in their chocks, so they couldn't have abandoned ship.

When the longboat was close enough, Hab jumped onto the *Xeul-liette*'s starboard ballast tank and climbed onto her deck. Tiq and Olle followed, first lashing the longboat to one of the *Xeulliette*'s scuppers. The Liars instinctively drew their weapons. The move surprised Hab. His own instincts for self-defense, never developed in the safe and complacent Paras, made even the notion of self-defense incomprehensible. But then this wasn't Paras anymore. Anything could happen here.

"Do you have an extra?" he asked Tiq.

"Olle, give him your dagger."

Olle tossed his stone dagger to Hab. Hab caught it easily, but instantly felt awkward with it. Tiq was right. He wasn't a fighter. He would just have to do his best.

A large hole had been blown into the middle of the deck, as if a great fist had come from the sky and punched right through the wood. What could have done that to hard vekeui? Hab peered into the hold, but it was far too smoky to see anything. The other two searched the deck, their weapons held out in front of them. Hab turned from the billowing smoke and watched them. He wasn't used to it. Men ready to fight. The brothers made a complete sweep of the deck, then joined Hab above the burning hold.

"We can't fight this smoke through here," he said. "Let's see if we can get below through the forward hatch."

They walked around the hole in the deck to the forward hatch. Olle twisted it open. Black smoke billowed out immediately, thickly at first. But then the smoke grew thinner.

"That's whale blubber burning," said Hab. "Let's wet our hats and use them to cover our mouths."

They wet their hats over the side, put them over their mouths, and descended the companionway into the forward hold. The smoke was so thick, Hab could barely see. They crouched. The visibility was a little better near the deck. Hab advanced into the forecastle. The smoke wasn't so bad in here. Crew hammocks hung everywhere. Dim sunlight filtered through the smudged portholes. A thin layer of smoke floated in a sharply defined strata near the ceiling. No survivors, no corpses. What in the name of Ouvant had happened to them all? The *Xeulliette* had become a ghost ship.

"Their gunnysacks are gone," said Tiq. "Their lockers are empty."

But they hadn't abandoned ship. All the longboats were still here. Hab and the two brothers continued through the boat until they came to the main hold. Hab half expected to find it full of corpses. But again, no corpses. The tide harnesses were empty, dangling. They got down on their hands and knees and crawled, gasping and sputtering, to the aft hold. When Hab opened the aft hold hatch, smoke billowed out in a thick black maelstrom of choking fumes. Here then was the source of the smoke. They backed away, strangling on the smoke, coughing, gagging, their eyes running with tears. They lay flat on their stomachs, their faces pressed to the bilge, waiting for the worst of the smoke to clear. The smoke pressed down on them like the black clouds of Oeil, leaving a gap of only eight inches between the slat floor and the bilge. Hab, looking into the aft hold, saw small flickers of flame dancing in and among thirty-pound chunks of salted whale meat. He heard the sizzling of blubber. He knew it was all ruined.

"Do you see anybody?" called Tiq.

"No," said Hab. "We'll have to abandon. The smoke's too thick."

They retreated, now squirming along on their stomachs, keeping their wet hats over their mouths. They inched their way back to the amidships hold, got to their knees, crawled to the forecastle, climbed to their feet, and hurried to the forward hatch. They ascended the companionway. On deck, all three gulped air. Soot blackened their faces and clothing. Hab gazed out over the water, thinking he might see a corpse or two, but there was nothing out there. No survivors, no corpses. Everyone vanished. Without a trace. A ghost ship. Here was a crew. And now it was gone.

᪥᪥᪥

"Land ho!" Jamas called a week later, just as the sun was coming up.

Hab, standing at the helm, looked up at the nest, tired, hungry, exhausted, not feeling the excitement he'd thought he would feel, nor any of the joy of discovery. What he felt was relief. He loved the sea, but after eighty days, enough was enough. Hands left their stations and walked with dull tired steps to the rail, having their own look, most of them skeptical of the boatswain's sighting.

"Doran, take the helm," said Hab.

"Aye, aye, Captain."

Hab trod to the nearest ratline and, with the slow method of a man who is near the end of his energy, climbed to the mainmast shroud. He hooked his right arm around the shroud, took out his telescope, and held it to his eye.

Far to the northeast, he saw a massive column of smoke trailing westward from what was the unmistakable caldera of a giant volcano. He felt an immense inner silence settle over him as he realized that Jamas wasn't mistaken, that this wasn't a fog bank or weather system or any of the other things that might masquerade as land out here in the open ocean. And, yes, he felt the excitement of discovery now, only he felt it faintly, like the thin pull of a magnet upon a nail resting a foot away. He scanned the horizon and spotted two other peaks, both volcanoes, both dormant, both a lot smaller than the giant active one.

"Can you see it?" called Esten from the deck, his voice now thick with illness; the scientist's hand wasn't getting any better; the sting seemed to be making him dizzy most of the time.

"I see three volcanoes," he called.

Silence from below. No cheering. No jubilation. Just a mute and weary thankfulness. "Do the volcanoes arise from islands?" asked Esten, his voice tremulous and reedy, hardly audible in its weakness. "Or do they arise from a land mass?"

"I see only their peaks."

"How far?"

"About fifty miles."

"And how fast are we going?"

"Five knots."

"So we'll be there in . . . eight hours?" ventured Esten.

"About that. If the wind stays steady."

The wind played in their favor, actually strengthened over the next few hours. By midafternoon they found themselves less than ten miles from a vast and barren coastline. Hab lifted his telescope to his eye. So here it was at last, the mysterious other continent, the world's other place. Black cliffs rose to craggy precipices. Low hills climbed to a bleak mountain range, and that first range of mountains in turn climbed to a higher range of mountains many miles inland, and all of these mountains were jagged, dark, and treeless. Deep in the interior he saw the largest of the three volcanoes rise out of the surrounding mountains, twenty times the elevation of any other peak around it, spewing a column of smoke and ash into the air that had to be at least a hundred miles across. This wasn't the Golden Land. This was a dark land, a forbidding and ashy place. This place was nothing like Paras the bountiful. This land was bereft, windswept, craggy, steep, ugly, treacherous, arid. Hab had a sudden impulse to turn the boat around and head for home. But he kept on. Here, finally, was the truth, a daunting wasteland, the antithesis of Paras, and he was determined to at last stand on its gritty black soil.

CHAPTER THIRTEEN

Two miles out, the sea bottom rose quickly out of the water in a series of strange, unpredictable rock formations.

"Those are hardened lava floes," said Esten, pointing over the side at the tongue of basalt four fathoms below. "You see the same thing on the south tip of Manense, near Mount Escalier."

The basalt, covered with algae, showed up dark green against the lighter green of the sea.

"A treacherous thing, these shallows," said Hab.

Jara stood beside them looking at the coastline through Hab's telescope. "I can't see any high-water mark."

"Let's see?" said Hab. She gave him the telescope. Hab looked. A narrow strip of beach fringed a steep cliff. After another moment's scrutiny, he said, "It's there. It's just so close to the low-water mark that it . . ." Most unusual. "The tides must be small here. These underwater formations must break them into . . . ripples."

They followed a channel through the basalt formations. The air was sticky, hot, smelled sulfuric. Hab climbed to the bowsprit and peered down at the underwater formations. Even this far out, they were alarmingly close to the keel of the *Fetla*, a seascape of underwater hills and gulleys that needed close and careful navigation. Tiq steered while Hab watched the bottom and called out commands.

"Two spokes to port," he cried. A few moments later, it was, "Three spokes to starboard." On and on, for the next two hours. They zigzagged through the channel. Hab's scrutiny of the shallows was unwavering, his concentration intense. His brow was covered with sweat. A merciless labyrinth, he thought, eerie with its coating of algae, its precipitous drops and sudden climbs. "Another three spokes to the starboard side!" he cried. The keel scraped against one of the formations; the boat shuddered, then drifted clear. He had the sailors reef every sail but the jibs. They traveled at less than half a knot. The surf rocked the boat gently, and the water was as transparent as glass. Hab saw every tiny underwater detail. No fish. No big green amphibious creatures such as they'd seen a thousand miles out. No food of any kind. What were they going to eat? Most of the whale meat was gone. "Ease her back to port." He glanced at the coastline. No readily discernible game. And the few trees and sparse patches of tough grass looked inedible.

The steep sides of the underwater channel finally converged a hundred yards from the beach. They could go no further without risking damage to the *Fetla*, or without grounding her.

"Cast anchor!" he called.

He chose a landing party: Esten, Jara, Chouc, Tiq, Olle, Doran, Antera, and Jamas. They lowered a longboat and rowed to shore. The beach had orange and black sand, with a strip of stones halfway up. The few trees, growing on the cliff above the beach in small clumps, were small, withered, with slender trunks and bushy tops, clinging precariously to small accumulations of soil on the steep rock face. Half of them looked dead. All were wind-beaten and salt-stained.

Ten yards out, the longboat nudged the bottom. Hab jumped from the bow and waded to shore. He stamped on the sand of the beach once he was there, as if he had to convince himself that it was real, then lifted a handful of the coarse particulate and rolled it between his thumb and fingers, letting it drift away in the wind, testing its texture and consistency. The others came ashore and looked around. They were stunned, bewildered, and wide-eyed. This new land was here after all. *"Paras is the Golden Land, the only land we know. Beyond her shores are only seas, and lonely winds that blow."* After hearing that verse all his life, Hab could hardly believe he was finally here.

⟅⟅⟅

They found a flat spot of beach grass among some protective boulders fifty feet up the slope, well above the high-water mark, on a wide terrace. What from the ocean looked like an unbroken cliff was really a series of terraces. They set up camp on the first terrace, one thatched all around with a tangle of small cliff trees, a good natural shelter if the wind got too strong.

Their first night there, half the crew stayed in the boat, half slept on the terrace. Hab, Esten, and Jara sat around the campfire eating a ration of hardtack and sharing a cup of drinking water. Tiq and his brothers sat at the edge of the camp staring out at the twilight, gazing down at the strip of beach immediately below them. Stars twinkled in a dark blue sky, and a golden band of dusk glowed at sea level in the west. The weather continued hot and humid, but with the sea breeze, it was tolerable, even pleasant.

"First and foremost," said Hab, "we have to provision the *Fetla*."

"Shouldn't we mount a search for survivors of the *Xeulliette*?" said Jara. "Some of them might have reached shore."

Esten shook his head weakly. The scientist was pale, lying against a gunnysack, his forehead moist with clammy sweat, his hand red and puffy. "I don't see how," he said. "They were over a thousand miles away. Their longboats were still on board. And if for some reason they couldn't use their longboats . . . if for some reason they abandoned ship clinging to something else—one of the extra spars, for instance—I doubt any of them could have landed anywhere near our immediate vicinity. This coast is broad. It's long. They could have landed anywhere."

The color climbed into Jara's face. "But . . . shouldn't we at least try?"

"I suggest we strengthen our toehold in this place first," said her brother. "Then we might possibly mount a search. Hab's right. We have to provision ourselves. What good's a search party if they're starving?" He cast a desolate glance about. "There doesn't seem to be much to eat here." He ripped a handful of brown grass from the ground. "Look at this grass. Look at how meager and dry it is. No wonder we haven't seen herds of wild chevuls roaming everywhere. No wonder there aren't any wild joadre. And there's no fish in these waters either. We're going to have to work hard if we're going to provision ourselves properly. This land hasn't had a chance to mellow and grow, the way Paras has. Let's worry about filling our stomachs. Then we might mount a search."

Jara was now staring at the fire. Hab felt sorry for her. She was a difficult young woman at times, but now she looked worried sick over her fellow crewmates aboard the *Xeulliette*. She cared. He reached out and put his hand on her wrist. She looked at him, her eyes glistening. How lovely she looked in the waning light of evening.

"Rest your soul, Jara," he soothed. "We'll look for them just as soon as we can. We'll search first by foot, and once we get the boat resealed and the sails mended, we'll journey up the coast and see if we can . . ."

But he trailed off. Trailed off because he noticed something odd about Tiq. The way Tiq was holding himself. Poised and ready. And not only Tiq, but his brothers as well, Olle and Doran, looking prepared to spring, cloaked in silence, staring down at the dusky beach.

"Tiq?" he called.

"Shhh . . ." said Tiq.

The brothers moved stealthily from their positions at the perimeter of the camp to the far edge of the terrace. They crouched behind some boulders, drew their weapons, and peered down at the beach. Tiq turned to Hab and waved him over. Hab felt the hairs on the back of his neck stand up.

"Douse the fire," he told Jamas.

"Aye, sir," whispered the boatswain. Jamas kicked some dirt over the fire.

Hab got up and joined Tiq and his brothers. When he reached them, Tiq pointed. One of the large amphibious creatures was standing down there on the sand now, not fifty yards away.

"I've been watching it for a while," said Tiq. "I watched it swim ashore. It swam right by the boat."

The creature stood with its long muscular legs slightly bent, a massive but docile-looking beast with a pale abdomen, a green back, and a great block of a head with tapering ears five inches long. Its hands hung like big paddles on the ends of its surprisingly slender arms. A long whip of a tail extended from its rump, curling on the beach like a snake. Though much of it was in silhouette, etched in black against the gold band of dusk in the west, Hab saw its eyes glowing dimly red in the gathering twilight. Chouc came up behind him and tugged his sleeve.

"Are we going to eat it?" he asked. "I'm hungry."

"Go back to camp," said Hab. "Stay with the others."

Chouc sulkily retreated.

The beast took a few steps toward them, craned its neck, then stretched its legs from their normally bent position, standing straight up, adding a foot to its already impressive height, getting a better look at them.

"Look over there," murmured Tiq. "There's two more coming ashore."

The two new ones surfaced, got up on their legs, and waded to shore. Animals, thought Hab. Their back legs had the lock, spring, and structure of animal legs. And their feet, with the heels poised off the ground, only the toes making contact with the sand, were just like animal feet. Yet unlike most animals, these creatures stood upright. Hab glanced around at the brothers. Their eyes were intent, unwavering. Here were three brothers, acting in unison, toward a common goal, something he and his own two brothers had never been able to do. Tiq had his hand pressed against the boulder, a large but spidery hand, with the blue veins popping out sturdily. Olle's face was set in his usual expression of surliness, his large hook nose prominent on his deeply tanned face. Doran, younger than Tiq by five years, a man who hardly ever uttered a word, whose hollowed-out cheeks were like dark shadows at this time of evening, had his mouth slightly open, as if he were about to sing a hymn. What was the dynamic between these three? Was there ever any discord? Why did Tiq, the middle brother, always take charge, and why did the other two so readily obey him?

"Olle, Doran, get your crossbows ready and climb to the next terrace," said Tiq. "See if you can attack them from the rear."

"You're going to attack them?" said Hab.

Tiq looked at Hab coolly. "That's our supper down there, Captain."

Hab steeled himself. "Then let me help."

Olle said, "It's a bit different than hunting whale, Captain."

"Get me a crossbow," said Hab.

Olle went to get everybody crossbows. When the four were armed, they set off.

Olle and Doran scaled the steep rock face to the next terrace. Hab and Tiq, crouching low behind the row of boulders, advanced toward the three animals. The amphibians bobbed, heads springing up and down. They were restless now, sensed something amiss. Hab and Tiq crept to the end of the terrace. Hab heard the creatures sniffing the air, faint reedy snorts, barely audible over the sound of the small waves.

"Olle and Doran are going to scare them our way," said Tiq. "When they do that, we let fly with our arrows."

"Understood," said Hab.

The three animals took a few steps forward. They looked awkward on their hind legs. They seemed unwary of human beings, having never seen any before, and were unabashedly curious. They held their arms out in front of them, bent at the elbow. Far in the distance Hab heard a faint whistle.

"That's Doran," said Tiq. "He and Olle are in position. Get ready, Captain."

Hab and Tiq raised their crossbows and aimed at the nearest creature. Far down the bluff, Hab saw two dark figures scramble beachward down the steep slope, Olle and Doran. They reached the sand and ran toward the creatures. They hollered. The creatures turned, looked at Olle and Doran, shuffled on their feet a bit, then hopped—hopped like Hab had never seen any creature hop before, ten feet into the air, in a long soaring arc that brought them gracefully into the sea.

"By the fires of Escalier!" exclaimed Tiq. "Did you see that?"

Hab thought they would flee, but they splashed into the shallow waters of the ocean feet-first, turned around, and stared again, their red eyes glowing. The first one made a sound, a chattering outburst that modulated through a half dozen tones. It stamped its foot in the water, made a big splash. Then it climbed onto the beach again and made some more chattering sounds. Tiq raised his crossbow and fired. The arrow hissed through the air but fell short. The creature looked at the arrow, climbed farther up onto the beach, then bent down and sniffed it. Olle and Doran meanwhile had stopped running, were down on their knees, their crossbows up, aiming. They shot two arrows at the creatures in the water, but the arrows, though this time they reached the creatures, simply bounced off their backs.

"Damn!" said Tiq. "They've got shells on their backs. No wonder they're not afraid. We'll have to try for a clean stomach shot." Behind them, Esten, Jara, and Chouc moved to some boulders nearby to get a better look at the creatures. Tiq glanced toward the west, where the last bit of gold was quickly disappearing. "We'll have to hurry. The light's almost gone. You go down there. Get in the water behind them. Try to cut off their retreat. I'm going to get in close and see if I can shoot that hopper right in the stomach."

Tiq climbed over the row of boulders and threaded his way down the steep slope through the patches of rough grass while Hab retreated along the terrace and descended the slope far to the left of the creatures. Hopper. A good name for them. Hab saw their quarry stooped on the beach twenty-five yards away, still sniffing the arrow, as if it thought the arrow might be something to eat.

Then it lifted its head, snorted the air a few times, and watched Tiq make his descent down the bluff. It made some more chattering noise.

The other two hoppers shuffled backward into the water, stopping when they were waist-deep, and watched the encounter from there, their heads twitching back and forth, as quick as birds.

The quarry hopper made the chattering sound yet again. Tiq made the chattering sound back, a near-perfect imitation. The animal hopped toward Tiq—not a big hop, no more than five feet, a mere twitch of its leg muscles.

That's when Tiq took aim. Tiq fired. The arrow hit the hopper in the leg, sank three inches, a clean shot into the soft part of its thigh. The barbs were firmly embedded.

Hab advanced quickly. The animal paused, as if it weren't sure what to make of its injury, then bellowed, an agonized howl that echoed up and down the beach. The hopper pulled the arrow out, but in so doing, yanked out a large chunk of flesh, widening the injury badly. It howled again, even more piteously.

The other two hoppers immediately dove. Hab caught a last glimpse of them, their tails flicking back and forth on the spume before they disappeared beneath the surface.

The wounded hopper bellowed a third time, its voice like a trumpet. It pivoted seaward, tried to hop, but couldn't. It didn't have any power in its left leg anymore. Couldn't hop. Fell to the sand instead.

"Kill it!" Tiq called to Hab. "Kill it before it gets away!"

Yes. Kill it. Hab was the closest. He strung an arrow into his crossbow and locked it into place. The wounded hopper tried to get up, kicking wildly with its right leg, clawing the ground with what Hab now saw were webbed hands, but it was bleeding all over the place; a small river of the dark liquid ran down the sand and curled into the surf. No matter how hard it tried to get up, it stayed on its side. Hab aimed his crossbow at its cream-colored abdomen. But he couldn't pull the trigger. This wasn't a whale. Couldn't pull it because the hopper was looking up at him. It had a face. True, just an animal face, but a face that now struck a chord in Hab.

He peered at the animal's face, a face as poignant and interesting as any human face, with wrinkles under its scaly chin, small dewlaps under each eye, and a scar on its upper lip. No. Not a whale. Not a game animal. Its eyes caught and reflected the last light of day, its nostrils flared, and it opened its mouth and clutched for breath. Hab felt sorry for it. The thing so obviously and desperately wanted to live. This wasn't like launching a harpoon from fifty feet into the broad and impersonal backside of a whale's air bladder. The thing looked at him; looked at him in desperation. But was that also resignation he saw in the creature's eyes?

No. Hab shook the thought from his mind. This was just an animal, he told himself. He was being nothing but a soft, complacent, and cowardly fool. A typical Parassian.

"What are you doing?" asked Tiq, running to his side, annoyed with his hesitation.

The Liar plunked to his knees behind the hopper's head, pulled out his stone knife, and slit the creature's throat as easily as that. A butcher's job, that's all. Dinner. Certainly not murder. Or was it? Hab watched the life fade out of the creature's eyes.

"I thought I . . . I thought I saw something," said Hab, now embarrassed.

"It could have rolled away into the sea," complained Tiq.

"I'm sorry," said Hab.

Tiq squeezed the animal's huge muscular thigh with his fingers. "That leg alone is enough to feed six or seven of us."

Olle and Doran came running up. Olle had a frown on his face. "What happened?" he asked Hab. "Why didn't you shoot?"

Hab stared at Olle. How casually these Liars talked of death. The three brothers looked at each other. Silent signals passed between them, something he had never had with his own brothers. Were they condemning him? He squared his shoulders. Tiq finally took a deep breath and grinned.

"Don't worry," he told his two brothers, covering for Hab. "We've got it." Tiq pulled a medallion from around his neck, a rusty iron likeness of the hunting goddess Disseaule, and kissed it. "That's all that matters."

CHAPTER FOURTEEN

Three days later, on a rocky point two miles north of their landing site, Hab and Olle lay on their stomachs, hidden under a blind of seaweed, their crossbows locked and ready.

"This Cloudesley place you sold," said Olle. "How many acres?"

Hab glanced at the eldest of the Liar brothers. "Fourteen hundred."

"And was it all under cultivation?"

"A third of it was vineyards," said Hab. "The rest was woodland."

"And you sold it all so you could come to a place like this?" The Liar seemed truly perplexed by Hab's actions.

"Shouldn't we hold our tongues?" said Hab. "We'll scare away the hoppers."

Olle pointed at the tidal pool down below. "I've never seen such a brackish lot of soup. I don't know why they come here."

"Keep quiet, Olle. It took Tiq a long time to find this place. Let's not ruin it."

Olle looked around the barren black point. "I don't know what's so special about this place." he said. "As far as I can see, it looks like any of these other points along here."

"We'll go back empty-handed if we're not quiet soon. Then Tiq will have to come out and do it himself. And Tiq needs a rest. He's been hunting day and night since we got here."

Olle looked away, peeved. "Tiq's all right, I suppose," he said. "A fine countenance, I'll give him that. My mug's never been one to make the ladies swoon. My forehead bulges, I've got bad teeth, and my eyes are too close together. Then you look at Tiq, that lovely brown hair of his, and those eyes, and that chin. I guess that's why he's next in line to take over from Javal."

Hab's eyebrows rose. "Javal? Who's Javal?"

Olle, for the last several minutes annoyingly loquacious, now lapsed into silence. He looked out at the waves, a hurtful expression coming to his face as a line of sweat etched its way down his hook nose. Hab stared at him, for the moment forgetting the brackish pool of seawater below, where there seemed to be an abundance of hoppers when the tide was in. Olle took a deep breath and scratched the black scraggly hairs on his chin that comprised his beard.

"He's our arbitrienne," he finally said. "Over on the Island. Our leader. Our chieftain. At least in our village he is. Very important, very powerful, organizes village defenses, distributes village food, and suchlike." More silence, and now a wistful moody look in his gray-green eyes. "He has a daughter, Olonia." His moodiness lifted, and a grin came to his face, but it was a melancholy grin. "I was supposed to marry her." Overhead, a few bird-animals flew by, the membrane on their wings transparent in the sunlight, veins clearly visible. Olle swallowed, his notch of Adam's apple bobbing in his throat. "But Javal picked Tiq instead." Hab stared at the eldest Liar. So there was discord between these three brothers after all? The small man nodded, more to himself than to Hab. "I'm not sure that Olonia ever loved me, but I'm positive I could have made her happy, given the chance." He glanced at Hab. "First born but second best," he said. "I try not to let it bother me. I love my brother Tiq. But sometimes . . ." He fiddled with a piece of seaweed. "In any case, who knows when we'll see Manense again?"

Hab considered. "So Tiq's going to be the new arbitrienne when you get back?"

Olle raised his eyebrows. "If Javal ever dies. But Javal's a strong old codger. He'll be around for a while yet."

They were silent now. Olle's perpetual expression of surliness came back as he watched the tidal pool. Brothers. Always politics between them. If Hab got back, he was going to make an effort with Romal. There was no reason why they couldn't sort it out. Then he remembered. He'd sold Cloudesley out from under Romal. That was going to take a lot of sorting. He was beginning to understand Olle's perplexity, why he would sell Cloudesley to come to a place like this, as he recalled the rolling woodland and pleasant vineyards of Cloudesley.

"Here comes one," Olle whispered, pointing. "Over there by those rocks." Hab looked to the right, where he saw the head of a hopper surface through the seaweed-choked scum of the tidal pool. "I'm going to let you take this shot," said Olle. "Don't miss. This will be number sixteen if we get it. We'll have enough. We'll be able to make the return voyage."

They watched the hopper for a few minutes. It swam up to the point as if it were looking for something on the rocks. Then it climbed out.

"It's a different color," said Hab.

This hopper wasn't green, like the other fifteen they'd killed so far, but brown, with a coppery tint to its scales. Hab watched the hopper closely. Not only a different color, but smaller as well, with a delicate cast to its frame. Was it female? So far, genitalia hadn't been readily obvious on any of their kills. The brown hopper hopped to the top of a boulder, turned around, and looked out at the sea. It stayed that way for a long time, contemplating the waves, as if it understood the waves, as if the waves were speaking to it and were offering it solace.

"Damn," said Olle. "I wish it would turn around. We need a clear stomach shot."

"The armor on its back doesn't look as thick."

"You want to risk a shot?" said Olle.

The hopper saved them the choice by suddenly hopping up onto the point. Perfect. Facing them. Easily within range. The skin of its abdomen was cream-white, soft, and tender. It stared in their direction, but as they were covered with seaweed, Hab wasn't sure it could see them.

"What are you waiting for?" whispered Olle.

Hab felt paralyzed. Again, it was the face. Yes, it had scales, like the green ones did, but the features were far more agreeable, the snout less pronounced, the jaw less harsh, the eyes bigger and not shiny with the same angry shade of red, but yellow, with a slit pupil clearly visible. Its brow was high and smoother. Why was it so much easier to kill a whale? He wasn't sure. But somehow his conscience wouldn't let him pull the trigger on these creatures. So far Tiq and his brothers had done all the killing.

Olle made a grunt of disgust and fired. His arrow sped through the air and pierced the creature right in the heart. The hopper looked down at the arrow—one of the new ones Tiq had fashioned from the extra vekeui spars in the aft hold—not sure what had happened. Then it curled its tail around its feet and sat down, the same look of resignation Hab had seen in their first hopper kill coming to its eyes. It coughed a few times, spraying blood out its mouth in a fine red mist, then toppled over and lay on its side, gasping for breath.

"Let's go, then," said Olle, now cheerful and brisk, flinging the seaweed from their backs.

Hab followed Olle, struggling desperately to bolster his nerve. Olle put his foot on the creature's head, took out his dagger, was about to slash its throat, but then looked at Hab, a challenging grin coming to his face. He handed the dagger to Hab.

"You do it," he said. "Show me your stomach, Captain."

Hab hesitantly took the dagger. He looked down at the hopper. Its eyes were half closed. Blood gushed from its chest wound, and its arms quivered. The thing was in misery. Hab raised the dagger, jabbed it into the hopper's throat, and yanked sideways, severing its windpipe, arteries, and cartilage in one clean jerk. Blood spewed everywhere.

"An effective surgery, Captain," said Olle. Then he looked down at the dead creature. "A small one, but I find the small ones make for the best eating." Olle took out a flask of water and had a drink. "I'll pull the longboat up to those rocks down there." He wiped the sweat off his brow. "Why drag the beast more than we have to?"

Hab was hardly listening. "What's this here?" he asked, pointing to the animal's groin.

Olle stooped next to him and peered at the fleshy bit of skin there. "I don't rightly know, sir."

They stared for the next several moments in silence. Hab finally came to the only possible conclusion. "It's . . . it's jewelry of some kind," he said. "Pinned right through that flap of skin there. And over here. Look. Another piece."

He glanced up at the eldest Liar brother. Was it murder, then, after all? He turned back to the creature. He touched what appeared to be a primitive talisman made of bronze, studded with multicolored stones, pinned through the flap of skin between the creature's armpit and chest. Several other pieces, all in a row, all the same, pierced the loose, cream-colored skin below the hopper's right wrist. Olle reached down and wiped some blood from the hopper's abdomen.

"Look at that," he said. Hab looked. Markings of some kind. "What is that?" asked Olle. "A tattoo?"

Hab looked more closely. Olle was right. A tattoo. A fish, a bird, and a volcano, with smoke and ash spewing from its caldera. Despite the heavy tropical heat, Hab felt a sudden chill. So it really was murder? Not only pictures of a fish, bird, and a volcano, but writing of some kind as well. And not just any writing. Writing he recognized. All the way down here, on this unknown continent. Impossible. The sound of the wind and the waves seemed to recede around him. Writing from the Wall at the Lake of Life. In the inner silence that descended around him, he could hear his own heart beating. A few more bird-animals squawked by overhead. Writing from the Great Code.

⟡⟡⟡

They now had the brown hopper stretched out next to the camp on the grassy terrace above the sea. Esten studied the tattooed characters on the creature's waist and chest, the glint in his eyes nearly maniacal, as if the discovery of these bits and pieces of Great Code on the creature's skin—such a startling and unexpected discovery, one that was so intimately and directly connected to the major endeavor of his life—had prompted partial insanity. His condition was further exacerbated by the fish poison. Hab glanced at Jara. Jara looked at Esten with worried eyes. Esten's hand was puffier still, and a purulent discharge oozed from underneath his fingernails. His forehead was clammy with sweat, and he was running a fever.

"You shouldn't feel bad, Hab," said the scientist.

Hab shook his head. "They're intelligent, Esten. We've murdered them."

A crease came to Esten's brow, as if he couldn't accept Hab's interpretation of events. "We had no way of knowing. None of the green ones showed even the slightest evidence of intelligence. None of them had tattoos. None of them had jewelry." Esten squinted in the bright sunshine, seemed to lose his train of thought. Then, in a soft, far-off voice, he said, "I wonder that our world should give rise to two distinct species of intelligent beings . . . a most startling thing . . . a most unusual occurrence."

"What about this Great Code?" asked Jara, pointing at the writing.

Esten turned his attention back to the brown hopper. "The question we have to ask ourselves is how the Great Code got all the way down here, on this continent. What connection does this brown hopper have to the Wall at the Lake of Life?"

"We're still going to eat it, aren't we?" said Tiq, always practical, as if the discussion about the creature's intelligence were now beside the point. "We're not going to bury it or anything, are we? We shouldn't let it go to waste."

Hab looked at his first mate, in a quandary over the matter. "We've killed sixteen of them," he said. "That's slaughter, as far as I'm concerned. They might retaliate. I think we should be prepared to defend ourselves."

Retaliate. The word sounded strange in Hab's ears. It was a word that wasn't used often in Paras, and then only in games of sport or intellect.

Tiq's eyes narrowed as he contemplated Hab with new interest. "Well-spoken, Captain," he said.

"Retaliate?" said Esten, grinning in a mellow, feverish way. "Why would they retaliate? They look like peaceful creatures to me. They carry no weapons. We'll just make them understand that we made a mistake, and that we had no idea they were intelligent. They're so remarkably different from us in every respect, how could we possibly know?"

"And how do you plan to make them understand?" asked Tiq.

Esten fished vaguely for an answer. "We could return their dead."

"We've got their dead butchered and salted," said Tiq. "I wonder about the impression we might make if we return their kin in that condition."

Hab pressed his lips together. "We make no gestures. We keep the food we've got." There was no point in giving back their dead when to do so would mean their own starvation. "Any gestures or efforts at communication might just lead to trouble. We break camp." The only sensible thing they could do, get off this terrace, out of the open, where they were vulnerable to attack. "Everybody sleeps on the boat." At least the boat might be more easily defended. "The boat will be our fortress, our haven, until we better understand these creatures." This wasn't Paras. He had to treat this place as if it posed dangers everywhere. "If we have to hoist anchor for Paras sooner than planned, then that's what we'll do." Because he wasn't going to stay in this place if it meant losing his last and only ship.

෧෧෧

So tired. Exhausted. The routine of double watches was grueling but necessary; two crew were needed as an extra measure of defense against a possible hopper retaliation. But it was draining. Especially in the dog-watches, in the middle of the night. The two moons climbed above the bluff, bigger and brighter in these southern latitudes, and the tides murmured against the beach, each one not more than four feet high, so different from the gargantuan ones in the open sea, even the ones in the Sea of Maju, rocking the boat gently, lulling him to sleep.

Hab's eyes closed. The heat was oppressive. The heat made him sleepy. He was taking extra watches. Too many extra watches, Jara said. But it was his responsibility. First the *Airamatnas*. Then the *Xeulliette*. He had underestimated. It was his responsibility, and he was going to shoulder as much of it as he could.

He slipped for a moment into a dream. He was sitting in the court-yard at home on a bright sunny day watching Thia brush her yellow hair. She sat on the ivy-covered swing near the west archway. The gentle sound of the tide permeated his dream. The tide was like music, rippling all around the boat. Thia stopped combing her hair and gazed at him, her lips curving into a gentle smile. He stared into her doll-like blue eyes, as bright as the buttons on his seaman's blues. The dream was vivid, clear. Those eyes were looking straight at him. He opened his own eyes, thinking she might be standing on deck, staring at him. But he saw not blue eyes but red eyes. Crimson eyes. Smoldering eyes. Eyes like two embers in a campfire. Staring at him from the other end of the boat.

He wasn't sure if he was awake or asleep. He must be dreaming, because he'd dreamed this dream before, the dream about the dark thing climbing out of the water. . . . Yes, a dark creature, such as he'd never seen before . . . climbing over the taffrail, standing on the poop deck, advancing in an awkward gait to the steps leading down to the main deck, stopping there, staring at Hab . . . then descending the steps and advancing toward the midships . . . stalking over the deck toward the sleeping boatswain, Jamas. A hopper, he wondered? Yes, a hopper, but an entirely different kind of hopper. His muscles stiffened as he quickly shook the sleep from his eyes. A different kind of hopper, one that wore battle plate made of thick leather over its chest, protective shoulder pads; a hopper that had black scales; one with no tail but with an assortment of metal weapons hanging from its belt—a battle-axe, a sword, a dagger, a mace—the weapons wet and glinting in the light of the full moons.

Hab peered at the thing. It was like a creature from Oeil, with its eyes burning like a lava pool. Its snout was much longer than a green hopper snout, its legs shorter, thicker, stronger, with huge hooked claws on the end of each toe. The black hopper pulled out a dagger and knelt beside Jamas.

"Ho, there!" called Hab.

But he was too late. The blade of the dagger sank deep into Jamas's throat, even before the boatswain had a chance to open his eyes. Hab jumped up, too stunned to do anything but stare at the thing. Then he ran to the tide bell and rang it with all his might.

"Ho, there! Ho, there! All hands! All hands!"

He rang the tide bell frantically. The black hopper looked up from his bloody work, got to his feet, and took a defensive stance, glancing calmly about, as if it weren't afraid of Hab's discovery. Crew roused themselves from sleeping spots all over the deck. Tiq and Olle scrambled up through the forward hatch, their weapons drawn. The thing bellowed with a deep throaty voice, then bellowed again, and this time Hab heard distinct syllables, not chattering, not animal noises such as the green hoppers made, but actual words.

"*Mawatingo pambango!*" the thing screamed. "*Mawatingo pambango!*"

It took out its battle-axe, hopped ten yards across the midships, and swung at one of the Dagulander crewmen. The blade severed the Dagulander's arm. The blade kept going, and sank deep into the left side of the Dagulander's chest. Blood shot like a geyser all over the deck. *"Mawatingo pambango!"* the thing screamed again. The black hopper lifted the Dagulander's severed arm and bit into it, ripping out a chunk of flesh between its teeth.

Hab, in all his life, had never seen such grisly bloodshed. He stood by the tide bell paralyzed. Jamas and the Dagulander, gone, just like that. Tiq ran from the slop-chest, bellowed at the creature, taunted the creature, as if he wanted to lure it into a fight. The black hopper saw him and hopped after him, bounding a full twenty feet in the air, landing on the forecastle head, its feet like thunder against the hard planks of vekeui. He swiped with his axe at Tiq, but Tiq, far more used to mortal combat than any of the Jondonqers, ducked, and the axe blade went thudding into the foremast. While the hopper struggled to pull the blade out, Tiq opened the tackle locker, grabbed a coil of rope, and ran back to the midships.

"Take this end!" he said, giving the line to Hab. "He's going to come after me. We'll get him in this rope. You run one way; I'll run the other. We'll bind him the way the Zairabians bind the wild chevuls."

"Right," said Hab, shaking himself out of his paralysis.

As Hab took the end of the rope, the hopper wrenched its axe loose from the foremast, hopped to the roof of the tackle locker, then hopped back to midships. Crew were running all over the place, trying to keep out of the way. Chouc stumbled up from the forecastle hatch, still half asleep. Olle ran around the starboard side up to the harpoon cannon.

"Chouc, go back inside!" cried Hab.

But Chouc opened his eyes wide and simply stared at the chaos and confusion on deck.

"Now!" cried Tiq.

Hab and Tiq pulled the rope taut. Hab ran clockwise while Tiq ran counterclockwise. The hopper took a swing at the rope but couldn't get the angle right and missed it. And in that time, Hab and Tiq managed to go once around.

"Pull tight!" cried Tiq. "It's going to get away!"

Hab pulled as tight as he could. A noise came from the hopper—not distinct syllables this time, just a grating hissing sound. Its arms were still free. What good was this rope if its arms were still free?

"Let's go again!" cried Hab.

But the hopper hopped, and Hab and Tiq were jerked right off their feet, such was the strength of the creature. The thing took a swipe at Chouc with its battle-axe, narrowly missing the boy.

"Chouc, move!"

Chouc moved back a few feet and stumbled over a washbasin. The simpleton fell to the seat of his pants. Hab, on his stomach now, strained at the rope, only wanting to save his brother from this vicious creature. The thing took a step forward. Odd to see it walk, not hop, as if walking was an unnatural and uncomfortable means of ambulation for it. It was getting ready to take another swing at Chouc. But then a harpoon sang out of the air and thudded into its chest. Olle! Hab's gratitude to the eldest Liar brother was instant and great. Yet had the harpoon penetrated far enough? The thing had that leather armor on. No, it wasn't enough. That armor was thick. The hopper pulled the harpoon from its protective breastplate, threw it to one side, and, lifting its battle-axe one more time, took another swing at Chouc.

This time the blade connected. Connected with Chouc's neck. With such force and swiftness that a long whip of blood went spilling across the back of the tackle locker. Chouc's head toppled to the deck.

"*Mawatingo pambango jipusha!*" the creature bellowed.

As if in a scene from a nightmare, the hopper stooped, using the haft of its battle-axe as support, and lifted Chouc's severed head from the deck, clutching his wispy blond hair in its brutish scaled hand, the blood spattering all over the vekeui planks like rain from a leaky eaves. Every muscle in Hab's body flexed as he witnessed the spectacle of his beloved brother's violent death, and the Jondonqian veneer of conscience, honesty, and peacefulness instantly evaporated. His rage was absolute and complete. He became an animal.

He dropped the rope, pulled out the stone dagger Olle had given him, and ran for the hopper. He leapt on the hopper's back, the passion of his hatred and need for revenge too strong to deny, and plunged his dagger into the black hopper's throat, plunged it again and again, finally twisting it one way then the other. He wrenched the blade around and around, making the wound as big as possible, all the time riding the cursed thing piggyback. The hopper staggered around the deck trying to shake Hab from its back. But Hab hung on, knowing he had to kill the thing.

He was only dimly aware that Olle had picked up the harpoon, that Olle was running toward the monster with the harpoon poised in front of him. He hardly saw Olle because he wanted only to cut this creature's heart out and stomp on it. His beloved Chouc was gone. His poor innocent brother, dead. And this thing was going to pay. Olle plunged the harpoon into the creature's stomach, ramming so hard so that it went right through the battle armor. The black hopper lurched back. Hab clung wildly to the straps of the pack the thing had on its back, continued to grind his dagger deeper and deeper into the hopper's neck.

Finally the creature fell, and Hab was thrown clear. He banged his knee badly against the deck, but he didn't feel it at all. He got up. He bellowed his own curse at the creature. His seaman's blues were soaked in blood. The deck was slick with it. Though still alive, the creature couldn't get up. Hab approached it. The thing drew its sword. Hab didn't care. He was going to finish the job. He was going to cut out its heart. But then strong arms held him back.

"Hab, he'll kill you!" cried Tiq. "Look how long that sword is. He'll cut you to ribbons before you have a chance to get near him. He's bleeding to death. Just let him die!"

"He killed my brother!" Hab cried. Tears came to his eyes, and his whole body shook with uncontrollable anger. "I'm going to kill it! I'm going to kill it!"

Tiq and Olle restrained him. Hab felt suddenly weak. Grief overcame him. The adrenaline ebbed away. His shoulders slumped. The creature, now seeing that it was in no immediate danger, dropped its sword. Its breath came and went with a sputtering sound. Hab looked at it with pure hatred. But he was done with mayhem. The hopper was, after all, clearly dying. Best just to let it die, he thought. But then it reached around and pulled the pack off its back.

"What's it doing?" asked Tiq, easing his hold on Hab.

The hopper took something from one of the pouches attached to its belt, a yellowish rock, bashed the rock against the deck, and to everyone's surprise, the rock caught fire. The hopper put the burning rock into the pack, then lobbed the pack with uncanny skill and accuracy right through the forward hatch into the forecastle hold.

"Ambiango ulio chongo!" it cried. Then the hopper grew still and closed its eyes, seemingly satisfied with all the destruction it had caused.

Before anyone had a chance to do anything, or to even investigate what might be in the pack, a violent explosion rocked the boat, splintering the deck, cracking the keel, blasting the forward hatch to pieces. A tongue of flame shot into the air. The shockwave knocked Hab, Tiq, and Olle off their feet. The boat immediately listed to port.

Hab got to his knees, not sure what had happened. Fire licked up around the giant hole that had been blasted into the deck. He remembered what had happened to the *Xeulliette*.

"There were crew members down there," he said, stunned.

"He used . . . some sort of big firework," said Olle.

Indeed, this was a new concept to Hab, to use the minor and undeveloped art of chemical pyrotechnics and fireworks display for the purposes of building a weapon. But if he knew nothing of bombs, he could certainly see that the boat was on fire, that it was sinking quickly, and that they had to abandon. Hab shook himself out of his shock.

"Man the longboats!" he cried. "She's going down!"

Jara stumbled from the aft hatch. Black smoke billowed all around her. Hab smelled meat cooking, all their slaughtered green hoppers

burning the way the whale meat aboard the *Xeulliette* had burned. He
ran to Jara.

"I find you safe," he said, greatly relieved.

She pointed to her ears. "I can't hear you," she said.

Tears ran down her face. The blast had done something to her
hearing. He looked down the hatch behind her. Esten pulled himself
awkwardly with his left hand, holding his lame and swollen right one
against his body. The boat lurched. Over the crackle of fire Hab heard
water spill into the bilge. Crew ran everywhere, some trying to put out
the flames, others lowering longboats, others dragging wounded or
dead from the various hatches.

He grabbed Jara's hand. "Away to the boats!" he shouted, hoping
she would hear him.

Her face was black with soot, her hair singed, and she was so
frightened she could hardly walk. Hab led sister and brother around
the gaping hole in the deck and handed them on to Antera, who was
helping wounded crew abandon. The *Fetla* lurched again, and her bow
rose into the air, and she started sliding stern-first into the water.

"Hurry!" cried Hab. "She's not waiting!"

The deck, angling more sharply, shuddered a few times as massive
amounts of air and water fought belowdecks. Hab grabbed the rail and
pulled himself up the slant. He glanced at his decapitated brother as if
in a dream. He saw his brother's cap, a plain blue paddock cap with the
Cloudesley coat of arms stitched onto the front, a cap such as any
teenaged boy might wear, lifted it from the deck, and shoved it into his
pocket. He heard the longboat lines singing through their boat-tackles
as unwounded crew lowered survivors into the water. Loose stores and
rigging began to slide down the sharp slant of the deck and the spanker-
boom suddenly creaked as it swung seaward on its mast. How had this
happened? He gripped the railing and pulled himself right to the bow.
He had meant nothing more than to mount a voyage of peaceful discovery. He had had nothing but the truest purpose in his heart.

"Captain!" cried Tiq, from one of the longboats. "Abandon ship! She'll take you with her if you don't get clear."

How could all his best intentions turn into a disaster like this? The stark reality hit home. They had no way of returning to Paras. They were stuck here. Unless they somehow made repairs and raised the *Fetla*. He gripped the rail and dragged himself up onto the bowsprit. The boat lurched again, and the deck angled yet more sharply. Then came another small explosion, the Affed oil going up, that which was to keep them leak-proof for the return voyage. Were they really stranded then? On this inhospitable continent? Where things came out of the night to kill them?

"Hab, please!" cried Jara.

He looked down. Only two boats. Only nine survivors. Nine out of an original complement of forty-five. His brother was dead. But Jara was still alive. And it suddenly became immensely important to him to keep her alive. So, as the water bubbled up over the midships, and the keel of the boat struck the edge of an underwater lava flow, he jumped. Dove. Like he and Chouc used to dive from the Cliffs at Alquay. He struck the water, surfaced, and, more dazed than ever, swam toward Jara's longboat.

CHAPTER FIFTEEN

Hab had never thought he would fear the night. In Paras there was never any need to fear the night. No one would ever dream of hurting or attacking anyone. But as the nine survivors—ten, including himself—sat in the dark on the grassy terrace above the sea, he stared into the shadowy distance, afraid that black hoppers would swarm them any second. He felt numb. He couldn't believe that Chouc was dead and that the *Fetla* lay in five fathoms of water, with only its masts rising above the surf.

"Should we light a fire?" asked Antera, the young Dagulander woman who helped Hadanas in the galley.

"No," said Hab. "The dark will hide us."

Antera fidgeted nervously. "What are we going to do?" Jara went over and held Antera's hand. "How are we going to get back to Paras?"

Hab wished he had an answer. Small pesky insects hovered around his head. "Antera," he said, as gently as he could, "we get through the night. We keep watch. We stay alive. Tomorrow, we think about getting back. Tonight, we concentrate on the black hoppers. How do we protect ourselves from such creatures?" He turned to Tiq. "Tiq, as a fighter, you'll have to help me on this. Do you have any ideas on what to do, how to defend ourselves?"

Tiq took a deep breath and scratched his chin. He looked around at the wind-scarred bluffs. Then he bent his right knee and folded his hands over it.

"Tomorrow we scavenge what weapons we can from the *Fetla*—the harpoons, the crossbows, and anything else that might make a good fighting implement," he said. "My brothers and I are good divers. We'll salvage a lot." He looked at Hab. "As for the black hopper . . . as far as I can tell—and I make my observations on the behavior of just one— they like to fight close, hand-to-hand. All his weapons—the mace, the axe, and the sword—are all designed for close hand-to-hand fighting. I didn't see a crossbow. I didn't see a spear. When he comes to kill you, he'll be standing next to you. In hand-to-hand fighting, his weight, size, and strength make him the winner every time. None of us will stand a chance in close combat with him. That's why we have to find the crossbows. That's why we have to find the whaling harpoons. Long-distance weapons, you see. We try to kill him before he gets close to us. Because if he gets close to us . . ." He shook his head. "Look what happened to Jamas. Look what happened to Chouc." He glanced at the moons. "Then we're going to need food and freshwater. We'll have no hope of protecting ourselves effectively if we aren't properly fed and watered. My brothers and I will dive to the larder to see if there's anything we can save." He looked around at the group. "Some of you can try to recover the black hopper's body. We might learn something from it. Something we can use against them." The Liar looked out at the dark terrace. "Who knows? Maybe we're lucky. Maybe that's the only one out there for miles and miles. A lone hunter, so to speak."

"Yes, but what do we do now?" asked Antera. "How are we going to get through this night? How are we going to protect ourselves now?"

Tiq glanced again at Foot and Lag, which were now starting to set in the west. "We divide into groups," he said.

"Won't we be safer if we stick together?" said Jara.

"That explosive he had," said Tiq. "If we're all in the same spot, and they have another big firework, we all die. If we split up, at least some of us will live." Tiq pointed along the terrace. "We'll sleep along these boulders. That way, they can come at us from only three directions." He glanced at Antera, looking concerned that she should be so overcome by her fear. "Live minute by minute for the time being,

Antera. Stop your weeping. Calm yourself. We're all here with you, and we're going to do what we can to survive this."

⛌⛌⛌

The survivors grouped off. Hab, Jara, and Esten settled near the end of the terrace. Hab stared at the moonlit grass and small stones on the ground, his back against a boulder, listening to the sound of the surf, knowing he had to get some sleep. The attack was now a few hours old. The adrenaline in his bloodstream was all but gone. He started to shake. Jara looked at him. Her green eyes captured the light of Foot and Lag. He couldn't stop shaking. He lifted his hand and looked at it. Jara put her own hand on top of it. He turned to her. She reached up and put her palm against his cheek.

"This has all turned out badly," he said.

"Hab," she said. Her hearing had returned.

"I never meant any of this to happen," he said. "I never meant Chouc to die." She got to her knees and held his head to her chest. Hab glanced down at Esten, who was dozing in a feverish half-sleep. "He was innocent. He didn't deserve to die. None of them did."

⛌⛌⛌

Daylight was like a tonic to the castaways. Their spirits lifted as the horror of the previous night receded. Tiq and his brothers made many successful dives to the *Fetla* and recovered not only crossbows and whaling harpoons, but several sides of salted hopper meat—enough to keep them going for at least a week.

Hab and Jara searched the surrounding waters in one of the long-boats for the black hopper body. The water was as clear as the water off the south coast of Maju. The sun was bright and hot, and burned their skin red.

They kept glancing over the side of the boat to see if they could spot any of the green hoppers, but the sea was empty. The bluff rose like a black wall to the east, and far to the north Hab saw the banner of ash and smoke from the volcanic eruption drifting in a large misty parabola over the aquamarine waves.

"Look," said Jara, pointing.

High on top of the bluff Hab saw two figures, both black, both staring at them. He let go of his oar, quickly put his telescope to his eye, and looked. He caught a brief glimpse—two black hoppers in armor, heavily armed. They hopped out of sight and disappeared among the sun-seared bush and trees higher up the slope.

Hab and Jara traveled another half mile along the beach, then, turning around, moved closer to shore and headed back to camp. Their dead hopper might have washed ashore. They were going to make a closer inspection of the shallows.

They found the dead hopper after another hour, snagged on an underwater outcropping of basalt, lying face down, his back three or four inches above the surface. As they approached, a swarm of insects lifted away from him, then settled back down. The stench of rotting flesh was enough to gag. Small pellet-shaped water parasites fed on the hopper's partially submerged leg. As the boat approached, the parasites scattered, disappearing into the cracks and crevices in the basalt.

Hab hooked the corpse to the side of the boat and they rowed back to camp.

At camp, Tiq and Doran helped Hab drag the corpse onto the beach.

"We saw two others," he told Tiq. "Black ones. Up on the bluff about three miles down. They were both armed."

Tiq nodded, as if he expected this. The Manenser knelt beside the dead hopper. "Let's roll him," he said.

The hopper's body, starting to bloat, split open as they rolled it. Trapped gases hissed out of the fissure, filling the air with a nauseating smell. Despite its obvious signs of early putrefaction, the hopper was in fairly good shape, and they were able to get a good idea of what the creature looked like in full daylight.

Black scales covered its face. It didn't have a nose, just two air holes at the end of a snout. Its neck was thick, strong, with the right side as ragged as minced meat from Hab's attack. It had thick powerful legs, similar in design to green hopper legs, four clawed toes on each foot, no footwear, just heavy black scales on the soles of its feet. The creature's hands were huge, three times the size of human hands, with three fingers on each, and an opposable thumb. Ornamental scars had been gashed into the back of each hand, and bronze wristbands studded with beryl circled the hopper's gigantic wrists. He was ten feet tall. He wore a loincloth made of thick hide, but part of it had torn away, and, unlike the green hoppers, this black hopper's genitals were obvious: a penis as thick and as long as Hab's forearm, and a sack of testicles, five or six in all, hanging in a scrotum as big as a water flask. Tiq tapped the armored breastplate with his knuckles.

"This is made from the back of a green hopper," he said.

Hab stared at the hopper, feeling awe. This creature was willing to cut a green hopper to pieces to make its armor. And that meant the attack last night could in no way be motivated by revenge. But if not revenge, then what?

☙☙☙

By midafternoon, with the sun still blazing hot, Hab decided they had scavenged enough for one day.

"We should strengthen our defenses," he said.

Tiq agreed, adding that the captain was beginning to think like a general. Hab couldn't deny it. Through the course of the day, he'd felt a change.

"We should scout the surrounding area." He felt a martial instinct taking over. "Over the next few days we'll try and find a more defend-able position inland, but for now we'll just try to booby-trap any obvious routes of attack to the terrace." But it was more than just martial instinct. Hab was, at heart, a problem solver. "We'll pile some stones into a wall." He knew he was, at heart, an inventor. "We'll string line and rigging from tree to tree." Now he was inventing a defense, just as he had invented a submersible boat. "We'll plant some pikes in the ground. Olle, take Antera and Risel out to scout the surrounding area. See if you can find a cave or something. Block any obvious pathways. And be on the lookout for footprints."

"Why bother?" said Antera, her voice thick with despair. "Don't you see? They're going to kill us no matter what we do."

Jara spoke up. "Keep your counsel, Antera. Belief is half the battle," she said, paraphrasing an old Parassian axiom.

So Olle, Antera, and Risel went to search the vicinity.

But Olle, Antera, and Risel didn't return. Not after one hour. Not after two hours. Not after three hours. Hab feared Antera's bleak prediction.

The sun was setting, and the first stars twinkled in the east. Hab looked around at the remaining six people as they went about the task of building the wall. They occasionally looked off into the trees, or up the slope, or down to the beach, waiting, hoping, wishing for the safe return of their comrades. Esten sat on a boulder, too ill to help. In spite of his weakness, he seemed lucid for the first time in days. Hab walked over to his friend.

"Should I send a search party after them?" Hab asked.

Esten's face was orange in the light of the setting sun. "Give them a bit more time," he said. "I trust Olle." Esten waved at the thin trees on the other side of clearing. "I'm just thinking we might build a boat with those trees."

Hab shook his head. "Those trees are softwood, even softer than the ileau tree back home. You might make a skiff for an afternoon row, but if you plan to survive the tides . . . a boat made of those trees would break apart like tinder."

"You're in love with Jara, aren't you?" said Esten.

The question took Hab by surprise. But then, so did the answer. "I think I am," he said.

𝕮𝕮𝕮

Hab chose Tiq and Doran to accompany him on the search. By this time the sun was a partial disk of fiery orange half sunk into the western sea, and the sky was thick with bird-animals, like charcoal check marks silhouetted in the pink dusk. If their situation hadn't been so desperate, Hab might have called the sunset beautiful.

The three searchers made their way through the brush trees along the north side of the terrace and climbed along a small ledge, a ledge spattered with the droppings of the giant bird-animals. Volcanic ash had settled in cracks and crevices, anywhere the wind couldn't blow it away, a fine gray silt rounding the edges of the rock face. Tiq lifted small fist-sized stones and put them in his backpack.

"What are you doing?" asked Hab.

"I'm collecting ammunition," he said. "I'm a good shot with a stone. I aim for the head. We keep the arrows for sure kills."

Hab collected stones as well. He saw Tiq's point. Close combat with a hopper was futile. The only way was with projectiles at a distance.

They climbed the rock face until they came to the next terrace. They searched this terrace for a while, found a few of Antera's footprints in some soft black clay, but other than that, nothing. So they climbed to the next terrace. The trees, though only twice the height of a man, were a lot thicker up here. The shadows among these trees darkened quickly as the sun finally slipped beneath the horizon.

"Which way?" asked Doran.

Hab held up his hand. "Listen," he said.

All three listened. Over the distant sound of the surf, Hab heard the distinct sound of insects buzzing—not just a few, but a swarm, thousands of them. Hab remembered the insects buzzing around the dead black hopper. He sniffed the air but couldn't smell the scent of rotting flesh.

"It's coming from over there," he said, pointing to a particularly dense copse of trees.

They pushed their way through the copse. Small burrs stuck to Hab's legs. The trees thinned and they came to a sandy patch in the middle of the copse. In this sandy patch, Hab saw what were unmistakably the four-toed footprints of a hopper, a deep impression cutting right through to the moister sand beneath, as if the hopper had landed here after a particularly high hop, perhaps a hop that had taken him right over the trees into the middle of this copse. Tiq pointed to a patch of grass farther along.

"Look over there," he said. "What's that all over the grass?"

Hab peered at the grass, tall grass, gone to seed, with broad blades extending out from a central stalk, the blades flecked with what looked like a black liquid of some kind. Was it blood? He hurried over. The other two followed. Yes. Blood. Speckling not only the blade but also the large seedpods, some congealed in drip patterns along the stalks.

The buzzing of insects got louder. Hab gazed across the small patch of grass. The trees started up again over there; the copse was ring-shaped, with this sandy clearing in the middle. He saw speckles of blood on some of the thin sawtoothed leaves, on the tinder-dry branches, and on the rough yellow bark of the slender, misshapen, dried-out trunks. Blood, showing up black in the dusky light, trailed inward to the thickest part of the trees. Hab drew his crossbow and strung an arrow into the lock. The string on the bow was swollen from being underwater, and he didn't know if it would hold, but it would have to do.

He followed the trail of blood. Tiq and Doran kept right behind him. The buzzing grew louder. He pushed his way into this opposite part of the copse and discovered yet another small clearing, a bubble of space in the rimlike formation of trees.

Olle lay in a pool of blood in this small clearing, his head half severed, attached to the rest of his body by a few fleshy strands of cartilage. The brothers entered the clearing. Hab didn't turn around, but he knew the brothers were looking at Olle. He heard Tiq take a deep breath.

"Bloody Oeil," said Tiq.

Doran, never one for words, said nothing at all, just stared at his dead brother, rubbed his hand through his hair, again and again, compulsively.

Antera lay next to Olle, on her side, her brown hair flung over her face, the insects swarming all over a foot-long gash in her hip. Risel hung from one of the stronger, taller trees, his back and abdomen pierced right through with a large metal hook, the blood still running from his fatal wound, seeping down his pant legs, dripping onto the sand.

"This couldn't have happened more than an hour ago," said Tiq, holding tight rein on himself, ignoring for the moment his brother's death, thinking only of the danger at hand. "That blood's still fresh."

Tiq knelt beside Olle. Hab heard him sigh, expelling every last molecule of air from his lungs, watched his shoulders sag, heard a nearly inaudible moan. Hab hung his head. He knew what it was like to lose a brother. He put his hand on Tiq's shoulder.

"Tiq . . ." he said. "Tiq . . . I'm sorry."

Tiq swiftly stood up. "The killers will be made to pay," he vowed.

"Why didn't we hear them?" said Doran, speaking up for the first time in days. "Why didn't they call for help?"

It was a question neither Hab nor Tiq could answer. Perhaps the attack had been too swift and deadly. Hab gazed at the three dead crew. He wondered if they had been able to fight back at all. They still had their crossbows. The only things stolen were their hardtack and fresh-water. Like the hoppers didn't know what the crossbows were for. Or like they didn't care. Only took what they could eat.

Then he smelled an odd smell in the air, like charcoal and body odor mixed, and at the same instant, Tiq said, "Shhh." The Manenser peered through the trees into the sandy clearing. "What's that noise?"

They listened. Voices. Hab held his breath. Hopper voices. Deep voices. Hab glanced at Tiq. Voices nearby. Not loud voices. Not bellowing voices, the way the black hopper had bellowed last night. Just hoppers talking to each other. In the deepening gloom, Hab squinted into the thick trees and saw them, not in the sandy clearing, but beyond the far edge of the trees, just outside the doughnut-shaped copse, their silhouettes pierced by a riotous and nearly obscuring tangle of thick branches. Two hoppers, big ones, ten feet tall.

The hoppers stopped talking, pointed to the copse, and started slashing their way through the thick bramble of branches with their swords. Hab, Tiq, and Doran watched, knowing that if they moved, or even so much as twitched, they might be discovered. The hoppers slashed until they finally hacked their way into the central clearing. They sheathed their weapons. One squatted, pointed to Hab's foot-print in the sand, then Tiq and Doran's footprints.

The hoppers looked at each other.

Then they looked across the clearing.

Could the hoppers see them when it was this dark out? Hab wondered. Could they see them through all the trees? How good were their eyes? One of them pointed. Pointed right at the three men. The one squatting got up. They exchanged a few words. Then they crossed the sand, not hopping but walking, an awkward cautious walk, their big square heads bobbing from side to side as they tried to see into the far side of the copse. Their eyes glowed red in the dusk. The scales on their faces were as black as coal.

This time, Hab didn't hesitate, the way he'd hesitated with the green hoppers. This time there was no question of killing them. He lifted his crossbow and shot an arrow through the thick trees. No point in trying to hide now. With their footprints out there in the sand, they were as good as discovered anyway. The arrow hissed through the lower branches and thudded into the left hopper's mouth, just as he was opening it. Blood spilled from his long black tongue. The injured hopper looked at his comrade, his thick brow rising, the feathered end of the arrow sticking out of its mouth like a stalk of grass. The other one immediately drew its sword and hopped. Hopped over all the trees, twenty feet in the air, and landed right in the middle of the small clearing where the three men were standing.

The three humans were so startled that they at first just stared at the thing. Then the hopper swung his sword at Doran, casually, not combatively, more like it was a simple chore, a piece of work, as if he were felling a tree. The sword sliced cleanly through Doran's neck and severed his head. Doran's head tumbled to the ground like an overripe melon and landed with a surprisingly loud thud. His body tumbled to the ground. The hopper turned, hoisted its sword again, and prepared to kill Tiq. But Tiq was fast.

Tiq pulled his knife, a stone weapon a foot long, and lunged at the creature, his face contorted with rage, veins standing out on his neck. The point of the knife found the hopper's throat. Found it, and sank right through to the other side. The creature stumbled backward, surprised, as if it hadn't expected anyone to fight back, dropped its sword, clutched for the stone knife that was now embedded eight inches through its windpipe, couldn't get a grip because of all the blood, and finally fell backward, dead, its head pounding against the ground like a hundred-pound kedge anchor.

Hab and Tiq heard a tree crack. The other hopper was making its way into the clearing. Why didn't it hop? Maybe with that arrow in its tongue, it had lost too much blood to hop.

"*Sikingo-mango dika diko!*" it shouted.

As it moved deeper into the copse, it stumbled. Hab lifted the dead hopper's sword, a weapon slick with Doran's blood. The sword was heavy, but Hab was a big man, with brawny shoulders and arms, and could lift the sword if he held it in both hands. The hopper looked at the sword, then turned its head and looked up the hill to the next terrace.

"*Tifu aumotongo dika!*" it cried. Hab and Tiq looked at each other. Was the hopper calling others? "*Dika diko!*" it cried. "*Dika diko!*"

High up the hill Hab heard several voices return the wounded hopper's cry.

"*Gaa tifu, gaa tifu!*"

Hab and Tiq looked up. They saw seven hoppers launch themselves from behind some boulders on the top of the cliff and plummet toward them, landing with ground-shaking thumps on the far side of the copse.

"Are we surrounded?" asked Hab.

Tiq pointed to a spot opposite from where the hoppers had landed. "Through there," he said.

Hab dropped the sword. He and Tiq ran through the copse, bursting to the other side, and headed for the far cliff. Hab heard two thumps right behind them and, glancing back, saw a pair of hoppers, each swinging snares — pieces of rope with a spiked ball on either end.

"Over the edge!" cried Tiq.

All those summers rock climbing in the Lesser Oradels now paid off. He lowered himself over the steep edge just as the hoppers let fly with their snares. Tiq was a skilled climber as well, and in seconds both men were down to the next terrace and running toward the path that led to the encampment. The snares flew over them. Only one more terrace to go.

But then he heard two more thumps, hoppers landing behind him, heard the jangle of their weapons as they swung and clattered on their belts. A second later he saw a hopper jump right over him from behind, land in front of him, turn around, and draw its sword, preparing to thwart Hab and Tiq's escape. Hab dodged around the creature.

The hopper tried to dodge with him, but its dodge was awkward—the creature lacked agility on the smaller scale of human movement. Hab narrowly evaded it. Tiq dodged his own hopper.

"Quick!" cried Tiq. "Behind these rocks. Pelt them with stones!"

Jondonqer and Liar made it safely to the rocks, took up defensive positions, and pelted the hoppers with the stones they'd collected, hoping to stall the hoppers as long as they could.

"Ho, there!" cried Hab, calling down to the next terrace, where their camp was. "Ho, there!" he cried again, warning the others that they were under attack, hoping to give them at least a little time to mount an organized defense.

He pitched three more stones at the hoppers. But the stones bounced off their breastplate armor, doing little more than confusing the hoppers for a few seconds. Hab and Tiq's only chance was to get back to the wall and defend themselves from a fortified position. They ran. But a few hoppers outflanked them, hopping to an outcropping of dusty black stone on the cliff above. Two more leapt right over them, again trying to cut them off. They had no choice. They had to go straight down.

They scrambled over the edge of the cliff to their right, down to the camp terrace. Hab saw the remaining crew hiding behind the wall of boulders. Hoppers thumped down behind Hab and Tiq, as if jumping from terrace to terrace was easy and natural for them. The two men, sweat now dripping from their brows, ran down the grassy slope, around the trees, and across the final clearing to the camp. A couple of hoppers hopped in front of them, and Hab again thought that they would be cut off.

But the hoppers continued to hop toward the boulder wall. They reached it in seconds. Without so much as a moment's hesitation, they yanked Siselen and Fleq, the last of the Dagulander crewmen, to their feet and decapitated them where they stood. Jara, Esten, and Hadanas sheltered behind the pitiful stone wall. Jara aimed her crossbow at one of the hoppers and got him right in the throat. The other hopper, seeing this, hopped away and regarded Jara from a distance. Hadanas, though she trembled, though she cried the tears of a terrified old woman, had her own crossbow aimed as well. Esten lay behind the wall in a feverish stupor, his hand now bandaged. Tiq locked an arrow into his crossbow, took aim at the hopper, and fired. The arrow slid neatly into the hopper's throat. The giant fell to its knees and toppled.

Hab and Tiq ran over the grass toward the wall.

Then Hab heard the plangent twang of a battle-axe spinning in the air behind him. He heard the thud of the axe as it cleaved into Tiq's back. Taking a close-combat weapon and turning it into a long-distance weapon, he thought. He turned in desperation to watch Tiq fall to the ground. Grabbed Tiq by the shoulders and dragged him the rest of the way over the grass to their wall of stone. Heard the battle cries of five black hoppers behind them. Saw another axe spin past him and, in a miraculously precise hit, slice cleanly into Hadanas's forehead, killing her outright. He dragged Tiq over the grass to the wall.

"Thank Ouvant you're back," said Esten, his eyes wild with fish poison.

Jara let fly with another arrow. "I got another one!"

The hoppers held back, still unsure about the crossbows.

Tiq lay on his back, bleeding profusely, gasping for breath, the blood spreading quickly out from under his seaman's blues, his face as white as evening clouds.

"Hab . . ." he said, his voice raspy. Hab heard the hoppers conferring with each other ten yards beyond the wall out on the grassy terrace. "Hab, you've got to . . . whatever you do, you can't . . . you've got to think like a Liar. . . ."

"I'm here, Tiq," he said.

"You've got to . . ." He struggled with his good arm and pulled his amulet of the hunting goddess Disseaule from his neck. "When you get back, make sure you give this to Javal. And tell Olonia . . ." But that was all he ever said.

"Tiq?" said Hab.

Tiq didn't answer. Tiq was dead. Hab heard a thump to his right, a hopper landing beside him. Then a thump to his left. Another hopper. Then saw two more hoppers peering over the wall at them. He stood up and faced them. He grabbed Jara and forced her behind him. Protecting her.

And then he simply waited. . . .

CHAPTER SIXTEEN

The largest of the hoppers lifted his battle-axe. Hab saw a festering growth in his armpit. They all had that peculiar smell—charcoal mixed with body odor—heavy, strong, gagging. The largest lifted his battle-axe even higher, was about to swing, about to end it all, when, from up on the terrace, Hab heard the angry bellow of another hopper.

"Buta ilango yathelu pambazo fantingo!" growled a smaller hopper, the smallest black hopper Hab had seen so far. *"Buta ilango fantingo!"*

The large hopper hesitated. Hab stared at it. Red eyes with a dark slit pupil, no iris. Intelligent eyes, focused eyes. Then he glanced at the small hopper, who bounded their way.

"Yethelu pambazo rango!" the large hopper cried back. *"Wea upaza pambango!"*

Hoppers talking to each other, the growls and grunts forming recognizable syllables, the vowels stretched and flat, the consonants sharp and hard. To hear them talk was as terrifying to Hab as to see them kill. He was numb with fear.

"Buta pambazo fantingo!" said the small one, bounding to the center of the group with one last hop. *"Inda fantingo. Inda!"* The small one gestured at Hab, then shuffled forward and looked over the wall at the stricken Esten. He turned back to the large one. *"Pambazo diko dika za fungo inda."*

Hardly discernible as words through the grunting and snorting, yet there could be no doubt—words were what they were. Hab felt faint, disoriented to be so close to the hoppers. Hadanas's hot blood oozed around his feet. He shoved Tiq's amulet into his pocket. He put his hand against the wall to steady himself. He looked from hopper to hopper. The large one had a narrow face with a thick brow, the slope of his cheeks angling nearly straight out from the hollows of his red eyes, his black scales dry and flaking. His penis coiled in a wicker basket outside his loincloth and had small white sores all over it.

The small hopper had a flat head. Wrinkles scored his face, fold after fold, like the face of a corpulent human, only each of these folds was covered with tiny black scales, like the scales of the black northern pekra. The small one craned its thick neck and peered over Hab's shoulder at Jara. He raised his hand and, in an unnervingly human gesture, beckoned to her. "*Diko dika*," he said. He was much smaller than the other ones, only four or five inches taller than Hab, squat compared to the other ones, pugnacious, and fat. His breastplate was made out of the back of a brown hopper, ornamented with several red lines dyed into the dried scales. He beckoned to Jara again, palm upward, flicking his three clawed fingers. "*Ip diko dika*," he said. "*Ipo ipa.*"

Jara cowered behind Hab. The small hopper grunted, as if in frustration. In a sudden lightning move, he grabbed Hab by the hair, pulled out his dagger, and held it against his neck; the small one was threatening his life as a way to entice Jara forward.

"*Ipo diko diki*," he said to Jara again.

Hab looked at Jara. Jara gave him a slight nod, put her crossbow on top of the wall, and stepped forward.

The small one let go of Hab and gently fingered Jara's red hair, lifting the long orange strands away from her shoulders, turning his head to one side, peering at her hair as if it were the most puzzling thing he had ever seen. Hab stared, aware that his breath was coming and going in short gasps. That gesture, that beckoning. He felt disoriented. Dizzy. He couldn't reconcile the alien nature of these creatures with that human gesture. He glanced at Esten. Esten looked at the hoppers with wonder in his feverish eyes. The small hopper bared his teeth, an inscrutable expression Hab couldn't figure out.

"*Omingo rango*," said the small one. Hab listened intently to the snarled and grunted syllables of the hopper's language, trying to make it out more clearly. The small hopper pointed to a large scar on his hairless black head, an angry red mark, leaf-shaped, the size of Hab's hand. "*Shakango rango*," he said. The small hopper pointed to his chest. "*Endango rango.*" Then in quick succession he pointed to Jara's hair, the red scar on his head, his chest, and while he was doing this he said, "*Rango, rango, rango.*"

Then a bellowing sound came from his mouth, and the others joined in: a raucous intimidating sound, a fearful thing to human ears. This wasn't talking. This was a war cry. This was the cry they cried before they killed someone. Hab was badly shaken by the sound. He mustered his nerve, forcing himself to think. *Speak to them*, he thought. *Make them understand that we aren't animals.*

"Don't harm us," he said.

The bellowing stopped immediately. They all stared at Hab. The small one took a step toward him, looked him up and down, his slit pupils growing larger, the wrinkles on his face shifting. He raised his hand and touched Hab's mouth, poked a black claw between Hab's lips, pulled Hab's lips gently apart, scratched Hab's front tooth a few times, looked at Hab's upper gum, then let Hab's lip fall back into place. The hopper's nostrils flared, its ridged brow sank, and its charcoal smell intensified.

He lifted his hand and, forming his fingers and thumb into the shape of an ungainly beak, imitated the movements of Hab's mouth. "*Eep . . . eep . . . eep*," he said. Hab felt his eyebrows rising. Was the thing mimicking him? Or was this a sincere attempt to communicate? "*Eep, eep, eep*," the small one went again, his fingers and thumb opening and closing with each syllable. Then, without even a hint of warning, the small hopper formed his fingers into a fist, pulled back, and struck Hab right in the face.

Easy enough to take the fist of a man, but the fist of a hopper was like a battering ram. Hab flew against the boulders and toppled to the ground, spots leaping into his eyes as he fought for consciousness.

The larger one, eager to take Hab's pummeling as a cue, once again lifted his battle-axe and prepared to decapitate him. The small one, tired of arguing with the large one, simply drew his dagger, reached up, and slit the larger one's throat, casually, easily, as if murder were the most common thing in the world on this black barren continent.

"*Butu pambango fantingo*," said the small one as the large one slid to the ground. The small one looked at the other hoppers, then jerked his head seaward. "*Rutisho mara fango fantingo.*"

The others lifted the big one, who was still alive, his breath sucking in and out of his throat wound. They carried him to the cliff and pitched him over the side.

The small one gestured at the three Jondonqers. "*Ip,*" he said. "*Ipa ipi.*" He beckoned again. Hab felt tingly all over. He glanced down at Tiq. Tiq's face was white, the brand of Ouvant showing up gray on his forehead. The hopper continued to beckon. Hab crouched. Hab helped Esten to his feet. Jara helped as well.

The scientist was at first unsteady on his legs but managed to get his footing after a few moments. Hab looked at the group of hoppers as if he were in a dream. Could the hoppers see that Esten was ill? And because Esten was ill, might they kill him? The hoppers contemplated Esten silently. Hab and Jara moved him from behind the wall out to the terrace. The hoppers closed in around the three humans. All now seemed intensely curious. From far in the distance came the sound of banging metal, a repetitive drumlike pattern. The hoppers glanced briefly up the slope, then turned their attention back to the humans.

The small one, the one Hab thought must be in charge, lifted Jara's crossbow from the wall, looked at it, then threw it over his shoulder as if it were no more than a toy. He then had a good close look at Esten. He lifted Esten's black hat from his head, sniffed it, bit into it, and dropped it to the ground. He stamped on it a few times. He then lifted Esten's arm and looked at Esten's hand. Esten winced in pain and began to shake with his fever. The small hopper carefully unwrapped the bandages. The scientist's hand was hardly recognizable as a hand anymore, was more like a glove filled to bursting with pus. The small hopper turned to one of his larger companions.

"*Nama-jivuno,*" he said. "*Dika diko yathelu nama-jivuno.*"

From up the slope Hab heard the drumming again.

"*Mu,*" replied the larger one. "*Nama-jivuno.*"

Hab listened closely to their words, trying to imagine how they would be spelled in his own alphabet. Making his mind work. Concentrating on their language as a way to control his fear. The drumming got closer.

Five hoppers bounded around the edge of the copse at the end of the terrace, leaping twenty feet at a time, the two drummers keeping a steady rhythm, even in midair. This new group of hoppers stood next to them in seconds. The fiercest looking of these new hoppers wore an assortment of primitive-looking jewelry: a studded collar, studded wrist bands made out of copper, big gold rings through the tiny nubs of its ears, a jewel-studded pin piercing its upper lip, and a silver ring through the foreskin of its exposed penis. The two drummers stopped banging their metal pans.

The mystery of what had happened aboard the *Xeulliette* now became apparent. Hanging on the jeweled hopper's belt was a human head. Jeter's head. His long blond hair was stretched up into a knot, his skin was brown and leathery, dried out in the sun, his eyes gummy, and his mouth was open in a silent scream. The jeweled hopper stepped forward and had a closer look at the humans.

"*Chungwa mizikani dika diki rango,*" he said to the small hopper, his voice deep, with a resonance that sounded like the distant rumble of an earthquake.

"*Gamka manga pashak,*" said the small one.

The jeweled one peered at Jara. He maneuvered closer to Jara and lifted Jara's hair. Like the small one, he seemed fascinated by Jara's red hair. He turned to the small one.

"*Omingo rango*," he said.

"*Mu pashak*," said the small one. "*Omingo rango.*"

"*Omingo rango rango.*"

"*Mu pashak*," said the small one. "*Omingo rango rango.*"

Rango, thought Hab. There was that word again. What did it mean? Why were they saying it again and again? He might be able to say that word. Not growl the "R" so ferociously, the way the hoppers did, but say it so they could at least understand it.

Before he could try, the jeweled one grabbed Jara by the hair, yanked her forward, bent her at the waist, drew his sword, and prepared to decapitate her. Hab jumped forward and punched the jeweled hopper in the eye as hard as he could. The jeweled hopper was so startled that he just looked at Hab.

"*Buta ilango yathelu pambazo pashak!*" said the small hopper. "*Buta ilango!*"

"*Dango?*" said the jeweled one, still bewildered that this human had given him an annoying tap in the eye.

"*Pambazo diko dika amba takasa mu wenda*," said the small one. "*Endango amba takasa pashak*," said the small one, forming a fist, and holding it to the sky. "*Amba takasa*," he said, pointing out to the sea. "*Takasa za diko takasa.*"

The jeweled one thought long and hard about these words. Hab could hardly believe he had punched the jeweled one in the eye. He could hardly believe he wasn't dead because of it. Jara, still bent at the waist, with her hair clutched in the jeweled one's hand, looked at Hab, her face pale, her whole body shaking. The jeweled one absently let go of her hair. She stood up slowly. The jeweled hopper was looking out at the sea. All the hoppers stared at the sea. Something solemn and respectful came to their eyes.

"*Takasa*," said the jeweled one.

"*Takasa*," a few of the others mumbled in response.

Hab, curious, looked out to the sea as well. The stars were out. A strip of murky salmon light rested like a blanket over the western horizon. Hab remembered how the brown hopper had stared at the sea. What did the sea mean to these hoppers? The small whitecaps glowed in the starlight. The jeweled hopper sighed, a melancholy sound, and finally slapped the small hopper on the shoulder.

"*Ogosha rango*," he said.

Rango. There was that word again. The small one turned to the jeweled hopper. The two looked at each other. The other hoppers were silent. Something was happening, but Hab wasn't sure what. The small one finally got to his knees. The jeweled hopper took hold of his tremendously large penis, uncoiling it from its wicker basket, aimed it at the small one, and urinated all over the small one's head. The stream was truly tremendous and steamed in the cool night air. The liquid trickled over the small one's shoulders and splattered to the ground, where it formed small beads in the black dust and gray ash before it soaked into the gritty soil underneath. The charcoal smell was stronger than ever.

When the small hopper finally got up, he was dripping wet, and smelled so foul Hab nearly gagged. The small hopper had bared his teeth in that inscrutable hopper expression again. Hab had no idea what was going on. The small one gestured at the humans.

"*Amba takasa*," he said. "*Takasa za dika diko.*"

Through his fear Hab felt a burgeoning relief. This small hopper had saved them. This small hopper had plans for them. And those plans were keeping them alive, at least for the time being.

♬♬♬

The hoppers put the three humans in iron shackles—shackles that in Paras would have cost a fortune. The shackles were too big, designed for hopper ankles. Hab's feet slipped right through. So the hoppers webbed the anklets with twine. This held Hab's ankles in place.

They walked for a long time. When Esten got too tired to walk, the hoppers made Hab and Jara carry him.

They walked into the hills and followed a meandering path, working their way north. Foot and Lag rose above the distant mountains in the east. Hab stared at the huge volcano to the north. The small hopper pointed at it.

"*Kimbia-kipugia*," said the small hopper. He pointed more vigorously. He seemed intent on Hab understanding him. "*Kimbia-kipugia*."

Hab tried the unfamiliar word. "*Kimbia-kipugia*," he repeated.

The hopper twitched its head from side to side, its eyes narrowing as it contemplated Hab.

Hab once again looked at the massive volcano, saw the banner of ash and steam trailing away into the starry night, and the orange glow of distant lava floes.

They traveled along the bleak coast for another two hours, three humans and nine hoppers, the hoppers bounding forward a hop at a time, then waiting for the humans to catch up.

Finally the humans got so tired that the hoppers stopped to let them rest. The hoppers built a small fire. Hab regarded them apprehensively while Jara sat some ways off beside the sleeping Esten. The small one came close to him, touched the dried blood on Hab's chin, then probed Hab's split lip. Hab began to shake again. He couldn't get his shaking under control. Had these been simply wild animals he wouldn't be so afraid. But they were intelligent. They spoke to each other. And though they were different from humans in many significant ways, there also seemed to be several salient similarities—similarities that made them more terrifying than an intelligent species of life derived, say, from a starfish or any of the other tide-dwelling creatures that were, at times, incomprehensible to the scientists of Paras. Two arms, two legs, a mouth, a nose, ears, eyes, all roughly in the same configuration as man's, but cosmetically so different, so terrifying to the human eye, that all Hab could do was shudder, despite the uncomfortable closeness of the campfire.

They sat there for an hour. The small one spoke to him. Spoke to him constantly. Repeated certain words over and over again. As if it were important to the small one that Hab understand him. The other hoppers looked on silently. Hab wasn't sure what the small one wanted him to do. Did he want Hab to speak? He wasn't sure. He didn't want to speak for fear of being knocked hard in the mouth with the hopper's fist. He was tired but too frightened to sleep. He gave the small hopper his undivided attention, even though the constant stream of growled, snarled, and expectorated syllables was entirely incomprehensible to him. Finally the small hopper left him alone. A half hour later they got up and began walking again.

They finally came to a path that led down to a small cove. A boat had been pulled up onto the beach. They got into the boat, a craft made out of the flimsiest softwood, twice as big as their own longboats.

Four hoppers took oars and rowed out to sea. The tides came in, each four feet high. The small hopper leaned forward and lifted Jara's hair again. Jara cowered next to Hab, still frightened but no longer trembling.

"*Omingo rango*," the small hopper said again, giving her hair a gentle tug. He dropped her hair and gave his chest a thump. "*Endango rango*," he said. "*Endango rango.*"

Rango, again. Was Rango the creature's name, then? Jara looked up at Hab. She squeezed his hand. Then she looked at the small hopper with defiance and surliness.

"*Endango rango*," she said, spitting the words out, mimicking the creature just as the creature had mimicked Hab.

"*Buto buto buto*," said the small hopper. He punched his chest again. "*Rango*," he said. And again. "*Rango.*"

"It's his name," said Hab. The nonstop one-hour stream of words he had endured earlier seemed to have the barest hint of sense now.

Jara looked at him in surprise. "How can you tell?"

Rango looked at Hab, then back at Jara. Rango tapped Jara on the shoulder. "*Omingo rango.*"

"You see?" said Hab. "*Omingo.* That's you. *Endango.* That's him. Rango's your red hair. Rango's that red scar on his head. Rango is his name."

Rango again looked at Hab. "*Omingo?*" he said. "*Endango?*"

Hab tried it, knowing he had to start somewhere. Even if he got hit again, he had to try. The better he could understand these hoppers, the better their chances for survival. "*Endango Hab,*" he said, tapping his chest. "*Omingo Rango.*" He tapped the small hopper's shoulder. "*Omingo Jara.*" He tapped Jara's shoulder. Then he pointed to the stricken Esten lying in the bottom. "*Omingo Esten.*"

Rango stared at Hab, his red eyes wide and glimmering in the starlight. "*Omingo Hab,*" he said.

So strange to hear his own name in this monster's mouth. It came out more like *AAWWBB*, loud and growly, a grunt, but still recognizable as his name.

ᘓᘓᘓ

An hour later, Hab saw a ship on the horizon, huge and daunting, its masts twice the size of any masts in Paras. As they drew near, he saw that the ship was made of metal, not wood, an innovation that, because of the desperate paucity of metal back home, had never even occurred to him. The keel was fashioned from great sheets of bolted metal, the masts were made of iron spars, the barnacle-encrusted anchors of steel. That ship was probably worth the entire fortune of the king's treasury. Great orange rust pocks bled along the side of the black keel. He tried to imagine what Jeter must have felt as he saw a ship like this heaving out of the waves toward the *Xeulliette*.

Fifteen minutes later, they climbed aboard.

Once on board, Hab saw at least a hundred black hoppers, all of them armed. Hab, Jara, and Esten were put in cage. A metal cage. The cage alone must have been worth several thousand decou.

After a half hour, hoppers set to and got the big ship under sail. Hab's fear, like a burden he had carried too long, evaporated as he looked around. As a mariner, he was curious about their seamanship. *Watch and learn*, he thought.

He wondered how such a monstrous boat of metal could float. But float it did. She was rigged with gaff sails, a style that hadn't been seen for five hundred years in Paras, huge ones, great trapezoids billowing in the wind. As the northwest breeze filled out the canvas—was it canvas or hide?—the ship lurched forward. Soon they cleaved the water at seven or eight knots, following the coast southeast.

Esten fell into a feverish half-sleep.

Hab stood up and looked over to the side of the cage, thinking he might see the large tides out at sea. With a boat this big, the tides might be an easy thing to manage. But he saw no large tides. He saw only small ones. The basalt collar around this continent was breaking the tides.

He sat next to Jara. He tried to think of comforting words, but how could there be comforting words in a situation like this? He put his arm around her.

"Your arm gives me strength," she said.

"And your eyes give me hope," he said.

She slept after that. He lay next to her, but he didn't sleep. He couldn't help thinking of Ouvant as the sails of the big metal ship snapped briskly overhead. The stars glittered harshly in the sky. He couldn't remember exactly how many years ago he had stopped believing in Ouvant, or when the 28 Rules of the Formulary had lost their power, but on this desperate night, as Foot hovered above the mainmast, so close Hab could see its barren mountains, he couldn't help thinking that he had offended Ouvant. Honesty was the way, the lifeblood of Paras, the tradition of his community and family, a strongly upheld belief. And he had lied. Lied again and again for the sake of this voyage. Was it any wonder that the journey had turned out badly? Ouvant was offended by his lies. Ouvant sought redress. Ouvant was going to make sure he never saw the Golden Land again.

Hab resolved then and there that he would never tell another lie. The truth was in his blood; he couldn't go against it. The belief of a thousand generations couldn't be denied. Honesty was the way, and he was more determined than ever that he would never stray again.

CHAPTER SEVENTEEN

They sailed most of the night. Hab slept for an hour, then woke up. In the moonlight he saw the surrounding sea and coastline. For the next hour he studied the coastline. At first it was deserted. But eventually he saw wisps of smoke from small coves and bays. Also the vague outlines of what appeared to be . . . houses? Cottages? Manors? Settlements of some kind. And the farther south the ship sailed, the more settlements there seemed to be. Out on the sea he saw boats— not ships as big as this metal ship, but primitive boats—gaberts, dhows, and keelboats similar to the kind of boats that sailed in the Sea of Maju a thousand years ago. They reached port, if such it could be called, just as the sun came up.

Here, the cliffs towered straight out of the sea, five times as high as the cliffs back at camp, at least a thousand feet high. Hab stood up in the cage and clutched the bars. He saw a deep inlet. The inlet was formed by high straight cliffs. Terraces had been carved into these cliffs. The terrace walls were honeycombed with caves. The ship sailed into the inlet. Jara stood beside Hab. Numberless hoppers hopped from terrace to terrace, fearless of the great height: small ones, big ones, old ones, young ones. Rango saw Hab and Jara looking up at all the caves hollowed into the rock. Countless cooking fires sent black plumes of smoke into the air, so much smoke that the air in the inlet was like a thick pall. Rango—for they had indeed decided that "Rango" must be the small hopper's name—waved his black scaly hand at this cliffside city.

"*Shakango Wagengo*," he said to Hab.

Hab nodded. *"Wagengo,"* repeated Hab.

The hopper twitched his head from side to side, not a negative, such as it would be construed in Paras, but a gesture, as hopper gestures went, expressing agreement, one of the gestures Hab had learned to interpret during the night's voyage.

"Mu mui mua," said Rango. *"Wagengo, Hab."*

So this place was Wagengo. A city as bleak as the rest of the landscape, so polluted with cooking smoke that the sun was but a murky disk overhead. Was this their capital? Was this their Jauny? Chiseled out of the rock of this inlet, where getting from place to place was more a question of up and down?

Hoppers came right to the edge of the lowest terrace and stared at them.

"Is that a woman hopper?" asked Jara.

A small hopper stared down at them, one still several inches taller than Rango, but with a more delicate build and a lighter coloring—gray scales that blended more slyly with the surrounding rock.

"I don't know," said Hab. "I'm thirsty." He turned to Rango. How to make his wishes known? First just by saying the hopper's name. *"Rango,"* he said. The hopper instantly turned, his head jerking as quickly as a bird's. So strange to see the head of a large creature jerk so instantaneously like that, when a similar move by a human might cause neck strain or injury. *"Rango . . .* we're thirsty." Hab gestured at the water, then at the cistern and ladle by the mainmast, then imitated the motions of drinking from a cup. "Thirsty, thirsty," he said. "Water, water."

Rango stared at him. Rango tried to understand. And as the small hopper tried to understand, he didn't look so horrible or fierce anymore. He looked . . . fascinated, interested, curious, as if humans had given him an absorbing subject for study. He glanced at the cistern.

"WAAA . . . TERRR," he said.

In one hop he was over at the cistern. In another hop he was back. The ladle was huge, the size of a small pail, meant to quench hopper thirst—so huge it wouldn't fit through the cage bars. Rango opened the door and came inside. He handed the ladle to Hab. Hab handed the ladle to Jara. Jara took a drink, then gave the ladle back to Hab. Hab took a drink, then knelt next to Esten. He lifted Esten's head, and was about to give Esten a drink when Rango leaped forward and hit the ladle out of his hand.

"*Buta, buta!*" he growled. "*Buta yathelu fungo.*" The hopper pointed at Esten's swollen hand. "*Shakango nama-jivuno. Pambazo fungo nama-jivuno.*"

Hab stared at Rango, trying to understand. He had to conclude that Rango had hit the water away for a reason. Something to do with Esten's hand.

"What did he do that for?" asked Jara. "Esten needs a drink."

Rango looked at her blankly. Hab put his hand gently on Jara's shoulder. "We'll just have to trust him," he said.

They sailed deeper into the inlet. The wind died and several hoppers went below, took up oars, and rowed the massive iron ship like a galleon. The inlet widened, and Hab saw several smaller ships at anchor, ones made of metal or softwood. After another hour they came to the inlet's terminus.

The terminus rose in a sheer cliff. A waterfall spilled more than five hundred feet from the top of this cliff in a narrow ribbon of frothy water. Thousands of bird-animals nested on the outcroppings and ledges. The hopper crew anchored ship and lowered boats. Hab, Jara, and Esten were taken out of their cage and bound with twine and shackles again. Hoppers put them into one of the boats. Rango went in the same boat with them. Hab looked around for the jeweled hopper but couldn't see him anywhere. He was relieved. He thought the jeweled hopper might change his mind and cut Jara's head off after all. The hoppers rowed ashore.

Several carts joined together with metal couplings waited for them on a stone pier. Hab, as an inventor, was intrigued by what he saw. The carts ran on two metal rails and were made of sheets of metal bolted over a frame of iron supports. The carts were so dirty that the grime was in some places an inch thick. Their wheels were made of iron, like large pie plates, molded precisely to fit the rails. Brown splotches of rust mottled the metal rails. The rails were held in place by metal ties. Though Hab knew that hundreds of years ago such a thing had been tried in Retelon using vekeui to make rails, vekeui simply hadn't been strong enough, and the invention had been abandoned. With metal, the rails worked.

Esten was now wide awake and looking around with great interest. The carts were twenty-five feet long and half as many wide. Some of the sheet metal had rusted right through and didn't look any stronger than cardboard. Esten pointed with his good hand.

"Green hoppers," he said, "in harnesses."

A team of twenty green hoppers stood at the front of the train. Their legs had been wrapped in strong binding to straighten them out. Green hoppers such as they'd originally seen on the beach, but these were bigger, a paler green, with no webbing between toes or fingers and a dull unresponsive look in their eyes. Their bindings were made of twine. The twine was sharp and abrasive. Some of the green hoppers were bleeding from their bindings, the blood drying brown on the crude textile, but none of the black hoppers seemed to care.

The black hoppers loaded their human cargo into one of these carts. A hopper on a platform in the front cart bellowed at the team of green hoppers. The green hoppers tugged, and the train moved out. The binding on the green hoppers' legs made them run rather than hop.

Soon the train whisked along at a fair speed. It veered left through a cutting in the rock and began to ascend.

"How are you?" Hab asked Esten.

"I'm thirsty," he said. "But I feel better than I have for the last several hours."

"They seem to be using these green ones as slaves," said Jara.

Jara's observation became conclusive when, after another hour of travel, they came to a large open-pit mine, similar to the smaller amber mines in Paras. In the mile-wide pit, nestled amid towering mountains, thousands of green hoppers labored with shovels, pickaxes, and sledgehammers, breaking the rock face, loading the ore into carts, and hauling it on rails to an immense smelting factory. The three Jondonqers could hardly explain what they witnessed. None of them had ever seen such a bleak, black, and polluted landscape. None of the green hoppers had tails. All their tails had been cut off. They were shackled in gangs of a dozen or more. If Hab understood nothing else, he understood that these green hoppers were captives, just like he was. Black hopper guards stood on various terraces supervising the mining operation, battle-axes and swords ready.

At this open-pit mine, their team of harnessed green hoppers was replaced with a fresh team. Of the old team, one had become lame during the journey, and he was peremptorily decapitated and his body pitched into a pit of what appeared to be rock salt, where several other similarly decapitated green hoppers looked as if they were being preserved. It was horrendous. It was terrifying. It was a scene from a nightmare a hundred times over. Never could Hab have imagined that Oeil existed right here on his own world.

Their new team pulled them farther into the mountains. The air grew cold and thin, and Hab, Jara, and Esten began to shiver. Hab saw patches of snow here and there. Over the clank of the wheels, Hab heard the wheezing of the green hoppers as they struggled for oxygen. They finally came to a wide plateau where the view was spectacular. Hundreds of mountain peaks stretched in every direction. Hab saw all the way to the ocean. He also saw the great volcano looming inland, twenty times as high as any of these other peaks. *Kimbia-kipugia*, he thought. To the northwest stood a much closer volcano. Rango saw him looking at it.

"*Shakango Mizikani, Hab,*" said the small black hopper.

Mizikani. Another volcano.

The train slowed and the driver finally braked. The driver and some other black hoppers got out and herded the team of green hoppers into a cart at the back. Then they all climbed back on. The driver released the brake and the train began to roll by itself, using gravity to pull it along. The train picked up speed, clanking along the rails, and soon they traveled much faster. On some straightaways they must have reached sixty miles per hour, faster than the fastest chevul back home. The wind was like a hurricane through Hab's hair. He was sure the train would careen completely out of control. But the train hugged the rails. The train lurched up onto banked curves whenever it had to make a turn.

At last they came to a long gentle slope through a massive rock cutting. Huge cliffs rose on either side. And carved into the left-hand cliff was none other than . . . the Great Code. They could see it from a mile away. Even though Esten was exhausted from the bone-shaking ride over the mountains, he pushed himself up from the steel bench, clutched the edge of the cart, and stared at the massive stone mural. He looked like a man who couldn't believe what he was seeing.

"All my life . . . all my life . . ." The scientist's voice was thick with emotion. His eyes moistened. "I've been trying to solve the riddle, to decipher and understand the Great Code, and now I find it here, and I . . . I . . ." He turned to Hab with wide eyes, awestruck by the sight. "Do you think they might actually understand it? Could they possibly interpret it for me?"

Hab put his hand on the scientist's body. "Esten, who knows what they're going to do to us once we get wherever we're going?" he said, raising his voice to be heard over the rattle of the wheels and the rush of the wind.

Yet Hab, too, was curious about the Great Code. How had it gotten here? Why were there two, one in Paras and one here? Was this Great Code carved before the Dark Time, that epoch of great stagnation and historical oblivion lasting thousands of years on Paras, a time long before the present age of reason and science? If so, this Great Code might be sixty thousand years old, like the one on Paras. It made Hab wonder about the similarities between humans and hoppers; the base coinage of their mutual behavior—a verbal language, body ornaments, an apparent social structure—seemed to have a common foundation, and with one Great Code here and another in Paras, was it possible that this base coinage could have found its origin in a previous contact between the two species?

The train descended. Hab's ears popped continually. Mile after mile they descended, through tunnels, over bridges, around mountain-sides, down, down, down, until the air once again became thick and warm. They rounded one last final mountain. Another, different inlet came into view, this one several miles wide and stretching endlessly to a vanishing point in the misty hot north. The mountains seemed to topple into this wide inlet. As they drew closer and closer, Hab saw another cliff city, this one much bigger than Wagengo. Rango gestured at the city.

"*Shakango Ketingo,*" he said. *Ketingo*, as bleak a city as Hab had ever seen. Rango gestured out into the inlet. "*Shakango Shindano-shtaka-shudo,*" said the hopper.

Ships crowded the inlet, a veritable forest of masts, massive metal vessels and smaller wooden ones. Manufactories huddled along the shore. A pall of black smoke hung like a shroud over Ketingo. The train rolled down a final slope, and Hab got his first look at some hopper buildings, not just caves in cliffsides, but real buildings: prim-itive, ugly, unruly, built without design, metal floors stacked one on top of the other in a diminishing sequence of size, no walls, the largest floor on the bottom, the smallest floor at top, a pyramid with terraces, the floors separated by boulders, or girders, or piles of junk, anything that might provide the necessary support between each level. No stairs. The hoppers simply jumped from floor to floor, terrace hopping. Many of these pyramid-shaped buildings seemed to be accommodation. The reek of hopper sewage drifted up from the inlet. The buildings were blotched with rust, some floors so badly corroded with it that they were partially caved in.

They came to a siding and a platform right in the middle of Ketingo. Black hoppers put Hab, Jara, and Esten in another cage, this one smaller than the one on the ship. Green hoppers lifted the cage onto a road cart and pulled it to a low, flat structure only two terraces high, right next to the waterfront.

The sun had disappeared behind the mountains, the moons were just up, and the inlet, Shindano-shtaka-shudo, whispered with the incoming tides. A fine coating of volcanic ash covered everything, in some places six inches deep. It looked as if no effort had been made to clean it up, and, for that matter, it looked as if it might stay there forever. The green hoppers dragged the cart under the first floor of the low, flat structure. Two black hoppers then killed one of the green hoppers, butchered it right then and there, and began cooking it over an open fire.

Despite the brutality, Hab was hungry. The black hopper kept adding ladlesful of tar to the fire to keep it going. The roasting green hopper was soon covered with a thin black residue. The smell of the roasting meat made Hab's mouth water. He hoped Rango would feed them.

Rango gave them each a large piece of meat. Esten, for the first time in days, was able to eat with a passable appetite.

As the light grew dimmer in the coarse iron shelter, Rango lit a torch and looked at Esten's hand. He stuck his finger in a leather pouch he had found somewhere in the back of the structure and pulled out a big glob of white paste.

"*Pambazo nama-jivuno*," he said.

Hab nearly understood the words. *Pambazo*. That meant to kill, to destroy, to decapitate. *Nama-jivuno*, he was sure, had to mean that fish with the stripes and poisonous dorsal fin. Rango rubbed the white paste over Esten's hand in a conscientious and gentle manner. *Pambazo nama-jivuno*. Yes. He was sure of it. *Kill the fish poison*.

For the first time in nearly twenty hours, they slept. Yet it was a light sleep. Hab dozed in a nimbus of fear, balanced on the edge of wakefulness, always conscious, even as he slept, that he was in a cage surrounded by hoppers, that despite Rango's efforts with the paste, and his attempts at communication, the hoppers could, at any moment, decide to kill them, torture them, or eat them.

Through the course of the night, Esten's fever broke. His finger-nails oozed a clear yellow fluid that smelled foul, like urine left in a chamberpot too long. At one point during the night the scientist was driven mad by itchiness all up and down the afflicted arm. But by morning the itchiness disappeared. So did the swelling. The white paste, now dried hard, had turned black and smelled so bad that even the hopper sewage in the inlet was like perfume. Rango peeled off the black hardened bits with a dagger and tossed them into the fire, where they sizzled, producing a bright blue flame. Esten raised his hand and worked his fingers. Though weak, he was again able to move them. The scientist gazed at Rango with wide eyes.

"Thank you," he said.

Rango contemplated the scientist in silence for several seconds, then said, "*Lira liretenengo, diko dika diki.*" He cuffed Esten on the shoulder in a comradely fashion. "*Lira liretenengo.*"

♪♪♪

The next morning, they were put on another train and hauled up the mountainside. This time their journey was short, not more than ten miles. They stopped on a wide area abutting a five-hundred-foot cliff. The cliff was honeycombed with caves and crisscrossed with terraces, and jutted with hopping platforms here and there. The wide flat area in front of the cliff looked like a training field. Hab saw lots of black hoppers. All wore armor. All carried weapons—battle-axes, swords, maces, snares, daggers. A hundred practiced with these weapons in the training field. They practiced on green hoppers. The green hoppers were unarmed. The black hoppers maimed them mercilessly and murdered them indiscriminately. Jara was badly shaken by the scene. They all were. They were Jondonqers. Peace was a habit. Wholesale slaughter like this was unheard-of in Paras, and could hardly be imagined by even its most jaded inhabitants.

Rango pointed to the training field, then up at the caves. "*Shakango Chungwa*," he said.

Chungwa, thought Hab. A place where they trained to kill. No female hoppers. No child hoppers. Only males. All wearing roughly the same kind of armor, carved from the backs of green hoppers, all armed with roughly the same array of weapons. Chungwa. Was this their final destination? Over the edge of the broad flat terrace he saw the inlet, Shindano-shtaka-shudo, and at anchor on the placid green waters rested thirty or forty ships, the big kind, metal, with tall masts. One of them was under way, its three dozen oars, eighteen to a side, moving in unison, making the ship look like a giant metal waterbug. Hab saw a puff of smoke come from the side of one ship, then a tongue of flame, and an instant later, heard a loud report. A storm cannon? No. They had once again turned explosives to destructive and warlike uses.

Green hopper slaves dragged their cage into a large cavern up on one of the terraces. Inside the cavern, green hopper carcasses, neatly butchered, hung on a series of overhead metal rafters. The slaves crammed the cage to one side. Rango hopped over.

"AAWWBB," he said. "AAWWBB *ipa ipi ipo*."

Hab went over. He stared at the small hopper. And for the first time he wondered how Rango had survived, how, as a virtual dwarf among these giants, he had managed to secure what seemed like a position of prominence.

"AAWWBB, *yethelu zufanana*," he said, and he pointed at the opening of the cavern. "*Ambiango Chungwa. Sit hua tifu*."

Hab had no idea what he was talking about. Something about

Chungwa. Rango turned and hopped away. Hab didn't like it. He didn't know where Rango was going. Rango was the only one who seemed interested in protecting them.

🌊🌊🌊

In the middle of the night, two large hoppers dragged him from the cage and tied him to a couple of pegs in the ground. They whipped him with a heavy metal chain. Jara screamed from behind the cage bars. The hoppers made that grunting sound, their laughter. They were having fun. One of them kicked him in the ribs. He felt an ominous crack. The other kicked him in the head. He had no idea why they were doing this. All he knew was that he had to do something to stop them.

"*Rango!*" he cried. "*Rango!*"

He kept calling Rango's name over and over again, even as he began to lose consciousness. Jara and Esten took up the cry. He wanted to tell them to stay quiet, that they were risking their own lives in their bid to save his, but his throat was dry, the hoppers kept kicking him in the head, he wasn't thinking clearly, and he couldn't stop shouting Rango's name, as if it had a lock on his throat.

He didn't know how long it took—he lost all sense of time—but just when he thought he was going to die from his injuries, Rango hopped into the cavern, bellowing like a Zairabian hurricane. He pulled out his sword, and in two neat strokes decapitated the miscreant hoppers. Then he knelt next to Hab and untied him.

"AAWWBB," he said, in a piteous kind of wail. "AAWWBB."

Then he said something in his own language that Hab couldn't understand. He carried Hab back to the cage. Esten and Jara helped Hab from there.

Rango brought ointments and bandages and, after examining Hab's ribs, fetched a binding, much like the binding used to cripple the green hoppers into harness.

From that day on, there were always two black hoppers under Rango's command standing guard outside their cage. From that day on, Hab began to think of Rango as his friend.

CHAPTER EIGHTEEN

Volcanic ash drifted into the cavern, covering the floor with a fine white dust. Esten got to his hands and knees at the edge of the cage, as if he'd been waiting for this ash. Hab watched the scientist with worried eyes. Esten reached out through the bars and drew a character from the Great Code in the ash. Then he called to one of the guards.

"Ho, there!" The guard turned. "Look at this!" said Esten. "I know your code! You have to take me to someone who understands it!"

Despite the improving condition of Esten's hand, his mind still seemed to be at times afflicted with fever.

"Esten," said Hab. "Stop."

But the scientist drew another one of the characters. The guard looked at the character with apparent interest, though what constituted interest in the facial expression of a hopper wasn't entirely clear to Hab.

"Esten," said Jara. "Please desist. Don't attract attention to yourself. Don't do anything that might make them hurt you. The Great Code can wait."

"Why would they hurt me over something like this?" asked Esten. His voice was shrill, and his eyes burned with an unnerving intensity. "We can help each other. We can learn to trust each other. What better way to trust each other than through the Great Code?"

An hour later, Rango hopped into the cavern. He stooped by the edge of the cage where Esten had written his characters. The small black hopper inspected the characters for several moments. Then he said, "*Amba takasa.*" *Takasa.* A word of reverence. A word that had something to do with the Great Code.

"Yes, yes, it's the Great Code," said Esten, smiling frantically, waving his hands. "You can tell me what it means. All my life, for the past twenty-five summers, I've been at Winterhouse trying to find out what it means. And now I find it all the way down here."

"*Butu, Esten,*" said the small hopper. "*Butu.*"

"He wants you to stop," said Hab.

"I know what *butu* means," said Esten, with uncharacteristic irritability. "I know what it means."

"Brother, temper yourself," said Jara.

Rango stood up and signaled to the guards. The guards opened the cage, tied Esten's hands behind his back, and, at sword-point, ushered him out of the cage. Jara leaped for the bars.

"Where are you taking him?" she asked.

But the hoppers ignored her. They took Esten away.

Hab put his hand on Jara's shoulder. She started to cry.

"Don't worry, Jara," he said. "I'm sure they'll bring him back. Rango's not going to let anything happen to him."

ᕪᕪᕪ

Day followed day after that, and Hab and Jara saw no sign of Esten.

A week later, Jara grew convinced that she would never see her brother again. Hab comforted her. He wouldn't give up hope on Esten. Until he knew one way or the other, he wasn't going to believe Esten was gone for good.

Rango came on a daily basis. He brought objects. Objects of all kinds. Weapons, armor, dead animals, rocks of different shapes and sizes, small statues out of metal. He also brought a stone tablet and a piece of limestone, and he drew pictures on the tablet with the limestone. He named these pictures. It quickly became evident that Rango was trying to teach Hab his language. But Rango's language was so different from Parassian, especially with its multiple noun forms, and with the conjugation of its verbs, that Hab was often overwhelmed trying to learn it, and Rango would get up in a fit of frustration and bound out of the cave.

Then they would be left alone for another day, in their cage just inside the entrance of the cave, with a view of the training field below and the inlet beyond. Day after day they saw the hoppers training on the field. Day after day they heard the boom of cannons out on the water. This small circumscribed view—this tiny cage, this reeking cave where the green hopper carcasses hung curing overhead—this became their whole world.

One day at the end of the second week, Rango brought an older hopper. The old hopper's black scales didn't have the same sheen as Rango's. His fingers and toes were horribly gnarled by arthritis, and except for two incisors, he was toothless. He didn't wear armor. He wore a robe of cured animal hide, not hopper hide. Burned into the old hide were the silhouettes of three volcanoes.

Rango and this old hopper entered the cage. Rango grabbed Jara and held her. The older hopper withdrew a pair of shears from his belt and snipped away her clothes. She struggled, cried, and looked to Hab for help. Hab rushed to help, but Rango lifted his leg and kicked him. The kick of a hopper, with a leg that's used to leap up and down mountains, was far stronger than the kick of human. Hab flew into the air and crashed against the bars.

"*Buta*, AAWWBB," said Rango. "*Buta.*"

So there was nothing Hab could do. The old hopper snipped away her skirt, her sea-woman's shirt, then ripped away her underthings with his gnarled old claw. She was left completely naked. She had nothing to be ashamed of—she was lovely, and in different circumstances Hab would have found her attractive—but she tried to cover herself with her hand, mortified that she should be standing naked like this in front of Hab.

"It's all right, Jara," he said. "It's all right. Don't be ashamed. There's nothing we can do."

"But I . . ." The tears streamed down her face. "Do they have to rob us of our dignity? Do they have to trespass upon our modesty?"

Dignity. Modesty. Two rules from the Formulary. He admired and respected her for it. It told him she was a true woman of Paras, that she was in no way like those Ladies of the Court who so fashionably flaunted their breasts and fornicated in public simply by raising the lavish silks and satins of their multilayered dresses and riding their consorts at the dining table in Summerhouse.

"Don't resist," said Hab. "Just let them do whatever they must."

They took her out of the cage and tied her to stakes in the cave floor, the same stakes Hab had been tied to for his whipping. Hab strained at the bars, pleading with Rango, but Rango ignored him.

Once they had Jara tied, they came back and they got him. Rango held him. The older hopper snipped away his seaman's blues, and in moments he was naked as well. They tied him to another set of stakes beside Jara. Hab thought they were going to be tortured. But he soon saw that Rango and the older hopper had no intention of torturing them. The old hopper knelt down and simply looked at them. He began to palpate Hab's abdomen, as if he were trying to get some idea of what organs lay within. Then he lifted Hab's penis and had a look at it, poked his scrotum and his testicles, then finally stuck his finger up Hab's anus. He smelled his finger once he was through. The old hopper fingered Tiq's medallion of the hunting goddess Disseaule Hab now had around his neck, but otherwise left it where it was.

The old hopper turned to Rango and made several comments, none of which Hab, despite his many language lessons, understood. The old hopper took out a bottle filled with red dye or berry juice and, using a crude paintbrush, dabbed a number of red spots over Hab's chest and abdomen, all the while talking to Rango. Rango looked on with great interest. Finally the old hopper, with a few grunts, got onto his knees and placed his small nub of an ear against Hab's chest. The scales on the old hopper's head were cool and dry, and several of them looked as if they were starting to flake away. Hab knew what the hopper was doing—he was listening to his heartbeat, to the respirations of his lungs. The old hopper was trying to figure out exactly how he worked.

Next, he worked Hab's arms and legs, concentrating especially on the joints, then made charcoal sketches on a piece of stretched green hopper hide of Hab's human anatomy. He had Hab open his mouth. He counted all of Hab's teeth, touched each one delicately with the claw of his index finger. Unmistakably counting. The thought unnerved him. They had science? They counted things?

After the old hopper finished with Hab, he moved on to Jara. He poked and prodded, and made note of the obvious differences between male and female. He spent a great deal of time palpating Jara's breasts, as if he were greatly puzzled by them. He finally drew a picture of an animal on the stretched hide, a bizarre rodentlike creature with a long beak and hoofed feet and a half dozen udders hanging from its underside. Hab had never seen such a creature before, but guessed the old hopper was making a comparison, trying to explain to Rango just what Jara's breasts might be used for. Obviously female hoppers didn't have breasts. Which meant the species wasn't mammalian? But if not mammalian, then what? Reptilian? Amphibian?

Rango took his own curious squeeze of Jara's left breast. Then he pointed with a claw to all Jara's freckles, which formed a tawny galaxy over her body, a strange but beautiful patina that seemed to accent the supple lines and curves of her slender figure. The older hopper said something, most probably about Jara's freckles, but Hab was curiously mesmerized by Jara, even in this present dire circumstance. Not sexually. She was more like a work of art. Despite the freckles, she was perfect. In fact, because of her freckles, she was perfect.

Rango leaned over him and said, "*Banya komesha, Hab.*"

Hab understood. Meaning every so often jumped out at him from their curious and complex language. *Banya komesha.* They were through. Finished. All done. Over. Rango untied their hands and ushered them back to their cage. The hopper lifted what was left of their clothes. He rubbed the fabric between his thumb and forefinger, curious about it. Then he rolled it up in a ball and carried it away.

"Are you going to give us new clothes?" called Hab, in Parassian.

But Rango ignored him. They were left naked. Together. In their cage. Like a couple of animals.

ᘓᘓᘓ

Though the forced intimacy was at first awkward, they soon grew used to each other's nakedness. Hab couldn't help speculating whether the hoppers expected them to mate, or if their nakedness was simply one of the conditions of an experiment to see how they would behave. At this high elevation, with the wind whistling in the crags around them, the nights were cool, and they slept huddled next to each other as a way to keep warm.

The first night or two the guards were curious, watched them, but soon grew bored and ignored them, often fell asleep at their posts. Hab and Jara talked. They talked about everything and anything. Hab found he could talk to her in a way he had never talked to anybody.

"No," he said, "I've never had a wife." The torches cast flickering shadows over the cave walls. "My grandfather wasn't a prudent man. I'm afraid he had many of the habits that Romal has. By the time he died he'd squandered much of the family fortune. My father had to drastically husband what was left. And my father had his interests. The tides and so forth. Not the kind of interests that made him great amounts of money. He wasn't there much of the time. He was at sea. Trying to figure out the tides. He was really a great scholar, even if he was self-taught. But the tides finally killed him. When that happened, we all expected Romal to take over. But Romal was raised a gentleman.

He wouldn't work. So I had to." He stroked the small of her back, kissed her on the forehead. "I had no time for a wife. I was young then, barely out of my teens. I had to look after everybody because I knew Romal wasn't going to."

"And you succeeded," said Jara.

"I have and I haven't," said Hab. "I had to give up school. I was in the Academy at Pieshe for a while. Learning my seamanship. But I had to quit. I suppose I'm like my father now, a self-taught man, squeezing in my education in a random and unsatisfactory way whenever I can. I made that voyage out to the tides when I was eighteen. I don't know why I did that. Part of it was restlessness. Part of it was curiosity. And I think part of me expected to find my father." He grinned at the memory. "I was more interested in the currents. Especially the Auvilly Currents."

Jara herself seemed to grow restless for a few moments. She pressed her lips against his collar bone and kissed it. She glanced at the guard, then turned back to Hab.

"Put your hand on my breast," she said. "I like it when you do that. You have such big hands."

"You enchant me," he said.

"Freckles enchant you?" she said.

"If they're yours, they do."

"And does my mind enchant you as well?"

"Your intellect is evident in every word you say."

She lay there silently for several seconds. "You've got to understand this about me, Hab," she finally said. "I've had to live in the shadow of my brother. He's looked after me. He's raised me. And I'll always be grateful for that. But when you're around such a brilliant man all the time . . . sometimes it's been difficult." She sighed. "Sometimes I think I've tried too hard to impress him. I've always wanted Esten to notice me, perhaps more than anybody else. But there's such a great difference in age between us, fourteen years. That separates us a good deal. I actually feel closer to you than I do to him."

The torches flickered overhead. He pulled her near. He put his hand on her breast, as she had asked. For one so slender, she had pleasingly full breasts, covered with freckles. He dipped down and kissed her left nipple. He was dirty, tired, and scared. Passion should have been the farthest thing from his mind, but it was as if because of their life-and-death situation that passion was now twice as strong, the will to live asserting itself in the sudden voraciousness of his desire. He reached down and pulled her thigh up over his hip. He was hard. He felt his penis pressing against her. She guided him. She pushed herself down on him. And she moaned. She looked at him with a soft and tender love in her big green eyes, eyes that kept their modesty and dignity even in this most intimate act.

He cradled her back in his thick forearms and in one quick move rolled her over so that she was now under him. She clutched his shoulders, and that made him feel the strength of his own shoulders, their muscularity and hugeness. He increased his rhythm, and she lifted her chin and closed her eyes. Balancing on one arm, he reached down with his other and rubbed her with his middle finger, all the while maintaining his rhythm. Her eyes opened wide in a kind of giddy surprise.

"Was anatomy one of the things you studied at Pieshe?" she asked.

"Aye," he said grinning. "That, and certain kinds of navigation only a seaman can know."

She licked his biceps. She was no longer petulant and difficult, no, not at all. She was like the fires of Escalier. Her cheeks began to burn with a pleasing glow. He was hard; so hard he couldn't remember a time when he'd ever been harder, as if the oil of her womb were playing upon him a magic alchemy, something to make him dance and spit as he had never done before. She bucked her own hips, meeting him, and began to moan again. He finally had to kiss her to make her stop moaning; he didn't want her to wake up the hoppers.

When she came, her body quivered like the strings of a Berberton wind-lyre in a full gale, and she arched her back and shook her head, as if she could hardly conceive that such pleasure was possible. A moment later, he flooded her, in rocking spasm after spasm. When he finally withdrew, they lay in each other's arms for a long time. They listened to the wind blow. Neither of them had been prepared for what had just happened. Hab felt uplifted. But he also felt frightened. Love was a frightening thing, especially when their lives lurched from one precarious hour to the next, and when their future was a moment-by-moment proposition.

෴

They took Jara away the next day. Two ten-foot hoppers came and got her. They tied her hands. She screamed and kicked. He could hardly believe that after his night of tenderness with her they would have the cruelty to take her away from him. She fought, but she was a slender woman, and despite her ferocity, was no match for the two brutes.

The last Hab saw of her was a flicker of her windblown hair and her pale freckled calf sticking out from under the black scales of a hopper arm.

෴

The green hoppers rebelled two days later. Hab saw them from the cave entrance. They came swarming up over the training field, three or four hundred of them. The sight of them momentarily shocked him out of his worry for Jara. They were crudely armored in softwood, and carried stone axes. Their green skin shone like emerald as they jumped up through the blue sky. The first wave valiantly clubbed many of the surprised black hoppers to death. But then the black hoppers regrouped and simply mowed their way through the green hoppers with their superior metal weapons.

Hab saw only a scrap of the action. He had no idea how so many green hoppers could get so close to the training field. Had a paddock of slaves escaped? No. These green hoppers were armed, and the slaves were too well guarded to have any hope of arming themselves. The advantage quickly turned in favor of the black hoppers, and the battle soon became a rout. Advantage in the battle seemed to be more a question of up and down, and the black hoppers could definitely hop higher than the green ones, sometimes as much as thirty feet into the air, descending from a dizzying height with a shrill battle cry and the lethal swinging of a sword or mace. Green and black hoppers bounced up and down, murdering each other, so that blood sprayed every which way, like a hundred red garden sprinklers going all at once; and in the distance, on the other side of the inlet, was that volcano, Kimbiakipugia, forever billowing its saturnine banner of ash and smoke.

When it was all over, every single green hopper lay dead, while only about fifty black hoppers, as far as Hab could count from his limited vantage point, had died. As crews of black hoppers went around cleaning up, Rango came into the cave.

"A full stomach to you, Hab," said Rango. So much easier to understand Rango, now that Hab at times was actually able to think in the hopper language. "A little bloodsport, yes?" said the small hopper, and chortled, flicking his head toward the massacre outside.

Hab was too shaken to say anything. But then the question of Jara came rushing back to his mind. "Where have you taken Jara?" he asked, pronouncing the hopper words with great difficulty.

"She's in the city," said Rango. "*Ketingo.*"

"Why have you put her there?"

Rango ignored the question. "Today we continue," he said. "Today we talk about geography."

Hab was too upset to concentrate, couldn't understand why Rango thought it was important for him to acquire a hopper vocabulary specific to geography, couldn't retain any of the new geographical terms the dwarf hopper tried to teach him. Were they at war with the green hoppers? Maybe that's why they took Jara to Ketingo. For safety's sake. He couldn't concentrate. At times he hardly heard Rango. Finally Rango grew frustrated. He smashed the limestone against the tablet, brought his face right up to Hab's so that Hab could smell the creature's foul charcoal scent, and clutched Hab by the hair.

"You will learn, Hab," he said.

It didn't sound like an order. It sounded like a threat. Like something bad would happen to him or to Jara if he didn't cooperate.

CHAPTER NINETEEN

Afew weeks later they moved Hab to a ledge overlooking the training field. They put him under an overhang of gray rock so that in the hottest part of the afternoon he was shaded from the sun. He wasn't sure why they put him here, only that he was glad to be out of the cavern, away from the overripe smell of curing green hopper meat, and in the fresh air.

"*Shakango Gashak*," said Rango, pointing.

The hopper language kicked in, Hab's mind shifted gear, and he tried to think, as best he could, in Abani, the dialect of the black hoppers. Rango pointed to the jeweled hopper, the one who had urinated on his head. *Shakango Gashak. That is Gashak.* Hab formulated his question carefully, thinking about all the words beforehand, still not clear on the multiple noun forms, whether they were feminine or masculine, intimate or formal.

"Is he your . . . your drillmaster?" he asked. He meant *leader*, but so far, this was the only word that came anywhere close in Abani. Drillmaster.

"Yes, he's our drillmaster."

Gashak stood at the end of the training field on the steps of a special stone building. The drillmaster lived in that stone building, known as the battle-house, the hopper equivalent of Parprouch's Summerhouse on the Necontreu. Rango launched into a long monologue about Gashak. Hab understood about a third of it. What came through was Rango's awe-filled respect for the drillmaster. What came through was Rango's loyalty and love for the hopper chieftain.

"They call him Gashak the Juggler," explained Rango, slowing down, as if he realized Hab wasn't getting a lot of what he was saying. "They call him the juggler because he has to keep so many factions happy. They call him the juggler because so many factions want to kill him. But I will never allow that to happen, be it the *bamkali-kalango* of the beaches, such as you saw when they tried to revolt a few weeks ago, or the *hari-bumuku* of the tar pools. What Gashak wants is for everybody to work together. And I make sure they do." Rango held up his arms, presenting himself to Hab. "Look at me, Hab. What do you see? You see a dwarf, a midget, a *sikingo-mango* regular of the mountain tribes who should have been killed long ago. Strength, agility, and battle skill are important among my people. And for my size, I'm a fierce fighter. But I'm no match for the giants of my race. I don't have to be. Gashak recognizes the skills of my mind. I've had to use the skills of my mind to make up for the deficiencies in my body. Gashak has given me a chance. For that, I will always love him. For that, he will always be my drillmaster."

♪♪♪

Nearly a month passed. The weather changed. The sun still baked the training field, the barracks, and Gashak's battle-house, but in the evening, a deluge of rain always whipped the mountains as regular as clockwork. When this happened, Hab crouched in the farthest corner of his cage, but it didn't do much good because the wind blew the rain right under the overhang.

They fed him. They made sure he had enough to drink. They even gave him a tunic of tanned *bamkali-kalango* hide to wear.

Rango came every day, and though they struggled hard with the more difficult forms, particularly the more descriptive words of the Abani language, Hab had reached an impasse, and was lucky to understand five or six new terms in any given session. There were too many permutations and subtle pronunciation differences in the many ways each term could be used. Rango often grew impatient. Other times Hab simply didn't feel like learning. He was depressed. He was sad. He was afraid he might never see Jara again. He felt alone. He was afraid he would never see Esten again. He felt isolated. All these things conspired to make concentration impossible at times.

Then they brought Esten back. They put him in a cage and placed him not protected by Hab's overhang but out in the open, so that the sun beat upon him mercilessly during the day and the rains lashed him all night. The scientist had been badly beaten, his hair had been shaved, and his ears had been cut off. He'd grown terribly thin. He was in a desperate condition, and needed the attention of a doctor, but the nearest doctor was on the other side of the world.

Esten recounted his story.

"They took me there," he said, his voice ragged from the physical abuse he'd endured. "To the Great Code. And they taught me some of their language, and I thought the reason they were teaching me their language was because they were finally going to reveal to me the meaning of the Great Code. But I found their language hard. My teacher beat me when I couldn't get something right. Why do they have five or six variations for every single word?" Esten shook his head in weary mystification. *"Takasa, takasi, takaso, takasango, takasango-kingo.* All the same root, with the same concept, but all meaning slightly different things."

Hab stared at his friend, shocked by his appearance. "They cut off your ears, Esten," he said. Esten now had scabby patches on the sides of his scalp, with just an ear-hole behind the right and left sides of his jaw, his ears cut clean off, pared right down to the skin.

"My teacher said I wasn't listening, Hab," explained Esten. "He asked what was the point of me having ears if I wasn't going to use them, so he cut them off. He ate them, Hab. Right in front of me. And the worst of it is, they had absolutely no intention of telling me what the Great Code meant. I would gladly lose not only my ears but also my nose to know what the Great Code means. But they kept the secret to themselves. I told them about Paras. I thought if I told them about Paras, they might tell me about the Great Code. But they didn't. They wanted to torture me by keeping it to themselves." Esten looked at Hab quizzically. "Did you know they call their own land Ortok?"

"Yes, Rango told me."

"And the inlet down there, Shindano-shtaka-shudo, that translates as 'The Mouth of the Monster.'"

Hab looked down at the inlet, with the black mountains and the volcano beyond. "Yes, Rango told me that too."

Esten glanced up at the cavern. "Is Jara still up there?"

Hab's face settled. "They took Jara to Ketingo. I haven't seen her in two months. Rango won't talk about her. I don't know what's happened to her. I'm sorry, Esten."

They fed Hab. They gave him the choicest bits of green hopper meat. They made sure he had lots to drink. On the other hand, they starved Esten, didn't give him any food, or anything to drink. And because Esten was out in the sun all day, the scientist's skin was badly burned. Hab couldn't understand it. Why the difference in treatment? Day after day he watched Esten grow weaker and weaker. Esten soon grew so weak he couldn't stand. Why did they have to shrivel Esten up like this? Why did they have to bake him all day and drench him all night? The heat addled the poor man's brains. His skull, in the intense heat, acted like a pressure cooker, and his brain a bit of stewing beef. His skin turned red, then purple, then blistered horribly as great open sores formed on his back. They oozed blood and pus all over the heat-baked rock of the black stone ridge.

"Hab, why are they doing this to me?" he asked. His voice rasped through swollen lips.

"I don't know," he said.

Hab asked Rango about it, but Rango wouldn't say a word, just kept pounding away at the more complicated forms of the Abani language, as if he were desperate for Hab to learn his tongue. Hab had to draw his own conclusions. Maybe they were making him watch Esten die of exposure and starvation like this as a way to motivate him. Maybe if he learned the complicated forms more quickly, and was able to express himself with more nuance and accuracy, they might pull Esten out of the sun, give him some food, and quench his thirst. Maybe he might save his friend by learning Abani in all its intricacies. So he redoubled his efforts.

One day in the middle of a language lesson, a train, pulled by green hoppers—the *bamkali-kalango*, as they were called—rattled up to the training field. Rango stopped the language lesson and watched. Hab surveyed the scene with growing interest. Esten was still alive, whimpering in a fetal position on the floor of his cage, his arms and legs now as thin as broom-poles, his hair and beard now growing back but infected with a voracious species of pesky red lice. Had it not been for the rainwater the scientist drank at night, he would have been dead long ago.

The train was unlike any of the hopper trains Hab had seen before. Not open cars, but tank cars. The hoppers riding on top of these tank cars were different from any of the hoppers Hab had seen as well. Their scales were coppery, spiky, tough, and they had a ridge of red spines along their backs. They wore similar armor, made from the back-plates of the *bamkali-kalango*, but much of their armor was splattered with tar.

"These are the *hari-bumuku*," explained Rango, "from the tar pools east of the mountains. They've come to make a trade. We buy their tar. It's a high-grade combustible, excellent for explosives as well as for cooking. We also use it in our smelting furnaces. We trade them metal. We have a lot of metal in these mountains. We control all of it." Rango pointed. "You see that big *hari-bumuku* there?" Hab nodded. "His name is Aychega. He's their drillmaster. You see how we had to make him a special suit of metal armor to keep him happy? Look at the way he hops, as if he owns everything, as if he forgets how the *sikingo-mango* are the masters of Ortok. He's a renegade. We have to watch him carefully. He's the single most dangerous drillmaster that we have to deal with. He thinks he might some day defeat Gashak. He thinks that just because he and his kind are treacherous to each other that the *sikingo-mango* might be the same, and that he might find one or two traitors among us to help him oust Gashak. But we *sikingo-mango* appreciate the truth, Hab. We worship honesty. Just as you do in Paras. We know what loyalty means."

Hab gazed at Rango with growing wonder. They worshiped honesty? One of the tar-pool hoppers went to the back tank car, twisted a valve, and, manning a pump, hosed a small puddle of tar onto the training field. Yet if they appreciated the truth so much, why wouldn't Rango tell him why they were killing Esten through starvation and exposure? Gashak leapt from the second terrace of his battle-house. The black hopper drillmaster said a few words to Aychega. If they worshiped honesty, why wouldn't Rango tell him why they were keeping Jara in Keringo? This was clearly an omission. Of course, their definition of honesty didn't necessarily have to match the rigorous definitions found in the Formulary. A *hari-bumuku* regular lit the puddle of tar on fire. Even if a looser interpretation applied, Hab still found the thought of a rough *sikingo-mango* honesty comforting. The puddle cracked and popped, and burst into flames. It made him think that someday, despite what they were doing to Esten, he might at last see Jara again.

ᘒᘒᘒ

The more complicated forms began to make sense to Hab. He and Rango were able to talk on nearly equal terms.

"I thought the green ones were amphibious," said Hab. "When we first came here we saw them in the water."

"Some are amphibious, some aren't," said Rango. "It's hard to catch the nomads of the coast. I'm surprised you were able to kill so many when you first came here. The wild nomads of the coast we generally let be. We raise our own slaves. It's our due. We're the *sikingo-mango*. Everything is ours."

"The tar-pool ones don't seem to think so."

"The *hari-bumuku* can think what they like," he said. "It's only by our good graces that we don't go in and take over their land. They've managed the tar pools for thousands of years. They know how to do it better than we do. It's easier for us to trade with them than to make war with them. But if we changed our minds we would kill them all. They're fortunate Gashak has such a benevolent regard toward them. There's nothing to eat where they come from. We trade them metal. We trade them food. They would die without us."

"But is there nothing to eat in the interior?" asked Hab.

The small hopper grunted and brushed some insects away from the big red scar on his forehead. "There used to be a few wild gourds, and some edible ground vines, and the occasional root or tuber. There used to be a lot of giant centipedes, ten-and-twelve-pounders, but they've either moved east, to the Dark Coast, or they've gone into the canyons, where no one can find them. Since the eruption ten years ago, everything is covered in ash. The *hari-bumuku* live in a wasteland now. The only useful endeavor for them is the harvesting of the tar pools. It's a dead land east of the Mouth here, Hab. Everybody has a hard time finding enough to eat, even we of the *sikingo-mango*. We've had to rely on a diminishing herd of *bamkali-kalango*, the green ones. We can't raise as many as we once could because there's nothing to feed them with. We've started fishing, but we've nearly fished out the coastal waters."

Hab remembered the fishless waters as the *Fetla* neared Ortok.

"Things are bad right now, Hab," continued Rango. "They've always been hard. But things are particularly grim because of the eruption. We're facing famine. Not that we haven't faced it before. But this is going to be a bad famine, and with famine there's always war. It's the ageless cycle of this land, Hab. Famine and war. That's why Gashak is keeping such a close eye on Aychega. We live in this bleak land. We live in hardship most of our lives. We never have enough to eat, and we have to fight for what little food there is." A wistfulness came to the hopper's red eyes. "Not at all like Paras, is it? Could you tell me about Paras again, Hab? Tell me about this Estuary next to Jauny. How deep is it? How wide is it? And is it really so full of fish?"

Hab smiled. Nothing gave him greater pleasure than talking about the Golden Land, even though it usually left him feeling homesick afterward. "You can stoop with your bare hands and catch a half dozen pekra just like that. And the Estuary's a most accommodating harbor, deep and wide, with room for hundreds of ships. And the children like to play in the shallows at the end of Ourrice Boulevard. And the banks are lined with apple trees so that everywhere in the spring the Estuary shimmers with the bright reflections of their blossoms. No one ever goes hungry. You can reach up to any tree anywhere and gorge yourself on apples of every variety till you're stuffed."

He talked about Paras for the next hour, giving Rango a thumb-nail tour of the four provinces and the two major islands, told the hopper about Cloudesley, about Summerhouse and Winterhouse, about the Lake of Life, the Wall, and the Great Code. He told the hopper of bladder whales so thick along the Dagu coast that you couldn't see any water, just their red bladders above the surface.

"Everything about Paras is soft and beautiful," said Hab. "Paras is bountiful. Paras is generous. Her forests are teeming with game. The growers in Berberton produce more grain than any of us can ever hope to eat."

"Grain?" said Rango, questioning Hab's use of the unfamiliar Parassian word. There was no Abani word for grain. They didn't have grain in Ortok.

"Seeds from certain cultivated grasses," Hab explained.

"You eat grass?" said Rango, obviously intrigued. "We've tried to eat grass but we . . . there's no value in it . . . there's nothing in it that can make our blood strong."

"Not the grass itself," said Hab. "We let it go to seed. We dry out the seeds, we crush the seeds into powder, we mix it with water, and we make a . . ." Hab thought. What word could he use for dough? "We make a paste with it. We cook this paste into . . ." No equivalent word for "bread" either. "Into bricks, and we eat it."

"You eat bricks made of grass seed?" said Rango.

Put that way, it indeed sounded strange, but Hab thought this was as close as he was going to get to a definition of bread when there were no specific equivalents in Abani.

Rango thought for several moments. "This land of yours . . . it sounds nearly too good to be true. Why was it that your people were so blessed? And why are my people so cursed? Look at this place. Ortok. It's an old word. It means burnt skull. You have the Golden Land and I have a burnt skull." Rango's eyes narrowed, his slit pupils focusing with a nearly unbearable scrutiny. "You wouldn't be boasting, would you? All this about the Estuary, and Berberton, and the east coast of Dagu, with all the bladder whales. You're not just making it up, are you, just so I'll think Paras is a wonderful place?"

"Rango," he said, his voice steady as he thought with pride of his homeland. "I would never boast. It goes against the Rules of our Formulary." He thought of his vow never to lie again. "We don't lie in Paras. We have a blessing we say to each other in Paras: Honesty is the way. Anybody who lies in Paras is banished to the Island of Liars. Honesty is the fabric of our society. We've been bred to honesty for thousands of years. Honesty is the mainstay of our religion, the foundation of our law, and the basis of our culture. We utter our true selves all the time. We are bound by the 28 Rules of the Formulary to speak the truth."

"Yet you embezzled your family estate to make the voyage to Ortok," said Rango, in an example of bewildering truth-telling that was equal to the most honest Parassian. "You lied to your drillmaster,

Parprouch. You fled without telling anybody what you had done." Rango lifted his snout in a contemplative manner. "Is this not deceit, Hab? Should you yourself not be banished to this Island of Liars? You see why I don't know whether to believe you? We value the truth as well. But we're not above suspicion. We like to have the truth verified. Can you explain your behavior?"

"Rango, what I did . . ." He struggled to come up with the proper Abani words. "I did it for the purpose of a higher truth. The purpose of finding this place. I did it to dismantle the mistruth all Parassians believed, that we were alone in the world. My hand was forced because my drillmaster schemed to dispossess me of my chance to find this place. I had no choice. And if I ever go back, he just might banish me to the Island of Liars. But I will at least have revealed to all Parassians the truth about Ortok."

Rango sat back, twitched his massive leg, as if it was getting sore from sitting in the same position so long. "Is everybody really so honest in Paras?" he asked. "Is it really in your blood?"

"Yes," said Hab. "We are honest and straightforward. Honesty is our way, Rango."

The small hopper gazed out at the training field, where five *sikingo mango* regulars arranged an obstacle course for a nighttime training exercise. The sun had sunk behind the mountains. Rain clouds prowled down the Mouth of the Monster. Rango grunted.

"Then we have much in common, Hab," he said.

৯৯৯

But if the *sikingo-mango* valued honesty above all other traits, Hab again wondered why Rango wouldn't tell him why they were slowly starving Esten to death. Dawn came, and the rocks were wet. Esten usually forced his face between the bars of his cage floor at this time of the day and licked what little moisture he could from the wet rocks.

But this morning he didn't move. Usually there were hoppers out on the field training by this time, but today, for some reason, the field was empty, the barracks still, and Gashak's battle-house silent. All he heard over the moaning of the constant wind was the squawking of the bird-animals above the inlet as they rode the updrafts.

"Esten?" he called. "Esten, get up."

But his friend wouldn't move. Hab cupped water from a small puddle in the rocks below the bars of his own cage and flung it at the scientist, but he was too far away, and the water was blown apart by the wind. He then tried to throw a chunk of cured green hopper meat. This was the hundredth time he'd tried to throw food to Esten. This time was no different. The food fell short. He couldn't angle his arm properly through the bars to fling it the whole distance, and a bird-animal swooped from a ledge above and gobbled the meat in one swallow.

"Esten, please . . ." The wind whistled hollowly, sounding like a hundred flutes. "Esten, you've got to try and drink."

But Esten wasn't really Esten anymore. What lay there was just some skin-covered bones poking out from a dirty leather jerkin. The insects began to buzz. No, that wasn't Esten anymore. That was just a corpse, and there was nothing he could do about it. His friend, this scientist who had saved him from certain death in the tides during their first attempt to find Ortok, was now dead.

CHAPTER TWENTY

They took Esten's body away. They also took Esten's cage. They left Hab on the same ledge under the overhang all by himself with only a guard to bring food and water once a day. Rango didn't come anymore. At first Hab thought it was because Rango had other things to do. Rango seemed to be what in Paras would be called a vice-chancellor, with a myriad of responsibilities and duties to attend to. Then Hab thought Rango was isolating him on purpose, as a kind of punishment. Day followed day and week followed week, and Hab grew so desperate to talk to someone, to share someone's company, that every day he tried to strike up a conversation with the guard. But the guard would say nothing, simply shoved his food through the door and hopped from the ledge back down to the training field.

After thirty days of this, Rango finally returned. The small hopper bounded across the training field carrying what looked like a large ball. Hab had nearly become unhinged from loneliness and was so glad to see his hopper friend that he couldn't help smiling idiotically. Rango leapt up onto Hab's stone ledge and shuffled toward his cage in an awkward walk.

"A full stomach to you, Hab," said Rango, using the traditional Abani greeting.

"And a full stomach to you, Rango," he said. "Where have you been? I thought you might have died. I've been up here by myself for the last several weeks." Hab couldn't stop talking. "Were you in Ketingo? Did you see Jara? Is she all right?"

Rango grunted. His breath smelled of carrion. "The red one is well," he said, referring to Jara with the pet name he'd devised for her. "You don't have to worry about her. She's learned the language. But she has an annoying habit of kicking her teacher in the shins."

"But where have you been?" he said, stressing the interrogative with three different pronunciations. "I've been so lonely up here all by myself. My beard needs a trim and I need a bath. I smell foul."

Rango sniffed. "You don't smell so bad to me."

"I've sorely missed our conversations, Rango," said Hab, the words tumbling out with manic speed. "That guard must have had his tongue cut out. He never talks to me. I thought you were never coming back. I thought you'd deserted me."

Rango opened the cage door and went inside, still carrying the curious ball. "I would never desert you, Hab," he said. He bared his teeth viciously, the hopper equivalent of a smile. "You and I are good friends now, and would good friends desert each other? In fact, I've come today for the exact purpose of having a long talk with you. We can talk all day if you like. You look like you need a long talk."

"Do you know what it's like up here all by yourself with no one to talk to?" said Hab, his voice shrill from lack of use. "And my limbs are wasting away. I never get any exercise. I'm surprised I haven't gone mad. I'm usually not much of a talker, but you're right, I stand in need of good conversation." He looked at the ball. "What do you want to talk about?"

Rango held up the ball, a sphere of thin metal twice the size of a human head, supported on a small metal frame. "Is the world round or flat?" he asked.

Hab's eyes widened. The hoppers might be technically advanced in the use of metal. But did they really not know the answer to this simple and most basic question? "It's round, Rango," he said. "As round as that ball you're holding."

Rango twitched his head in the affirmative. "I thought so," he said. "Ortok, then, must be on top of the world, and Paras must be somewhere nearby."

Hab's brow creased. "What makes you assume Paras is nearby?"

"Because we both have to be on the top of the world or we would fall off."

Hab stared at Rango. The hopper said this in complete seriousness. Hab searched the Abani vocabulary but failed to find a word for gravity. So he explained the concept with the available words he had.

"And this force you speak of," said Rango, struggling to understand, "it pulls at you the same way with the same strength no matter where on the world you stand?"

"*Mu, mui*," said Hab.

"But if you're standing on the bottom of the world, wouldn't the blood rush to your head?"

"No, your blood is pulled groundward as well. On the bottom of the world, up still seems like up, and down still seems like down."

"So Paras could be anywhere on this ball?"

"Anywhere at all," confirmed Hab.

Rango took out a sharpened piece of charcoal and drew something on the sphere, an inexpert but recognizable attempt at cartography. When he was done, he held the globe up for Hab's inspection.

"This is Ortok," said Rango. "Here is the Mouth of the Monster, here's *Kimbia-kipugia*, and beyond these ashlands is the Dark Coast."

"You've drawn it much too big," he said.

"I have?"

"There's a lot of water out there, Rango," said Hab. "When you account for the land masses of Paras and Ortok, our world is eighty-seven percent water. Our lands might be continents, but they're small continents. Paras is about two thousand miles from north to south and about fifteen hundred from east to west. I think Ortok wouldn't be much bigger. In fact, I think it's probably smaller."

Rango handed the globe to Hab. "Why don't you draw how big you think Ortok is?"

The bit of charcoal, while small in Rango's hand, was large and unwieldy in Hab's, but he managed to draw with it. "Have you traveled much in Ortok?"

"Everywhere," said Rango.

"Have you sailed around Ortok?"

"Yes."

"In one of the wood boats or in one of the metal ships?"

"Both."

"And the wood ships are faster, aren't they?"

"By about twenty percent."

Hab spotted one of the wood ships down in the inlet and estimated how many knots she could pull in an average wind. About ten. "And in a wood ship, how many days does it take you to sail around Ortok?"

"Twenty days when the wind is with us."

Hab did some quick calculations. "Then Ortok is about two-thirds the size of Paras." He studied the shape of Rango's charcoal Ortok on the globe, then drew a much smaller one inside it, a tenth the size. "There," he said. "That's Ortok." He rubbed out Rango's large Ortok with the back of his hand. Then he turned the globe over and drew Paras on the other side. "This is the Golden Land." He sketched quickly and accurately; he had studied cartography extensively at Pieshe, the Mariner's Academy. "This is the Island of Maju, the Sea of Maju, which narrows at its northernmost point into the Estuary. Jauny lies on the west bank of the Estuary. The Estuary then narrows farther to become the River Necontreu, the Golden Land's great heartland river, and finally finds its source in the Lake of Life. As you can see, there's a great deal of water between our two homes. Your unit of measurement is the *kuthi*. That's just a little smaller than one of our miles. You say no one's ever sailed farther than a thousand *kuthi* away from Ortok."

Rango grew visibly uneasy. "That's where the water turns dark," he said. "That's where the world ends."

"You would have to travel fifteen times that distance, like I did. It would take you sixty, maybe even eighty, days to get there."

"Eighty days!" said Rango, as if he couldn't conceive of such astronomical distances. "No wonder neither of us knew the other existed." A new expression came to Rango's face, one Hab had never seen before; was it admiration? "You are brave, Hab. But I still feel as if I don't know Paras as well I'd like to. Its land features and so forth. I'm going to take you on a tour of Ortok. We'll look at land features. You tell me what features are similar. You tell me which features aren't. We are all so curious about the Golden Land. We can never go there because it's much too far. But at least you can tell us about it."

ﾟﾟﾟ,

They sailed the next day up the Mouth of the Monster, northward toward the open sea. They sailed for two days. The mountains on either side grew smaller and smaller. They became foothills. These foothills changed into wide rolling plains covered with tough brown grass.

"Stop," said Hab. "Let's pull ashore."

Hab and Rango got in a small boat and rowed to shore. "What you see here is terrain similar to the terrain you see around Jauny. We have a range of mountains just north of Jauny, similar to the smaller ones we passed ten or twelve hours ago. These mountains are called the Lesser Oradels. But that's not the reason I stop. Let's take a look at this grass. This grass looks like some of the cultivated grasses we have in Berberton."

"This cultivation you speak of," said Rango. "I'm not sure I understand it." He gestured at the dead brown grass. "How can you harvest something like this? We've tried to eat it, but it's no good."

"You mean you don't cultivate it?" said Hab, now beginning to wonder if the hoppers had any organized form of agriculture at all. "You don't farm it?"

"This word farm, *yafunjeo*. I don't think we mean the same thing by it. *Yafunjeo* literally means to take from the skull. And cultivate, *yakukolewa*—you're using it in a way I've never heard it used before.

Why would you want to cultivate grass? You cultivate friends and allies. You cultivate political and military strength. But to cultivate grass? This is a strange new idea to me, Hab."

The bow of the small boat knocked against the shore, and the human and hopper got out. "What I mean by *yafunjeo*," said Hab, "is to influence the conditions by which this grass will grow. You hardly get any rainfall east of these mountains. But look over here. A small sinkhole filled with rainwater. You see how green the grass grows there?"

They went over to the sinkhole. The grass was taller, greener, more succulent, and the seeds at the top of each stalk were rich and full. Hab plucked one of the seeds, peeled the chaff away with his fingernails, and popped the heart into his mouth. He chewed. And he instantly knew that this grass could become a staple. He picked another seed off, removed the chaff, and gave it to Rango.

"Try it," he said.

Rango tried it. "Bland," concluded the hopper.

"In its raw form, yes," said Hab. "But you can make . . . bricks from it. What we call bread."

Rango tested the unfamiliar Parassian word in his mouth. "BRROUDD."

"Yes, bread." Hab waved toward the ship in the inlet. "Have the regulars come ashore and collect some of these seeds. When we get back from our travels we'll plant them."

"Plant them?" said Rango.

Again, Hab had to wonder. The hoppers were technically advanced in the arts of war and metalworking but seemed to know nothing of the more peaceful sciences. "Yes," he said. "These seeds will produce other plants." Hab gave Rango a quick overview of organized agriculture. "You don't just have to collect these gourds and vines you told me grew in the interior before all the ash came. You can grow your own. You can virtually solve all your food problems with *yakukolewa*."

Once the regulars had picked three bushels of grass seeds, the ship continued north along Shindano-shtaka-shudo. Soon they reached the ocean. A small chain of mountains, black and treeless, rose on the east bank of the Mouth. These mountains surrounded a volcano, one not as big as the gigantic Kimbia-kipugia, but still at least seven thousand feet high, with an impressive caldera nearly a half mile across. A small town, mostly stone pyramids with the usual hopping terraces, ringed the bottom of this volcano.

"This town takes its name from the volcano," informed Rango. "They're both called Zingira."

They stayed in Zingira for the night. Its inhabitants, all black hoppers, were thin and undernourished.

"You see the toll starvation takes on my land," said Rango. "It's getting worse. Zingirans were at one time famous for the mollusks they scraped from the tidal pools. They did a good trade. They used to export to Chungwa, Ketingo, even as far away as Wagengo. Now there are not enough mollusks to feed even themselves. They've been over-harvested, and consequently there are not enough left to breed in proper numbers. In five years I expect they'll all be extinct."

"Do they not raise the green ones here?" he asked.

"They haven't the resources," he said. "They're poor here. And there are no birds here." Hab assumed he was talking about the bird-animals. He hadn't seen any of these creatures for a few days now. "That's how we raise the green ones, by feeding them birds. When the birds run out, which happens seasonally during the migration time, we let the green ones eat their own young. No, we've had to bring our own *bamkali-kalango* with us. We'll be traveling by train into the interior tomorrow."

The next morning their team of green hoppers waited outside their pyramid, hitched and ready to go. The iron rails curved around the base of Zingira.

"We go to the Black Desert," said Rango.

The Black Desert, a region of low mountains and barren bleak valleys, looked as desolate and deserted as the surface of Foot on a clear night. Nothing grew there. The air was filled with flakes of ash from Kimbia-kipugia's eruption, and the ground was covered with it, in some places a foot deep. From behind certain mountains, Hab saw great clouds of black smoke rising. It was as much like the classical depiction of Oeil as Hab could imagine.

"Why are you taking me here?" he asked Rango. "There's nothing like this anywhere in Paras. I thought you wanted me to point out similar land features."

Rango's expression was now grim. He said nothing. They crested a rise, the green hoppers climbed in, and the driver, taking firm control of the brake, eased the train down a long gentle slope. The smell of the air thickened, grew redolent of tar, and the slopes of the mountains hissed and billowed, and occasionally shot flame. The ground became slick with tar puddles. They passed through one particularly thick bank of smoke, a choking black smog that made Hab cough, and when they came through, he saw a lake of tar, a body as black as pitch, maybe two miles across, with a small town clustered at one end.

"That's Bwasiarika," said Rango.

As they drew near, Hab saw barges out on the lake of tar manned by teams of the copper-colored spiky tar-pool hoppers. The tar-pool hoppers ladled tar into large metal urns. The lake bubbled and steamed, and occasionally whirlwinds of fire danced up.

They pulled into Bwasiarika, a town of caves and ledges carved into the steep mountain at the foot of the tar lake. A gigantic train yard stood at the base of the mountain, with close to two dozen sidings crowded with tanker trains. A huge corral of bound and blindfolded green hoppers sat beyond. The sky overhead was black with smoke, and the sun appeared as a pale and wavering yellow disk, sometimes disappearing altogether. Hab felt as if he had entered a giant furnace. The heat was tremendous, and he was instantly covered with sweat.

"Do I have to tie you up, Hab?" said Rango. "Or will you promise to stay in the train?"

"Where are you going?" asked Hab, alarmed that he should be left alone in such a place. Some spiky, ugly *hari-bumuku* were coming over to take a look at this strange creature from another land.

"I must pay homage to Aychega," he said. Their train creaked to a halt. "He's over there."

The *hari-bumuku* drillmaster stood on top of a series of impressive stairlike terraces carved into the black rock. Huge torches flamed on either side of him. He casually hopped from one terrace to the next, one of the largest hoppers Hab had ever seen, easily twelve feet tall. In one final bound, Aychega stood next to the train.

"You've brought the pale one," he said to Rango. "Can I poke him? I want to see if he jumps."

"Not now, Aychega," said Rango. "We have things to discuss."

Rango jumped out of the car. Together the two hoppers leaped to the top terrace. Hab watched them. Amid the smoke and fire, in the stench of tar, and with heat that felt as if it might burn his skin off, Hab watched the conference between the large and small hoppers take place, as fearsome a spectacle as he had ever beheld. *Hari-bumuku* gathered on both sides of his car, their coppery scales splattered with tar, their eyes gleaming red in the choking air, and stared at him. One did indeed poke him, treating him like he was no more than animal.

Hab was glad when Rango finally came back.

ઠઠઠ

Once back at Chungwa, Rango put Hab in his cage again on the ledge above the training field under the overhang.

Weeks passed, and he pined for Jara. The weather changed again and the evening rains stopped, and now it was just as hot and dry at night as it was during the day. Hab stared up at the night sky, mentally cataloging and positioning the different stars on this side of the world for the day when he might possibly add them to his navigational charts back home. One in particular seemed to shine with a fearsome beauty, a bright blue star he called Jara. The star mesmerized him. It made him think of Jara. He sustained his hope by looking at that star. His impossible goal of he and Jara somehow sailing back to Paras together didn't seem so impossible when he looked at that star.

His loneliness felt like a palpable weight closing in around him. He gripped the bars and looked out over the dark inlet. Rango came once every third day. That wasn't enough. He glanced at the uneaten green hopper joint on the floor of his cage and felt no appetite for it. Even if he were miraculously offered a box of Gougou's bonbons, he doubted he would have much taste for them. He needed company. And not hopper company. Human company.

He heard a sudden thump at the edge of his ledge. Rango approached out of the darkness. He had something in his hands. He raised the object.

"BRROUDD," he said, using the Parassian word with difficulty. "You were right, Hab. Gashak extends his gratitude. We've made a thousand loaves. The regulars seem to have enough to eat for the first time in their lives."

"Shouldn't you ship some to Zingira?" said Hab.

"The army must be fed first," said Rango. "There's no point in feeding the populace if they don't have a strong army to defend them."

Hab's lips came together. "In Paras, we outlawed war five centuries ago."

Rango's black scaly lips twisted to one side, an expression that meant puzzlement on a hopper face. "How can you outlaw war?" he asked, perplexed by the notion.

"We can outlaw war because everybody has enough to eat," he said.

"So you have no army, no navy?"

"No army, and a navy for only civil uses."

Rango took a deep breath. The hopper seemed amazed by these revelations. "Every night we go to bed fearing for our lives," he said.

"We think we'll be attacked in the night. We fear what little food stores we have will be pillaged." Rango turned and gazed out across the inlet. Far in the interior, an orange glow filled the sky, the lava floes of Kimbia-kipugia. He handed the bread to Hab. "Here," he said. "Try it. We followed your instructions as closely as we could."

Hab took the bread and nibbled. Hard, dry, more like biscuit than bread, salty, but at least edible. "That's not bad," he said.

"We've got a thousand acres under . . . cultivation now," said Rango, "or at least partially worked. We've dug wells, as you've instructed. We've converted some tar pumps to pump the water up to the fields. The fields are green. It doesn't look like the Mouth of the Monster anymore."

Hab took another nibble of the hopper bread; even if he had no appetite, it was at least nice to taste something different than cured green hopper meat.

"I was watching you just now, from up there," said Rango, pointing to a ledge above them. "I sometimes come here and observe you. You were looking up at the stars. I've seen you do this on numerous nights now. Why do the stars fascinate you so much?"

Hab glanced up at the blue star, Jara. "Because I'm a mariner, Rango," he said. "The stars are my stock in trade. I find my way around the sea using the stars as signposts. I use star charts. Unfortunately, I lost all my charts when the *Fetla* went down. But I've been looking up at the stars in this sky, mentally cataloging them. And I remember all the ones from my old charts. I plan someday to collate the lot of them into a comprehensive chart."

Rango seemed deep in thought. "I could bring you some hide and indelible ink. You could make some of these . . . these star charts. I would be most interested. You really use them to find your way around the sea?"

Here it was again, a deficiency in their science. "The *sikingo-mango* don't use stars to navigate?" asked Hab.

"No," he said. "We're always within reach of the coast. We never venture into the dark water. We navigate by landmarks. We navigate by depth-sounding. Our best navigators have charted the underwater topography around Ortok. By taking numerous soundings, we can pinpoint exactly where we are. We never thought to use the stars. And this word, 'stars,' *wenda*. Again, you're using it a little differently, shaping it to fit a Parassian idea. *Wenda*, yes, stars, but *wendia*, volcanoes, like Kimbia-kipugia, Mizikani, and Zingira."

"The stars aren't volcanoes, Rango," said Hab. "The stars are suns."

"And the Sun," said Rango. "*Wendia-kupango*, the big volcano in the sky."

"They're not the same thing, not really, though I can see how you might think that, in a land where there are so many volcanoes."

"I'll bring some hide and ink, and you can make some star charts." A sudden hissing sound came from Rango's throat, one that signaled sadness in a hopper. "We are ignorant, Hab," he said. "I'm small, I've been forced to use my mind. I'm considered one of the most brilliant diplomats and scholars in Ortok, but when I talk to you, and I learn all the wondrous things you and your people know, I feel like a barbarian. We *are* barbarians, Hab. Make no mistake. We have to fight all the time. I tell you we value honesty. But none of us trusts each other. We know we would kill each other for a scrap of food. In all my life, you're the only one I've ever trusted. And that's because I know you come from a land where honesty is the way. Or maybe it's because I can keep you in a cage. You can't stab me in the back while I'm asleep."

Awful hopper laughter erupted in one of the distant barrack pyramids.

"But you have no one you trust?" asked Hab. "No one you love? Don't you have a wife?"

"I have several wives," said Rango. "We don't love our wives the same way you seem to love them in Paras. We use them to satisfy our loins and to raise our children and to run our households. We kill them if they misbehave. We treat our women badly here, Hab. We were all of us so surprised to find women in the crew of the *Fetla*. In fact, what amazes most of the regulars here on the base is how your women find an equal place in your society. The women of the *sikingo-mango* are treated not much better than the slaves of the *bamkali-kalango*. They have no protection. They're raped, mistreated, abused, and murdered on a daily basis. We have no laws here, except the law of might. Sometimes the women are killed simply because the *sikingo-mango* male has nothing else to eat. And it's all because of Ortok. It's made us brutal, Hab. It's made us ignorant. About the only thing we know how to do with any skill or ingenuity is kill one another."

ϟϟϟ

The next morning, a tar-pool train rattled up onto the training field, the largest tar-pool train Hab had ever seen, seventy-five cars long, pulled by a team of fifty green hoppers. Gashak stood on the steps of the battle-house decked in his jewelry, still with Jeter's head tied to his belt. Rango stood beside him. As Hab watched what he surmised was another trade, maybe the one Rango had negotiated with Aychega in the smoky and forsaken town of Bwasiarika, he felt sorry for Rango, thinking that they had their loneliness in common. Rango was probably more lonely. He couldn't trust any of his fellow countrymen.

There he was, down on the training field, with hundreds of hoppers everywhere, yet he was more isolated than Hab was. Did he at least trust Gashak, Hab wondered, as he clutched the bars and watched the proceedings. Hadn't Rango spoken of his love and loyalty for the *sikingo-mango* drillmaster? Wasn't it Gashak who had given him all his chances? Rango must have at least had a friend in Gashak, even if Gashak struck Hab as somewhat pompous and foolish.

Aychega hopped off one of the middle tank cars and approached the *sikingo-mango* drillmaster. He got halfway to the steps of the battle-house. An unexpected silence fell over the field. A palpable tension followed. A sudden shifting and stiffening of the black hoppers in the field ensued. Something wasn't right. Aychega drew his sword and held it in the air. A piercing battle cry bellowed from his throat. To Hab's astonishment, all seventy-five tank cars burst open, like the lids of seventy-five giant bread boxes opening, and hundreds upon hundreds of tar-pool hoppers, in a canny deception, sprang from the dummy tank cars and attacked.

Rango hopped to the alarm bell and rang it fiercely. Black hoppers poured from the barracks, and soon a ferocious battle raged on the training field. Gashak the Juggler hopped to the roof of the battle-house. Rango hopped after him. The *sikingo-mango* drillmaster bellowed commands to his subordinates from the roof while a blockade of personal guards surrounded him. He stayed out of the battle, directed it from afar. Not so with Aychega. The gargantuan tar-pool hopper entered the fray with his regulars. He was a consummate hopper, attained heights of sometimes thirty and forty feet, crushing skulls and breaking backs when he landed, hewing with an axe in one hand, slashing with a sword in the other.

The fighting continued for nearly fifteen minutes before a strange and unexpected thing happened. Some of the black hoppers chalked their armor with white crosses and then turned against the black hoppers without white crosses. What was this? Hab's grip tightened on the bars. A coup d'etat unfolded before his eyes.

On the roof of the battle-house, Rango drew his sword, and pressing the point against Gashak's jugular vein, thrust the sword right through the drillmaster's neck, twisting the blade this way and that until he finally decapitated the *sikingo-mango* leader.

CHAPTER TWENTY-ONE

A day later, with the bloodshed finished, and the *hari-bumuku* drillmaster Aychega now in control, Rango came to see Hab up on the ledge. Hab was overwhelmed by Rango's treachery, but Rango seemed to think nothing of it.

"I've been . . . cultivating support within the ranks of our regulars for several months," explained Rango. "But I didn't get the strength in numbers I'd hoped for. So I had to go to Aychega. He's drillmaster now."

"But why?" asked Hab. "I thought you loved Gashak. I thought you were fiercely loyal to Gashak for giving you the chance to use your mind. You say you've been plotting against him for months, yet every day you pretend that nothing is different, that you're not holding a knife behind your back, and that you're going to be loyal to him no matter what. I thought you valued honesty, Rango. This isn't honesty. This is deceit. You've lived a bald-faced lie. And you've included me in your treachery by professing your love and respect for Gashak. All this time I thought he was your mentor. All this time I thought he was your patron. And now this. *Yethelu pambazo Gashak!* The coldblooded murder of the drillmaster who helped you to your high position in life."

The small black hopper gazed at Hab coldly. "Human, there's no dishonesty here," he said. "There's no treachery or deceit. There's not even treason. There's only a coup. And a coup is as honest, at least in *sikingo-mango* politics, as the edge of my sword. Gashak has been drillmaster for a long time, longer than anyone in recent memory. There's more to this coup than you might think, Hab. And I do value honesty.

Like yourself, I was forced into regrettable but necessary acts of deceit and subterfuge for the sake of securing a greater truth. The Great One of the tar-pools has finally come to take his rightful spot. It's time for the *sikingo-mango* and *hari-bumuku* to unite. Together we are stronger. Together we just might save Ortok. Together we might make Ortok as bountiful as Paras. This is my higher truth. So please, no more of your censure. Our politics are complicated and dangerous. The coup yesterday is but a chapter in a much larger story. Someday when the story is finished, you'll understand why I had to kill Gashak. Now, let's get to our usual business." The hopper pulled a slate tablet and piece of chalk from his bag. "I want to talk to you today about ships. Look at this drawing I've made."

Hab struggled to get his confusion and sense of betrayal under control. He looked at the drawing. The drawing was of a typical metal ship, like any of those down in the inlet, tremendously long, with a single mast and a single sail, a longship such as sailed the seas around Paras five hundred years ago. The galleon oars showed clearly as white chalk strokes.

"We've had a look at your *Fetla*," he said. "And we've seen the *Xeulliette*. They've each got three masts. The foremast and the mainmast have three sails each. Why?"

"For a number of reasons," said Hab, disconsolately, still put out by the magnitude of the treachery involved in yesterday's coup. "With more sail you get more speed. You get more maneuverability, and you have a greater number of options when handling the wide variety of winds you'll encounter on the open seas." He tapped the hopper longship. "This is good enough in its way, for coastal voyages, especially because you have the galleon oars, but what happens if you rip this sail? Undoubtedly you carry extra sailcloth with you. But what if you lose it in the middle of a storm? You need maneuverability in the middle of a storm, but with that sail ripped, you'll have none. Chances are you'll be swamped."

Rango twitched his head in agreement. "We've lost a good many ships in storms, you're right."

"And then you've got no bulkheads on these ships. One hole, and the entire boat sinks. You've got to have walls dividing the boat." He took the chalk from Rango and drew three quick strokes. "Here, here, and here. That way, if you run aground and break her open, only one of the compartments will flood and you'll stay afloat."

"We're going to try to build a three-masted ship," said Rango. "In fact, we're going to try to convert all those ships down in the harbor into three-masted ships. You've helped us so much with our food, I thought you . . . you must be familiar with shipbuilding in Paras."

"I studied shipbuilding at Pieshe."

"So how would you modify our . . . our metal boats?"

"For one thing, you'd have to forget about the *Fetla* and the *Xeul-liette*. You've got a longship, and it's not going to take the same kind of sail. The keel is all wrong for the typical three-masted rigging. You're going to have to rig them more like a barkentine."

"A barkentine?" said Rango, hardly able to pronounce the strange Parassian word.

"A kind of ship with a straight, low-lying keel. I rent five barkentines every year. I use them for whaling. You have to rig the foremast and mizzenmast with gaff sails. Gaff sails are triangular in shape, so you'll have to retrain your sail cutters. The foremast you can rig with regular sails. You've also got to rig them with shrouds and ratlines so sailors can get up and down to do the reefing and furling. Then you've got to rig some jib sails. Before that, you've got to fix a jib boom to the bow by cutting away that ridiculous prow and rigging a straight piece of metal to a bowsprit and bobstay."

Over the next hour, Hab made several drawings. He might not understand hopper politics, but that didn't mean he was going to stop helping them. And if the coup meant the tar-pool hoppers and the mountain hoppers were going to work together to make Ortok a better

place, then he couldn't deny the chance to try, even if he didn't necessarily agree with their means. By the time he was finished, he had given
the small hopper a complete set of blueprints on multiple tablets.

"And our ships, overhauled in this manner, will be suitable for
more than just coastal travel?" asked Rango.

"If you know your tides and your winds, you can take them anywhere in the world."

ᔕᔕᔕ

Aychega, the new drillmaster of the tar-pool and mountain hoppers,
came to see the human the next day. He was accompanied by Rango.

"So this is the strange one from the other side of the world," said
Aychega. "He is like the maggot, is he not, white and smooth, and all
like jelly on the inside."

"We've taught him to speak, drillmaster," said Rango.

Hab was still unnerved by the appearance of tar-pool hoppers.
Whereas Rango's black scales were smooth, tiny, and configured like a
shingle roof, with one row overlapping the next in such regularity that
from a distance the scales actually looked like skin, Aychega's coppery
scales protruded randomly in a series of sharp points, so that he looked
as if he were completely studded over in hobnails.

"He speaks, does he?" said Aychega. "Then have him say something."

"Hab, say something to the drillmaster."

"A full stomach to you, drillmaster," said Hab.

Aychega bared his teeth, amused by the familiar greeting. Then he
seemed to ponder. "Is there not some sport we can play with him?" he
said. "Could we not set him loose and hunt him down? Imagine the
squeals he would make. And imagine the mess all that jelly inside him
would make once we took our axes to him."

"Yes, drillmaster, but we are learning things from him," said
Rango. "He's taught us how to make the seed bricks. He's taught us

that we can sail out into the dark water and beyond. And he's taught us that the world is round, not flat."

The drillmaster grunted. "The world is flat, Rango. As for the dark water, I forbid it. Would you have all our fleet fall from the edge of the sea into the abyss?" He pointed to Hab. "The white one here is a demon and a trickster. You talk to me of Takasa, but this demon doesn't come from Takasa. Takasa is a place where the creatures are beautiful. This one's a maggot. He's a demon from the abyss. He came from the dark water. He came from where the monsters roam. He came from the place where our sailors have gone and never returned. Tell me, Rango, why do you think they never return? Come, scholar, tell me."

Rango looked at the floor. "I don't know, drillmaster."

"I'll tell you why," said Aychega. "And so will any child. They don't come back because they reach the end of our world, out where the sea buckles strangely, and where the currents are strong. Of course the sea buckles. Of course it pulls and drags. Because at the edge of the world the sea acts like the Great Falls of Wagengo. It drops precipitously into the abyss." He turned back to Hab. "I think we should cut him open and see what he looks like on the inside. That might serve your science better than a voyage to the dark water, scholar."

Rango's neck muscles rippled strangely. "I think we should preserve him for the time being, drillmaster."

Aychega hopped to the cave entrance and looked down at the training field. "No," he said, with his back to Rango. "I think I should like some sport with him after all. This plain down here is broad and inviting and should make for a good chase."

But Rango wasn't listening. Rango, with his usual birdlike quickness, pulled his battle-axe from his belt and flung it with uncanny expertise at the new drillmaster. The axe spun through the air and sliced cleanly through the *hari-bumuku*'s heavily scaled back. Here was the ultimate treachery, coldblooded murder, killing an intelligent creature while its back was turned, something inconceivable in Paras, with no warning, no chance for Aychega to defend himself, no opportunity to plead for mercy, a direct violation of Rule Number One of the Formulary. Blood spurted like wine from a punctured wine barrel. Aychega collapsed sideways to the ground. A gurgling sound came from his mouth for a few seconds. Rango knelt beside Aychega and slit his throat. Then Rango looked at Hab. Hab stared at him, mystified.

"Why?" said Hab.

Rango stopped wiping the blade of his dagger and rose. The axe remained embedded in Aychega's back. "I didn't bring him up here to see you, Hab," he said. "I brought him up here to murder him."

"Another treachery? Another deceit?"

"Another necessity."

"How can anyone ever trust you?"

"They must trust me because I grasp for a higher truth, just like you do. Did you hear his ignorance? Did you hear his abominable unwillingness to accept what might be new and strange? Gashak was the same way. That's why they both had to die. I used one against the other. I was too weak to kill Gashak by myself. So I had Aychega help me. I promised him full command of all our mountain tribes. He's a fool. He believed me. Now he's dead. And I'm the drillmaster. Another treachery, yes, another deceit, true, but in time, you will see that my goals are as honorable as yours. In time, you will know my full plan."

ᘝᘝᘝ

A week later, after Rango had consolidated power—after he had conducted a violent and bloody purge to root out and destroy any and all opposition—he broached with Hab the subject of the monsters out in the dark water.

"They have eyes as big as suns, they shoot geysers of water a hundred feet high, they're bigger than our biggest ships, and they have teeth as tall as trees."

"They're not monsters, Rango."

Hab stared out at the inlet. Twice as many ships lay at anchor. Many of them had been refitted with three masts. Some were under way on practice runs.

"If not monsters, then what?" asked Rango.

"They're bladder whales," explained Hab. "They're the ones we encountered halfway to Ortok. They're ten times larger than the ones I hunt in the Channel of Liars, but fundamentally, they're the same creature."

"Then they're not monsters at all, just animals?"

"Yes."

"And they can be hunted?"

"Rig any of your cannons with a harpoon and plenty of line, fire when you're within range, pierce both bladders, and wait for the creature to suffocate. When both bladders are pierced the whale swims for shore. The whale has an internal bladder called a swim bladder. This will float the creature for a while after it dies. This gives you about two days to harvest and butcher the animal. Don't kill it outright. Let it suffocate. If you kill it outright, it releases a poisonous substance into its meat and the meat is ruined."

"So if a ship were to run out of provisions while sailing far from shore in the dark water, she could conceivably restock herself by killing one of these whales?"

"Yes. One kill would provision a whole fleet."

Rango pulled from a long narrow bag several rolled-up pieces of hide. He unrolled them. They were the star charts Hab had been working on. "Do you want to work on these anymore?" asked Rango. "Is there anything you can add, anything you think you might have forgotten?"

"No," he said. "They're accurate and complete."

"And with them, our ships can sail the dark waters without getting lost?"

Hab hesitated. There now seemed to be a palpable frisson in the air. What was he feeling? He wasn't sure.

"You won't get lost."

Rango lifted the globe of the world. "Yes, but how can you navigate simply by using the stars? I've thought about it, and I've talked to our most experienced mariners. I've shown your star charts to them, and they've decided that you would need something to correlate the stars to the surface of the world. And we're not sure how you would do that."

Was it apprehension he was feeling? No, it was a much stronger emotion, something he rarely felt, something he'd been taught never to feel.

"It's easy," said Hab. "Do you have your charcoal?"

"Right here," said Rango.

Hab took the charcoal and drew lines of latitude and longitude on the globe. "We make a gridwork of the globe. By charting speed and degree arc, and by using triangulation with the stars, such as I explained to you last week, you can pinpoint your position anywhere on the world."

What he felt was suspicion, deceit's inauspicious counterpart, her opposite number in the ever-changing and ambiguous ether of dishonesty. And that suspicion was like an arrow piercing through all of Rango's comradely dissimilitude. For the first time he now knew that the small hopper's friendly interest was more than just scientific curiosity.

"Now what of where the sea buckles?" asked Rango. "Near where we once thought the edge of the world was?"

It all made such perfect sense to Hab now. The methodical inquisition, first the older hopper performing his bodily exam, marking points in red where a human might be most easily killed, the intense instruction in Abani, the unending curiosity about Paras, Rango's particular interest in the Estuary and Jauny. Then had come the questions about shipbuilding. And of course there was the globe, now beautifully lined with marks of latitude and longitude, and the star charts, a map that would enable the hoppers to find their way to Paras. He remembered Rango's questions about not having any army or navy in Paras, his in-depth inquiry about the ethic of honesty, his undying interest in the Golden Land's bountiful resources. Then there was the trip down the inlet to find landforms similar to ones in and around Jauny. War was a forgotten art in Jauny. But he saw Rango's motive clearly now. And he felt like the biggest dupe in history. He had built their ships. He had taught them how to get there. With the new bread and the whale hunting, he had fed their armies. The only thing they didn't know about were the tides. How could they possibly know anything specific about the tides when Rango simply described it as a buckling of the sea?

Now Rango wanted to know. Despite Hab's efforts at penance, to redeem himself in the eyes of Ouvant, a God he didn't believe in, he knew he had to lie. Here was deceit in its vilest form, clothing itself in the fabric of truth, so skillfully handled by the small hopper that in fact it was more than just sleight of hand, it was an art, a science: the science of deceit. And at last he had learned its cruelest lessons.

"The sea buckles?" he said innocently. He was surprised by how glibly the lie rolled from his tongue. He knew he had the distinct advantage now. The hopper believed him because he believed that on Paras honesty was the way. "I've never encountered such buckling."

"Then why do we get reports of . . . some of our sailors stray from time to time into the dark water, and through their telescopes the sea seems to rise of its own accord."

"I can't say I've ever seen that," said Hab. "What quality are your optical instruments? I've known the glass on many telescopes to warp and shift the sea, but that's not because the sea rises. That's just an optical effect from an imperfect lens."

He was amazed by how easily the misrepresentation continued to weave itself into a believable whole. He had told Rango everything he needed to know to wage war on Paras, but he hadn't told him about the tides, those monthly moon-tides, those devastating tides, the tides that had swept his father away.

"And in the whole twenty thousand miles of your journey you didn't once see the sea buckle?" said Rango, seeming to be greatly relieved by this news. "You didn't see the ocean as if it were tipped on its side?"

"No," he said. "Of course there are the tides, but from what I've observed, your seamen know about the tides."

And even this was new and devious to Hab, telling the truth but turning, by art of deception, the truth into a lie.

"Oh, yes, of course we know about the tides, the rising and falling down here in the inlet every day, the natural respirations of the Monster's Mouth that vary no more than four feet from night to night. But the scant descriptions we've received indicate more than just our gentle tides."

"I think what they saw was fog," said Hab.

"Fog?"

"You plan to wage war on Paras, don't you?"

The hopper grew as still as a corpse and stared at Hab, his slit pupils seeming to fluctuate. A few bird-animals screeched by overhead, diving into the inlet. Rango turned to watch them. He curled his black lips in on his sharp teeth and puffed some air out his large round nostrils at the end of his snout. The training field shimmered with heat and was alive with bugs. A cannon report sounded down in the harbor.

"I'm sorry, Hab," said Rango. The hopper exhaled, then grunted. "I'm sorry I've had to deceive you this way. I like you, I respect you, I admire you, and under other circumstances we might have been true friends. Your priests teach you that honesty is the way, and in a place of plenty like Paras, it can *be* the way. We're taught something entirely different here. Our fathers tell us, our crèche-masters tell us, and finally our drillmasters tell us." Rango bared his teeth in a smile, but it was a wistful smile. "And do you know what they tell us, Hab? They tell us exactly the opposite of what your priests tell you. They tell us that the lie is the thing." The hopper grunted again. "The lie is the thing, Hab. A crude little maxim crafted in the crude and common language of the people. Deceit is your friend, they tell us. Subterfuge is your second skin. Dishonesty is the air you breathe." The new drillmaster picked a bug off his ear and ate it. "You live in the land of truth, Hab. I live in the land of deceit. When there's nothing to eat, you have to lie to survive."

"That's not true."

"There is no truth, Hab. Truth is an illusion. In Ortok, only fools aspire to the truth. And sometimes the truth is too hard to bear. Gashak couldn't bear the truth. Aychega couldn't bear the truth. Only I was strong enough to bear the truth. Only I was strong enough to believe in the Great Code, as your Esten called it. Only I was strong enough to see that the coming of the *Fetla* and the *Xeulliette* was more than just a coincidence." His eyes narrowed, and his slit pupils seemed to burn with an inner darkness. "Do you believe in providence, Hab?"

"I don't," said Hab. "It's too easy to blame everything on providence."

"*Look* at my land," said Rango. "There are no fish. There are no gourds or vines or centipedes. My land is buried under ash. I'm sick of famine and war. My land is dying. I want a better place. That's the higher truth I strive for, Hab, the higher truth Gashak didn't want to believe, the higher truth Aychega didn't want to believe. I told them you were a sign. I told them the Great Code was true. I told them you were proof that Takasa exists and that it's not just a legend."

"Takasa and Paras are one in the same?"

Rango twitched his head in the affirmative. "But neither of them wanted to believe me. They ridiculed my claims. They believed Ortok would come back. But I don't think it will this time. The eruption's been going on too long. By the time Ortok comes back, we'll all be dead. If I had a way to reach our moons and make our new world there, Hab, I would. But we will sail for Paras, and we shall conquer Paras, and we shall be the rulers of Paras. We will subjugate your people and make them our slaves, such as is prophesied in the Great Code. We will sail first in a fleet of twenty wooden expeditionary ships, crossing the ocean quickly in the light crafts. We will establish our beachhead on the Island of Maju." The mention of Maju felt like a blow to Hab. He wished he had never told Rango about Maju. "Then a fleet of a hundred metal—" He tried the Parassian word carefully. "—*barkentines* will invade the Estuary and bombard with cannonade your capital of Jauny. When Jauny is flattened we will invade. Our infantry will secure your coastal cities, then move inland along the River Necontreu." Another blow, the River Necontreu. "We will occupy your seat of royal power at Summerhouse, then flank left and right to secure the provinces of Berberton, Zairab, and Dagu. We will finally send a small amphibious force to the Island of Liars and wipe out any final resistance there." The hopper looked down at the globe he was holding, as if the whole world were already his. "I'm sorry, Hab. But there can't be two of us. One of us must be supreme, and I'm afraid that's going to be us. You will come as an emissary. Jara will be an emissary also. You will try to convince your countrymen that it is futile to resist. That would be the best way to do it, Hab. From what you tell me, you're woefully unprepared to fight. You hardly have any metal to make decent weapons from. On the other hand, I'm going to send five thousand battle-hardened troops into your country, regulars who have done nothing but practice the arts of war since they were boys, regulars who have seen campaign after campaign in my war-torn Ortok. Resistance is futile. It's better that you all surrender immediately. More of you will survive that way."

Part Three

WAR

CHAPTER TWENTY-TWO

Ten days later six black hopper regulars, under the new regime of Rango the drillmaster, moved Hab, cage and all, onto a rail cart and braked their way down a series of switchbacks to the harbor at the foot of the bluff. Jara was sitting in her own cage on the shore of the inlet. As a crane lifted Hab and his cage off the rail cart and swung him toward the ground, Jara got up from her crouched position, gripped the metal bars, and stared at Hab with blank disbelieving eyes.

Rango stood beside six cannons on the pier. The drillmaster hopped over, covering the thirty-foot distance in one graceful bound. As Hab got closer to Jara, he saw that she was trembling, and that tears stood in her eyes. He hadn't seen her in several months. She looked as bereft of human company as he. She was a lot thinner but otherwise seemed well. She wore a scrap of hopper hide, barely enough to cover her. He was so glad to see her, his legs felt weak. He sank to the floor of his cage.

"Hab?" she said.

How strange to hear another human voice after all this time. Was the human voice really so musical? So sweet? Or had he grown too used to the sound of harsh hopper voices all the time?

"They've made you a tunic of hopper hide," he said. He was so glad to see her, he could think of nothing else to say.

The regulars placed his cage right next to Jara's, metal touching metal. Hab struggled to his feet and went to Jara. He touched her, put his hands on her shoulders, pressed his face to the bars, kissed her, wanted to wrap his arms around her but the bars were too narrow and he couldn't thrust much more than half his forearm through. Jara's arms, more slender, slipped right through, and she put them around his waist. Here it was again, that energy whenever they touched each other, like together they created a force that was greater than themselves, something that was brilliant and sublime, and so wild and unpredictable it was hard to control. Despite the hopper preparations for war all around them, the sexual tension was immediate, magnified through a love that was desperate, and as they kissed, the taste of Jara's lips was as sweet to Hab as the sweetest apple along the Embankment Road back home.

"They said you were in Ketingo," he said.

"I was," she said.

Rango stepped forward, peered at them curiously. "You . . . you love each other?" he said. The drillmaster was still unfamiliar with the idea of human love. The sudden inclusion of Abani into the conversation was like a club striking a skull. Neither of them answered. They were both too startled by his inquiry. Rango, sensitive to this, backed away, showing respect no other hopper ever showed them. "I'm glad you . . . you love each other," he said. "I wish we *sikingo-mango* could love each other the way you humans do." He contemplated the humans for several seconds, then grunted. "You'll have a few days to share before we ship out. If you do all that is asked of you, I'll make sure you're reunited when we reach the Golden Land."

Coercion, thought Hab. Sly and gentle, but unmistakable coercion. No wonder Rango was drillmaster.

"You mean we're not going in the same ship?" asked Hab.

"You'll be going with the expeditionary force, Hab," he said. "Jara will follow with the main force."

The hopper hopped away.

𓏤𓏤𓏤

During the next hour Hab and Jara got to know one another again.

"He's lied to us all along," said Jara. "War was the last thing I suspected."

"Did he show you the globe?" he asked.

She nodded, then looked at the train. "I thought my brother would be with you."

Hab glanced out at the Mouth, where blinding tropical sunlight reflected off the water. "I'm afraid your brother's dead, Jara," he said.

Hab told her about Esten's death. Her eyes again clouded with tears. The man she had tried so hard to impress all her life was gone. "Why did Rango make him suffer like that?" she asked, bewildered. "Why did he starve my brother to death?"

Hab shook his head. He looked at Rango, who was now back beside his six cannons supervising some regulars as they loaded them onto a barge. "I wish I knew," he said.

⟨⟨⟨

During the next few days Hab sat as close as he could to Jara and watched the battle-fleet prepare. Sat close, even though the annoying metal bars were always in the way. There was no possibility of lovemaking. Despite this frustration, it was enough for Hab to be near her. Just to hear her talk, to have a conversation with her, was enough for him.

Rango separated them on the morning of the fourth day. As they hoisted Jara away from him, Hab looked up at her. His lungs felt empty. He couldn't breathe. He felt as if he were being exsanguinated. The cargo crane lifted her out over the water to a waiting barge. She looked paralyzed with misery. The crane lowered her onto the barge, which six hoppers then rafted out into the inlet with long poles. Hab watched the barge grow smaller and smaller as it advanced out into the Mouth. It rounded one of the wooden ships, and Jara gave Hab a final piteous wave. Then she was lost from view.

ᕬᕬᕬ

His turn came an hour later. Two *sikingo-mango* regulars secured grappling hooks to the overhead crossbars of his cage. Two others worked the crank-handles of the crane. He rose steadily into the air. From up here, thirty feet above the harbor, he saw skids of every kind of materiel needed for the effective waging of war: weapons, stacks of dried *bamkali-kalango* meat, barrels of *hari-bumuku* tar refined into high-grade explosives. Battleships and frigates crowded the inlet. He saw Rango farther down the pier talking to some regulars, giving them directions. They were trying to load a particularly heavy cannon onto a special barge. The crane swung Hab out toward his own barge. The overhead bars of his cage creaked ominously. He looked up at them nervously and saw that the rusted metal support was starting to bend. Was it going to break? The cage quivered. A few rivets popped loose.

"Ho, there!" he called. "The cage is going to break!"

The hoppers looked up, but they were too late. The top crossbar broke at one end, the grappling hooks slid upward toward the break, made a loud twanging sound as they slid off the end, and the cage plummeted toward the sandy lip of beach. The cage struck the ground. Hab fell heavily against his shoulder. The cage exploded around him, the bars falling outward like a big iron flower. The roof fell on top of him. He looked up, dazed. He got up.

Before he could take even a single step, the hoppers attacked him, thinking he was trying to escape. One clubbed him. He raised his hand, trying to protect himself, but the hopper clubbed him again. Another hopper kicked him with the sole of his massive foot. The air rushed out of Hab's lungs. He tumbled halfway into the water. He clutched for air, but it was as if his lungs were frozen. Another hopper bounded into the water and poked him with a slave prod. The hopper lifted the slave prod high, was about to smash Hab over the head with it, when Rango, leaping all the way over from the pier, landed right on top of the offending *sikingo-mango* regular.

"*Buto!*" bellowed the hopper drillmaster. "*Buto yethelu pambazo diko dika diki, sikingo-mango!*" He kicked the stricken hopper out of the way and waded with awkward steps into the shallows. "What happened?" he asked Hab. "Why did you provoke them?"

"I didn't provoke them!" said Hab. "My cage broke!"

The drillmaster glared at his miscreant troops. "What do you think you're doing?" he bellowed. "You've got to be careful with this creature. It's delicate. It's like a jellyfish. You can't go poking it. You'll break it. And it's important we keep it in one piece. It speaks our language. It's going to help us defeat our enemies in Takasa. If I ever see any of you ever harm it again—and that goes for this whole army—I'll personally cut off your heads and wear them on my belt."

The hoppers grunted the six or seven pronunciations of *mu*, then sullenly went about gathering up the broken cage. Rango helped Hab to his feet.

"Are you hurt?" asked the drillmaster.

Hab felt sullen. "You call me an *it*," he said. "I'm not an *it*."

Rango sucked at his lips, a hopper expression of exasperation. "I know, Hab," he said. "But look who we're dealing with? They all think you're an animal, a strange little pet who knows how to mimic our words. They're ignorant, Hab. They're barbarians. You have to talk to them so they'll understand."

ᏃᏃᏃ

He rode aboard a timber barkentine called the *Vuna*. She was eighty feet long, refitted with three masts, displaced about twenty tons, and rode so high in the water she nearly skimmed the surface. She was fast, far faster than any Parassian ship, but was made of such soft flimsy wood she creaked even in the gentle swell of the inlet.

The expeditionary fleet was comprised of forty such ships. They cleaved the water quickly northward.

Hab was fitted with a metal collar and chained to the mainmast; as terrible as it sounded, it was better than being in a cage. The chain was twenty feet long, and he was able to wander more freely. He stood at the rail watching the parched bank of the Mouth slide by.

"Will the iron ships follow directly?" he asked Rango.

"No," said the drillmaster. "They leave in ten days. Depending on the wind, they'll reach Paras ten to twenty days after us. They're not as fast as these sprightly wooden ships, Hab, but they still make good time."

"So there'll be up to twenty days between the first and second waves."

Rango's eyes narrowed. "Your probes are suspicious, Hab."

"I intend nothing, Rango," he replied. "I'm anxious to see Jara again, that's all."

They watched the inlet slide by in silence for a while. Then Hab said, "You've given your soldiers new metal armor."

Rango twitched his head affirmatively. "The leather breastplates wear out after time," he said. "We're not going to have any *bamkali-kalango* to make new ones with. We had to give them durable armor."

The new armor might be more durable, but it would sink like a stone once these ships broke apart in the tides.

"Why aren't you wearing metal armor?" asked Hab.

"Because I don't like it." Rango gestured disconsolately at his troops. "Look at them. Have you ever seen such bombast and vanity? Look at the way they prance around in their new armor." The new armor would sink like a stone, but the hoppers were so enamored with it they showed no signs of taking it off. "If I'd realized something so frivolous would make them so happy, I'd have had Gashak make it for them years ago."

They made seven knots all day and night. Hab was worried about Jara. And of course he was desperately concerned about the fate of Paras. But what he felt bad about was what he had done to these hoppers. They were all going to die. These ships would be like flotsam against the true moon-tides. And these hoppers, in their metal armor, were like the walking dead, marked for Oeil even as they strutted about in what for them passed as ostentatious finery. He could have stopped it with a word. *Butu.* But the word didn't come. He could have told them to take off their armor so they could swim, but he didn't. He let them trust to what they perceived as the infallible seaworthiness of their war vessels. The hoppers would sink. But he might float. He didn't expect to survive. But he was chained to the mainmast, locked to what was virtually the largest life preserver on the whole ship. He reached up and rubbed the amulet of Disseaule, hoping that when the desperate time came, the hunting goddess would see him safely through.

The next day the fields and pastures on the banks of Shindano-shtaka-shudo went from brown to green. Here it was, his immense good deed. Grass. Cultivated and high. Heavy with seedlings. Thousands of acres of it. Enough to make a million loaves of bread. With water, this particular grain grew quickly. Two months was all it took. They could have ten crops a year if they wanted to. Here it was, his gift to the lords of Ortok, organized agriculture, the gift that would feed their armies and make them strong against the fussy and effeminate lords of Paras. Yet what was this? He looked over the bow of the ship. What strange metal city was this, and why did it look so familiar?

"Do you recognize the spot?" asked Rango. "We were here a number of months ago. This terrain . . . it's the terrain you marked out as terrain similar to Jauny's. We've made a mock-up of Jauny. Remember that day you drew a map of Jauny for me? I had you mark all the streets, all the districts, had you describe in detail the buildings we'd encounter, their size, shape, and location. See over there? That's Triser." Yes, Hab saw it, up on the hill, even recognized some of the more famous brothels. "And over there, that large metal construct? That's Gorolet, Parprouch's palace. There's the Lagaine and that's Pendagal, where your priests reside. That's the Liars' Prison down by the waterfront, and over there is the Escrolage, your banking district."

The buildings were hollow iron shells, mostly black but with great ochre rust splotches all over them. It was like a nightmare version of Jauny, bleak, deserted, with the roads no more than ruts in the dirt, no fountains, gardens, or cafes, no blossoming apple trees lining the Embankment Road, not a hint of Jauny's predominantly tawny color, no flags or banners, no wagons or carriages, no chevuls, nothing but a dark and silent replica.

"Some of the buildings have been destroyed," Hab remarked.

"Target practice," Rango said simply. "When the second wave passes here in ten days, they'll flatten it completely. We train for war the same way you train for honesty, Hab—with complete and utter thoroughness."

ᏣᏣᏣ

The wooden ships of the expeditionary force passed into the dreaded dark water on the night of their tenth day out. Here, the thousand-mile basalt collar of hardened underwater lava floes terminated. Here, at least for the hoppers, the end of the world began.

"You've changed course," Hab said to Rango, surprised.

"We'll ply the equatorial route as opposed to the polar route, Hab," said Rango. "Our mariners have considered carefully your own trek across the frozen seas. The equatorial route might be longer, but we won't be plagued with ice walls. And the wind will be at our backs for much of the way. At least until we reach your Laisse Winds."

The tides began to surge an hour later. Hab looked up at the moons. They were still five days away from their eclipse, but now that the fleet had ventured beyond the subsurface breakwater of basalt, the tides had depth to build, to pull up from the bottom and form into massive walls of trillions of gallons of saltwater. Hab heard nervous grumbling from the crew.

"Hab," said Rango, "what of these tides?" The small hopper gazed out at the twenty-foot swells, the moonlight glowing purple against the scar on his forehead. "Is this usual for the high seas? Observe the way they roll toward us in even walls, each one a little higher than the next? Listen to the way the ship creaks."

"She's a fine ship, Rango," said Hab.

Evasion, Rule 20 of the Formulary.

"But what of these tides, Hab?"

"These are but the natural fluctuations of the sea, Rango, such as all sailors know."

The next night, the tides were forty feet high.

"Hab, the crew is getting restless," said Rango. "Why didn't you tell me about these tides? Look how the *Vuna* climbs and dips."

Hab contemplated the ship. If it weren't for the massively strong metal spikes holding the *Vuna* together, he feared the ship would have already encountered trouble. Spikes like these they simply didn't have in Paras.

"These are the tides, Rango," he repeated.

"Will they get any bigger?"

Hab looked up at the moons, still four days apart. "I doubt it," he said. Hab felt as if he were being turned inside out.

"Of course we know the tides," said Rango, as if offended that Hab should assume otherwise. "But the tides we know are four and five feet high and ripple against the beaches and coves as harmlessly as the moons spill their light over the slopes of Kimbia-kipugia. But never have any of our mariners seen tides like these. We know the tides as an effect of the natural respirations of Ortok, a thing alive, a thing that needs to breathe. You see it plainly in the Mouth of the Monster, the inhalations in the evening, the exhalations at dawn, the Monster breathing, softly and evenly and never with such a flood as this."

Hab cocked a brow. "Was this what you meant when you said the sea buckled?"

ꞁꞁꞁ

On the night of the eclipse, storm clouds stalked the convoy and blotted out the last light of day like an ink spill. Sky and water were gray, and the thin slice of clear air between the two was heavy, thick, and wet. Hab felt resigned. He sat with his back against the mainmast. He was glad Jara was sailing with the metal fleet. The metal fleet stood a much better chance of getting through. Conversely, his own chances were slim. Without question, all these flimsy ships would sink in the tides. First he had to survive the shipwreck, then survive as a castaway, then somehow construct a raft out of the wreckage and find his way back to Paras to warn everybody that the second wave was coming— he was sure most of the metal ships would get through.

His task seemed impossible. If it weren't for his rigorous training at Pieshe—castaway instruction included a month alone in the Sea of Maju—he might have given up. But he had survived his month in the Sea of Maju. Not only that, he had sailed to the great tides by himself when he'd been eighteen years old. That at least gave him a little hope. What gave him the most hope was the thought of seeing Jara again.

As he sat looking up at the boiling gray sky, feeling the first thick warm drops splash his face, the *Vuna* began to rock and heave as the wind freshened. Foot and Lag rose somewhere behind those storm clouds, building the tides a gallon at a time in their age-old cycle. The wind grew stronger and stronger, and hoppers hopped all over the masts and yards reefing and furling sails.

High overhead the lookout cried: *"Jivuno jipusha! Jivuno jipusha!"*

The first moon-tide had been sighted. Rango hopped all the way from the poop deck and landed beside him. Hab continued to sit with his back against the mainmast as the boat rocked in the storm. Over the storm Hab heard the deadly ripple of the moon-tides.

Hab could have turned and looked at the oncoming tide, but instead he looked at Rango. He'd never seen fear in a hopper face before, but he saw it now. Rango's lips stretched up over his snout, and great creases of scales furrowed his forehead. He looked for all the world like a gargoyle, his yellow teeth protruding like spikes from his black gums, his neck muscles bulging, his long thin black tongue flickering spasmodically from his mouth. His legs were bent at the knee, and he was poised on the balls of his feet. His right hand had gone instinctively to the hilt of his sword, and the characteristic charcoal smell that came from all black hoppers was stronger than ever. The drillmaster turned to him. Rango's red eyes glowed like hot metal.

"You lied to me!" he said.

Hab regarded the hopper calmly. "You never told me why you killed Esten," he said.

The air seemed to vibrate between them. Despite the noise and confusion of *sikingo-mango* sailors hopping madly all around them, preparing for the onslaught, Hab and Rango were wrapped in their own little bubble of preternatural stillness, seeming to understand each other for the first time.

"As a way of getting you to tell the truth, Hab," said Rango. "Why else?"

At that moment, the *Vuna* lurched violently upward. Hab looked up, straight up, his sight aligned directly with the mainmast, and saw a hundred-foot wall of water towering directly above them. The wind tattered the peak of the wall into tendrils of mist. The *Vuna* climbed the wall. The mainmast shifted. Hab pressed his feet hard against the deck to stop from sliding. Hoppers everywhere clung to the nearest available support. The rippling of the tide sounded like the gnashing of teeth. Hab stood up and clung to the mainmast.

"I'm sorry, Rango," he said. "I've never seen them this bad."

Which was the truth. He looked out over the railing where he saw the ships of the expeditionary force floundering on the slope of the first massive tide, their hulls dark shadows in the flood, their sails flapping like wayward ghosts. Storm lanterns—pots of tar hanging on stanchions—flickered in the wind.

Even as he watched, three ships tumbled sideways and disappeared beneath the foam. The *Vuna* climbed higher, reached the top of the tide, and slid down the other side. The second tide rushed toward them quickly, like a judgment, right behind the first, a gray frothy wall of water, stippled by rain and whipped by the wind. The *Vuna* hit the second tide with a shudder. Hab heard a crack below, part of the keel caving in. The bow tilted upward. The ship climbed steeply. The rain intensified, the wind grew stronger, and in the distance Hab saw a water funnel rise out of the water like a black snake. A slim tear in the clouds appeared, revealing a glimpse of Foot and Lag, the orange and silver moons overlapping in their murderous embrace. The sea pitched crazily, gripped the *Vuna* like a child's toy, and shook it from side to side.

Hab looked up. The crest of the second tide curled above him, forming a perfect tube. The swamp of the massive tide was upon them.

"Hang on to something!" he shouted to Rango. "She's going to go!"

The tide crashed down on the deck of the *Vuna* like a fist. The ship lurched sideways as the water rushed over her in a ten-foot flood. The foremast broke. Hab caught one last glimpse of the sails collapsing; then the water was on top of him. He clung to the mainmast fiercely, but the water was simply too strong for him. The surge pried him from the softwood spar the way a shipyard worker pries mussels from the hull of a trawler. He floated free of the mainmast. He was caught short by the length of his chain, his neck yanked fiercely. His metal collar dug into his windpipe. He couldn't breathe. They might as well hang him. He thought the force of the water would break his neck. But then the current eased, the water drained away through the scuppers, and the ship, miraculously righting itself, plowed through the tide and came through the other side.

Hab struggled to his feet, looked around, and saw that many of the crew had been washed overboard. The mizzenmast had been snapped a quarter of the way up and now hung over the taffrail, its ratlines and shrouds tangled in the rudder. Rango lay next to the bulwark, his hand gripping a scupper.

"You're going to have to clear those shrouds from the rudder if you want steerage!" he called to Rango. His seaman's instinct took over. "You'll have to cut those ratlines too." He steadied himself against the mainmast as the boat heaved. "Are there any crew below?"

"No," said Rango. "The fools stayed on deck."

"Aye, they mistake prudence for cowardice. And the deck not strung with lines." Hab looked toward the forecastle. "And no helmsman either?"

"I saw him sink like an anvil."

"You better take it yourself then, Rango," shouted Hab. "Get me out of this chain, and I'll see if I can untangle the rudder."

"Why didn't you tell us, Hab?" The hopper roared the words. "Hundreds are going to drown!"

The hopper struggled to his feet. The third tide, still a mile off, rolled steadily toward them. "Are you going to get me out of this chain or not?" asked Hab. "The tide is almost here! I can help you save this ship!"

The drillmaster puffed a few times, forcing himself to get his anger under control, then jumped over to the mainmast. He looked at Hab's forehead. "You're bleeding," he said.

Hab touched his brow. He had a huge gash there. He pulled his hand away. It was covered with blood. A lot of blood. A severe injury, but he couldn't even feel it. Rango lifted the chain to his mouth and bit it in two.

"There!" he said. "You're free, human! Enjoy the few moments you have left!"

Hab grabbed Rango by his breastplate and shook him. "Man the helm, *sikingo-mango!*" he commanded. "Do as I say and we'll survive this! Keep her dead ahead! The winds will blow her to port, so correct the helm three spokes to the starboard side! Be steady, be true, and hold firm! I'll go aft and see if I can untangle the shrouds and ratlines from the rudder."

Hab climbed to the stern as the ship slid bow-first down the backside of the second tide. Rango hopped to the helm. Hab looked over the back of the ship. The mizzenmast hung over the taffrail; its rigging had jammed and looped itself between the brace and the rudder, locking the rudder in the port position.

"She's not moving!" cried Rango over the wail of the wind.

Hab realized manning the helm was pointless until they cleared this mess away. "Come help me with these shrouds!" he cried. "It's the only way we'll get some steerage!"

In one bound, Rango stood beside him. The drillmaster took the shrouds in his clawed hands and ripped them apart as easily as thread. He tore apart the sails like paper. Then he yanked on the ratlines.

"I'm not on the right angle!" he called. "That tackle has to be pushed down. Once the ropes are out of that cutaway, they'll come free."

The hopper leaped over the taffrail and, hanging onto it with one hand, dangled from the stern of the boat and kicked at the jammed ropes, trying to push them down with his feet. But time was against him. The third tide crashed over them in a monstrous deluge, sweeping across the deck in an onslaught of foam, spray, and seawater. Hab got to his knees, hooped his right arm around the nearest scupper while he offered his left to the dangling Rango.

"Hang on!" he cried. "The flood's upon us!"

The hopper latched onto Hab's arm just as the water slammed into the taffrail. The rail broke away like a twig in a gale. The surge of the water knocked Hab flat to his chest. He was lucky enough to get his foot hooked into another scupper. He looked down at Rango as the water bubbled and cascaded around them. A momentary flash of lightning lit up the drillmaster's face, and on it Hab saw unmistakable sadness, a keen regret forming itself into the folds and lines of his scales.

"I can't hang on!" cried Hab.

Rango's head twitched in the affirmative, accepting death and forgiving Hab with the same slight gesture. "I almost believed you,

Hab," he said over the roar of the water. "I almost trusted you." As if to trust, just for once, another living intelligent being was the zenith and pinnacle of all the hopper's goals and aspirations. Then the water surged even harder, Hab lost his grip, and the hopper was washed away into the sea.

CHAPTER TWENTY-THREE

The water rose higher and higher around the *Vuna*. Hab still clung to the scupper, flat on his stomach. In seconds, he was under twenty feet of water. He held his breath. He clutched the scupper with all his might, hoping the bulwark wouldn't rip free of the deck, his ears ringing in the sudden underwater silence. The bow of the ship lifted, the angle of the deck sharpened, and Hab was sure she was going to capsize, but she suddenly surged. The angle of the deck abruptly changed. The stern leaped out of the water, now became the highest part of the ship. She broke through the tide, lunging through its backside. As the flood drained from the deck, Hab, still clutching the scupper, lifted his head and looked around.

The *Vuna*'s deck was now wiped bare, the forecastle head ripped clean away, no masts, no fittings, no tackle, no rails—a flat wedge-shaped expanse of soaking wood. The ship was no more than hull now. He looked over the stern and saw that the rudder was badly cracked, virtually useless. With no steerage the *Vuna* was bound to capsize in the next tide. He got to his feet and looked desperately around the deck for the broken mainmast, thinking he could rig a temporary rudder by bracing it through a scupper. But the mainmast was nowhere to be seen.

The fourth tide, a wall of water higher than any of the others, surged straight for him, the tallest tide he had ever seen. He ran for the midships hatch. No stairs. Hoppers hopped. And he would just have to do it the hopper way. He jumped into the hold.

Three lamps still burned in wall mounts. He looked around, desperate to find something that might float, or provide him with a rudimentary raft. He worked his way to the stern, where he saw a great weapons rack hanging on the wall, a gridwork of wood held together by a thick frame—not the best substitute for a raft, but he didn't have time to find anything else. He had to get away from the ship. The ship was doomed.

He pitched the weaponry to the floor while the ship heaved and bobbed. The wind howled fiercely all around the *Vuna*. He lifted a battle-axe, chopped the rack away from its mounts, and yanked it from the wall. As the rack fell to the floor with a bang, Hab heard a grunt behind him. He swung round. A hopper regular stood there.

"What are you doing?" the regular asked.

Hab didn't hesitate. "*Yathelu pambazo!*" he cried, and swung the battle-axe at the regular's neck.

The blade, supersharp, sliced right through the hopper's neck. The *sikingo-mango*'s head toppled to the ground. The body stood there for a few seconds, the blood pumping from its neck, then collapsed on its side, twitched a few times, and grew still.

Hab dropped the axe and ran to the lazarette, where the ship's stores were kept, at the back of the ship. He pulled open the door and quickly found some rope. He put the coil of rope over his neck, ran back to the weapons rack, lifted a sword, slid it through his belt, then dragged the weapons rack to the forward hatch. Rain pelted through the hatch and, looking up, he again saw lightning, sickly and green, flash in the low black clouds. He hoisted the rack lengthwise into an upright position, leaned the top against the hatch frame, then, in lieu of what on a human ship would be a companionway, climbed the gridwork like a ladder.

The tide was now no more than a hundred yards away, towering above the ship, fearful to behold, sucking the seawater up from the bottom with such force that even the pressure in the air seemed to change with its deadly advance. Hab yanked the weapons rack out of the hold, dragged it to the edge of the ship, threw it into the water, and jumped. He latched onto the end of it. He gave his legs a good scissors kick, swimming with his usual economical precision, and pushed the weapons rack away from the ship. He kicked and kicked. He felt the first rise of the water. He dragged himself onto the weapons rack, pulled the coil of rope from his shoulder, and lashed his body to the gridwork of wood as quickly as he could. He hooked his feet under the gridwork, then gripped the side braces with his hands. The tide pulled him up higher and higher. Far below he saw the *Vuna* listing badly to starboard in the swell. She turned on her side, rolled, and capsized. She sank, an insignificant bit of wood, into the tremendous breach of the ocean.

ᶜᶜᶜ

The next morning, with the tides over, wreckage and debris floated all around him. The wind had died, but the rain was still coming down steadily, splashing against the calm surface of the sea like a million silver coins. The weapons rack rode admirably high on the water. The sky was gray, and despite the rain, the air was oppressively hot. He undid the rope and rose on shaky legs. After battling the tides last night, he was exhausted. He looked for hopper corpses but saw none. If he thought at all about his desperate circumstances—how he was thousands of miles from the nearest land, how he had no water, no food, how he was lost and adrift in uncharted waters—it was only briefly to take stock, and after taking stock, to decide what had to be done. He was a seaman. He was a problem solver. He lived and breathed the sea. He knew how to survive out here. He was a natural. He knew what to do. He had to search this wreckage to find things he could use. But first he had to determine if there were any living hoppers around.

"A full stomach to you!" he cried. No answer. He called the greeting to an empty sea. "A full stomach to you!" he cried again. But he heard nothing except the steady whisper of the rain as it fell into the steamy water.

He got down on his knees and paddled with his hands. He gathered some planks from the scattered wreckage and placed them on top of the weapons rack so that his knees would have a flat place to rest. One of the planks he used as a paddle.

A piece of hopper-hide sailcloth floated by. He snagged the end of it with his makeshift paddle and hauled it aboard. The sea was green and dotted with islands of foam. Seaweed floated in the undulating swell. He pulled some onto the raft. If worse came to worst he would eat it.

The rain continued hard all morning. With part of the sailcloth he made pockets in the exposed gridwork. The tarred hide made several watertight catch basins, and with the rain coming down hard, he soon had a supply of freshwater. With the rest of the tar-treated hopper hide he made a crude sail. Using his sword, he fashioned one of his planks into a serviceable rudder, and a small mast, and fastened the sail to the mast. With steerage and sail, he now searched the wreckage more quickly, taking advantage of the light puffs of wind whenever they occurred. He didn't think about direction. His course was dictated simply by the piles of junk floating in the water.

Late in the day, he found a chest floating in the water. He headed for the chest and hauled it on board. The rain had stopped and the clouds were burning off, and here and there orange spears of sunlight pierced through. He pried his sword under the latches and broke them open. He found seedloaves inside, thirty in all, each encased in its own coating of dried tar. He chipped the tar away, glad to see that it fell from the loaf cleanly, and bit into the bread. Bland, tasteless, and hard, but it would at least sustain him.

The tides came again the next night, but they weren't as bad. He lashed all his possessions to the raft with his rope. He rigged his sail so he could raise it or drop it with one hand, while with his other he was able to reach the rudder. He navigated the tides as best he could. A fresh breeze blew from the southeast while the flood came from the northwest, and the two forces suspended him in the same square mile of sea for most of the night.

Then the ebb came. Both tides and winds were now with him, and the small makeshift craft made about five knots all night so that by the time dawn came, he reckoned on at least fifty miles; fifty miles closer to Paras—not much, but at least it was a start.

He spent the next ten nights in a similar fashion. Each night the tides grew less and less. These were what the sailors in Jondonq called the quadrature tides, those weak tides teased from the sea during the farthest opposition of the moons. He didn't think about how far he had to go, or how Paras could be as much as fifteen thousand miles away. He simply concentrated on observing the sea around him, hoping to find a current or stream that might carry him toward his goal, the bountiful and peaceful Golden Land, charting distance traveled by taking note of the stars at night and by measuring the angle of the sun in the morning.

Each night the blue star Jara rose a little farther to the south. Each night its trajectory in those latitudes described a smaller and smaller arc on the horizon. Some days, he saw volcanic ash drifting high in the sky; other days he saw none. He spent hours each night contemplating Jara, wondering about her, knowing she was just a sun, but perhaps a sun with planets around her. He also thought of the star's namesake, Esten's sister, Jara Pepteri, and prayed often to Ouvant to give her a safe passage. Each morning, he scanned the southern horizon for the fleet of metal ships, but never saw anything but the flat unbroken surface of the sea.

$$\mathscr{S}\mathscr{S}\mathscr{S}$$

Twenty-three days after the destruction of the expeditionary fleet, Hab ran out of water. The sun beat down mercilessly, and the temperature was so hot the sea steamed.

At midday, with the sun directly overhead, he took down his sail and hid underneath it. He felt weak. He peered out from under the sail at the flat blue sea. His bones ached. He needed fruit, he knew that.

But all he had was seedbread. He was sweating. He rubbed his hand over his perspiring forehead and licked the sweat from his palm.

Though he was hot, he shivered, and felt feverish. He tried to stop shivering, but he shook and shook. He wasn't afraid of the sea, but he was afraid of this shaking. This fear was small, nothing he couldn't endure, yet it reverberated inside him persistently, and after a while seemed to open a clear and vivid window into greater fears. He was a single man on a scrap of wood in the middle of the ocean, and nobody knew where he was. In Paras it was different. If a ship didn't return to port the king's cutters went looking for it. But he knew no one was looking for him. He let his head rest against the planks. Twenty-three days at sea, six thousand miles from Ortok, and still another nine to Paras. He was out of water, and half his seedloaves were gone. Now he was shaking. Now he had a fever. The tides were growing bigger again. Would he have the strength to navigate the next moon-tides?

That night, as the sun set, he saw rain clouds on the horizon. Rain slanted like gray film from their flat undersides, and their tops billowed into wondrous cumulus castles. Rain fell over there, five miles away, but none fell here, where the sun's reflections rippled like a streak of fire over the sea. Tears of frustration welled in Hab's eyes. He hoisted sail, but the wind was against him, so he tacked, approached the rain at maybe three knots in a zigzag pattern. He sailed toward the rain clouds for nearly an hour. He was just about there, no more than a half mile off, when the slanting film of precipitation stopped. He was left panting and parched, with nothing to quench his terrible thirst.

The tides came that night. The violent surge of saltwater, by the time it reached its predawn ebb, left him thirstier and more exhausted than ever. His hair and beard were caked with salt. Salt smears ringed his limbs. His lips and throat were so swollen from the high concentration of salt in these waters that he could hardly touch them. He was hungry, but his mouth was so dry he couldn't moisten the seed-bread sufficiently enough to swallow it. The sun rose above the eastern edge of the ocean, and in his fever he had the delirious conviction that the sun was alive, not just a star around which his world circled, but a cruel and evil entity, an intelligent phenomenon with the singular intention of broiling every drop of moisture out of his body, its heat so strong, even this early in the day, that he didn't know how he was going to survive it.

At the hottest part of the day, when the sun was directly overhead, he lowered the sail and lashed it over the deck of his raft. He took some rope and his sword, jumped into the ocean, and swam under the weapons rack. Holding his breath, he hacked away some of the grid-work, enough to fit his head through. The rack was of double-frame construction, with twelve inches between upper and lower frames. This allowed for a sun-protected breathing space. It took some doing, but he finally managed to fashion an underwater hammock from his rope. He slid into his hammock, pushed his head through the hole he'd made in the gridwork, and in this way stayed submerged for the whole day, the back of his head resting against a cross-support between the frames while his body hung submerged under the raft in the hammock of ropes. He fell asleep. He stayed cool.

ᘐᘐᘐ

He spent the next several days working his way northwestward in this way, sailing only at night to escape the fierce rays of the sun, sleeping in his underwater rope hammock during the day. On one or two occasions it rained and he was able to quench his thirst—enough to keep going.

The days piled up into a week, then into two weeks. Sometimes he felt clear-headed, but on other days he was delirious, the way Esten must have been when he was afflicted with the fish poison. When he was in this condition, time seemed to become disjointed to Hab, so that sometimes an hour seemed to last a day, while a day could blink by in an hour. He felt like he became a creature of darkness. He spent all night on the dark sea sailing. Sometimes he sailed through huge banks of mists miles wide, and he grew convinced in his delirium that he had sailed into a land of spirits, that any moment the ghosts of Chouc, Esten, Tiq, and all the others he had lost on Ortok would rise out of the ocean like an army of phantoms and point accusatory fingers at him. When the sun came up, he would slink under the raft, like a pill bug or earwig seeking shelter under a rock. He became nocturnal. And because of it, a darkness crept into his spirit. He had always considered himself a happy if taciturn man. Now he was witnessing a bleaker side of himself.

Was it depression? He tangled with the question for a whole day, because he knew depression was just a step away from despair, and despair but a hair's breadth away from hopelessness. So he fought it. Fought it as hard as he had ever fought anything. Yet it was difficult because he was so lonely. Still, he pressed on, day after day, fighting the moon-tides a second time and winning, thankful for the strong spikes that held the rack together, keeping track of his course by the stars, notching the days into the raft with the edge of his sword, stroking out the groups of five, watching thirty days turn into forty days, then forty into forty-five.

Once, just as he was getting ready to crawl beneath the raft for the day, the weapons rack nudged a dead bird-animal floating in the way. What absolute luck! His spirits revived instantly. What could it be doing way out here, when he hadn't seen a bird-animal since the wreck? Drifting. Maybe someday he would make a study of the currents in this part of the ocean. He butchered the bird and ate it raw. His strength returned, and the next evening he was able to sail with renewed vigor. He was convinced, if his charting of the stars was in any way accurate, that he must be halfway there by now. If only the sun weren't so hot. And if only his water weren't running out again.

ᔕᔕᔕ

When he woke up at sunset the next day, he heard a strange hissing sound all around him.

He opened his eyes. He stared at the planks above the gridwork on the upper frame. His muscles tensed. He knew the sound well. A percussive sputtering followed by a long hiss. And he knew that smell as well. He felt something brush against his leg. Bladder whales. But were these the small ones he hunted in Dagu, or were they the gargantuan ones the exploration fleet had found halfway to Ortok? He slipped free of his rope hammock and sank into the water. He gripped the edge of the weapons rack and climbed up onto his crude raft.

Red bladders, like giant balloons, each as big as a house, stretched as far as he could see. These were the big ones. The whales swam past him, heading northwest, moving quickly, making at least ten knots. He tried to calculate the season. He'd been gone at least eight months. So up in Paras, it was early spring. Which meant the whales were in migration. Here was a bit of fortune. Heading northwest, in the exact direction he had to go. Not only that, the whales always found gaps in the tides to swim through, the so-called whale tides. When they migrated they stayed surfaced for days.

He immediately hoisted sail. Maneuvering the rudder far to the right, he angled closer and closer to the pod. One of the whales lifted its head out of the water and glanced at him. Its eyes were so big his heart jumped. Why did they grow so big down here? The behemoth lowered his head back into the water and continued to swim. Hab sailed right into the stream of whales. One was coming straight for him. The trick was to have an even head-on collision so that he slid up the slope of the creature's forehead while at the same time hoping he didn't break his raft into pieces. He yanked the rudder from its brace and used it as a paddle to align the raft. The whale drew closer. A small ripple of water preceded it. The raft bobbed on this ripple. Hab saw the whale's nose slide underneath him, about a fathom below. The bladders came right at him. He dropped his paddle and dove for the deck. He clung to the edge of the gridwork. The bladders slammed into him. He lost his grip and slid off his rack onto the slippery back of the giant bladder whale. He dug his fingers into the whale's blubbery skin and steadied himself. When he was sure he wasn't going to slide into the water, he looked up.

The change of speed brought a cooling and refreshing rush of wind. He got to his feet and stood on the whale's back. He saw his weapons rack sliding off, dove for it, and at the last second grabbed it. He arched his toes, digging his toenails into the whale's skin, hoping to get some purchase. At the risk of angering the whale, he drew his sword and plunged it into the whale's back. The whale jerked its head once or twice, but otherwise didn't seem to notice. This was all blubber, at least three feet of it, and the sword was like a fly bite to the whale. To Hab, it provided the necessary purchase he needed. Using the sword as a handhold, he pulled himself up, all the while hanging onto the weapons rack.

He hauled the weapons rack onto the flatter part of the whale's back, up near the bladders. From there he took a last few steps and nestled himself and the raft between the whale's two huge pulmonary organs.

The pod's pace never slackened. Red bladders everywhere, geysers of spume shooting straight up into the air, massive tails slapping the surf. The pod rushed forward at ten knots, sometimes twelve. Hab tried counting the number of whales. Thousands.

The tides came that night, and, as was their instinct, the bladder whales found convenient gaps, sometimes racing north or south at twenty knots to make it around the tidal terminus. As the tides began to ebb, and the whales slowed their pace, Hab fell asleep. He slept on the whale's back for nearly an hour, until fresh rain woke him. He got up and checked his hopper-hide catch basins in the gridwork of the weapons rack. The rain fell from the sky in thick close drops, soothing the salt from his body. In the dusky light of dawn, he watched the rain fill his catch basins. They filled quickly. He lifted one out of the gridwork and drank. Cloudesley was said to produce some of the best vintages in all of Paras, but never had Hab tasted a vintage so sweet as this simple equatorial rainwater. The relief the water brought to his throat was nearly painful, stretched the dried-out surface of his raw esophagus, trickled into his stomach like a cool spring deluge, and raced to every pore of his body so that in seconds he felt them open with a cleansing sweat.

He rode whale-back through the tides again that night. He ate. Dry though the seed-bread might be, he was easily able to make a repast of it with his new supply of freshwater. His strength returned, and with it came hope. The tides were small. Lag had overtaken Foot again. He hadn't seen a living Ortokian bird-animal in weeks. He hadn't seen birds of any kind, except for the dead one he had found. The whales kept swimming through the early morning, never still, always moving.

At dawn, with the sky turning peach-colored to the east, he stood on the back of the whale and faced south. Was the metal fleet still out there, plowing the surf somewhere behind him? Or had the second wave already overtaken him? In all this big ocean they could have easily passed on one side or the other, even at a distance of ten miles, and he wouldn't have known the difference.

He traveled with the whales for the next fifteen days. He stayed alive on seedbread and freshwater, was even able to carve away a few pounds of blubber without the whale noticing much.

On the night of the fifteenth day he saw, far to the north, stars he recognized: Labre, Frande, Neiale—stars that were usually far to the south when viewed from Paras. In the south, Jara, the blue star, was gone. He had two seedloaves left.

Two nights later, the bladder whales finally dove. They dove all at once, as if they'd been spooked by something. Their bladders deflated, and they sank slowly and gracefully, leaving behind only a myriad of star-glimmering whirlpools and a mantle of bright foam. Hab clung to his weapons rack and climbed on top. How strange to again see the ocean deserted like this, no whales, no coast, no ships, just the endless panorama of green waves advancing toward him, and the empty birdless sky overhead.

The next day a stiff wind blew from the northwest. The smell of the wind was familiar. These were the Laisse Winds, originating in the heartland of Zairab, the ones that swept over Paras and combed the seas south of Maju to a distance of five thousand miles. He tacked into this wind as best he could. But it was hard work, and in order to sustain himself, he had to eat the last of his seedloaves.

Bad enough that he faced a headwind, but the next day the wind died altogether, and he was left with a slack sail. He resisted his water all day but finally got so thirsty that by evening he drank the rest of it in a few desperate swallows. Judging from the slant of the stars, he was five thousand miles from Paras, still far from the traditional fishing grounds. Five thousand miles was still a great distance. And with the Laisse Winds dead ahead he might as well be halfway back to Ortok.

The next three days drained him of his strength. He had to sail all day even to gain ten miles, and he was reluctant to sleep at night because he was bound to drift if he didn't keep his crude sail unfurled.

He was hungry. Fish now teemed in the water, and the water itself was nowhere near as salty as the water a thousand miles back. He saw many red-scaled southern pekra, but there was little he could do to catch any. He kneeled on the edge of his makeshift raft looking down at them. They schooled no more than a fathom below, a kaleidoscope of tails and fins. He jabbed the water with his sword, but the southern pekra was a smart fish, not like its lumbering northern cousin, and easily dodged his multiple thrusts. His mouth watered at the sight of them. He took down the sail and tried to use it as a net, but the southern pekra were sharp-sighted as well, and swam around it. Then their numbers dwindled. Hundreds became one or two, then none at all. Hab gave up trying and struggled to get used to his painfully empty stomach.

Two days later, the wind shifted, about-faced, blew from the southwest. He made five knots, and the sailing was easier, even though the swell was four to five feet, a constant rise and dip of aquamarine whitecaps, a decent following sea if it hadn't been for the constant spill over the back of his raft.

His thirst began to bother him again. Lack of food made him weak and faint. Still, the favorable winds and following sea pushed him forward. He braced the rudder a few degrees to port, made fast the sail, and in this way was at last able to lie down and let the small raft ply these seas by herself.

As tired as he was, Hab couldn't get to sleep. He suffered from sailor's fatigue, a nervous restlessness, and an unaccountable apprehension. He kept lifting his head and looking to the south. He was afraid that the great metal war fleet of the *sikingo-mango* would be visible on the horizon. He thought it ironic. He had promised Parprouch mountains of metal, and here they were, mountains of metal, coming the monarch's way.

The sun wasn't as hot, now shone indirectly from a more southerly direction. Spring in Jondonq. He pictured the Estuary with all the apple trees in full blossom. Then he pictured hopper warships at anchor in the Estuary, rust-pocked monsters with giant sails made out of skin. Then the quayside, fringed by all the color and frivolity of the Parassian spring: women promenading along the boardwalk in the latest fashions; lovers paddling in rowboats on the flat and gentle waters of Ourrice Harbor; gentlemen in riding breeches and codpieces, with feathers in their hats, trotting on their finest mounts down the Embankment Road. Then the warships again. What a contrast. What starkness. He felt guilty. His intentions had been pure—to discover a new world. But hadn't this new world really turned out to be the end of the world?

He must have dozed, because when he woke up the sky was tangerine-colored. A few wispy pink cirrus clouds floated high overhead, and there was nothing but a fingernail of sun left above the horizon. A bird was perched on the top of his small mast. A nuiyau bird. His heart lifted. Here was a familiar friend indeed: the gold crest feathers, the black mask, the brown wings, the white breast feathers, and the carrot-orange beak.

"Ho, there, nuiyau," said Hab. "Are you far from home?" The bird twitched its head, curious about the croaking dry voice that came from Hab's throat. "Do you hail from Alquay?" Hab realized he was talking to a bird, something he had never done before, but he'd been over sixty days at sea, and was desperately lonely, and had to talk, especially to an old friend like the nuiyau bird. "Why don't you fly south and see if you can spot the hopper armada?"

But the bird spread its wings and flew north instead.

The next morning he was awakened by a splash not sixty yards off. He sat up. A lone bladder whale floated on the surface. Not a giant one. A Parassian one. What was it doing way out here by itself? The speckling on its back indicated a bull; bulls swam in gangs of five or six; it was unusual to find a single bull so far south with no other bulls, cows, or calves around. Then Hab saw a harpoon buried deep into the animal's hide just behind its crimson air bladders. The animal was injured. Could opportunity smile with such good fortune after all these hard days at sea? Here was a harpoon ready and waiting for him. All he had to do was yank it from the bull's back, puncture the bull's bladders, and get a tow toward Paras.

He hoisted his sail and made for the whale. In less than a minute he was alongside the stricken creature. Blood and pus oozed from its wound. Its breath came and went from its forward blowhole in a sickly wheeze. The skin around the wound was inflamed. The harpoon line dragged in the water next to the whale. Hab lifted the line and yanked.

The creature immediately reared up and let out a tremendous howl. With a slap of its tail and a twist of its body, the bull turned on Hab. The harpoon popped free, taking a chunk of flesh with it. How quickly opportunity turned to catastrophe. The bull swam toward Hab, its mouth wide open. Before Hab could do anything to maneuver the weapons rack out of the way, the great jaws enveloped him, and he found himself inside the mouth of the whale. The whale's jaws closed, cracking his raft in half. Hab dove farther into the dark abyss of the whale's mouth to avoid getting sliced to pieces by its teeth. Seawater bubbled up around him. Except for two reddish membranes—the openings into the whale's air bladders—all was dark.

He glanced back at the raft, seeing if there was any way he could salvage it. The reek of brine and rot was overpowering. Despite his weakness, he sprang to his feet, his body pumped with adrenaline. He could hardly believe it. He was inside the mouth of a whale, a big bull who could easily swallow him. His raft looked beyond repair. He was closer to death than he'd been at any time during his voyage. This wasn't an opportunity. This was a disaster.

The bull's tongue rolled and shifted underneath him as the peristalsis muscles of its swallowing mechanisms tried to push Hab down its throats. The whale opened its mouth again, ejected Hab's raft, then closed it, leaving only the pink light from the whale's bladder apertures above. The tongue lurched upward and crushed Hab against the roof of the mouth, scraping him badly on the rough surface, then pulled him back toward its uvula, forcing Hab farther and farther to the rear of the bull's throat. A sudden thump came from somewhere down the creature's throat. A rank acidic smell wafted up from somewhere down there. The tongue sank to the floor of the mouth, and seawater swelled up around Hab's body. How was he going to fight this? He couldn't die now, not when he had traveled over ten thousand miles through uncharted waters on a barely seaworthy scrap of wood. Not when the metal warships were somewhere behind him, and Paras lay pathetically unprepared to fight a war against the *sikingo-mango*. Not when Guenard and Jeter had died, not when Esten had died, not when his beloved brother Chouc had died.

Hab struggled to his feet. He poised the harpoon upward. The bull's swallowing muscles again constricted. The tongue lifted. And as it lifted, Hab aimed the harpoon right at the left air bladder membrane. The harpoon pierced the membrane, and the barbs lodged in the fleshy musculature of the air aperture. Hab gripped the shaft of the harpoon with all his strength as the whale's tongue once again settled to the floor of its mouth. He was left dangling there.

He lifted hand over hand and climbed the shaft of the harpoon. When he reached the aperture, he punched his fist through the torn membrane and gripped what sailors called the whale's collar, a thick elastic ligature at the base of the bladder. The collar was creased with several folds of flesh, and he dug his fingers into one of these, got a good grip, and pulled himself up through the aperture into the air bladder itself. The ligature spasmed and closed like a lock behind him, tough cartilage that was like iron.

The air inside the bladder was thick, close, hardly breathable. The sea was a blurry sheet of pink outside. He pulled out his sword and sliced through the bladder. Fresh air rushed in, as sweet as perfume to Hab after the stench of the whale's gullet. He sliced some more, widening the opening, then got to his knees and clung tightly. The whale dove. Foam and spray splashed up around him, and in seconds he was four fathoms underwater. Sometimes bulls did this. They were fooled by the sudden emptying of air. They believed that they themselves had expelled it. And that, of course, was a signal to dive. They didn't realize they were injured.

Hab hung on as tightly as he could. He was dragged through the deep. A minute passed, then another, and he knew he couldn't hold his breath much longer. So he struck out with his sword at the other bladder. Bubbles of air suddenly burst around him everywhere, rising to the surface like giant pearls in these gemlike southern waters. The bull bellowed underwater, a haunting and soul-disturbing sound, one that made Hab momentarily sorry for the creature, then slowly lifted toward the surface.

The creature understood now.

The whale angled itself due north and swam for shore, the only shore it knew, Paras.

CHAPTER TWENTY-FOUR

No, it hadn't gone as planned, not at all, because he was now without a raft. The whale swam faithfully shoreward—yes, every whale did the same—but the distance was so great Hab knew the whale wouldn't make it even halfway to Paras before it died. The whale would die in the open sea. Its swim bladder would keep its corpse afloat for two days, but after that, the whale would sink. And Hab would still be thousands of miles from shore without anything to cling to.

The whale kept a steady pace over the next three days but then began to take rests. With the incessant spray from the animal's blowhole, Hab couldn't keep dry. In the constant Laisse Winds coming from the northwest, he grew terribly cold. He shivered. He was hungry and thirsty. The moon-tides were growing bigger. The bull whale didn't have the strength to navigate through the gaps, and Hab was often swamped, had to hang on tightly to the tattered air bladders so he wouldn't be washed away.

On the morning of the fifth day, it rained—a cold spring rain that turned Hab's flesh blue. He cut away part of the whale's air bladder and fashioned first a crude basin to catch rainwater, then a cloak of membrane that he draped around his shoulders to shut out at least some of the cold and wet. He drank his fill of water, but didn't risk eating any whale blubber: the meat, because of the animal's original wound, might now be poisoned. So he stayed hungry and grew weaker, but that was better than dying quickly from toxic shock.

The tides of the eclipse came that night. He thought they would be the massive tides of the open sea, but they were small, the biggest not more than forty feet high, with a gentle slope that stretched out nearly a mile, a kind of tide common in the shallower waters of the Great Reef. Was he near Alquay then? He and the whale made it through the night, but then the whale stopped. One last sputter of spray came from its blowhole and it didn't breathe again. Hab poked it with his sword. The animal didn't even quiver. He knew the whale was dead. He thrust his sword into the creature and sliced away a chunk of raw blubber. He almost ate it. He was terribly tempted. But then he smelled the blubber. A scent of bitter almonds rose from the blubber. He knew the whale had poisoned its body. He tossed the chunk of blubber into the sea.

He looked down at the left bladder's blow hole. He hacked away with his sword. He wondered if there might not be at least a few boards of his raft left somewhere in the creature's mouth. It was, he knew, his only chance. He had to get into the creature's mouth and see.

He worked well into the afternoon, dug right down to the creature's skull, hacked through the closed ligature, difficult work because with all the blood he kept slipping, couldn't keep his footing, fell into the water several times. Once he almost lost his sword. Above all, he had to keep that sword. The sword was proof. Proof that Ortok was out there. Proof that Ortok was coming.

Kneeling in the bloody pit he had gouged into the whale's head, he hacked at the tough ligature cartilage well into evening, but it was virtually as strong as bone and came away in small grudging chips. The tides came again, but they were smaller still. When the tides were finished at dawn, Hab worked for another hour, the white chips of blow-hole ligature flying everywhere. Finally he grew too tired to work anymore. He lay down between the deflated bladders and slept.

He slept until he felt the water come up over the sides of the whale. He sat up, startled out of his sleep, and looked around. The whale was sinking. Before he could even think about what he was going to do, the water was up to his knees, then up to his waist. The angle of the whale's back shifted sharply as the bull went down head-first. A second later Hab found himself treading water.

He was stunned. He was shocked. He was out in the middle of the ocean with no possible way to keep himself afloat. The bull's tail lifted behind him and slid with barely a ripple beneath the surface. As the bull's swim bladder finally gave out, expelling its air, huge bubbles rose all around him. He was frantic. He didn't know what to do. Then his training from Pieshe took over, and he gained control of himself.

A minute later, a few planks, presumably from his raft, shot to the surface like rockets, leaping clear of the waves and landing with three loud smacks on the water. He stared at them. A meager bit of luck, because he knew, even as he stared at them, that they wouldn't be enough to keep him effectively afloat, but he had to make for them nonetheless. He fixed their positions in his mind, knowing how easily he could lose them in the dip and swell of the waves, even though they were no more than fifty feet away. He swam slowly toward them, conserving his energy.

The first plank measured only four feet long, two inches thick, and eight inches wide. And while it gave him some buoyancy, it wasn't enough to keep him afloat independently. Holding the board straight out ahead of him, he kicked toward the next plank. He was sure it was just over the next wave, but when he reached the crest, he saw nothing in the trough. So he swam to the next wave. Nothing. He kicked through three more waves. But the plank was gone. He scanned the ocean in every direction, hoping to get a glimpse of the third plank, but he couldn't see it anywhere.

He searched for the remaining two planks over the next hour, but the waves hid everything. Proper elevation was impossible. The other planks could have been within easy reach. But because he couldn't see them, they might as well be a thousand miles away. He finally gave up. He concentrated on how to make the best use of the plank he had.

He tried to tie it to his back with the piece of twine he had around the waist of his tunic, careful not to lose his sword, but the plank kept slipping out from under the twine, no matter how tight he tied it. He tried sitting on it sidesaddle. Lying on top of it. Using it as a pillow with the idea that it might at least keep his head afloat. But all these positions required a modicum of balance, and balance meant effort. Effort meant exhaustion. And exhaustion out here, in the open sea, meant death. He finally sat astride it, riding it like a chevul. He sank up to his neck. He still had to smooth the water with his palms to stay afloat. And yes, it took some balance. But it seemed to be the best of all the positions he had tried.

Hab was a strong man, broad-shouldered and barrel-chested, muscular and tough, but he was no match for the sea when all he had to stay afloat with was a four-foot plank. After an hour of sitting astride the board, he had to change position. He lay on his back and hugged the board to his chest. While this gave his arms and back a rest, the surf kept washing over his face, and he swallowed so much seawater that his throat burned. So he turned over and, bracing his chest against the board, breast-stroked, just fast enough to keep him afloat.

He did this most of the day, despite his dire hunger and thirst, and by evening his arms were so tired he could hardly feel them. As the stars came out he rolled over on his back and took their position. In this way, he calculated that he had traveled roughly two hundred miles on the back of the whale, which meant he was now well within charted waters, or at least at their fringe, and that he conceivably might be close to the Auvilly Currents.

Two hours later, he began to float steadily northward at about three knots. He *was* in the Auvilly Currents. This lifted his spirits. He kicked, hoping to make four knots, but his legs were heavy, and he weakened through the night. The tides came, but they weren't nearly as massive now, and he didn't concern himself with navigating them so much as simply staying afloat. His body felt numb. The sword dragged at the twine belt around his tunic. He might float better if he got rid of his sword, but he knew he had to keep it. It was the only way he would convince Parprouch that the hoppers were coming.

But then it dawned on him: Why did he need proof? He was going to Paras. Nobody lied in Paras. Yes! Everybody would believe every word he said, even without his sword. He closed his eyes. He was falling asleep. All he needed was his word. Honesty was the way. Why should anybody doubt him? He was a Parassian. And the sword was so heavy. He loosened his belt and let it slide into the deep.

But it didn't seem to do any good. He felt heavier than ever. He couldn't feel his legs anymore. He kept swallowing seawater. He couldn't stay awake. The stars twinkled above him, indifferent to his plight. His skin was horribly wrinkled from the water. He clutched the board, but the board seemed useless, and he had a sudden urge to give it up and let it drift away. Wasn't it fitting that he should drown out here in the middle of the ocean? What better way to go? He thought of his father, Duq, remembered his father's reddish hair and beard, his faded seaman's blues with the crest of the House of Cloudesley stitched upon the breast, remembered his father's blue eyes, those wide and startled eyes that always looked surprised at everything.

"Father?" he called, so exhausted and confused that he thought he might actually rouse his father's ghost from the bottom of the ocean. "Father, can you hear me? It's me, Hab. If you can hear me, please help me. I'm sinking. I can't keep going. And they're coming. The hoppers are coming. You've got to help me. I've got to get to Paras."

But no ghost appeared. The sea murmured with the ebb of the tides. Hab stuck his face in the water. Did there have to be a mad struggle? Could he not slip peacefully into the embrace of his beloved ocean without clutching and panicking for air?

He fell asleep with his face in the water. And he dreamed. He dreamed that he sprouted fins and a tail, that he became a fish. He dreamed of sinking deeper and deeper into the water, of his lungs filling with water, of finally letting go, forgetting the hopelessness of the Golden Land's fate. He swam deeper and deeper, through the green, into the blue, and finally into the dark, where only those strange-eyed creatures of the most extreme depths ever went.

But then he felt a great pain in his chest, and he awoke with a strangled cough, his eyes sprang wide, and he realized he was several fathoms underwater, that in his sleep he had slipped from his board. He kicked frantically. He had to get to the top. He had to breathe! Perhaps there was going to be a mad struggle after all.

He broke the surface, sputtering and coughing, and couldn't understand how morning had come so quickly, or how the middle of the night could have disappeared so suddenly. He looked madly around for his board but couldn't see it anywhere. He was confused, disoriented, and so full of saltwater he felt sick to his stomach. Where were those voices coming from? Was he hearing things? He swung round. He saw a boat. A schooner, a small one, a fishing smack.

"There he is!" shouted a sailor, his foot on the bowsprit, his hand hanging onto a halyard. "Two spokes to port, helmsman! I see him! I see him again!"

Hab looked at the smack bearing down on him. He felt more confused than ever. He couldn't feel his body. He must be dead. This had to be a dream. Hands on board took in sail, and the smack slackened her pace. Hab saw her name along the side, painted in orange script along her black hull: *Oissette*, a word from the Berberton dialect meaning "small bird." The helmsman steered her expertly until she was alongside Hab. Hab looked up at the sailors leaning over the bulwark with dull blinking eyes. One threw a ratline over.

"Ho, there, seaman!" called the captain, a gangly youth of about twenty-five. "We've heard of no shipwrecks in these waters!" The Parassian tongue sounded strange to Hab—familiar yet foreign at the same time. He tried to answer, but he found his lips and throat wouldn't cooperate. "Can you manage the climb?" asked the captain, when he saw Hab wasn't going to answer. None of them could realize that he had made his way in a small raft all the way from the other side of the world. "Come now, grab hold, the boat's bearing off. We nearly lost you once already."

Hab looked at the line as if he weren't sure what it was, then weakly gripped it. None of them could realize that, combined with his initial polar voyage to Ortok, and his subsequent equatorial trek in the raft, he was the first man to circumnavigate the globe. He tried to pull himself up, but his arms were too weak.

"Captain," said the first mate, "he can't do it. Look at his condition."

The gangly young captain pondered the sea-logged wastrel clinging to the starboard ratline. "Then go down and give him a hand, Mr. Tenebrille."

The first mate, with a few others, climbed down overboard shrouds and helped Hab onto the *Oissette*. When they got him up on deck he couldn't stand. He looked at his legs. Were those his legs? They were as scrawny as oar shafts.

"You've been adrift for a while, haven't you, seaman?" said the captain.

Hab, sitting quickly to the deck before he collapsed, looked up at the captain with squinty eyes, only one thing on his mind. "Are you heading for port?" he asked.

Was that his voice? It sounded so ragged, so dry.

"We made our last haul this morning," confirmed the captain. "We're on our way home."

"And where do you sail?"

"Calundi."

"Then let's make sail, seaman," said Hab. "Let's make sail."

𝄞𝄞𝄞

He rested the whole way. The *Oissette* was a quick ship, made ten knots, even tacking into the Laisse Winds. Mr. Tenebrille, the first mate, a tawny youth of twenty-one with an unruly mop of brown curls, a mouthful of snaggle teeth, and brown eyes that possessed all the openness and honesty of his Berberton origins, looked after Hab, brought him soup and fish, and ointment for his salt burns, and plenty of freshwater, and a glass of decent cordial to ease the pain in Hab's spent muscles.

"Where did you get that strange tunic?" asked Mr. Tenebrille. "I've never seen anything like it."

"Are there many boats leaving Calundi for Jauny?" he asked.

"I thought you were a Jondonqer. It's hard to tell, you're so tanned."

"Do they leave every day?" persisted Hab. "Twice a day? I must reach Jauny as quickly as possible."

Mr. Tenebrille lifted his chin. "The folk in Calundi don't have much call for Jauny."

"I can pay."

"I'm sure you can."

"We're in danger," said Hab.

Mr. Tenebrille squinted. "Danger?" he said. "Danger from what?"

He pondered Mr. Tenebrille, wondering if there were any point. No. The tale would have to be told, but not to Mr. Tenebrille. But if not to Mr. Tenebrille, then to whom? Lord Cloudesley, his brother? Lord Teur? Parprouch? One way or the other, he had to enlist the help of the nobility. They were the only class with resources enough to raise an army.

He fingered his tunic. Hopper hide. With green scales. Too bad several of the larger aquatic reptiles on the south coast of Maju had green scales. Too bad tanners were constantly making purses, shoes, and doublets out of their hides. Too bad anybody who saw this tunic would think it came from the hide of one of those large aquatic reptiles. And too bad he was already deemed a Liar. He was beginning to regret the loss of his sword. His tale, after all, was so bizarre, would anybody believe it without incontrovertible proof? Or was he just thinking like a *sikingo-mango*?

"If they don't ship out often for Jauny," he said, "what's my fastest way there?"

The first mate scratched his head, snorted, then spit the products of his nostrils onto the floor. "Well . . . take a barge up the river," he finally said.

"Which river?"

A hint of incredulity came to the young man's eyes. "The River Gerleni, of course," he said, as if there were no other river worth mentioning, not even the Necontreu. "Take it as far as Kenetin. Do you know Kenetin at all? It's famous for its gourds. They grow more gourds there than any place I know. They grow all kinds of 'em."

"Do they?"

"Especially peacock gourds. Have you ever seen a peacock gourd?"

"Yes."

"They have the biggest peacock gourd ever grown sitting on the quayside there," said Mr. Tenebrille proudly. "Two thousand six hundred and twenty-two pounds, with all the colors of the rainbow. She's a dandy, she is. You can take a coach from Kenetin to Jauny. One leaves every other day. It's primarily a mail coach, but I'm sure they can put you on the roof if they have room."

≈≈≈

The cook had all sorts of stewed fruits and vegetables stowed aboard the *Oissette*. Feasting on these fruits and vegetables restored Hab's health more than anything. By the time the south coast of Maju came into view, he was on his feet and helping out on deck. His salt sores had scabbed over. And he was able to trim his beard, albeit badly, with a pair of scissors. He told the captain he was of the Miquay clan, the House of Cloudesley, and on the strength of this connection the captain gladly loaned him three hundred decou. The captain knew he would get his money back. This was Paras, after all. A bad loan was unheard-of.

They crossed the Sea of Maju in just over a day. When Hab caught his first glimpse of the Golden Land, tears came to his eyes. He wasn't a devout man, not by any stretch, but he sent fervent thanks to Ouvant and vowed to reinvestigate the 28 Rules of the Formulary thoroughly.

The *Oissette* eased into the small estuary of the River Gerleni on a bright morning in late spring. Her hands tied her fast, and Hab jumped to shore. He hurried to the nearest spot of grass and kissed the ground. He wore an extra pair of seaman's blues Mr. Tenebrille had had hanging about, two sizes too small, and in a satchel he carried his hopper-hide tunic. He said good-bye to the crew of the *Oissette*, thanked her captain, and within an hour found a barge bound northward on the Gerleni for Kenetin.

The green fields bent with spring grains, and the fruit trees were in full blossom. On his lazy way up the Gerleni, with the warmth of the sun easing the last of his aches away, he decided he had neglected Berberton too much of his life. Especially this part of Berberton, which, after all, was on Jondonq's doorstep. The peasants and landholders were decidedly wholesome-looking, with their curly brown hair, dark eyes, and rosy cheeks. Cloudesley was gone. But if his countrymen could push the *sikingo-mango* back into the sea, might there someday arise the opportunity to buy a small farm in one of the more remote counties of Berberton, and start building the family name, with Jara Pepteri as his wife, all over again?

The world's biggest peacock gourd came into sight an hour later. The gourd was a truly tremendous squash, lacquered over with Affed varnish to protect it from the elements, Kenetin's unique and decidedly peculiar landmark. He found his way to the mail office, where the clerk gave him the once-over. Hab looked down at his clothes. His arms protruded four inches from the end of his sleeves, and the cuffs of his trousers rode well above his ankles.

"Ho, there," said the mail clerk indifferently, then busied himself with some parcels.

"I want to take the coach to Jauny."

The clerk stopped fussing and stared at him. "The coach, as you call it, left five minutes ago. I'm afraid there won't be another for three days."

"I was told they run every two days."

"Three days," corrected the clerk.

"I can't wait three days. I have important government business to conduct in the capital."

"I thought you said you were going to Jauny."

"I am."

"Ionis is the only capital around here."

"I meant Jauny."

"That's not our capital," said the mail clerk. "Speak in plain words, friend. Say what you mean."

The clerk began with his parcels again.

"Then I mean Jauny," said Hab.

"The coach, as you call it, leaves in three days," repeated the clerk. "And as it will be loaded with parcels, I doubt there'll be room for you."

"I would pay any townsman a hundred decou to take me there today."

"We're not much for traveling," said the clerk. "Especially to Jondonq. I doubt anyone will take you."

"You said the mail coach left just five minutes ago?"

"We call it the mail cart around here," said the clerk. "No point in being fancy when you can be plain."

"But it's just left?" said Hab, losing patience.

The clerk glanced at the clock on the wall, disgruntled that he wasn't going to thwart Hab after all. "Seven minutes ago," he said churlishly.

꙳꙳꙳

Hab ran fast and hard. As he climbed out of the valley of the River Gerleni, he saw the mail cart at the top of the hill. It took him fifteen minutes, but he finally caught up. He was out of breath, covered with dirt, and sweating, but when he waved his money in the driver's face, the driver made a small spot for him on the roof.

᠈ᕬᕬᕬ᠈

He arrived in Jauny late the next day, just as the sun was going down. All was as it had been. The happy and carefree citizens of Jondonq's capital were oblivious to the imminent arrival of the hopper battle force. The usual decadent and inebriated rabble thronged the cafes along the Estuary, the lights in Triser burned with their usual crimson glow, and the streets were so thick with the surfeit blossoms of the ubiquitous apple trees that the whole place stunk of sweet tea-biscuit jelly. Everybody's chief concern was pleasure. It was as if none of them had ever heard of the 28 Rules of the Formulary. Couples made love openly in the deepening shadows. Compared to the bleak, rugged, and destitute Ortok, Paras was like a bit of girl's lace, a silk handkerchief, or a box of Gougou's favorite bonbons.

He made his way to the family compound in Bosiler Boulevard. He was surprised to see a half dozen to-let signs in the windows. He tried the front door, but the front door, always left open, was now locked. He knocked on the door. No one came. Knocked again. Still no one. Knocked loud and long and hard, knocked until Uvet, the maid, finally opened the door. Her eyes widened. Her petite features showed shock, amazement, fear, puzzlement, confusion.

"Mr. Miquay . . . you're alive?" she said, in a small frail voice.

He gestured at the windows. "What's happened here?"

"You . . . you . . . went away," she said, her voice now breathless. "And you took all your brother's money . . . and Lord Teur came with a writ . . . and we had to . . ." She looked up at the family compound. "It's a hostelry now. We have to pay a tithe to Parprouch. We barely have enough to live on . . . and when we heard about the wreck, we thought you were never coming back, so we went ahead and we—"

"What wreck?" he said.

"A ship," she said. "Found during the thaw up north last summer by some whalers in the Bay of Vabreulle. Drifting on an iceberg. A strange ship. One of the ones you built. The *Airamatnas*."

Hab pondered. "And you thought I was dead." He pushed past Uvet. "These rooms are rented by boarders now?" he asked, looking up and down the long corridor.

"It's the only way we can . . . the family's confined to three small rooms in the southeast wing . . ." As Uvet said this last sentence, some annoyance crept into her voice, as if, far from being happy to see her master alive and safe, she actually blamed him for everything.

"And is my mother well?" he asked.

Sadness crept into Uvet's round blue eyes. He peered at her more closely. Uvet looked away. "Your mother died during the winter, sir," she said.

His heart skipped a beat. Somehow, in going away, he'd expected everything in Paras to remain the same. But obviously it hadn't. "How did she die?" he finally asked.

"Thia found her dead in her wheelchair in front of the hearth. The doctor says a stroke."

A stroke. Not so bad. Quick and easy, if it was massive enough. "And is Romal here?" he asked.

"I don't know. I doubt it. I don't keep track of his comings and goings. I'm not really a maid anymore. I . . . run this place," she said, looking around the hostelry. "Thia wouldn't know how."

"Is Thia here?" he asked.

Uvet nodded. "Mistress doesn't go out much anymore," she said. "She keeps to her rooms."

CHAPTER TWENTY-FIVE

He found Thia in the new cramped family quarters on the second floor of the southeast wing. As they stared at each other over the stone floor, Thia's shoulders rose, her fingers splayed, and her blue eyes brimmed with tears. She wore a sleeveless sheer gown. She had bruises all over her arms. Her lip was swollen, split, her left eye was black, and she had a bandage on her forehead. She was thin. She looked starved.

"You've returned," she said.

Was that really Thia's voice? He didn't remember it being so thin and brittle. Her voice sounded like a badly strung lyre.

"He's mistreated you," he said.

She looked at her hands. Her hair fell limply around the sides of her face.

"Where is he?" he asked.

"Don't hurt him," she said. "It's been hard for us." She looked up, mustering what dignity she could. "Why did you . . ."

He regarded her levelly. "Thia, I found it," he said. "I found it."

"We have nothing," she said. She fidgeted, then looked at the floor again. "Nothing at all."

He moved nearer. He put his arms around her. He felt sorry for her.

"Thia, I'm sorry," he said. "I had to go."

"You always looked after us," she said. "You were the only one I could trust."

Was she blaming him, then?

"Thia, I think you should leave Jauny." But it was as if she weren't listening, as if she had no room in her mind for anything but her own misfortune. "It's going to get bad here," he continued. He explained about the hoppers. "Don't you have an aunt in Renay County? I think it might be best if you go there for a little while."

She glanced at him vacantly. "I haven't been to the dressmakers since last fall." As if she hadn't heard a word of what he had said to her about the hoppers. "I have nothing but rags to wear. I can't go out."

Hab fingered the material of her shift. "This gown is of the finest silk," he said.

"Come to the divan with me," she said. She pulled him toward the divan. "Sit." He reluctantly sat beside her. "I'm sure the tides will get them." So she'd been listening after all? "You look thin, Hab. You should gorge on apples. I wish we had some joadre."

"Thia, they mean to harm us. Renay is two hundred miles from here. You should be safe there."

She stroked his badly barbered beard. "Why would they harm us?" she asked. "We've done nothing to them." Then she looked at the seaman's blues he was wearing. "Where did you get these?" she asked. "They stink."

"They're going to harm us because that's the way they are."

"I haven't been to a soiree in over a month," she said. "We don't get invitations anymore. No one wants us. The baker and the fishmonger won't give us credit anymore. What am I going to eat? If I eat another apple . . ."

"We're going to be slaves." He looked around the room, searched his mind for the words that might make for a more eloquent apology, but he couldn't find them. He glanced at her. "He shouldn't beat you," he said.

She hesitated, but finally she told the truth, as was the way. "He tries not to. But it's become a . . . a habit."

"Where is he?"

She looked away. "Triser," she said disconsolately. "In the arms of another."

ʕʕʕ

But Romal wasn't in Triser. He was in a gaming house, one of the shabbier ones, just south of the District of Lagaine. He played cards with some young nobles, not his usual gang of cronies, in a mist of cheroot smoke under weak lamplight that spilled across the table like dirty dishwater.

Romal looked up, the weak glow of the lamp playing in the brown curls of his pompadour. A grin came to his face, but it was a grin Hab couldn't readily interpret. Romal showed no surprise at seeing him. If anything, he seemed amused by him. He lifted a slender white-gloved finger and pointed at Hab.

When Romal had all his new friends looking at Hab, he said, "Is that a ghost I see?" Romal looked thin, but thin in the way alcoholics looked thin. "Or a Liar?"

Hab looked at all the dissolute young nobles; at their effeminate stylish clothes, their silken hands, and their girlish complexions. He wondered if they were capable of taking his news seriously. He wondered if he should even try to enlist his brother's support.

"Brother, I am no ghost," he said.

"Then perhaps you're an embezzler," said his brother in the same casual tone. "I thought an embezzler might wear a different mask than a thief and a Liar, but I see the mask's the same for all three."

Hab studied the faces before him, all so young, naive, and affected. Had his brother taken up with boys, then? Romal was easily twice the age of every lad here. What kind of bed-sport was he engaged in now? None of them looked like soldiers. Were these the men he had to trust to defend his land? The task of telling them the harrowing news about the hoppers suddenly seemed daunting. They all looked somehow sly to him, as devious in their way as the hoppers were in theirs.

He thought of his father, Duq. His father, when he'd had something to say, said it simply, in a loud clear voice, with the most prosaic words he could find. So Hab began his tale, his voice low and determined. He remembered the mail clerk in Kenetin. Speak plainly. Which was what he did. He told the young nobles of the hoppers without embellishment, adding none of the linguistic flourishes or labyrinthine constructions he might use when speaking to the higher nobles of the Court. These were boys, after all, and he had to speak to them as boys.

He told them everything. And he wasn't much surprised when none of them believed him. His mood settled. He felt cantankerous toward them. But he persisted in his tale, bearing down in the face of their ridicule the way he might bear down against a strong wind at sea. He pressed on, even though some of them began to talk among themselves. Hab was forty, young still, but among this lot he felt middle-aged. Romal slouched in his chair, steepled his fingers, rested his elbows on the armrests, and stared at Hab over his manicured nails, waiting for him to finish. Yes, a fantastical voyage home, months at sea alone in a raft, a length and a method of sea travel that sounded extravagant even to his own ears. No wonder they didn't believe him.

Romal raised his hands. "Brother, please desist. You've told us enough. We don't need to hear more. Suffice it to say that while you were gone you were convicted in absentia by the king's highest magistrates for embezzlement, thievery, and—" He looked around at all his friends, smiling broadly. "—lying."

Everyone got a good laugh out of that. Especially after Hab's extravagant tale. And he had to admit, Romal's timing was impeccable. When it came to public humiliation, his brother was the best. A waiter came over and poured wine in everybody's glasses. The waiter offered Hab a glass, but Hab waved him away. His eyes narrowed and he stared at Romal. Was no one going to believe him?

"We must raise an army," said Hab, angry, his words dropping like bricks from his mouth.

"Brother, did you not hear me?" asked Romal, his voice shrill with suppressed delight. "The king's highest magistrates have convicted you of three felonies. Now you blithely speak to us of committing another. Have you not learned your lesson?"

Hab again looked at all the young nobles—at their fine silks, velvets, and gold rings. Some wore ribbons in their hair, and the lot of them smelled of perfume. Dissipated with drink and gambling, as delicate and untrained as puppies, they certainly wouldn't make an effective fighting force.

"Still and so, Brother, we must raise an army."

Romal got to his feet, yawned, stretched, and scratched the small of his back. His hair needed a trim. So did his beard. Lord Cloudesley looked disheveled.

"Come, Hab," he said, taking Hab by the arm. "Let's sit in this back room here. You're tiring my friends with your story. I'll order a bottle of brandy, and you can tell me of your adventure in more detail." They entered a small private room where a few candles burned dimly in wall-mounted candleholders, and where a few scattered bread crumbs lay moldering on the red tablecloth. "Sit, Hab," said Romal, gesturing at a scarred spindle chair. The room smelled of human sweat and old wine, a gagging smell that nearly suffocated Hab. "I'd say an occasion like this demands a bottle of their best."

Hab waited impatiently while his brother went to order a bottle of brandy. He looked down at his clothes, Mr. Tenebrille's seaman's blues. Then he looked at himself in the mirror. His beard was badly cut and his hair was dirty. Romal returned a few minutes later with a bottle of brandy and two snifters.

"What took you?" asked Hab.

"The waiter had to nose around in the cellar for a while. We wanted the best, didn't we?" As Romal sat down he cuffed Hab on the shoulder. "For the first time in my life, Hab, I think I admire you."

This was unexpected. Romal admired no one but himself. "Admire me?" said Hab.

"Yes," said Romal. "The way you had me sign all that money away. I couldn't have mounted a better deception if I were to do it myself."

Hab looked at his hands. "I'm sorry about the family money, Romal," he said. "I had no choice."

Romal lifted the brandy and poured. "I should have realized that you had some of Grandpa's blood. So much for the Formulary in our family, eh, Hab? Aye, we were never much for Pendagal, not us Miquays." Romal's eyes narrowed, and he leaned forward. "The only thing I can't understand is why you ever came back. You should have stayed wherever you were hiding."

"I wasn't hiding, Romal."

"You expect me to believe that?"

"Romal, they're coming. You must use your title. You must influence those in power."

"Hab, my title means nothing," said Romal. "Unless you have the money to back it up, a title is worthless." He took a sip of his brandy and looked at Hab with bold eyes. "I was wondering if you could write me a note for a few thousand decou."

Romal could think of nothing but his own misfortune.

"I have no money, Romal," said Hab. "I spent it all."

A wry grin came to Romal's face. "Come, Brother, don't jest. You've jested long enough tonight. Your swindle is perfection itself. Grandpa would have been proud. Don't ruin it by playing coy. A bank note for five thousand decou will do."

"But Romal, I tell you truthfully, I have no money. The money was spent on my three submersible boats."

Romal paused. "Boats?" he said. He shook his head, took a sip of his brandy, then put his glass down with the care a surgeon might take when making an incision. "Not the best investment, but they'll make for the necessary collateral."

"Romal, the boats are gone." Had Romal not been listening at all?

Had he not heard anything Hab had told him about the fates of the *Fetla*, *Xeulliette*, and *Airamatnas*?

Romal's grin disappeared, and a feral moody look came to his eyes. "What happened to them?"

"I've told you. One gave way to the ice, the other was gutted, and the last was scuttled."

"What about your whaling fleet?"

"Except for the old family ketch, the rest of my boats are rented for a percentage of my kills. The family fortune, even before I sold Cloudesley, was hardly enough to maintain my own whaling fleet."

Candle wax dripped from the wall-mounted candle and splattered on the table. "Well . . . then . . ." Romal looked incredulous. "Then I suppose it's a good thing there's a price on your head. I, too, am capable of a good deception, Brother. I, too, have learned a thing or two from Grandpa."

Hab stared at his brother as Romal's meaning became clear. Now he knew why Romal had gone to get the bottle of brandy himself instead of having the waiter bring it. Here was treachery. Here was deception. He thought of Gashak. He thought of Aychega. He knew how they felt. He sprang from his chair and bolted for the door.

ᶜᶜᶜ

As he left the private room he saw two officers of the Civil Guard charging down the corridor toward him. Hab rushed across the room and launched himself out the window like an Ortokian bird-animal, the glass falling around him in a million pieces. He landed on the cobblestones of the street below and rolled. He came out of his roll and, struggling to his feet, darted into a lane. He heard the Civil Guard jump out the window and run after him. But he was fast. He dodged down another lane, yanked the grate from the sewer opening, and hang-jumped into the pipe below.

He followed the sewer, passing grate after grate, and finally stopped at the junction of another pipe. He was out of breath. His legs were shaking. Too many months in a cage without enough exercise.

A second later he heard footsteps pass by overhead. He waited until the footsteps disappeared. Then he climbed the rungs and pushed the grate aside. He quickly got his bearings. Across the street, hidden behind magnificent apple blossoms, he saw the monarch's in-town palace, Gorolet, a beige structure of turrets, towers, and a large sweeping portico with a dozen carriages parked underneath. He wondered if Parprouch might be there. Should he risk it? No. It was late spring. By this time Parprouch would undoubtedly be at Summerhouse.

He climbed out of the sewer. The gates of Gorolet opened. Out came a company of Civil Guards in a wagon. Had they been alerted? He pressed his back to the trunk of an apple tree as they passed. Suddenly he felt like a stranger in his own land. He was a fugitive. He was a criminal. He had been convicted in absentia of the heinous crime of deceit, sentenced to branding, and to banishment on the Island of Liars. How was he ever going to raise an army against the hoppers under those circumstances? Yet raise an army he must.

He turned up his collar and walked down the street toward the Estuary, feeling off balance, in conflict with himself. He was a far more honest man than any of those young nobles back at the gaming house. Yet now he had to sneak along the streets like a common criminal. It was as if he had been asked to fit himself into a different skin.

He came to the Embankment Road, where chevul-drawn traffic rattled by. The Estuary, glimmering with a last peach-colored light, was a forest of masts. He walked with his hands in his pockets, descended a few steps to the Grand Promenade, and continued southward toward Ourrice Harbor. If he couldn't enlist the help of his brother, he would have to somehow get a message to Lord Teur. Lord Teur might arrest him on the spot, but it was a chance he would have to take. The globe lamps on their amber posts cast a milky light over the green tiles of the Grand Promenade. Or perhaps he should first talk to his lawyer, Orvint

Vencal. Orvint Vencal might keep him out of custody for a while. And he could entrust the lawyer to get a message to Lord Teur.

Upon reaching Place Ourrice he saw a crowd of sailors and yachtsmen gathered round the harbormaster's tower. He looked around for Civil Guards but saw none. He stood next to a warehouse for several minutes watching the men. Why were they all gathered together like that? Had the word gone out? Were they talking about Jauny's newest fugitive? No. A man in a blue coat and a red sash—traditional yachtsman garb—was speaking to the crowd. Hab grew curious. What could the yachtsman be telling them? And why was there something familiar about the yachtsman?

Hab walked along the low stone wall beside the Grand Promenade and unobtrusively placed himself at the edge of the crowd. He recognized the yachtsman now, a professional racer, a man by the name of Landarde, fifty years old, a five-time cup-holder, a man who designed boats for speed and maneuverability.

"I was a hundred miles south of Maju when I saw them," said Landarde, his face red, his eyes glittering like opals. "I didn't know what they were at first. I was skimming along at seventeen knots with the Laisse Winds fair at my back. It seemed as if the Lesser Oradels had removed themselves into the sea. I put my glass to my eye. And I discovered that they weren't mountains at all. They were ships. Ships such as I'd never seen before. Ships of black iron, about fifty of them, tacking at five knots into the wind, heading straight for Maju."

Just then, a commotion erupted on the other side of Place Ourrice. Hab turned and saw Civil Guards, eight in all, running toward him. He broke free of the crowd, but it was no use. The Civil Guards were on him in seconds.

〰〰〰

They put him in a wagon. The wagon had bars. He was in a cage again. They drove down Eleger Avenue into Place Giofre and passed the imposing pillared edifice of the Fanille, the law courts. They followed an alley around the Fanille, down a small slope, where they came to a marsh farther along. Beyond the marsh he saw Jauny's main cargo and shipping docks. Beside the marsh he saw the bleak structure of the Liars' Prison. The prison was made of the characteristic beige stone so common in Jauny, but the windows had bars over them.

They put him in a cell on the second level in the east wing overlooking the penal docks.

"You'll wish to notify your lawyer," said the jailer, an old man who smelled like cabbage.

Hab fished out the money the captain of the *Oissette* had given him and handed it to the jailer. "Marrouin and Vencal," said Hab. "In the Fanille."

Vencal came an hour later. The lawyer sat down on the motwood stool, looked around the cell, then folded his hands over his small paunch. "Mr. Miquay, I don't know if there's much I can do for you," he said.

Hab stared at the lawyer. "I found it," he said. Hab recounted the events of his adventure. "Have your clerk find Landarde," he urged. "Hear it for yourself." Then he asked Vencal to go to Lord Teur. "We're going to be invaded," he said. "They mean to crush us. You have to get me out of here."

Vencal made a face. "Do you think I can simply have the high court overturn your conviction in a few days?"

Hab sighed. "Talk to Lord Teur," he said. "Tell him what I've said. You've got to get him to come and talk to me."

CHAPTER TWENTY-SIX

No one came. He expected Orvint Vencal to return with Lord Teur no later than the following morning, or if not with Lord Teur, then with an agent from Lord Teur's office. He stayed up all night, waiting. Dawn came. But no lawyer, lord, or agent appeared. He was tired. He finally lay down on the cold stone floor. No sleeping pallet. Liars were treated . . . like liars.

He dozed, slept, and woke near noon. Where was the hopper fleet now? he wondered. He got up and looked out the barred window. Had it rounded the Point of Clarity on the eastern tip of the Island of Maju? From here he got a good view of the marsh, thick with nesting nuiyau birds at this time of the year. He saw, as well, part of the port section of the harbor. Perhaps by now, thousands of Majuelles had seen the *sikingo-mango* warships. And what of the residents of Jauny? He turned from his barred window and paced. Had Landarde's story spread through the capital yet? He waited all afternoon, and still no one came for him. He was the only one in all Paras who had any direct knowledge of the *sikingo-mango*, the only man who understood how they fought and what their weaknesses were, yet he was trapped here, unable to do anything about it.

By sunset, standing at his window again, he couldn't help noticing an unusual flow of traffic out on the Estuary, ships coming and going, cramming the water, some nose to stern, as big a jam as he had ever seen on the Estuary at this time of day. Many of the boats were small, containing single extended families. Many were heaped with personal belongings and household possessions—tables, chairs, beds, even a small chevul on one, bleating miserably as it was jostled in the boat. A royal cutter tried to keep traffic separated into northbound and southbound lanes, but there were so many boats the task proved impossible. What he saw on the Estuary, he realized, was the beginning of an exodus. And he knew the news was out. Landarde's story had spread. He was heartsick at the sight of all the boats and ships out on the Estuary, and weary with impatience. The war had begun. And, stuck in here, he was unable to join it.

🌀🌀🌀

That evening, he walked to his cell door.

"Please!" he called through the little window. "Please! I must see my lawyer!"

But there was no answer. In fact, the corridor was empty, and had been empty for some time. There were no guards, no jailers, no caretakers. The chamberpots had remained uncollected. Some poor Liar in a cell near the end of the corridor was crying miserably for his supper. The guards hadn't brought Hab any food yet either. His stomach growled. He was thirsty.

He called down the hall. "Ho, there, Liar! What's your name, and where are you from?"

Silence. Then a thin voice drifted out of the darkness. "My name is Ennetos," said the Liar down the corridor, "and I come from Onrahey, in the Province of Zairab."

"And how long have you been in the Liars' Prison?"

"Six days."

"And how many times do they feed you each day?" asked Hab.

"Twice," said the Zairabian.

"But they haven't come today."

"No," said the Zairabian. "They haven't."

◞◞◞

An hour later, Ennetos the Zairabian called out of the deepening gloom. "Do you hear that?" Hab listened but heard nothing. "Is that thunder?" asked Ennetos.

Hab listened again. Yes, a distant rumbling, but it wasn't thunder. *Boom!* Getting closer. He walked to the window. For fifteen minutes Hab watched the war fleet of the *sikingo-mango* approach from the southern reaches of the Estuary. He saw them sailing five abreast up the most beloved and storied waterway of the Golden Land, cleaving her placid surface the way a butcher's knife cleaves a side of joadre. He saw five puffs of smoke from five different ships, all in unison, and then heard horrific explosions along the Embankment Road, the ordnance pummeling the residential district of Bleissue. *Boom! Boom! Boom!* He saw the projectiles, black blurs in the peach-colored sky, like phantoms released from Oeil to destroy the urban idyll of Paras. The ships deployed rank upon rank, targeting precisely, a calculated bombardment that lit the dusky sky with hundreds of white flashes. *"Boom! Boom! Boom!"* He heard the sound of citizens shouting and screaming in the distance.

Then a deafening report resounded directly above him. Flying mortar raced through his bars, leaving him with a gash on the back of his hand. Dust and smoke filled his cell, and he coughed violently. Another boom, then a crack, and the penal docks exploded into splinters. Then yet another hit, not ten yards from Hab's cell. The percussion from the blast knocked him down.

He lay on his stomach with his hands over his head as rubble fell on top of him. Rubble. But rubble from where? From the roof? Would he be able to get out through the roof now? The thunder of the bombardment continued unabated all round him. The dust was so thick he felt grit on the back of his teeth. He looked up at the ceiling and saw a large crack.

He got to his feet and had a closer look, squinting in the dust. The crack was a handspan across—not wide enough to get through. He struck the wall with his fist, exasperated, only wanting to get out of here, more restless than ever. But he was stuck here. He had to accept that. Despite his best efforts—his desperate struggle to survive the tides, his fifteen-thousand-mile odyssey across uncharted waters, and his futile attempt to convince his brother and the young nobles to raise an army—he was stuck in here. He sat with his back against the wall and prepared himself for a long frustrating evening.

The bombardment continued for most of the night, but became more sporadic toward dawn. He paced off and on throughout the night. As the sun peeked over the eastern shore of the Estuary, Hab walked over to the window to see what he could see.

Up in the city, piles of rubble made unfamiliar hills where none had been before. Several areas had been flattened entirely. Looking northwest up the hill to Triser, the view was entirely unobstructed, a clean slope of broken stone and rubble scorched black, still smoking in places, unnatural-looking, when, for as long as he could remember, that particular hill had been terraced with pretty little row houses. Strange, also, to see so far. The aggregation of beige buildings, spacious boulevards, and twisting lanes that had once been the hallmarks of his city were now gone. Survivors wandered about this plain of rubble, so far away from the prison that they looked like bugs to Hab. Triser was in flames, the old wood buildings engulfed, billowing black smoke. He counted sixty-two fires in all.

After another fifteen minutes, the slowly slackening bombardment stopped altogether. Then, silence. After a night of thunder, the silence sounded huge and empty to Hab's ears.

He stared at the armada of black rust-pocked ships in the Estuary. The air smelled acrid with the reek of burning buildings. The sails made of *bamkali-kalango* skin had been reefed and all ships were anchored, their great chain-link hawsers dipping into the placid waters of the

Estuary like umbilical cords. He heard the shouting of Abani from the ships. Regulars in metal armor lowered boatloads of other regulars into the water. As the hulls of the various attack boats touched the surface, Hab felt his shoulders sag. He didn't know what he could do to stop them. Then he thought he was hearing things. His ears were ringing so badly from the night-long bombardment that he didn't want to trust them. But he was sure he heard a voice coming from downstairs.

"Hab?" the voice called to him.

The voice was a woman's voice. He ran to the door. "Jara?" he called. He at first didn't wonder how Jara could have escaped from the hoppers or how she could have found him in the Liars' Prison. He was too happy to hear her voice to think much of anything.

"Where are you?" she called.

Then it occurred to him that she might be with hoppers. "Are you alone?"

"I can hardly hear you," she said. "Where are you?"

He listened intently. He heard no hoppers, no jangling of weapons or growling voices.

"Up on the second level near the back."

All he heard was the tap of her light footsteps on the stairs. He looked out his door and in the light of dawn saw that the outside latch had been blown off, that if it weren't for the big pile of rubble standing in the way he would have been able to push the door open and get out. She came into view. He was happy to see her, but now he was also curious. He asked her how she knew he was here in the prison.

"I found your house in Bosiler Boulevard," she said. "Your sister-in-law told me you were here."

She was alone. He asked her how she had escaped. She still wore her hopper-hide tunic. Her hair had been roughly shorn, cropped close to her head. Pale beams of morning light came in through the cracked roof, lighting the rubble here and there. She carefully picked her way over and around the piles of rubble.

"I was allowed to walk freely over the deck," she said. "I jumped overboard last night. The fools had their armor on. They weren't about to jump in after me. And by the time they lowered a boat to chase me, I was gone. They never thought I would try to swim all the way from the middle of the Estuary. It's over two miles wide at that point. I went to your sister-in-law's at four bells. I stayed there for a couple hours, then came here. She's hiding in the wine cellar."

Jara looked at the pile of rubble in front of his door and began to dig.

"Look at your hair," he said.

"It'll grow back," she said. "Rango wanted it. He had to give it to Mivuno."

"Rango survived?" he said.

"We picked him up from the wreckage of the expeditionary force," said Jara. "He's commanding. But it's hard for him with Mivuno there."

"Who's Mivuno?"

Jara stopped her digging and looked up at him. "Aychega's brother," she said. She spoke of Mivuno with great apprehension. "Rango's had to make some concessions." Then she began to dig again. "Rango and I talked about the tides," she said. "He still wants to believe you."

Hab sighed. "I know."

She pitched a sizable chunk of rubble away. "He's convinced himself that you misunderstood him, that you would have told him the truth about the tides if he'd explained it to you in a better way. That's not good, that he wants to trust you. Mivuno's just waiting for an excuse to kill him."

❧❧❧

The first hopper touched the soil of Paras just as Hab pushed his cell door open. Hab and Jara embraced with no words exchanged; why use words when the embrace was complete in itself? No time for more than a quick kiss. No time for more than the sketch of a caress. Then it was hand in hand down the corridor, and out into the morning sunshine. Out into the smell of smoke, dust, and death.

On the hill just before them, the Fanille lay broken and smoldering. Three jailer's carts lay overturned on the marsh lane, and the field next to the prison was now no more than a black expanse of burned grass.

They walked up the lane to the law courts. The black domes of the much-vaunted palace of justice were gone. The civil wing was rubble. Knots of people moved about Place Giofre, some tending wounded, some pulling handcarts of household possessions, some just standing wide-eyed in bewilderment, everybody dirty, covered with dust, not sure what had happened.

Hab lifted the splintered spoke of a blown-up mail wagon. He wanted a weapon.

They made their way into Triser, where the buildings were still burning, and where various district fire brigades were still fighting the flames. From here, Hab and Jara got a clear view of the city below. The hoppers hopped, black specks leaping out of the rubble. The killing had begun. The enslaving had begun.

Hab and Jara walked along Cabeau Lane, crossed Orierre Circus, attempted the Rousse Warren, but saw hoppers down there, so quickly backtracked and hurried along Amadre Road. In a small square at the foot of Amadre Road, a baker's cart had been overturned and flour strewn everywhere. Many of the cobblestones looked as if they were covered with snow. Looking farther along, they saw two men, two women, and three children, all decapitated, their bodies hacked with battle-axes, their clothes half charred by fire.

They finally reached Bosiler Boulevard. Most of the front part of the family compound had been blown to rubble. Hab could see right into the courtyard from the street. Strange to see the courtyard from the street, the lemon trees all in blossom, the fountains still bubbling, the gardens untouched by the destruction. Hab and Jara climbed over a mound of rubble into the courtyard and entered what was left of the west wing.

Much of the plaster had crumbled away from the walls, but the structure otherwise looked stable. They worked their way to the south end of the east wing, where the new family apartment was. The windows were all shattered. Dust covered everything.

"Thia?" Hab called. "Romal?" No answer.

They walked to the wine cellar. From the top of the wine cellar stairs, Hab saw flickering lamplight emanating from below.

"Thia?" he called again. He saw shadows down there.

"Hab?" called Thia from below.

She appeared at the bottom of the stairs holding one of Romal's crossbows in her hands.

"Stay there," he said. "We're coming down."

Hab and Jara descended the narrow stairs. At the bottom they found a handful of house servants sitting around on upended wine kegs. Thia wore a heavy blue cloak. Burn marks scorched the back of it.

"Where's Romal?" asked Hab.

"I don't know," said Thia. Dirt covered her face, and tear marks streaked white lines over her cheeks. "He never came back."

Hab and Jara looked at each other. Jara stepped forward and put her hand on Thia's arm. "Thia, you should come with us. It's not safe here anymore. We're going to head north."

In a calm voice Thia said, "I'm going to wait for him."

"You have to come with us," insisted Jara. "We'll saddle some chevuls and leave by the Port Road."

"I won't leave my husband."

Hab stared at his sister-in-law. Did she really love Romal? Despite the way he mistreated her, and how he was always off drinking and gambling, was there something of a marriage between them after all?

Before he could think of words that might convince her, he heard a thump upstairs. Thia immediately raised her crossbow. Hab heard scuffling—clawed toes in an awkward gait along the stone floor. And then he smelled it: that odd charcoal smell. A dark shape hopped down the stairs and landed right in front of them, a black hopper in full battle gear, sword in hand, eyes glowing like embers, scales like obsidian.

Thia fired her crossbow, but she missed. The servants cried. The hopper pulled some rope from his weapons belt. He raised his other hand and beckoned to the group of humans. "*Ipi, ipa, ipo,*" he said. Hab and Jara looked at each other. "*Ipa, ipi, ipo, dika, diko, diki,*" growled the hopper, obviously growing impatient.

Jara moved slowly to a wine keg. The hopper watched her closely. She raised her hands, showing him that she wasn't going to try anything. She lifted a stoneware dipper from the top of the keg, held it under the spigot, turned the spigot, and filled the dipper. She bared her teeth in an approximation of a hopper smile, then drank some of the wine, knowing that any hopper would be naturally suspicious of poison, then offered the dipper to the *sikingo-mango.*

"*Abungo tifu?*" asked the hopper. Is it drink?

Jara again bared her teeth in hopper fashion. "*Mu,*" she said. "*Mua, mui, muo,*" she said.

The hopper stared. "*Yathelu abungo Abani?*" he asked. Do you speak Abani?

She raised the dipper higher, baring her teeth farther, and said, in Abani, "A full stomach to you."

This distracted the hopper immensely, that this human should be speaking its language. And in the hopper's moment of distraction, Hab launched himself at the hopper. He went right for its neck with the wagon spoke and plunged the splintered end through the *sikingo-mango*'s throat. The hopper spasmodically swung its sword, but Hab was already out of the way, pulling the regular's battle-axe from its weapons belt. Close hand-to-hand combat was a fool's trick with a hopper, but what choice did he have? Surprise was the only thing that worked in a situation like this, and Hab thought he had never seen a hopper so surprised. With the spoke through its throat, and blood spurting out from its carotid artery, the creature stumbled forward and took a feeble swing at Jara with his sword. Jara jumped out of the way. The regular crashed to the floor. Hab hacked the creature's head off with the battle-axe.

When he was done, both he and Jara were splattered with blood.

Thia and the servants stared in shock. Hab and Jara were, by this time, inured to bloodshed. Hab stepped over the dead hopper and put his hand on Thia's shoulder.

"Thia," he said, as gently as he could. "It's war." He nodded, trying to get past the shocked look on her face. "After five hundred years, it's finally war."

She stared at him. "Go away," she said. Thia looked at Hab, then at Jara, her hazy blue eyes glassing over. She looked old. "I'm waiting for Romal," she said.

Hab stood there staring at the woman. "We'll try to come back," he said. "Or if you can make it to Summerhouse—"

"I'm going to wait for my husband," she repeated.

Hab saw that it was pointless.

He and Jara were just riding away on the quickest chevuls, Hab armed with the hopper's battle-axe, Jara with its sword, when five hoppers hopped into the family compound courtyard. Two entered the west wing. Three went to the south part. A minute later, looking down from the Port Road, Hab saw Thia and her servants standing in the courtyard, chained together one to the next, guarded by armed *sikingo-mango* regulars.

CHAPTER TWENTY-SEVEN

Traffic jammed the Port Road north of Jauny. Carts, wagons, carriages, buggies, and runabouts streamed away from the city. Refugees. The antique word, long vanished from common use, echoed uneasily in Hab's mind. Some of the refugees sat on the side of the road in bewilderment. Some headed back to Jauny. Now that the bombardment was over, many thought it might be safe to return.

When Hab and Jara reached the Vellaisson Plain, the broad flat plain overlooking Jauny where the circus came every year and where some ruins of the ancient Jauny could still be seen, Hab turned around and looked back at the capital. Several columns of black smoke rose from the rubble, and, as the smoke reached a certain height, it was carried southward by the wind. The *sikingo-mango* warships still sat at anchor in the Estuary, looking like toys from this distance. Hoppers were like fleas on a dog's back, leaping twenty and thirty feet into the air out of the rubble, thousands of them. Hab was reminded not so much of an invasion but of an infestation.

"Let's cross the plain," he said. "We'll never get through all these people otherwise. Cloudesley's eighty miles off, and Summerhouse only a hundred."

They reined their chevuls over the Vellaisson Plain. Once they crossed the plain, they rode for five hours through the deciduous forests south of the Lesser Oradels, and stopped at two bells to let their chevuls eat and drink. The horns of Hab's chevul needed a trim, were two feet long, so he took Jara's sword and began to whittle away. The chevul clucked in pleasure and scuffed its hoofs against the grass as the molt of its horns was scraped away.

"Do you think you'll convince him?" asked Jara. She was speaking of Parprouch.

"He's undoubtedly heard by now," he said.

"But how will he raise an army?" asked Jara.

Hab scraped a particularly troublesome knob of horn away. "Over half the nobles in Jondonq live within ten square miles of Summerhouse," he said. "Many of those nobles control the strongest fiefs in the country. They have at their command thousands of men and women. We'll be on high ground at Summerhouse. And that counts when you're fighting hoppers. Summerhouse is where we'll make our stand. I don't want them sailing any farther up the Necontreu than that."

They made love in the sunshine while their animals drank and ate. In the arms of Jara, in the leaf-dappled glade, with the musical sound of the brook nearby, he could nearly believe that everything was back to normal. But even at the height of their desperate pleasure, he was plagued by that last haunting image on Bosiler Boulevard, Thia and her servants chain-ganged and enslaved by the hoppers.

By the time they had their clothes back on, he was anxious, worried, and restless to be on his way.

They rode for the rest of the afternoon. They passed Cloudesley at sunset. Hab gazed at the gray stone walls, spied the amber gazebo in the south grounds, and the mill wheel spinning lazily in the stream under overhanging trees. Cloudesley was gone now. Liquidated. Sold. He turned away. He was back home, but home wasn't the same anymore.

They reached Summerhouse as the first stars came out.

"We bring news of the invasion," Hab said to the five Civil Guards who peered nervously out the gate. "We must speak to Parprouch. I am Hab Miquay. I am returned from the land of the barbarians. I have news that will help us defeat the barbarians."

The guards, after talking among themselves for a minute, swung the gate open. Hab and Jara rode up the hill to the amber towers of Summerhouse. Hab remembered Gashak's battle-house above the training field in Chungwa, a bleak and drab structure of stacked metal floors, the *sikingo-mango* equivalent of Summerhouse. In contrast, the Parassian seat of government rose in elegant spires—bright, enchanting, dazzling—built of the choicest amber mined from the best amber mines in Zairab, an iridescent conglomeration of vaulting towers luminescent in the starlight. The king's ostler took their chevuls at the top of the hill, and, once they explained their business to one of the king's many chamberlains, they were shown directly into the Council Hall, where Parprouch conferred with many of the kingdom's highest-ranking nobles.

ᔆᔆᔆ

Parprouch and the nobles stared at Hab and Jara as they entered the Council Hall. A great fire burned in the hearth, and the council table was strewn with the remains of a feast—a joadre, roasted whole, glazed with applesauce, of which only the head remained.

Parprouch was without his crown. His gray hair hung limply around the sides of his head. His narrow face looked particularly drawn this evening, and his eyes were like black marbles, numb, uncomprehending, catching and reflecting the candlelight on the table.

Hab glanced around at the other nobles. Lord Teur was there, looking old and decrepit, as small and fragile as a nuiyau bird nestling. So was Lord Raq, a robust middle-aged man, as tall as Hab, bald, but with a bushy black beard, dressed in red silk and black boots that came up to his knees. There was Lord Martene, dressed in pink, his hair dyed purple, his eyes ringed with eyeliner, wearing striped pantaloons and a jeweled codpiece. And there was Lord Iolas, a sallow and undemonstrative man whose dour eyes contemplated Hab and Jara as if he pitied them for their existence. Finally, there was Lord Terrarre, a man about Hab's age, forty, an ardent patron of science who on his estate in Calleux funded a thriving community of inventors, alchemists, astronomers, mathematicians, and philosophers, the only lord among them who wasn't wearing a codpiece.

Parprouch rose slowly. Hab and Jara bowed.

"You are a criminal, Hab Miquay," began the monarch. "You are in direct violation of the compact you signed with your king. You have embezzled from the rightful heir to Cloudesley his proper fortune."

Hab rose to his full height, squared his shoulders, and stared at the king, unable to hide his displeasure, and got right to the point. "You've by now heard reports of the invasion, Sire?" he said.

"I have," said Parprouch.

"The capital is sacked and the Golden Land overrun by creatures more strange and brutal than any in Oeil. I sailed to their land. I am not a criminal. And I am not a Liar. I am the truth, Sire. The truth is me in my small boat sailing to the other side of the world and finding these creatures. The truth is me leading them back here. The truth is me telling you that we've got to stop them. My little ship, across the sea and through the tides, my lords, that's the truth. I bounced against Ortok, and now Ortok—for this is what the invaders call their land—bounces against Paras. This is the truth, my lords. That it's happened now, in our time, is our misfortune. That it's happened now, in our time, is also our challenge. Because I say to you, if not now, then ten years hence. If not ten years hence, then a hundred years hence. And if not me, then another sailor like me. And if not him, then someone else. Whatever the time and whomever the man, happen it did and happen it must. Sooner or later we would breach the tides. And now that we've crossed those dangerous and infernal waters, the truth is war, my lords. I am not a criminal, Sire. I am here to help."

For a long time nobody spoke. They all just stared. Parprouch's eyes were wide, bulging, and his brow was pinched. He finally sat down in his throne. He poised his bearded chin between a thumb and two fingers and looked pensively at the remains of the feast. The other lords shifted uncomfortably in their seats.

It was Lord Terrarre who finally spoke. "My liege," he said to the king, "if we don't quickly reconcile ourselves to Cloudesley's words, we'll be lost. The time has come for action. The rulings the court has taken against Cloudesley while he was gone mean nothing in the face of what he's telling us. And he's telling the truth. The truth burns in his voice. We must act, Sire, and we must act now."

Hab examined Lord Terrarre more closely. Lord Terrarre had shoulder-length brown hair, a mustache that was curled up at the ends, a long nose that tapered to a point, and fair blue eyes the color of a Berberton summer sky. He wore the brown frock and breeches of a common squire, plain and durable-looking clothes. Hab glanced at his sovereign. Parprouch was looking at Hab with a pained expression, as if life had become hopelessly perplexing to him. Parprouch's eyes then alighted on Jara.

"Do I recognize you, girl?" said the monarch.

Jara stepped forward and curtsied. "Sire, my name is Jara Pepteri. My brother was Esten Pepteri. You graciously extend your patronage to us in our endeavor to decipher the Great Code. You also show your munificence on Maju, where we recover the fossilized bones of creatures long extinct."

"Yes, now I recall," said Parprouch. "And can you confirm what the mariner's telling us?"

She curtsied again. "I can, my liege," she said.

"Then you have my ear, Hab Miquay of Cloudesley."

Hab told his story—his voyage into the polar sea, south through the ocean on the other side of the world, his arrival in Ortok, his capture, his time with Rango, and his subsequent voyage back to Paras. Then he spoke of the hopper as a species.

"He is large and he hops. He can walk, but walks awkwardly. His world is bleak and inhospitable, and he faces starvation on a daily basis. He has been taught since birth to lie, cheat, and steal. Everyone must fight for food. Survival is by no means assured. Murder is rampant, even tolerated, and never goes punished. Suspicion is admirable, and the double-cross the mainstay of their diplomacy. Slavery is the chief mode of commerce, cannibalism the preferred method of sustenance."

"Then it is Oeil you have discovered," said Lord Martene.

"No, not Oeil, but a place much like it. Ortok is a volcanic continent two-thirds the size of Paras. It lies roughly fifteen thousand miles to the southeast of Paras, or twenty thousand miles to the southwest, in a tropic zone just beneath the equator. Its interior is virtually uninhabitable. They call the interior the Black Desert. Most hoppers live on the west coast, where there are cooling winds and occasional heavy rains. Only a few live in the Black Desert."

Hab then urged the lords to spend all available resources on building an army.

"An army?" said Lord Iolas, tapping his fingers against his paunch with nervous agitation. "And what are we going to use for weapons? If the reports are correct, these creatures are armed with weapons made of steel. How can we fight them when all we have is wood, amber, and stone? Spending money on an army would be futile." He looked around at his fellow nobles. "Can you imagine the expense of such an endeavor? I for one think my decous would be better spent trying to appease these creatures with imaginative gifts or elaborate feasts. Tell them we mean them no harm, that there's plenty for all, and then throw them a lavish party. Open our best wines. Slaughter our finest livestock. Dazzle their eyes with our brightest gems. Compose for them graceful symphonies. Devise clever entertainments. My pocketbook could certainly afford that. But to arm a force to meet these indomitable creatures when such a challenge from the outset is doomed to failure . . . where's the good sense in that?"

"Lord Iolas," said Jara, rather sternly, "the *sikingo-mango* won't be dazzled by your symphonies or entertainments. They simply want to conquer. They don't want jewels or feasts. They want war. They want to fight. They like to kill. There's no negotiating with these creatures. They mean to defeat us. They mean to subjugate us. Forget about your pocketbook. Your pocketbook will mean nothing once you're roasting live over an open fire."

They all stared at Jara in silent shock. Lord Raq shifted apprehensively. "Then . . . then . . . I suppose we better surrender immediately. If it's going to stop widespread bloodshed then—"

Hab interrupted the big bald lord. "No," he said. "If we surrender, we die. We must fight. But we must fight to the end. The *sikingo-mango* fight hand-to-hand. That's their way. They don't use crossbows. They don't use spears. They might pitch a snare at you, but other than that, they prefer to kill you with their bare hands. To be killed by a hopper you must come within arm's reach. This is the way they fight. This is their code of honor. They might use cannonade to bombard a city, but once their regulars are on the field it's the sword, the battle-axe, and the mace. This is their code. This is their honor. And this is our advantage. If we fight with crossbows at a distance we might stand a chance." He looked at each of the lords. "I ask you, Iolas, Raq, Martene, and Terrarre, to return to your fiefs and enlist as many yeomen, peasants, and farmers as you can. Find as many crossbows as you can. We can rip down the vekeui pikes from the fence around the palace and use them as spears. We can douse the hillside with Affed oil and light it on fire. We can plant some of the pikes in the hillside. This might stop them from hopping."

"But they wear armor," said Lord Teur, speaking up for the first time. "Our marksmanship will have to be superb. We'll be restricted to head-shots."

"Then head-shots it will be," said Hab.

"But can our amber arrowheads penetrate the carapaces of these creatures?" asked Lord Teur doubtfully.

"We'll make stone arrowheads. We'll scrounge up as much metal as we can and make metal arrowheads."

"Metal arrowheads?" said Lord Iolas, clearly aghast at the notion. "As expendable ammunition? One might as well take one's decous and pitch them off the Cliffs of Alquay."

ᶋᶋᶋ

Lord Teur led Hab, Jara, and Lord Terrarre down a long winding passageway deep under the palace of Summerhouse early the next day. Lords Raq, Martene, and Iolas had already departed for their fiefs to raise as many foot soldiers as they could. The corridor was so long and winding that Hab began to mark his paces. When he counted over a thousand he knew they had to be far from Summerhouse, somewhere out under the pastures and parkland that surrounded the palace. The corridor was no longer a corridor but a tunnel, with an arched ceiling made of stone and mortar, smelling of earth, with small puddles collecting in the unevennesses of the stone floor. The only light came from Lord Teur's lantern.

"These weapons are old," said Lord Teur. "They haven't been used for hundreds of years."

At last they came to a large wooden door at the end of the tunnel. Lord Teur pushed the door open. Inside they found a cone-shaped chamber with twelve sides arranged in a dodecahedron, the twelve different walls rising halfway up, then curving to a point at the top. The chamber had a diameter of twenty-five yards. Metal weapons hung on racks everywhere, weapons much like hopper weapons, only smaller, made to human scale: swords, battle-axes, spiked maces, hundreds of crossbows, and at least a hundred bushel baskets of arrows with metal arrowheads. A milky light filtered in through a half dozen overhead vents. Lord Teur extinguished his lantern because there was now enough light to see by.

"The House of Zadeaux has been collecting these weapons for the last two centuries," said Lord Teur. "When I became adviser to Parprouch I engaged a hundred smithies. We live in a peaceful land. There hasn't been war for five hundred years. But as the king's adviser I plan for all contingencies, even ones I can't foresee." Lord Teur walked across the chamber. "These wagons are filled with weapons as well. And these are battle plans over here," he said, waving to several scrolls stacked on a shelf. He pulled one down and flattened it on the work-table. The others gathered round to look. "This battle plan outlines a defense of Summerhouse from a southward attack. I drew these plans twenty years ago, when I was younger and had more energy. I have other plans, one for an attack from the north, another from the west, and another from the east—an amphibious attack from the Estuary. In fact, the Estuary's just down the hill here. If Cloudesley and Terrarre could be so kind as to open this door, we'll all have a good view of it."

The door was large, wide enough for wagons to pass through, and had three stone gargoyles sitting on pediments above. Hab and Ter-rarre opened the door. Bright morning sunshine spilled into the chamber. Hab took a few steps outside and saw that, indeed, they were on a hillside overlooking the Estuary. A cart track led from the door through a grove of young motwood trees. The leaves of the motwood trees were out, glowing golden in their characteristic yellow of spring.

Lord Teur emerged and stood beside him. "This is another contin-gency," he said. "In case we have to retreat. See that building over there through the trees? We stable three teams of chevuls in there. If and when we have to retreat, we harness the teams to these three wagons full of weapons. We must make certain we have weapons to protect our flank as we retreat. We have another cache of weapons at Winterhouse. Winterhouse is the fallback position in my plan. We have high ground at Winterhouse, and we're upstream from any attacking amphibious force along the Necontreu. . . ." Lord Teur trailed off; he looked at Hab speculatively. "What's wrong, Hab of Cloudesley? Why so downcast? I thought you might take hope from my secret cache."

Hab took a deep breath of the spring air. "Your prudence is admirable, Lord Teur. But these close-combat weapons will be useless against the *sikingo-mango*. Our soldiers must avoid hand-to-hand fighting at any cost. We can take the arrows. But I sincerely suggest you block this tunnel and hide this gate. This is a weapons cache the hoppers don't need to know about. If such weapons fell into their hands, their significant arsenal would be that much increased, and so would the threat to ourselves. Give our yeomen and peasants these superior arrows and tell them to shoot well. That's about the best we can make of this weapons cache."

ᕷᕷᕷ

By the next day, Hab and the lords had raised an army of eleven hundred yeomen and peasants. The metal-tipped arrows were given to the best archers. Two hundred and seventeen men and seventy-six women could hit groupings within a three-inch range, even with the Laisse Winds blowing fair from the Lesser Oradels. Each of these archers received between five and seven metal-tipped arrows. The other less skilled archers were given stone-tipped arrows.

Parprouch sent riders south to spy on the *sikingo-mango*.

One came back three days later, a lad of eighteen by the name of Oddarme, a wisp of a boy, a natural-born jockey who raced regularly at the derbies in Calleux. By this time pikes had been planted on the hillside surrounding Summerhouse, the ground saturated with Affed oil, and, taking an idea from the hoppers themselves, bottles filled with Affed oil and stuffed with rough cloth wicks, ready to be used as bombs. Two hundred had volunteered for close-combat assignments, despite the high risk, and, consequently, over half the close-combat weapons were brought up from the armory and given to these brave souls. The messenger, Oddarme, out of breath and hot, made his report.

"They're moving up the Port Road, killing and maiming any and all refugees they see," he said. "The fields flow with blood. An amphibious force of thousands sails north on the Necontreu. They wear our heads on their belts. Some of us fight back. Reports confirm that anywhere between two and three hundred of the black ones have been killed. But I'm afraid most of us just run or hide."

Chapter Twenty-Eight

The hoppers came just before dawn, in the darkest part of the night, as Hab had known they would. If it hadn't been for Lag beaming peacefully over the peaks of the Lesser Oradels, Hab wouldn't have seen the *sikingo-mango* army at all. The regulars showed up like dark shadows on the moonlit plain below. And on the glittering waters of the Estuary three miles away, Hab saw attack boats, smaller than the ones left behind in Jauny, made of flimsy wood, carried on metal ships across the ocean all this way. Hab handed his telescope to Jara. Jara scanned the field below.

"Should we give the order to attack?" she asked.

"No," he said. "Wait till they come closer."

Jara handed the telescope to the king. The three stood behind a low stone wall overlooking the valley and floodplain of the Necontreu. Parprouch held the telescope to his eye.

"I thought you said they hopped twenty or thirty feet at a time," he commented. "They're not hopping much more than five or six right now."

"They move cautiously, Sire," said Hab.

The *sikingo-mango* army approached in a loose stretched-out front two miles across. Hab heard the faint jangle of their weaponry, like an old refrain. The king stared intently at the enemy through the telescope. Hab looked at Parprouch. He saw something he had never seen before in his monarch, a resoluteness and determination. Terrarre came clopping past the fountain on a black-and-white chevul.

"Our archers are prepared," he said. "I've received word that the enemy is within range. The archers await your order, Sire."

Parprouch turned to Hab. This, too, was new, the way the monarch now looked to Hab. "I require your advice, mariner," said the king.

Hab nodded. "Have west battery circle to the rear. North battery attacks first. East battery will pinch them at the flank."

The monarch turned to Terrarre and gave him a grim nod. "As the mariner says," he commanded. "Send the orders down the line. Make Raq, Martene, and Iolas stand prepared."

Five minutes later, Hab heard the *sikingo-mango* bellowing at the foot of the hill. He saw them hop up the steep slope, leaping as much as forty feet at a time. Many of them landed right on top of the camouflaged pikes, impaling themselves, unprepared for this tactic on the part of the Parassians. Hab heard their grunts and their cries. Hoppers in the second and third ranks held back, realized they couldn't hop up the hill, so walked, weaving their way around the pikes and their skewered fellow soldiers. To the east the barest glimmer of dawn appeared on the horizon, marking in silhouette the advance of the hopper army, providing a clearer target for the archers. Beside him, Jara fit her crossbow with an arrow.

They watched the hoppers climb the hill. Some grew impatient and hopped in spite of the pikes, only to find themselves skewered like their less fortunate fellow regulars. Hab raised his hand. He knew Lord Teur was up in the tower watching him with a telescope. From the tower, a moment later, a rocket burst forth, an ornamental and flowery bit of pyrotechnical display, the kind of firework saved for the Year-End. The rocket screamed into the air, etching a trail of orange sparks behind it, and exploded into seventeen starbursts, all bright blue, the national color of Paras, lighting the battlefield for miles around, illuminating every single hopper in sharp detail. All the hoppers looked up, an army of monsters, a thousand pairs of ruby eyes staring skyward. This was the signal. Arrows filled the air. From up on the hill next to the palace Hab watched the hoppers fall by the dozens as the expert marksmen of the king's new army let fly with a barrage of tempered steel arrowheads. The hoppers looked around in confusion and surprise. Then, as expected, they fell to defensive positions on the ground, put their hands around their necks, and curled into fetal positions. In this position they were invulnerable to the metal arrowheads.

Hab called down the line, "Light the fires!"

He heard his order echoed along the hilltop and finally down into the valley.

Over the next five minutes a wall of flame crawled down the hill. Hundreds of kegs of Affed oil planted around the field exploded, adding great roaring bursts of flame to the already burning field. The hoppers had no choice but to get up. Which they did, in the hundreds, and this in turn opened them to crossbow fire again. The arrows sang in thick flocks through the air while the *sikingo-mango* regulars hopped frantically to escape the flames. Already Hab could smell the well-remembered scent of roasting hopper flesh. The Affed oil burned with a distinctive white flame that crawled in ragged and luminescent tongues, like an unstoppable tide toward the hedgerows to the left. The hedgerows, painted with the thick sticky derivative of the Affed bush, ignited all in a piece with an audible *poof!* The smoke billowed thick and black into the brightening morning sky, and down on the field, hoppers fell everywhere. Hab thought it was working. He thought they were going to drive them back. The heat from the field was so intense that he could feel it up here. But then he saw that it wasn't enough, that behind the second and third ranks of hoppers there were at least a dozen more ranks.

These next ranks quickly stamped out the fire with their big hopper feet, and taking a closer look through the telescope, Hab saw that this new rank was comprised of the spiked and fearsome tar-pool hoppers, the *hari-bumuku*, and that they stamped out the flames as if the soles of their feet were impervious to it. Hab saw a thicket of arrows fly from the rear, knew the intent of the west battery archers was to slow the advance of these tar-pool hoppers, but the metal-tipped arrows simply wouldn't penetrate the spiny ugly necks of the *hari-bumuku*, and worse still, the volley of arrows revealed the location of the west battery. The archers were spread out in a grove east of a farmer's thatched cottage.

Sikingo-mango regulars immediately moved in. And then the screams started. Human screams. The screams of brave men and women subjected to the blade. Hab and Jara looked at each other, their eyes growing wide. Despite the heat from the burning hillside, Hab felt cold. Human butchery and dismemberment. War. Parprouch stared down at the grove near the cottage with grim eyes.

"I fear the battle now favors our enemies," he said.

And so it continued as the sky grew brighter and brighter. Contingents of black hopper infantry flanked left and right and pincered the remaining batteries of archers, cutting them off from the main body defending Summerhouse. Even more ominous was the movement out on the Estuary, eight assault boats taking advantage of an unexpected change in the wind, moving with full sails against the weak current of the outgoing tide, each boat filled with at least two dozen hoppers.

The dawn sky was now purple, gold, and pink. The fires were nearly out. *Sikingo-mango* regulars advanced up the hill to the palace, pulling out pikes one by one, making way for a full hopper assault. Hab made a rough count of hopper corpses, about five hundred, far more than he could have hoped for, but still not enough.

"What of our archers?" asked Parprouch.

Hab looked at the king. The priests of Pendagal preached optimism as part of the standard liturgy. In a place like the Golden Land, optimism was easy. The king desperately clutched at this optimism now. But Hab knew this wasn't the time for optimism. This was a time for blunt pragmatism.

"Dead, Sire."

Parprouch's face grew solemn. He looked down the hillside at the *sikingo-mango*. "They advance," said the monarch.

"My liege, take note of those boats down there on the Estuary," said Hab, growing ever more concerned. "Those troops are going to land near the mouth of the Necontreu. They are going to attack us from the rear. I want to take Terrarre and Jara, and thirty of our soldiers, and ride to the mouth of the Necontreu before they get there. I saw some smacks harbored there. We'll take them out into the harbor and ram their boats. The river is wide there. The hoppers wear heavy armor. If we ram their boats they'll sink before they can swim to shore."

"Of course, Cloudesley." The monarch nodded distractedly. "But what about these hideous creatures whom this very moment are dismantling our defenses and advancing up the hill?"

Hab gestured at the rack of firebombs. "When they're about halfway up, Sire, give the order for the bombs." Hab put his hand on Parprouch's shoulder. "Lead your people, Parprouch. Show them that you are their king."

𓆟𓆟𓆟

Hab, Jara, Lord Terrarre, and twenty-five peasants, yeomen, and farmers saddled chevuls and followed an old cart trail toward the mouth of the Necontreu at the northern end of the Estuary. Though not expecting any close combat with the hoppers, everyone was armed with either a sword, battle-axe, or spiked mace from the armory. Hab wore a sword. All carried crossbows and a quiver of metal-tipped arrows. The trail wound down the hillside, curving toward the Estuary. The sky was gold, teased with curls of pink cirrus clouds. Through the trees Hab saw the water, flat and still, with dimples of ebb-tide here and there. The road angled closer to the Estuary, and rounding a final bend, they came to a small quay, where two smacks rested against the dock.

The small group of fighters tied their chevuls in and among the trees and quickly manned the smacks. With sails soon set and anchors hoisted, the vessels set off down the Estuary toward the approaching group of hopper boats. Terrarre commanded the *Shiffeau*, a winsome craft with a black hull and eyes painted on her bows, while Hab commanded the *Feulleulle*, a heavier boat with a higher mast and a bigger sail. The Laisse Winds, so consistently from the northwest at this time of year, refused to cooperate, had snuck around the windward side of the Lesser Oradels and doubled back from the southwest, making progress for the two smacks difficult. They had to tack, and this compromised their maneuverability. Their only advantage was the outgoing tide.

Jara joined Hab at the helm of the *Feulleulle*, slipped her arm around his waist while he turned the wheel a spoke or two to port. She rested her cheek against his shoulder. He thought she would say something, but she didn't. He glanced down at her. She was a stalwart and silent support.

The *Feulleulle* and the *Shiffeau* bore down on the eight hopper boats. Over the still water Hab heard the hoppers bellowing in alarm. He turned the helm a few more spokes to port and rammed the first of them. The smack plowed into the boat, cracking her gunwale, forcing all the regulars to jump overboard. The *Shiffeau* plowed into its own boat with the same result. The assault crafts were loosely aligned into two columns. Thus, their dispositions couldn't have been more favorable for ramming. Down went a third boat, then a fourth, the hoppers bellowing madly. All went quickly to the bottom in their heavy metal armor. Down went a fifth, but this time, some of the hoppers were able to get their armor off quickly enough. They swam for shore, fantastically good swimmers, fast and tireless, nearly as good as the beach hoppers.

"Archers, to your stations!" cried Hab.

The archers let go with volley after volley at the escaping hoppers, aiming expertly for their unprotected necks. In moments, bright runlets of blood appeared in the water. The *Feulleulle* rammed the sixth boat, while the *Shiffeau* rammed the seventh, the crack of the wood echoing over the flat surface of the Estuary. Jara climbed to the bow as they approached the eighth and final boat. She hoisted her crossbow and prepared to shoot. But then she hesitated. She turned to Hab.

"It's Rango," she said.

Hab looked, and sure enough, there he was, Rango, the hopper who was different, the hopper who wanted to believe, who wanted to trust. Hab swung the helm violently to the starboard side. But he was too late. The *Feulleulle* rammed the boat. Hab gave the helm to the yeoman and ran to the bow. He saw Rango, the healed scar bright red on his scalp. The drillmaster fell backward into the water. He caught Hab's eye. He wasn't wearing hopper-hide armor. He wore metal armor.

"Archers, leave off!" he cried. Rango floundered in the water, struggling to stay afloat in his armor. "Yeoman!" cried Hab. "A line!"

The yeoman hurried forward with a rope. Hab took the coil and flung the line to Rango. While the other regulars around him sank to the bottom, Rango latched onto the rope. "Lend a hand," Hab said to Jara. Jara joined him. Together they pulled Rango toward the smack. Rango looked up at them with desperate eyes.

"*Shakango yathelu haminingo, Hab?*" he sputtered. Are you going to save me?

Hab didn't answer, kept pulling. The archers gathered on the bow. They stared at Rango in astonishment.

"Archers at the ready," Hab commanded. "We have a prisoner." Out on the water, Terrarre was coming about in the *Shiffeau*. Hab saw the big man, dressed in his brown squire clothes, raise his hand, giving his own archers the command to stand ready. "You there," shouted Hab to a sturdy lad, "lend a hand!" The lad came forward and helped them haul the four-hundred-pound drillmaster up onto the smack. Hab and Jara reached down and, gripping Rango's scaly clawed hands, pulled the *sikingo-mango* on board.

Rango gained his footing and, dripping wet, looked around, his red eyes like dull rubies in his face. Though a runt among his own kind, Rango towered above all the humans on the *Feulleulle*. The black hopper took quick stock of the fifteen archers ranged around him, then glanced over his shoulder into the water. His penis hung out like a long black rope from under his loincloth, a crude immodesty that somehow made him all the more terrifying to look at. Hab spoke to the drillmaster in Abani.

"Throw your weapons to the deck, drillmaster," he said.

Rango threw his sword, battle-axe, and dagger to the deck. "I don't need these weapons," he said, his growling voice seeming to rend the air with a deep vibration that Hab could feel in the pit of his stomach. "I can kill any one of you with my bare hands."

"Your life for Summerhouse, Rango," he said. "Tell your troops to retreat."

The hopper's eyes narrowed, his shoulders rose, and he turned his head to one side. "Am I hearing these words from the mouth of the peaceful one?" he said. "You barter my life? How well you've learned your lessons, Hab."

"I have to bind your hands, Rango," said Hab, lifting the rope. "Don't try to fight us." Rango raised his hands and allowed Hab to tie them. Hab ran the rope down to the hopper's ankles and bound them manacle-style.

He turned to his archers and switched to Parassian. "Guard him," he ordered.

He walked to the helm, signaled to Terrarre, and soon both smacks were heading back to the dock.

ʒʒʒ

At the dock, Hab tied three ropes around Rango's neck, making three leashes. He gave the leashes to the strongest yeomen in the group. This would stop the hopper from hopping.

He forced Rango to walk in the awkward gait of a hopper until they were a hundred yards up the road. Some farmers ventured into the woods and retrieved the chevuls. As the animals came clopping out onto the road, Rango cowered. The chevuls apparently unnerved him.

"Are you afraid of these creatures, Rango?" asked Hab. Rango just grunted. Hab turned to the three men with the leashes. "Tie him to the back of the biggest," he said.

Rango, once he saw that they were going to put him onto the back of a chevul, resisted only for a moment or two. As long as he was behind the hoofed creature's horns, he didn't seem to mind. He sat awkwardly on the saddle, his long muscular legs hanging over the left side of the beast. The chevul grew skittish with the hopper on its back. It took two peasants to settle it down. Everyone else mounted, and they started for the palace.

"You should have warned us about the tides, Hab," said Rango. Hab didn't answer. On the road ahead five white joadres trotted across the cart trail, one of them carrying an oversized apple in its mouth. "You might as well forget this trade, Hab," continued Rango. "Power is an elusive and shifting thing in my world, and I don't have as much of it as I did before the tides. There have been challenges." He glanced at Jara. "There have been threats. What happened in the tides severely undercut my authority. I've had to make concessions. Ask Jara. She knows."

Jara's eyes narrowed. "He's speaking of Mivuno," she said.

"A faithless, lying, ruthless, greedy, power-hungry son of a cut-throat," said Rango. "He doesn't see Takasa as salvation, Hab. He sees it as plunder. That I've now been captured will further undermine my authority. You should let me go. Get me off this beast. Mivuno will never make a trade."

"I don't care about Mivuno," said Hab.

"You have a choice of who conquers you, Hab. Don't let it be Mivuno."

"No one conquers us, Rango. You're going to be defeated."

"If Mivuno conquers Takasa he will destroy it. If I conquer Takasa, I will preserve it."

"You play for power, Rango."

"I offer mercy."

"You have nothing to offer except a shut mouth, *sikingo-mango*."

As they crested the rise to Summerhouse, Hab saw that despite the last-ditch defense of the firebombs, the palace had been overrun with *sikingo-mango* and *hari-bumuku* regulars, and that the king's fighting force had at last, under the force of superior numbers, surrendered. Hopper regulars shackled the humans together and herded them down the hill along the main wall toward the Estuary. Hab immediately saw the battle was lost, and that he would have to save what he could of the situation. These weren't soldiers. These were just peasants, farmers, yeomen, commoners, and landsmen cobbled into a mob that pretended to be an army. He wasn't surprised. But neither did he give up hope. He would defeat the hoppers, if not today then some other day, if not at Summerhouse, then at some other place.

"You see?" said Rango. "Mivuno conquers."

"Mivuno smells," said Hab.

Hab saw Parprouch, tallest of the humans, in chains, shackled together with his subjects, just another slave now. Hab paused, considering all the possibilities. He would trade for the king. The king would probably die in the attempt, but the death of the king might serve as an integral piece of the deception he was even now planning against the hoppers. His mind now worked in sly and devious ways. His mind now worked seven steps ahead of the game. Was the death of the king worth it? He had to try. He had to set the stage for the future defeat of the hoppers. The trade would be one for one. And Ouvant help the king. He turned to Jara.

"Which one's Mivuno?" asked Hab.

"He's the tallest. The one with the two human heads tied to his belt."

Hab spotted the tallest *hari-bumuku*, Aychega's brother, his pointed copper-colored scales ugly all over his body, a ridge of red spines sticking out the back of his head. He stood well above the rest, a giant, twelve feet tall, twice the height of a man, six hundred pounds. Hab raised his telescope and had a closer look. Even from this distance Hab saw a yellowish discharge oozing from his left eye.

"What's wrong with his eye?" he asked Rango in Abani.

"No one knows," said Rango. "He's had that ever since he was a boy. Sometimes it gets better, sometimes it gets worse, but it never goes away entirely. He's blind in that eye. And it oozes pus all the time."

The *hari-bumuku* was hideous with that eye dripping like that. He knew Mivuno was a brute and that the king was as good as dead. But dead, the king might provide the ultimate deception. As Hab looked through the telescope, he saw several hoppers point. They were discovered. He took the telescope away.

"They've seen us," he said.

"You should flee, Hab," said Rango, "while you still have a chance."

But they kept going up the hill toward the hopper army. "How many are still loyal to you?" he asked the drillmaster.

"About half," said Rango.

"You see the tall man there, with the gray hair and the long arms?"

Rango grunted affirmatively.

"He's our drillmaster. That's who I want."

"Deal with Mivuno at your own risk, human," said Rango, now exasperated with Hab. "You deal with a monster."

"Dismount," said Hab.

"As you wish," said Rango, sliding from the back of the chevul.

Hab raised his hand and flicked two fingers forward. Guarded by archers on every side, three yeomen tugged Rango toward the palace. Some hoppers immediately hopped forward, bounding thirty feet at a time, flanking out in all directions through the well-tended flowerbeds and gardens of Summerhouse. In ten seconds the humans were surrounded. But the hoppers didn't attack. They saw Rango.

"The Takasan comes to palaver," Rango grunted at them. "Make way, make way, or I'll crush the skulls of your firstborn between my teeth."

The hopper regulars backed away, their gait awkward, ambulating cautiously, their weapons drawn, taking small graceless steps into the flowerbeds, crushing all the flowers underfoot. The humans moved forward. The regulars in the flowerbeds moved slowly back with them. The line of slaves stopped to watch. A hundred *sikingo-mango* sat on the grass tending to their wounds. Hab was disappointed. He thought the metal-tipped arrows might have killed more. But he now saw that the metal arrows simply didn't have the power to be consistently fatal, and that a better weapon would have to be devised. Even as he edged his way into this dangerous situation, part of Hab, ever the problem solver, ever the inventor, tinkered with a solution. He took a deep breath, squared his impressive shoulders, and faced Aychega's eye-oozing brother.

"*Omingo mangi shakango mawatingo Rango,*" bellowed Hab to Mivuno. "*Inda boleano ganyiko ambiango afyango kifusa Rango.*" Hab pointed at Parprouch. "*Ipa, ipi majingo dango dangi danga.*"

Mivuno hopped forward. "We make no trades," he growled. "The tall one is ours. Keep Rango."

Hab raised his voice yet further and bellowed directly to the hopper troops. "Do you really want to be led by this cutthroat piece of sewage? Look at him. He's as stupid as a palango. Rango is smart. You are here in Takasa because of Rango. You owe your glory to Rango. And now you let this lowly piece of tar-pool excrement tell you what to do? He thinks he's better than the rest of you. You give us the tall one." Hab drew his sword and put it to Rango's neck. "Or you will be ruled by that cutthroat piece of *hari-bumuku* garbage."

Disconcerted grumbling swept through the army of hoppers. Mivuno looked back nervously. Many gazed at Mivuno with open hostility, while a half dozen others huddled near him as bodyguards. Finally, the giant *hari-bumuku* signaled to guards near Parprouch. The

guards unshackled Parprouch and shoved him forward. Hab wasn't
fooled. He knew the monarch was spending his last minutes alive. And
he hoped that when the moment came the king would understand. To
surrender, an army had to be defeated. Or at least look defeated. And
what looked more defeated than the murder of the army's leader?

The Parassian king and Rango approached each other slowly over
the open expanse of lawn. Parprouch's face was white. Silence fell over
the grounds. Parprouch and Rango passed each other, glanced at each
other, a strange and silent summit of the two leaders. Then Parprouch
looked at Hab, his eyes shining with gratitude. And that's when it all
went wrong, as Hab knew it must. For it was easy to understand what
a hopper would do, once you understood deceit.

Mivuno pulled his battle-axe from his belt and flung it expertly at
the sovereign. Rango cried, *"Buto, buto, buto!"* but the axe was already
twirling through the air, hasp over blade. Hab heard the sickening
thud as the axe sank into Parprouch's back. That was that. The king
stumbled, fell face forward to the ground. Done. Blood gurgled profusely from his back. Finished. Parprouch clawed the ground a few
times and died. The deception was complete.

Hab jerked on the reins of his chevul and galloped down the road.
His troops followed. The groundwork was laid. Hoppers hopped after
them, but the chevuls were too fast and whisked them quickly to the
quay and the waiting smacks. His archers let fly with a volley of
arrows, killing a half dozen pursuing *sikingo-mango*. Down to the dock
they went. The deception was planted. The king was dead. And Hab
knew, at last, such as every young hopper on Ortok knew, that, contrary to everything he had ever been told, honesty wasn't the way.

No, not at all.

The lie was the thing.

CHAPTER TWENTY-NINE

Winterhouse, when not used by the king, was a place of priests. Hab stood in the council chamber up on the third floor looking out over the Grand Sward, twenty acres of emerald green grass stretching in a narrow strip for nearly a mile in front of Winterhouse. The Wall rose to his right, stark, gray, a natural precipice several hundred feet high. The Great Code was carved into the Wall. Hab remembered Esten. He could understand why Esten had been so fascinated by the Great Code. A thing so old—and the Great Code was acknowledged to be sixty thousand years old—was a thing of great interest and fascination. A thing made before the Dark Time, that great and long age of historical stagnation from which this present glittering age had emerged only a thousand years ago. At the foot of the Wall stood the metal ruin, neatly preserved. This, too, was of great interest. No one knew what the metal ruin was, only that it was even older than the Great Code. Hab turned around. At the table sat Jara, Lord Terrarre, and Winterhouse's most senior priest, Damonel, a dour bald-headed man about seventy years old with a beak of a nose and humorless eyes. A messenger scout stood before them, a native Zairabian with dark skin, his name, Tubob.

"They move slowly northward," Tubob reported. "They encounter no resistance. They kill and maim wherever they go, and make slaves by the thousands. With the king now dead, the people feel defeated. The invaders occupy village after village, town after town. They burn and destroy."

Hab walked to the other side of the room. A large bay window faced the Lake of Life. The lake sparkled beyond a forest of conifers. Hab turned around and looked at Tubob. The people felt defeated. That was a good sign. The hoppers would feel this defeat. The hoppers would believe in quick victory. And they would be fooled.

"And there are many boats on the Necontreu?" asked Hab.

"Several dozen," said Tubob. "The invaders are able rivermen."

"I, for one, think we should evacuate," said Damonel, his brow set in what was turning out to be his perpetual frown. "My priests aren't fighters, Cloudesley. I forbid the use of Winterhouse as a redoubt. This is a holy place. This is a shrine."

Hab took a deep breath and sighed. "Damonel, we stand at Winterhouse," he said, growing tired of the priest's constant objections. "Evacuate your priests if you like, but not before you go to Dagu and recruit an army of one thousand men to replace them."

ぐぐぐ

Hab and Jara traveled to the east coast and sailed north to Fadil, the capital of Dagu. They carried in their ship's hold most of the metal weapons from the second secret armory at Winterhouse, over a ton of good hard steel worth hundreds of thousands of decous.

In Fadil they met Aigre the boat-builder. Hab showed Aigre his new designs. The aging boat-builder raised his bushy eyebrows in admiration at the ingenuity of Hab's deadly invention, then dispatched his most trusted apprentices to find the best metalworkers in the province. The master of the metalworkers' guild in Fadil, Fod, a man of forty with thick eyeglasses and salt-and-pepper hair, was the first to show up at Aigre's shipworks. Fod looked at Hab's design with growing interest.

Hab explained his rationale for such a design. "Our foes are twice our size and hop twenty to thirty feet at a time. This gives them an immense physical advantage over us. They fight with superior metal weapons. Our own weapons are made of amber or stone, are brittle and weak, meant to hunt game, and barely strong enough to penetrate the hopper's skin. We need metal. We must put what little metal we have to its best use. We must make from metal a weapon that can be used effectively at long range. Hand-to-hand combat with the physically superior hopper is out of the question. The metal arrow fired from a crossbow is only partially effective. In order for a metal projectile to be consistently fatal to a hopper, the missile must be hurtled at great speed. I steal designs from a harpoon cannon, but I make them small." He tapped the design. "This I call a handcannon. I saw many large cannons while I was in Ortok. We can't build large cannons in Paras because we don't have the metal. So let's build small ones, weapons we have the metal for, weapons we can use at long range, big enough to kill a single hopper, but small enough to carry around on the battlefield."

Fod nodded. "This rod," he said, pointing. "What's it for?"

"For packing," said Hab. "The soldier will first load the tube through the end with a crystalline derivative of Affed sap. Jara Pepteri knows how to make this crystalline derivative and will undertake to supervise its manufacture. Once the soldier has packed this crystalline derivative, he will then add some fodder to help with the ignition. Finally, he will pack his projectile."

"And what's this wick for?" asked Aigre. "And this hook?"

"That wick is soaked in slow-burning Affed tar. The hook holds the wick in a spring-lock mechanism. When the soldier pulls the trigger—and you can see that the trigger design is the same one we have on our crossbows—the spring releases, the hook and wick snap forward, the wick ignites this primer, and the primer in turn ignites the interior load. The resulting explosion is confined to the tube. The explosion naturally finds its way out the other end of the tube, pushing the projectile with great velocity toward the intended target. This pressure, then, is what drives the projectile forward." Hab looked at Fod evenly. "Can such a weapon be achieved, guild master?"

"With the proper materials, anything can be achieved, mariner," replied the guild master.

"I have old weapons from Winterhouse," he said. "Nearly two tons of tempered steel. The hopper army approaches the Lake of Life slowly, stopping often to consolidate its occupation. Even so, I'm more concerned about the time this will take than I am about the materials. We have the materials."

"Then we'll work round the clock until it's done," said Fod. "What to use for a projectile, though?"

Hab nodded. "The lead keels from the royal clippers anchored at Owsheau on the Island of Liars," he said.

ᔑᔑᔑ

So often, whenever Hab sailed in the Channel of Liars, the surface was apple red with the air bladders of whales and the sky was dark and misty with the autumn fogs. But now the channel was empty and the sky was bright with the sunshine of early summer.

They sailed, he and Jara, in an ancient trawler called the *Cenqu*, so named after the small intelligent dolphinlike creatures that found their sustenance by nibbling algae off the backs of bladder whales. They stood at the rail looking out over the waves. The Channel of Liars was usually a place of boats and ships. In fine weather like this they should have seen at least a half dozen on the horizon. But the sea was empty. Commerce had been strangled. Pleasure cruising had been suspended.

The Island of Liars came into view just as the sun set. A bleak and rocky coastline, yes, but certainly less forbidding than the coastline of Ortok.

The *Cenqu* angled gracefully toward the small port town of Owsheau, leaving a dainty silver wake on the water behind it. Liars, dressed in rags, gathered on the docks to watch. Beyond the point in the protected harbor, Hab saw the masts of the royal launches he had sold to Joulis. A moment later, Joulis himself came out of the purser's shed and walked onto the dock.

"Ho, there!" he called. "What ship are you?"

"Ho, there, Joulis!" called Hab.

Joulis's eyes widened. The *Cenqu* came neatly alongside the dock. Hab jumped from the gunwale to the dock and lifted Jara over. Joulis stared at him.

"I thought you were dead, mate," he said.

"I came close several times," admitted Hab.

"You bring news of the war?" asked Joulis.

"I do."

"Then let's retire to my shed." He turned to some of the Liars. "Feed this crew and make sure they're well looked after," he said. He offered his elbow to Jara. "Come along, then. We'll fix you up with some brandy and smoked pekra."

In the purser's shed, Joulis had several of the older Liars listen. Hab told them about the war. The hoppers ravaged Paras. They moved slowly northward. How long before they finally sailed across the small bit of water to Manense? some of the Liars asked. Hab didn't know, but he intended to fight them. Hab told Joulis about his new invention, the handcannon, and that he would need the lead in the keels of the royal clippers to make ammunition.

"Yes, yes, of course," said the purser.

"And I'm going to recruit an army of Manensers too," Hab said.

Everyone, including Jara, was stunned by this suggestion. That Liars, even in this gravest of situations, should be allowed to return to Paras hadn't occurred to any of them. But Hab remembered Tiq. He remembered Olle and Doran, and how well the three brothers had fought. He pressed on. "Manensers know how to fight," he said. "This barren island has made them strong. I need them. Paras needs them. Manense and Paras are no longer divided. We are at last joined in war."

᠂ᘓᘓᘓ᠂

Hab and Jara met Javal, the arbitrienne of Tiq's village, the next day. Javal was a thin but strong-looking man of sixty, with the brand of the six circles of Ouvant showing white against his wind-burnt wrinkled forehead. He wore a stone axe and a dagger in his belt. He had a large scar on his bare forearm.

Several young men stood around him, some with their stone axes in their hands, ready to protect the arbitrienne. Other young men were up in nearby trees with crossbows poised and ready. They were as suspicious as could be, and this was good. Hab lifted the amulet of Disseaule from over his head and offered it to the arbitrienne. Javal looked at the amulet, his eyes widening. The old man's lips tightened. Then his eyes grew misty with sadness as he realized what Hab had to tell him.

"You bring news of Tiq's death," he said. Javal looked at him quizzically. "You were the captain, weren't you? I recognize you now."

Hab nodded. "I was."

Javal raised his hand. All the young men standing around him eased their vigilance. "Come to my hut," said the old man, in the voice of one who was used to command.

In the hut, Hab told Javal how Tiq, Olle, and Doran had died.

"Then they died bravely," said Javal.

He described to Javal his long incarceration on Ortok and how he had been tricked into revealing tactical information about Paras.

"These creatures are deceivers," said Javal.

"All that time they meant nothing but war with us," said Hab. "I had no idea. I trusted them."

"Trust is a fool's commodity," said the arbitrienne, his voice like bedrock.

"Tiq told me of your raids."

"Yes?" said the arbitrienne.

"You are fighters. I need you. I need battle-experienced soldiers, and here on Manense is the only place I'll find them. The hoppers advance northward daily. The king is dead. The House of Zadeaux has fallen. You are now all free. The banishment laws are null and void. I have had Lord Teur proclaim them so. I can't force you to fight. Even so, you remain free."

The arbitrienne grinned, but it was a melancholy grin. "There cannot be freedom with these barbarians in our land," he said. "We will fight, as we have always fought. Only in fighting can we find our freedom."

ᔈᔈᔈ

Javal raised an army. For the first time in centuries, feuding villages patched up differences, and thousands of young men and women volunteered, eager for the chance, prompted by the same motives as Tiq, Olle, and Doran, looking for an opportunity to be free, to live in a place where they could do more than just subsist, even if it came at great cost. Two thousand recruits boarded nine ships—the three royal launches and six purser freight sloops. Children and elders crowded the docks and hillsides of Owsheau, ready to see the army off.

In the purser's shed Hab held a council of war with Jara, Joulis, Javal, and ten other local arbitriennes.

"When we get to Fadil, I will send Jara south to meet the *sikingo-mango* forces." Hab felt his shoulders sink. Here was the lie. Here was the deceit. "When she meets with the drillmaster, she will offer him unconditional surrender. They will of course send scouts forward. And to their scouts our army will look like an army of surrender. Jara will further convince the *sikingo-mango* by stressing the death of Parprouch and the fall of the House of Zadeaux, which they've seen for themselves. They know we can't lie. They know honesty runs in our blood. Because so many have surrendered already, they expect surrender from everybody. They believe in their own superiority as fighters. Even so, their scouts will come, because they are, by nature, a suspicious species. And their scouts will see an army ready to surrender."

❧❧❧

Upon Hab's return to Fadil, Fod gave him one of the new handcannons to try. The target was an expensive piece of sheet bronze roughly the size and thickness of a hopper's armored breastplate. Hab raised the handcannon, smelled the acrid scent of the slow-burning Affed wick, steadied his finger on the trigger, and sighted along the barrel. He squeezed the trigger, trying to keep the slender cannon as steady as he could. The primer hissed, a loud report came from the barrel, the cannon recoiled, and smoke filled the air. A crunching *pang* resounded from the bronze breastplate. Instantly, a huge hole appeared.

❧❧❧

Hab tried to imagine Jara's journey. Swiftly downstream on the Necontreu surrounded by five bodyguards; the dangerous approach to the forward line of the hopper forces; her uneasy reunion with Rango. He spent many anxious days and nights in Winterhouse waiting for her return. He expected, and was ready, for anything. He had an army of a thousand Dagulanders sitting in and among tents on the Grand Sward, his army of surrender. His army of Liars were deployed in the forest on top of the Wall, in the woodland surrounding the Grand Sward, and along the road south of the Grand Sward, ready to snipe, kill, and wound. Each Liar had his own handcannon and two dozen loads. Having spent two weeks training with alternate loads—stones, glass, amber—the Liars had improved their marksmanship considerably, and most were certain of a sure kill at twenty-five yards.

Jara returned a few days later accompanied by a platoon of twelve hopper regulars. A spiny tar-pool hopper held Jara at knifepoint as he and his platoon shuffled around the immense army of dejected-looking Dag-ulanders on the Grand Sward. Here was the bluff. Here was Hab's army of surrender. But there was more to Hab's strategy than just this grand deception. As Hab expected, the hoppers stared at the Great Code, cowed by it, superstitious, nonplussed that they should find it here, all the way on the other side of the world. Here was a distraction he could use. Not for the first time, he was profoundly curious about the Great Code. What did it mean? Something about Takasa, yes, but that's as much as Rango had ever told him. What story did it tell? And why and how had there ever come to be two Great Codes, one in Ortok and one in Paras?

The spiny tar-pool hopper, still holding Jara at knifepoint, approached Hab. Jara looked peeved at the tar-pool hopper, ready to kick it. "He stinks," she said. "He's had the runs for the last three days. I told him not to eat so many apples. Now he stinks. They gorge them-selves sick."

The tar-pool hopper shook her and spoke in Abani to her. "Don't squeak like a bird. You've exasperated my patience long enough, red one." He looked down at Hab from his ten-foot height, his scarlet eyes glowering. "You are the quisling?" he asked.

Hab winced. Yes, he was the quisling, a general who was about to surrender his army without a fight in the hope of securing favorable terms. "I am," he said.

The hopper's tongue flicked in and out as he considered Hab's response. He let go of Jara and gave her a shove. Only three of her bodyguards had returned. The spiny tar-pool hopper bared his teeth. "We will tell the drillmaster that your army is ready for surrender, quisling," he said, glancing over the field of Dagulanders. "I will rec-onnoiter, first your battle-house, then these woods, then up there in the forest, above the Creed of Takasa."

For the next six hours the twelve hoppers combed the entire area, looking for a hidden army. But the Liars, adept at hiding, at camouflage, and at silence, melted into the trees, burrowed into the ground, sank into bogs, wedged themselves into grottoes, and retreated on small boats into the mist of the Lake of Life. The hoppers left Winter-house and sailed downstream on the Necontreu. The hoppers were going to tell their drillmaster that the Takasan army was indeed ready for surrender.

ᔕᔕᔕ

A Liar scout by the name of Fialle came to Hab just before dawn the next morning.

"They're ten miles away on the South Road," reported Fialle. "They approach quickly. They hop."

"And how many did you count?" asked Hab.

"Two thousand."

He turned to Lord Terrarre. "Terrarre, prepare the Dagulanders for surrender."

ᔕᔕᔕ

Hab and Jara took up positions on the roof of Winterhouse. On the Grand Sward below, word was passed along, and the restless Dagulanders stirred from their tents and prepared to play their part as decoy. Hab lifted his telescope and looked across the Grand Sward to the South Road. Tall conifers lined either side of the road. Hidden in the branches of those conifers waited hundreds of Manenser snipers.

Minutes later Hab saw the hopper army—leaping, bounding, jumping—small black figures lifting puffs of dust from the road. Two thousand, yes, such as the scout Fialle had told him, a mass of hoppers stretching back three miles down the South Road, a black snake, alive and bristling, with the occasional flash of copper, *hari-bumuku* regulars jumping into the morning sunshine. Somewhere behind the last cloud of dust, Liars flanked over the rear of the hopper column, cutting off retreat, Javal's part of the plan.

Finally, the hoppers entered the Grand Sward.

"Look, there's Rango," he said, handing the telescope to Jara.

Jara took the telescope and looked. The churlish set of her face softened, and she shook her head to herself. She handed the telescope back to Hab. Hab again looked through it, concentrating on Rango. The short drillmaster stared up at the Great Code not so much with fear as with wonder. Hab saw his lips and jaw moving. To his great astonishment, Hab realized that Rango was reading it.

Before he had time to ponder the mystery further, Hab heard the Liars open fire. *Crack, crack, crack!* An endless series of reports erupting from both sides of the South Road. Hoppers immediately fell down dead. The hopper army looked around, trying to figure out where their death was coming from, why so many were dropping down dead in the road. Gunsmoke drifted up through the branches of the conifers. Hundreds of hoppers unsheathed their weapons, but with their assailants up in the trees, out of hopping range, they were defenseless against the barrage from the handcannons.

All the Dagulanders fell to their stomachs and put their hands over their heads. Volley after volley thudded into the column of hoppers. They broke rank. They panicked. They hopped. But there were so many, they kept getting in one another's way. Some managed to hop forward into the Grand Sward and, thinking that the invisible death came from the Dagulanders, began to maim and kill as many as they could. Hab drew his weapon, lit his wick, then primed the firing plate with Affed powder. Jara did the same. They both went down into the field. A hundred Liars emerged from positions around Winterhouse and advanced through the prostrate Dagulanders. They fired at the hoppers. Along with Hab and Jara, the Liars advanced with impunity. They had the advantage. The advantage to fight a hopper well beyond arm's reach with ammunition that could pierce their armor plating.

The advantage to lie so baldly that these born deceivers were themselves deceived.

But then, much to Hab's alarm, he saw Rango felled by one of the lead balls. He saw Mivuno take command. Yet was it command when the *sikingo-mango* and *hari-bumuku* regulars were too panicked by the withering hail of lead to fight back effectively? No. Mivuno had no command. And now that Rango was down, troops loyal to the drillmaster deserted. As Hab gazed down the South Road he saw hundreds of hoppers killed and wounded, their blood shining wetly scarlet under the light of the climbing morning sun. Hoppers broke rank. Hoppers fled.

"Archers!" cried Hab. "At your will."

Two hundred Dagulanders with concealed crossbows rose from the Grand Sward and fired a volley of metal-tipped arrows into the retreating phalanx of hoppers. Far down the South Road Hab saw Javal and his Manensers swarm onto the thoroughfare and arrange themselves into a kneeling row and a standing row. They fired a simultaneous volley, a hundred lead balls at once, ripping into the retreating hoppers so effectively that many tumbled to the ground in midhop. Hab hated it. He didn't want to do this to the *sikingo-mango* or the *hari-bumuku*. But he knew he had no choice.

Out on the Grand Sward, Rango tried to get up. The hopper drillmaster bled badly from the head. Rango got to his feet, stumbled a few steps, and fell back down. He couldn't get up. Hab and Jara approached the drillmaster cautiously. Rango was the only hopper Hab was willing to spare. The hundreds of wounded hoppers lying about the Sward had to be killed. Hab raised his hand and shouted to his Dagu army.

"Infantry!" he cried. "At your will!"

Five hundred Dagulanders rose from their positions on the Sward and, scavenging hopper weaponry from dead regulars, hacked to death the wounded *sikingo-mango* and *hari-bumuku* soldiers. *How easily we've become murderers*, thought Hab. He turned his back on the mayhem. He didn't want to see it. He and Jara knelt next to Rango. Rango's eyes had gone dull, like dust-covered pieces of garnet.

"So it ends," said Rango, "as it always ends. In a lie." The drillmaster bared his teeth as he clutched for breath. "Only this time a little different, Hab. The believer deceives. And the deceiver believes. I am you and you are me. We have changed places, Hab." The irony of the thing pained Hab. "My army is a remnant now, Hab. You should have no trouble wiping it out." Rango gestured at the Great Code. "This . . . this Creed. This is why I believed. I always knew it had to be true. I always knew it had to be here, somewhere on the other side of the world."

Hab looked up at the Wall. "What does it say?" The handcannon fire was growing remote as the Liars tracked down and killed the remaining hoppers.

Rango's eyes narrowed and he read:

The ghosts came in castles of steel out of the sky, pale and wispy, bearing with them the tools of an evil magic. They drove us from our home, in the heart of our beloved Takasa, where the lake water is pure, forced us to flee down the great river, where the water tastes like salt, and finally out to the sea, into the womb of the world. Their eyes were not the true red of our brothers and sisters but the color of mud and the color of sky. And when they spoke, it wasn't in the noble tongue, but in the tongue of birds, discordant, wrathful, and hideous to hear. They planted strange trees and grasses in our land. They came out of the sky at the beginning of time and destroyed us in their fire. Now we must flee. Down the river and into the sea we flee. But we leave this creed in the oldest stone of Takasa. To the ghosts from the sky we say, be warned. We flee to the land of the cloudmaker, and there the cloudmaker will make us strong, and one day we will return to take what is ours, and oust from our home the pale ones from the sky.

Hab and Jara looked at each other. Neither of them knew what it meant. Hab got up and took a few steps toward the Wall. He looked at the metal ruin. He was just becoming deeply absorbed in the puzzle when he heard a commotion behind him.

He swung round. He saw Mivuno leap a distance of thirty feet, battle-axe ready. The giant hopper decapitated Rango in one vicious stroke, gripped Jara around the waist, and hopped, not down the South Road, but toward the forest beyond Winterhouse.

ࣸ ࣸ ࣸ

Mivuno hopped around the side of Winterhouse and disappeared into the woods along the south shore of the Lake of Life. Hab followed, but he was no match for the hopper's speed. He quickly lost sight of the hopper. If it hadn't been for Jara hollering petulantly over and over again, he would have lost Mivuno.

He chased after them into the forest, the saplings and bushes whipping into his face and legs, a cold sweat of apprehension beading his forehead. In shock at first, he soon came to a deeper comprehension of what was at stake. In spite of war, in spite of hardship, and the slimmest hope for survival across the tides by himself, he carried within him, just as he had carried the amulet of Disseaule, a notion of a future for himself and Jara, a life together. Now that life together was in jeopardy.

He was joined by others. They fanned out in a search. He could no longer hear Jara. He couldn't help fearing the worst. What made a hopper trail difficult to follow was, of course, the hopping, the trouble finding takeoff points and landing points, especially in the thick forest.

Through the course of the afternoon, Hab became farther and farther separated from the main search party. But he managed to keep track of Mivuno's trail. He would find one landing spot—broken bushes, broken grass, the unmistakable claw marks of the hopper footprint—and then he would circle the landing spot in an ever-widening spiral until he located the next landing spot. In this way he accurately determined the hopper's direction.

He came to a brook. It quickly became apparent that Mivuno had hopped in the brook for a good distance. For several hours Hab thought he had lost the trail. But at sunset he found it again, far upstream, miles away from the rest of the search party. He thought he might go back and tell the search party. But if he did that, he might lose the remaining precious daylight hours. So he followed the trail by himself.

He followed it for the next two hours, noted that the distance between hops was becoming shorter and shorter. This made the trail easier to follow. And because Mivuno was such a big *hari-bumuku*, he left obvious breakages through the vegetation. But it was getting dark, and soon it would be hard to follow even this most obvious trail. Hab pushed on, tired, hungry, thirsty, desperate to know if Jara was alive. The early-summer flies came out and bothered him constantly. A crumb of the misshapen Foot rose, in crescent phase, followed by a sliver of Lag. Meager light, even with the stars, and certainly not enough to penetrate the overhead canopy of the forest. He finally sat down, exhausted. If Mivuno continued through the night, he would be long gone by morning. Given a few days, Mivuno might make the coast, get a boat, and set sail. Once the *hari-bumuku* did that, Jara was as good as gone.

ﭼﭼﭼ

He saw a brief flicker of firelight through the trees an hour later, far up the gentle rise of a hill he was climbing. He opened his eyes wide, willed his pupils to stretch to their fullest, tried to gather as much light into them as he could. And he saw it again: a flickering orange glow on the underside of some branches. He pulled his handcannon from his belt and, working by touch, prepared the load, the wick, and the primer. He approached the firelight, moving with great stealth, maneuvering so he was upwind, taking nearly twenty minutes to cover the distance.

When he was close enough, he saw that the fire was in a small clearing. Mivuno hunched over the fire on his knees, blowing on the flames. Hab moved closer, out from behind some bushes, obtaining a better line of sight.

Jara hung upside down from a rope tied to a branch. She was still alive but badly beaten. Mivuno was making the flames bigger and bigger. Jara struggled. Her mouth was gagged, and her hands were tied behind her back. She squirmed and lurched, despite her injuries, trying to get away. Mivuno was going to roast her over that fire. He was going to roast her alive, such as was the hopper way.

Hab raised his handcannon and sighted along the barrel. So it had finally come to this, he thought. Coldblooded murder, shooting an intelligent creature unawares in the back, with no warning, no chance to defend itself, no opportunity to plead for mercy, the ultimate treachery, in direct violation of Rule Number One of the Formulary. He had come a long way down the road of deceit, and he knew he couldn't stop now. He felt sick at heart, but he had no choice. First he had made promises to the monarch he couldn't keep. Then he had embezzled the family fortune. Then he had lied to Rango about the tides. Then he had defeated the hopper army with the largest and most premeditated deception Paras had ever seen. Now he was going to shoot Mivuno in the back. The believer had become the deceiver. And there was nothing he could do about it.

The irony of the thing pained him.

He gently squeezed the trigger of his handcannon and closed his eyes as a deafening report filled the air.

CHAPTER THIRTY

The army of Liars chased the hoppers downriver along the Necontreu over the next several weeks. Parassians were at first afraid of the Liars, remembered all the stories they had heard about the Liars as children, but when they realized that the Liars were actually here to save them, they didn't call them Liars anymore, they called them saviors, and saw that, despite all those stories, they were just ordinary men and women who, because of the hardscrabble nature of Manense, had learned how to fight.

Hab warned the Liars constantly about close combat with the retreating hoppers, but many went ahead and fought the hoppers hand-to-hand anyway, using weapons scavenged from dead regulars, taking to the heavy metal swords and battle-axes as if it were second nature. While many Liars died in close combat with the hoppers, many others racked up kill after kill. Hab was stunned and at times shocked to see how violent the Liars could be, how wickedly adept at inflicting blood-shed and death. They quickly and naturally probed for hopper weak-nesses and discovered that while the hoppers were superior fighters in open spaces, where they could hop without obstruction, their effective-ness diminished considerably when they were in enclosed spaces, where they were forced to ambulate in their painful and awkward way. The preferred method of engagement, then, was to lure the hoppers into dense bush or forest, into buildings or caves, and to fight them there.

Fod and his metalworkers followed up the rear, taking possession of any and all ships and boats with lead-lined keels, making round after round from these keels, or otherwise digging the lead slugs out of dead hoppers and recycling them. In this way, Fod made sure Hab's marksmen always had enough ammunition.

Some hoppers managed to escape into the mountains; they were, after all, extremely adept at mountain living, being able to hop so easily from ledge to ledge, and for years afterward mountaineers would come down from the highest peaks of the Oradels or the Pan-Pans and report sightings of bands of hoppers living in caves together. The same tales that children were once told about the Liars were now told about the hoppers: how they would eat you for their supper, how if you weren't a good boy or girl they would cut off your head and wear it on their belt. If you ever went above the snowline of the Oradels or Pan-Pans you were always advised to take a handcannon and plenty of ammunition.

Most of the hoppers fled south along the Necontreu. A band of two hundred managed to make it all the way to Jauny, and they were then joined by the hopper army of occupation in Jauny. But Jauny was a particularly bad place for the hoppers to fight, with all its buildings and enclosed squares, and even though much of it was in rubble, the Liars found plenty of places to hide in that rubble, old cellars and small crawlspaces that the hoppers simply couldn't fight well in.

A great slave camp had been erected on the Vellaisson Plain above the city, pen after pen filled with half-starved humans. Hab searched this camp for Thia and Romal, but they were nowhere to be found. Once the capital was liberated—only one hopper ship managed to squeak down the Estuary to the sea—Hab searched its streets endlessly, but he couldn't find Thia or Romal or any of the house servants. He turned to Jara. Jara put her hand on his arm.

"Maybe they escaped to Renay after all," she said.

Hab nodded. He knew this was unlikely. He knew that he would never see Thia or Romal again, that he no longer had any immediate family, and that in fact the only family he would ever have again was the family he had in Jara.

And so the war ended, the first war Paras had seen in five hundred years, but Hab knew the conflict wasn't over. One hopper ship had squeaked away. He knew the hoppers would return one day. It was the Creed.

People began to rebuild. Everyone sensed the same thing Hab sensed: The world would never be the same again. They would have to be on guard now. They would have to be vigilant. They would have to raise, train, and maintain a standing army. They would have to make a navy out of the metal ships the hoppers had abandoned in the Estuary.

Finally came the question of government. People clamored for Hab to be the new monarch, wanted the House of Cloudesley to replace the House of Zadeaux. But Hab didn't want that. He proposed something different. Instead of a monarchy, have a governor answering to a council of advisers, who in turn answered to a body of elected officials. The governor would rule for a term of seven years, and then a new one would be appointed by the body of elected officials. This way, no one could abuse power, the way Parprouch had. Hab would never forget the disastrous and financially ruinous compact he had entered into with the king. He suggested Lord Terrarre as the first governor, and the people readily accepted such a likable and practical man.

🐚🐚🐚

Hab and Jara went to the Island of Maju six months after the war on their wedding trip. They spent some time at one of Esten's old paleontology digs. Hab remembered well the conversation he had had with Jeter about the strange bones of old creatures long extinct that the Pepteris had discovered on Maju. He and Jara now brushed dirt away from the fossilized remains of such a creature.

As they brushed more and more dirt away with their delicate chevulhair brushes, they realized they had a full skeleton, something not yet found by the Pepteris, and even more startling, that the skeleton was none other than the skeleton of a *bamkali-kalango*, a green beach hopper.

They both stopped their work and stared at the skeleton. The bones were brown and dusty. The skull showed the same unmistakable snout of a green hopper. The legs were the same powerful swimming legs, and the tail stretched out six feet behind in small articulated vertebrae.

"So the Great Code is true?" said Jara. She turned to Hab. Her hair had grown back, was now shoulder-length, and her abdomen had rounded out nicely with the child she carried.

Hab stared at the skeleton. For the first time in his life he felt content. The restlessness that had dogged him for the last fifteen years was gone. He pondered the mystery: the *bamkali-kalango* driven from Paras; two Great Codes, one in Paras, one in Ortok; the *bamkali-kalango* making the great migration all the way to Ortok, the cloudmaker; creatures who, back then, were far more aquatic, hadn't changed into the mountain, beach, and tar-pool hoppers yet; creatures who could survive their whole lives at sea; some of them using the great seaweed pods to get part of the way to Ortok; diving deep whenever the tides came; making the long migration over the course of several generations. These thoughts swirled lazily through his mind as he gazed at the skeleton. Who knows how this particular hopper had died here on the Island of Maju? He began brushing the bones again. Interesting to speculate, to guess, to tinker with the evidence, but he no longer felt a driving and destructive obsession to know about these things. The world was at peace with itself. Hab felt the same way. At peace with himself.

"I suppose it is," he said.

He felt as if he had finally put his father's ghost to rest. His chronic feeling of emptiness was gone. He wasn't going to worry about all these old mysteries. A cooling wind blew over the hot dusty hill, revealing yet more of the green hopper skeleton. He was going to let them slip back into the mists of time.

What mattered was Jara. What mattered was the child that she carried. He rubbed his hand over Jara's burgeoning abdomen. She looked up at him, surprised but touched by the gesture.

There were far more important things to think about than what might have happened here sixty thousand years ago.

About the Author

SCOTT MACKAY is the award-winning author of eight novels and over forty short stories. He has been interviewed in print, Web, TV, and radio media. His short story "Last Inning" won the 1998 Arthur Ellis Award for best short mystery fiction. Another story, "Reasons Unknown," won the Okanagan Award for best Literary Short Fiction. His first Barry Gilbert Mystery, *Cold Comfort*, was nominated for the Arthur Ellis Award for best mystery novel, and his SF novel *The Meek* was a finalist for the prestigious John Campbell Memorial Award for Best SF Novel of 2001. His novels have been published in six languages. For more information, visit his Web site, www.scottmackay.net.